CHERRI CHASTISED

'I've never been spanked before, miss.'

'I had a first time, Cherri, as every girl does. Take your time, reflect if you wish to proceed. It's easier for me to spank you over my knee, because of my prosthesis, but many girls prefer their spankings standing, and bent over holding their knees or ankles. It's up to you. In either case, you'll have to lower your panties, if you're wearing any. Spankings are on the bare.'

CHERRI CHASTISED

Yolanda Celbridge

This book is a work of fiction.
In real life, make sure you practise safe sex.

First published in 2002 by
Nexus
Thames Wharf Studios
Rainville Road
London W6 9HA

www.nexus-books.co.uk

Typeset by TW Typesetting, Plymouth, Devon

Printed and bound by Mackays of Chatham

ISBN 0 352 33707 9

Contents

1

Needababe

The girl's face shone wet with tears of rage.

'It's not right. How come I always get to be the victim?'

She stood, thumb up, by a southbound on-ramp of Interstate 5, her torn skirtlet whipped up by wind, to show pantiless, wealed buttocks.

'I was never a scapegrace, but they've made me one. It's not right.'

That night, she'd been lonely, and the big moon always gave her funny feelings inside. That was the only excuse Cherri could think of, although she'd been *more* than punished for her behaviour – her smarting butt was proof of that – and it wasn't even *her* behaviour. Mickey was guilty, dragging Cherri along as his victim. Him, and the moon, and her job at NeedaBurger – although it wasn't so bad, apart from the weird rules – and Chehalis, and the whole state of Washington, and the big pink Corvette Mickey had cruised up in, they were all to blame, except Cherri herself. Mickey Donahue, with a 'Vette! She should have known he'd boosted it. She saw the California plates, and chose to believe his bullshit story about making big money in LA, and driving all the way up the interstate to see sweet little Charity Black – and he did have California plates. He still melted her heart. It was only Mickey's absences that kept Cherri virgin, when her high school peers from the trailer park at South Chehalis had swollen bellies. Those absences, and her fear of pain.

It wasn't a proper, managed trailer park, just a clump of dwellings grown like swamp fungus, with Interstate 5 a ribbon of lights to freedom, only yards above the moonscape of shacks, broken by the shiny aluminium domes of the trailer trash aristocracy. Cherri dreamed the aluminium pods housed aliens, who would awake and devour people, at full moon; she imagined them, one day, all awaking at the same time. The trailer park was across the railroad, by the river, amid the ruins of wharves, long since broken for firewood. Far away towered the snow-cap of Mt Rainier, brooding over the forests. It was a dank, windy place for a girl to grow; it didn't seem like America, not the sunny Californian dream in the movies. The trailer park was a weal in the wooded landscape, festering with human insects that stole, worked casual jobs, or eked welfare cheques. There were seasonal Mexicans, drifting north from the Sacramento valley, for fruit-picking jobs. Cherri wanted to be friendly, but they seemed scared of her, making a sign. Cherri didn't know what sign it was. A car not up on blocks was rare in South Chehalis: a shiny pink 'Vette with all its wheels, unheard of.

Cherri's job at the NeedaBurger, by the off-ramp halfway to Centralia, was almost glamour. The NeedaBurger chain, like everything else in the rainy pacific northwest, operated out of Miami, or LA – somewhere sunny, anyhow. Its founder, D. Bob Niederburger, realised early in the twenty-first century that Americans faced too much fast food choice, and that minutes spent menu-browsing meant lost profits. NeedaBurger operated like a gas station: fast food customers needed to fill up, without wasting valuable seconds choosing with or without, large or small. Every NeedaBurger was identical: a 4-ounce patty of proteiny mush, slopped in secret sauce, with a 4-ounce portion of fries, microwaved: both served in cardboard packs, pyramidal in shape, for easy storage, and because it felt and tasted the same, any way up. NeedaBurger was proud that all ingredients were 'local produce', even the obligatory serving of icy NeedaCola, in its pyramidal pack.

Cherri preferred the night shift – all NeedaBurgers were drive-thru only, to save on fixtures – and, because skimpily uniformed NeedaBabes were blatantly chosen for big breasts and butts, there was no dialogue with customers, who ordered by pressing a keyboard. Customer choice was limited to quantity. Only her titties were seen through a plexiglass surround, but the NeedaBabe had to waggle her butt to fetch stuff from the microwave, and the NeedaBabe uniform teased on purpose: a short skirt, tight blouse and stockings, of gauzy chiffonnette, showing blurred bare skin. The panties, too, were translucent.

The chain's slogan, registered with the US Patent office, was 'We Got 'Em!' Its logo was a pyramid like that on the back of a dollar bill, with the big eye at the top as the 'o' in 'got'. At first, the no-choice idea was scorned, but D. Bob rightly reckoned most junk foodies were too tired, lonely, or stupid to care, and Americans would go for anything titillating but lawful. No one knew what was in his burgers, or his sauce, and customers found the monthly changes in flavour cute rather than alarming: they did have a choice, and, hey, D. Bob made it for them. South Chehalians consumed many NeedaBurgers.

Mickey had escaped from the trailer trash: he was, at different times, allegedly at junior college, in nearby Centralia, digging for gold, enlisting in the marines, or some other bullshit. Cherri listened, as he pawed her breasts, trying to sneak under her panties to her wetly closed pussy, in some junkheap car, because she had no

3

one else. Mickey told her she was beautiful – no one said that, ever. He said she was too beautiful to be good. Even then, her thighs remained shut. No one in trailer trashland was to take her precious virgin membrane – but she made sure he, like the others, got his relief. In fact, she liked relieving males, taming them. Cherri longed to please.

She *was* too beautiful. You didn't make friends in South Chehalis by standing out, and Cherri was cursed with looks so striking that lank-haired, zit-scarred trailer girls hated her, and beer-bellied men drooled. 5'10" made her too tall; the perfect harmony of her breasts, jutting without the need of a bra, and her full, firm, massively ripe buttocks, tapering to muscled, coltish legs, made even the kindest comment unseemly, as in, what triple-X movie did her 44-22-44 figure escape from? It was her shiny blonde hair – the girls said it came from a bottle – and her glowing bronze skin that made her both desired, and resented. In Chehalis, like everywhere in the pacific northwest, it rained all the time, and a girl who had never been anywhere else had no right to the perfect tan.

Except, Cherri's skin wasn't tan. It was the colour of gold, bronze, or copper, shining with an eerie luminescence, and the colours flowing and changing in the light, with her eyes a deep, luminous green. It had not always been so. Until well into her nineteenth year, she'd been a stringbean, an ugly duckling. Her oddity kept her virginity safe, even from her own fingers, which had never strayed to her sensitive areas. Her breasts and ass were scrawny, her pubic hair lank and sparse. She blossomed at nineteen, her pallid skin assuming its uniform bronze sheen, her breasts and buttocks swelling to ripe melons, her pubic down growing to a jungle in weeks. She discovered the pleasure of her body in masturbation, and to be wary of the desire it provoked. Men wanted, yet feared, their fantasy come true: her

4

strapless tan proclaiming her a nudist, a gamer. How she longed, as a young adult, inspecting her nudity in the glass, for pale bikini patches on her bottom and breasts! Her huge pubic bush interrupted her even bronze skin, but from the rear, her ripely swelling buttocks formed a clear, unbroken harmony of bronze, from spine to ankle.

Under the thick blonde curls of her pussy mane – which she never trimmed – under the strongly extruded clitoris, and the well-developed lips of her vulva, lurked another secret. Cherri was small, inside: really small. When she squatted to pee, she sprinkled. Her pussy was so tight that it hurt even to get her finger inside, but during her daily masturbation at the mirror, she had only to stimulate her nipples, and extruded clitoris, to bring herself off. Her come flowed copiously, as she tickled the stiff nubbin, but the lubrication – she was later identified as an unusually heavy juicer – made her channel no larger. Her anus was really squishy and flexible: she had complete control, and could squeeze it tight as a clam, or relax it to a balloon, so that defecation was never a chore, but a pleasure. It was as if nature had her two holes mixed up.

It wasn't often that she had long in the bathroom, nor even at home, when Mom was 'entertaining' – guys with pickup trucks, mostly, meaning long, shivering walks in the rain for Cherri, and leers from behind drapes. Her lush of a father had run off, tired of his wife and her entertaining, when he was away at the logging camp; tired of the sneers about the younger Cherri's pallid body. He was too drunk to spank her, so her mom took the strap, when he was mad. Cherri could run faster than anybody minded to thrash her. Her long legs carried her like a gazelle, even barefoot, and she was sure she had been blessed with that power, to preserve her hymen. After her sexual blooming, she ran a lot, and, once enclosed by fir trees, would strip off her shorts and halter top, to run nude, barefoot, for miles, until her sweat poured, and she seemed almost within grasp of the snowy cone of Mt Rainier. What mysteries hid beneath that peak, Cherri gasped – the climax of her run being her own masturbation, as, excited by the power and beauty of her nude body, she frigged her throbbing clitoris to orgasm, until her knees buckled. She worshipped the forest and the cold air on her skin, as she worshipped her own body, caring for it, in readiness for its blossoming far from the cold northern woods.

California! If only she had the money to ride south! It was always lack of money; whatever part-time job she had, at high school or after, her mother leeched from her. *Charity*, she would say, *you owe me*, laying a guilt trip on her daughter, as if everything was her fault, which wasn't right. She watched what she ate; inspecting her dungs, tracking them from rectum to anus, to plop into the bowl, and reassuring herself that they were of requisite darkness and quality for her health. Her piss, too, she checked, for a clear or golden sprinkle. She went to the dentist, to be reassured her teeth were perfect. Her body was her only treasure.

Her mom was not the only woman in the trailer park who 'entertained', and the place was never silent. There were always whimpers, moans, cries, crashes of broken glass – and the dull thud-thud-thud of a hand or strap, with shrieks of a girl's pain in between. Spanked women were common in South Chehalis. Karen Souter used to show off the bruises on her bare ass, in the washroom at the high school, and invite the other girls to feel her beltmarks, laid by her own mom, for peeking, when she was with one of her many 'friends', or even, she hinted, whipped bare-ass by the 'friend', as Mom watched. Karen, in fact, was proud of her endurance, boasting of her welts as though they were designer panties.

Fascinated, despite her repugnance, Cherri had run her fingers over the scarred skin, marvelling at how deep and dark the strap had dug, and at Karen's coos of delight as the girls touched her there. Cherri got a funny feeling inside when she thought of Karen's bare ass, with the girl crying as she was whipped. Or did she cry? Maybe she just moaned, or maybe she screamed. Maybe Karen just laughed. What did it feel like to take a whipping? She wondered if there was more than whipping, especially when the social department took Karen away, although rumour claimed she'd been jailed for hustling, or skipped back east with one of her mom's boyfriends, a trucker from North Carolina or someplace. A lot of girls besides Karen showed their bare asses, with whipmarks, but they didn't like doing it. Girls would gang up and tease them, until, crying, they dropped their panties in the washroom and showed their weals, although nobody could match the awesome dark blotches on Karen Souter's ass. Often, they wouldn't say who had whipped them, or why, no matter how much they were teased.

Cherri had masturbated enthusiastically since the blossoming of her body, as few of the available males did anything to inspire her or arouse her potent sexuality. After one of those spanked peekaboo shows in the school bathroom, she couldn't wait to get alone and masturbate, sometimes twice without stopping, and thinking of a girl's bare whipped ass. Whipping would be a different kind of pain than vulval penetration, but no less awesome. She dreamed of herself spanked or whipped, in the nude, and roped tight, like a slave, cowgirl or wanton princess in the old movies, and once blurted something about that to Johan Benz, the dentist, who was kind of uncly. That was why she got the NeedaBurger job, for Paula Dupree, his hygienist, listened in, the rustling of her nylon lab coat and stockings betraying her aroused curiosity. She was a rangy, thin-lipped girl, a few years older than Cherri, with a big ass and titties, her figure 39-24-39, with dark roots under her bouffant peroxide mane. Johan said he

7

was no psychiatrist, and told Cherri to find somebody to spank her, if that's what she wanted.

'Shouldn't be hard to find, round here,' he added. 'You'd be surprised how many people enjoy that kind of thing at home.'

Paula grinned as she rinsed Cherri's gums.

'Not only at home, huh, Johan?' she said. 'Office spankings aren't exactly rare, and the county sheriff keeps a paddle on his desk for wayward girls.'

'Now, Paula, that's just talk.'

'Cherri mentioned the subject first. She's looking for a job right now – I'd suggest NeedaBurger. The pay's outstanding, if you can put up with the, um, quirks of the job. She'd be a great NeedaBabe, *if* what she says is true.'

'Paula, there are people waiting.'

'How do you think I got the money to train for hygienist, anyway? And what keeps me here? I'm a lousy hygienist.'

'Nonsense, Paula,' Johan protested.

'But I make so many mistakes.'

'You're only human, Paula. That's it for now, Cherri.'

Paula raised her lab coat and her short skirt beneath: she wore no panties, and Cherri gasped as Paula blatantly mooned her. Her bare bottom was rosy with spankmarks.

'You earn your money at NeedaBurger,' she said, showing Cherri out.

'You mean, girls are spanked if they screw up?'

Paula nodded.

'Some of those spankmarks look kind of new, Paula,' Cherri blurted. 'Or different than just spankmarks.'

'So you've seen spankmarks before?'

'Uh, yeah, at school, you know?'

'I make mistakes, and Johan is too sweet to fire me. I pay for them the simple way,' Paula said, smiling. 'I make sure I make mistakes.'

'I can't believe – you get spanked on purpose?'

Paula paused, before showing in the next patient.

'Twice a week,' she whispered, 'over that very dental chair. You know why only twice a week? Because Johan canes me as well as spanks me, and that hurts *so* much, as well as leaving different marks.'

'But why?'

'Because I'm a girl, dummy. Like you.'

Shortly after, Cherri got her job at NeedaBurger. Her interview took place in the regional office, in Centralia, which looked more like a motel room. The area manager, Tracee Pyle, brunette, twenty-five years old, 5'8" tall, and 39-24-37, originally from Tacoma, had been with NeedaBurger for six years. Her lush mane swung at her shoulder in a shiny ponytail, and she limped slightly, explaining that her left leg below the hip was an artificial prosthesis.

'I'm sorry,' Cherri said.

'Don't be!' said Tracee, with a radiant smile. 'I'm not, so don't waste sympathy on a girl who's perfectly happy! Anyway, this prosthesis is only temporary, until the company has my real one ready.'

Cherri expected questions, but Tracee did most of the talking, convincing her what a wonderful company it was, and how Cherri was *just* the girl they needed.

'You have no problem with our glamour girl policy? I mean, we only hire girls who are – excuse my French – stacked, like you.'

Cherri said she was happy to be a glamour girl, if the pay was right. The pay was indeed outstanding, and Cherri said she could start next day.

'First, I must ask if you heard about us from any former employees.'

Cherri mentioned Paula Dupree.

'Dear, sweet Paula! So, you know of our, uh, methods?'

Cherri blushed.

9

'She said something about spanking,' she murmured.

Tracee put her fingertips together.

'Exactly,' she said. 'The essence of NeedaBurger is simplicity, and cutting costs to the bone. Fast-food outlets have a high staff turnover, much of it because of instant dismissals, for small errors, or even alleged deceit. Either way, recruitment is costly. In return for generous pay, we ask our NeedaBabes to pay for errors in a simple, non-judgemental way – by taking a weekly spanking, from their area manager, *if there is an* error. Just the time saved on arguments makes it economic sense.'

Cherri shivered.

'You mean I might be spanked?' she said.

'Yes.'

'By you?'

'Yes. Do you have any problem with that?'

'Why, no. I'm sure I won't make mistakes.'

'I'm sure, too. But, before offering you the job, I have to submit you to a test. That is, give you a trial spanking. Some girls can't take it very well.'

Cherri felt her loins tingle and a moistening in her quim, and blushed.

'I've never been spanked before, miss.'

'I had a first time, Cherri, as every girl does. Take your time, reflect if you wish to proceed. It's easier for me to spank you over my knee, because of my prosthesis, but many girls prefer their spankings standing, and bent over holding their knees or ankles. It's up to you. In either case, you'll have to lower your panties, if you're wearing any. Spankings are on the bare.'

'You want to spank my bare ass, miss?'

'It's company policy, Cherri. Off the record, I'll say that in your case, I do want to spank you on the bare. I spank many bottoms on duty, but yours will be a pleasure.'

She gave Cherri a photo album and invited her to scan it. Inside, Cherri saw photos of girls' bare croups,

10

pale, over lowered panties, and then blushing pink, after spanking. Some were deep crimson. She blushed, lingering over certain pictures, that excited her.

'One of those girls is me,' murmured Tracee.

Cherri picked one of the photos. Only scarlet buttocks, above the thighs, were in frame. Tracee smiled, nodding.

'How many spanks will I get, miss?' Cherri blurted.

'A NeedaBabe never knows how many her spanking is to be,' said Tracee, 'not even her test, although of course she can stop it any time she wants. Spanking is always at the manager's discretion.'

Cherri bit her lip.

'OK, I'll take a test spanking, miss,' she blurted.

Cherri was glad her face was lowered, as she pulled down her panties – Tracee was not allowed to do that – while bent over her spanker's thigh. She blushed, and her heart thumped, not least for fear Tracee might see the glistening liquid oozing from her quim. She kept her bare ass-cheeks tightly clamped. Tracee wore a pleated grey business skirt, with nylon stockings in a fishnet pattern, perched on high stilettos, so that her prosthesis was unnoticed. It wasn't right that a girl should be wet when about to get hurt, surely? Cherri was afraid her seep would stain Tracee's skirt, and she'd be stuck with a dry-cleaning bill, but Tracee pulled her skirt up so that Cherri's pubis rested on her stockings, which would be easier to clean. One of those powerful thighs quivered beneath Cherri's moistening pubic curls. Tracee laughed.

'Listen, I know you're wet down there, Cherri, and it's quite normal for a girl to get excited by spanking. I was, my first time. Also off the record, I still am. Spanking, or being spanked.'

'You? Spanked?'

'In fact, caned, and on the bare bottom. Managers are also subject to discipline, but with higher status chastisement. Shall I begin your spanking?'

11

'I guess so.'

'I require a "yes", Cherri.'

'Yes, then. Spank me.'

Slap! Slap! Slap!

'That hurt?' said Tracee.

Cherri felt pin-pricks, and said so.

Slap! Slap! Slap!

'Mm . . . those hurt a little.'

Slap! Slap! Slap!

'Oh! Those were hard!'

Slap! Slap! Slap!

'Ah! Ooh!'

Cherri's bare ass clenched, and her pubis wriggled on Tracee's thigh as her buttocks squirmed. Juice seeped from her quim as the warmth in her spanked bottom sent tickles up her spine and into her clitoris.

'Smarting, huh?'

'Yeah.'

'Want to stop?'

'Then I wouldn't get the job.'

'That's right.'

'Don't stop.'

Slap! Slap! Slap!

'Oh! Those really stung!'

'Good. Your ass is blushing well – you'll be pleased when you look in the mirror. Teenage girls always do that.'

Slap! Slap! Slap!

'Ooh!'

Cherri's buttocks clenched and squirmed furiously as the glow of her early spanks turned to hard, throbbing pain. Yet the flow of come from her writhing cooze increased, as her squirms made her clitty rub Tracee's stocking. The spanks rained on her seared bottom, seeming harder and harder; Cherri's cunt gushed come, and her breath came in harsh, anguished gasps. Tracee did not pause in her spanking, but asked:

'Cherri, this is off the record, too – do you masturbate a lot? It's just, my stocking's wet, under you. You don't have to answer.'

'Yeah, I do masturbate, miss.'

Slap! Slap! Slap!

'Ooh! Hey, it really hurts! Surely most girls masturbate? Does that mean you won't hire me?'

'No, Tracee, you already have the job. You got it at your hundredth spank.'

'A *hundred*?'

'Didn't think you could take that many?'

'No!'

'I can stop now, if you like.'

'No. Don't stop.'

Slap! Slap! Slap!

'Ooh! Ahh!'

Cherri's naked ass-globes jerked and shuddered, squirming, and clenching furiously, as her whole body writhed, and she rubbed her come-soaked pubic bush against Tracee's wet nylon stocking.

'It gets lonely, working shift,' Tracee said, 'and sometimes girls get bored and, well, you can masturbate if you like. In fact, each shift, you put on clean panties and leave in clean ones. Ones wet with your juices, you dispose of in a green Tupperware box. For heavy juicers, like you – and you *are* a heavy juicer, Cherri – there's a green Tupperware juice cup that fits between your thighs. You leave that behind, as well.'

The spanking continued to over three hundred slaps, until Tracee looked at her watch and terminated the session.

'Congratulations, Cherri,' she said. 'There's a mirror in the bathroom, which you might like to use.'

Cherri went to the bathroom with her panties around her thighs, and gazed at her flaming crimson buttocks, rubbing the ridged spankmarks wealed by Tracee's fingers.

Her cunt dripped with come; she put a finger to her stiff clitoris, pressed it twice, and brought herself off, trying to disguise her orgasmic panting as cries of surprise. Tracee rose from the chair, leaving a dark wet stain where her own panties had pressed. She told Cherri where and when to report for duty, and said she looked forward to the pleasure of spanking her every Saturday.

'Miss, you said I'd be spanked only if I made an error.'

'Cherri, no cash roll in America ever quite balances at the end of a week. There will always be an error.'

'Guess you got me there.'

'Do you mind?'

'No. Hey, I really am sorry about your accident and all.'

'Accident? Oh, yeah. Sure.'

Her thighs clamped together, Tracee spoke to Cherri's buttocks.

'Bye, then. See you soon.'

Tracee and she soon tacitly agreed that her weekly bare-bottom spankings allowed them to separately, then mutually, masturbate, and always filling the green pots with come. Tracee let Cherri see and touch the cane-marks she received when her area figures did not quite tally. Both stuck to the pretence that they feared their chastisements, and that masturbation was relief from pain rather than its fruit. It did not occur to Cherri that spanking might take place outside of the workplace. On conventional dates, she accepted boys' backseat fumbl-ings with eagerness: unzipping them, and getting their cocks into her mouth, to suck, until the sperm came. Her mom, in sisterly mood, had confided to her that a male was tame, once despermed. Cherri didn't mind the taste and happily swallowed it, so that she got a reputation; she stopped, realising that what she wanted to tame boys for – escape from South Chehalis –

14

was no longer on the menu, once their cocks were softened. She gave up on boys altogether, being content to relieve her longings by frequent masturbation. The NeedaBurger night shift got her away from the noises of the trailer park and, apart from the hum of the interstate, it was quiet enough to let her masturbate in peace, often fantasising about her weekly spanking. Tracee made it clear that spanking was not a *relationship*, but an end in itself. Mickey Donahue was the exception to her boy fatigue, but he wasn't around most of the time, and when he was, he was always some new kind of crazy. She loved sucking his cock, it was such a monster. In fact, when she was alone at the NeedaBurger window, at 2 a.m. that night, she was masturbating, with his cock in her fantasy. Her panties and stockings were wet with come so when he was there, in that pink 'Vette that looked just like a cock, she didn't need much persuading to jump in.

Nor did she mind, when he said he would rush her away to California – she had no reason to go back to the trailer park at all. Some shabby shoes and skirts, six pairs of thong panties, two bikini cut and two regular, making eight in all, plus four scalloped uplift bras, one peekaboo bra and three regular 44Ds, didn't make a lost fortune. She knew there would be urgent business first, when he drove up a track into the forest. They stopped by a lake with only one dwelling visible, silhouetted at the crest of the ridge: preacher Ellum Tod's house, which he called the 'house of the lord', and where he had his revival meetings. Cherri often saw big fancy cars, with out-of-state licence plates, going up the track. Preacher Ellum was a familiar figure, very young and fashionable for a preacherman, with long curly hair and beard, as he drove his Cadillac around Chehalis, even into the trailer park: folks said his revivals were only for rich people. They said he and his brother Sheriff Josiah owned most of South Chehalis, to serve as a showroom of sin.

15

As Cherri climbed into the back seat, which seemed to recline for them automatically, she hoped that after she'd sucked him a good long time, and swallowed all his stuff, Mickey *would* take her to California. They both got naked: Cherri's buttons and zips and elastic popping fast, and her breasts bursting from her bra. The NeedaBurger uniform was so flimsy, it hardly needed removing, but she did anyway. Mickey was in such a hurry, he tore her skirtlet and her stockings. She didn't mind, as long as her black garter belt and straps were intact – real nylon, they were, and the belt too tight, pinching her flesh, which helped her focus, and mastur-bate, during the hours alone. As the last shreds of clothing left her body, Cherri's pussy was awash.

She hadn't seen Mickey in four months, and sensed his alleged time in California had made him less tolerant of her virginity and less content with oral sex, however expert, and however much she humiliated herself and played with herself as she sucked – which, Cherri knew, boys liked. Oral sex was good enough for most, in fact it was what they really wanted, because they had the illusion of power. The back seat of the car seemed to vibrate and billow as the two naked bodies caressed, and Cherri's lips closed around the glans of Mickey's stiff cock. While she sucked, she masturbated her erect clitty between two fingers, accepting that Mickey wouldn't eat her pussy, considering it 'dirty'. She assured herself that it didn't matter, that a girl's fingers could bring more pleasure than a male's tongue. Mickey did suck her toes, taking the whole of her big and second left toes into his mouth. He gasped that it was called 'shrimping', so she figured he really had been to LA, and learned a few tricks. She felt his cock throb and shudder, harder and harder, as her head swooped, to take the shaft right to the back of her throat, where she had learned to make her uvula vibrate, tickling his piss-hole. That was a trick that drove boys wild.

16

However, after a grunt, Mickey pushed her face away from him, and upended her, so that his cock nuzzled her clit, under her massive pubic thatch, now soaking in sweat and come from her gushing pussy-lips.

He said he wanted more than a blow job – that it was time she really put out – that he knew 'for sure' she opened up for other guys, and didn't mind – after all, she must take after her mom – so this time he was going to fuck her little tight cunt. He laughed when he said that gross thing about her mom, and then laughed some more, after telling Cherri he'd fucked her own mom. He said her mom loved it up the ass, too, with a bare-ass spanking thrown in, and she suggested he did Cherri and her together, that way. Cherri panicked – that was *beyond* gross! – but Mickey's glans was pressing her perineum, and he rammed her slit with his cock, getting nowhere, despite her flood of come. The pouch wouldn't open, and Cherri wasn't sure if it was natural reaction or her own effort. Understanding a male's need to ejaculate, she urged him to throat-fuck her again, but Mickey wanted to penetrate her down there, and called her a fucking tease. *Maybe I am a tease*, she thought. *Who am I to judge Mom?*

Fingers parted the cheeks of her ass, and Cherri felt his cock thrusting against her anal pucker. Cherri pleaded, no, no, *no* – yet his glans entered the anal aperture, slowly, painfully, and all her buttocks' squirming and writhing only seemed to increase the penetration of the cock into her anus, which became increasingly elastic, despite her sphincter's efforts to close her channel. Mickey snarled that he was doing her a favour, respecting her virginity, and that millions of virgin bitches were regularly butt-fucked to their satisfaction. Cherri sobbed, as her anus opened wider and wider, penetrated to an agonising inch by his throbbing monster of a cock.

It was the first time anyone had penetrated her sex organs. Oral sex didn't count, she reasoned, as, with a

17

guy's dick in her mouth, she was in charge. She thought, *I'm wrong, even thinking my butt-hole's a sex organ* – but recalled her pleasure at her anal elasticity as she dunged a really hard stool, which was as near sexual as could be. *At least I'll still be a true virgin*. She sighed, opening her anus and relaxing the sphincter, and feeling the cock withdrawing to its tip, ready to plunge right into her – felt her pussy gush with oily come, all over the seat of the Corvette – swallowed and shut her eyes, dreading and craving the pain a cock must inflict, bigger than the hardest dung.

There was a roar; Mickey's cock left her butt-hole with a loud plop; and both bodies were flung back against the seat as the car's engine sprang into life. Automatic seat belts shot from the velour upholstery to snare both bodies by their waists and ankles; all the lights went on. The steering wheel jiggled; the shift locked into drive. The parking brake snapped off, and the Corvette began to move up the track, towards the crest of the hill. When it reached the house of the lord, it stopped. Two hooded and robed female figures emerged from the house, carrying metal. They opened the car's rear door, and manacled Mickey and Cherri, with their wrists and ankles chained in front of them, to three-foot steel bars, and those two bars fixed together by a third. When they were secure, their safety belt was loosed, and they exited the vehicle, obliged to hold themselves, stooping and unable to walk at more than a hobble. Rev Ellum Tod, wearing a black satin robe, joined them. His long, shiny curls danced in the breeze, and his eyes twinkled.

'Welcome to the lord's house,' he said. 'Perhaps you would care to come inside and discuss how to get you out of this embarrassing situation. My helpmaids here wanted to summon my brother, the sheriff, but girls tend to be headstrong – don't they, Cherri, you dirty scapegrace? A little talk, man to maid, should put things right.'

'Let me go! What is this?' Cherri cried, shaking.

'Car theft, to start with,' said Rev Ellum.

'Let's go with the asshole, Cherri,' said Mickey gloomily. 'I did boost the car.'

Cherri squirmed, white with rage, in her clamps.

'You tricked me, fucker!' she hissed, as they followed Rev Ellum, with the females prodding their backs, into a lounge lit by green candles that gave off fragrant smoke.

On a table stood a wooden pyramid with an eye, like the NeedaBurger sign. Two walls were covered in video screens above rows of twinkling computers.

'All your misdeeds are recorded,' said Rev Ellum, 'right from the car theft. My car is wired and transmits directly to the sheriff's office. Dumb trailer trash! You suspected nothing, even when you didn't need to hotwire the car?'

'That's entrapment!' Mickey growled.

'The car is wired inside, too.'

A monitor showed Mickey and Cherri, with a close-up of Mickey's glans penetrating Cherri's anus. Cherri shuddered. The images flickered on successive monitors: Mickey driving away the 'Vette, Cherri's climbing in, the stripping, the caresses, and then the tiny cubicle at Needaburger, Cherri's wet fingers masturbating her extruded red clit, her thighs and stockings moist with come that she licked from wet fingertips; the arrival of the stolen Corvette, and Cherri's breaking open the NeedaBurger cash desk to remove a pile of money.

'*Wait!*' Cherri cried. '*That's not right!*'

The Rev Ellum shrugged.

'Only the lord knows what is right,' he said. 'Call it computer enhancement. It's what you'd have *liked* to do. The car theft is beyond doubt, so no court would doubt the rest, where trailer trash are accused.'

2

Scapegrace

'I'd ask you to make yourselves comfortable,' said Rev Ellum, 'but I'm afraid that isn't the object of your visit.'

'Hey, man, can we make a deal?' Mickey said. 'Look, man, I only borrowed the fucking car, you know? I mean, it was her that talked me into it. Like, she insisted.'

'So the car theft was her fault,' said Rev Ellum. 'That fits in with the facts: robbing her workplace, and inducing a young man to commit sodomy – that is, butt-fucking. My brother, Sheriff Josie, can return the vehicle to its rightful owner, while I spare the taxpayer the expense of court proceedings. Someone must be punished and it seems fair that it be the young lady.'

'But that's crazy! Can't you tell he's lying?' Cherri cried. 'I never even drove the damn car.'

'The female is temptress,' said Rev Ellum.

'What do you *want*?' she blurted.

'What the lord wants,' he purred.

'This is no lord I ever heard of,' she said.

'You must learn, then,' said Rev Ellum. 'We may call the sheriff's office and you'll go to jail, or we may settle the matter here and now by cleansing you.'

'Cleansing?' Cherri spat. 'Let me go, you fucking creep!'

'That might be less than wise. I suggest you accept the lord's chastisement – a whipping of your back and caning of the buttocks, taken in the nude.'

'Whipping? Caning?' Cherri gasped.

'It sounds painful, and it is, though you shall be glad of your penitence afterwards. Aren't NeedaBabes used to corporal chastisement? You do have a choice, of course – chastisement is not real, unless the miscreant desires it – but not an appealing one, scapegrace.'

'I don't *b-believe* this,' stammered Cherri.

'The lord,' said Rev Ellum, 'does not require belief, only penitence.'

'Look, this is some kind of set-up. I want to call my manager, Tracee Pyle.'

'Scarcely necessary.'

The two helpers removed their robes and hoods. Apart from sneakers and fluffy white socks, one was in the nude, the other wearing only peach-coloured panties. Both girls carried hickory canes, three feet long, with cattle whips coiled around their waists. Their backs faced Cherri, showing bare buttocks bruised with fresh crimson weals and ridges, and purple blotches amid the crimson.

'I cleansed my helpers, awaiting your arrival,' said Rev Ellum. 'They are eager to witness your own cleansing.'

The two girls turned.

'Seems I'm no longer to be your manager. I'm disappointed in you, Cherri,' said Tracee Pyle, grimacing, as she rubbed her bare ass.

'Yeah, me too,' said Paula Dupree. 'I mean, I practically got you that job, and what does this do for my cred?'

'Tracee!' Cherri cried. 'Your leg!'

Tracee flexed her left leg.

'This is my new, real one. I wear panties so you can't see the join, though my friends say it's seamless. How could you be so ungrateful to NeedaBurger, Cherri? You really ought to take cleansing, for your own peace of mind. You did walk out on the job, you know.'

'OK, but –'

'And Mickey was going to butt-fuck you in the stolen car, wasn't he?'

'Yeah, but he didn't. I mean, he only got in an inch.'

'Does it make you feel good about yourself?' said Paula.

'Not really, I guess,' Cherri said. 'Look, I could think better if I wasn't shackled up.'

'Just say you accept the lord's punishment,' said Tracee, 'and you'll take your beating naked but free. A chastised girl unbound suffers not just strokes, but the pain of choosing to take them.'

'How many strokes?' Cherri asked, in a whisper.

'NeedaBabes never know,' said Tracee. 'And, until I fire you, you're still a NeedaBabe. We only want to cleanse you, Cherri. Trust me.'

'OK, then,' Cherri said. 'I'll take the punishment. It can't be too much worse than spanking.'

Paula and Tracee looked at her, and each rubbed her wealed buttocks, smiling at Cherri's gaze, and staring pointedly at the captive girl's glistening cooze-flaps.

'Don't be too sure,' Tracee said.

'Hey,' said Mickey, 'the bitch was to blame, right? So that means I'm outta here?'

'No, young man,' said Rev Ellum, 'you have the lord's work to do. Girls, free the maid, but not the stud.'

Mickey remained, growling, in his shackles, while Cherri stood freely naked. She was to be back-whipped first, and Rev Ellum directed Cherri to go to the wall and cling to two rope nooses that hung four feet apart, seven feet above the carpet. Then she slipped her feet into two ankle-nooses, five feet apart, which Paula tightened without knotting.

'Believe me, you'll be glad of the support,' she whispered. 'Whipping makes a girl go crazy. Hey, is your pussy wet, or what?'

Cherri's come was an unmistakable trickle, seeping down her thighs from the gash. She was to take her whipping at the wall, but her caning bent over the back

22

of the sofa. Tracee would whip her, then Paula would cane her bottom. Awaiting her duty, Paula pushed the shackled Mickey to his knees before the sofa, then sat and spread her legs with her cunt-flaps wet and open, placing her fingers in her jungly cunt-bush, and teasing her stiffening clitty with the crook handle of her hickory rod.

'I'm kind of scared, Tracee,' Cherri whispered, as Tracee uncoiled her cattle whip. 'Please don't be brutal on me.'

'When I'm so mad at you? Get a clue, bitch.'

Thwap! Thwap!

'Ah!' Cherri groaned, as the heavy leather whip rocked her bare back.

'Eat me, shit-kicker,' spat Paula to the crouching Mickey.

'What? I never do dirty stuff –'

Vip!

'*Ah!*'

Paula's cane lashed Mickey's bare ass.

'Lick good, trailer boy.'

Mickey's tongue penetrated Paula's wet cunt, and began to lick her clitoris.

Whap! Whap!

'*Ahh!*'

Cherri was slammed to the wall, crying out, as the heavy whip wealed her naked back. Needing time and distance to most effectively launch the thong, Tracee stood feet away, allowing the full length of the leather to snake across her victim's bare skin.

Whap!

'Oh, please, Tracee, not so hard!'

Whap!

'*Ah!* Tracee, it hurts! Spanking was never this bad!'

She looked round to see Tracee masturbating as she whipped. Cherri clung to her wrist-nooses, with her feet kicking against her ankle-ropes. Her back was striped red, but her whole body stiffened, shivering, as the leather slapped her naked skin. Her cunt-basin slammed against the embossed wallpaper, pressing her wet, throbbing clitoris. Her come seeped down her thighs and dripped onto the carpet beneath her sweat-soaked pubic jungle.

Whap!

'*Uh!* Oh, please, please, Tracee!'

Cherri's groans became a drooling wail. Her flogged back was raw; her wriggling groin rubbed her erect clitty against the wallpaper, making come flow in a torrent from her swollen red gash flaps.

Whap!

'*Ahh!* Stop, Tracee, that's enough! I've never hurt so much, ever!'

Tracee put her hand between Cherri's legs, and thrust her palm to Cherri's face. Cherri spluttered, as she swallowed her own come.

'And you don't like my whipping, bitch?'

Whap!

'*Ahh!*'

Cherri was flogged for seven minutes, during which thirty-four strokes striped her back in a latticework of red crimson and purple weals. Her cunt gushed come; sobbing in docility, she slipped from her bonds and bent over the sofa, just as Paula was writhing in orgasm from Mickey's tonguing. Tracee coolly continued masturbating, while replacing Paula on the sofa. Paula stood behind Cherri's raised bare bottom with her hickory cane. Before Cherri stood Rev Ellum; he ordered her to spread her hands on the sofa seat and swept his robe aside, revealing his naked cock erect.

'No,' Cherri cried, even before the first cane-strokes lashed her bared buttocks.

Vip!

'*Oh!* Please, please, it's too hard, Paula.'

Vip!

24

'*Oh!* Please, no! I didn't realise caning was so cruel.'

Paula caned every inch of the buttock skin, painting a uniform crimson glow, then concentrating her cane on the weakest, most tender points where welts would blotch most lividly and ridges rise hardest: the haunches; the top fesses; the inner thighs, just by the cleft. The fleshy mid-fesses, too, soon showed an artful criss-cross pattern of weals hardening to ridges. As the rod wealed her, Cherri's pain deepened along with the shame that her caned bare was on view. Her buttocks clenched and twitched, as she tried to diffuse the smarting, unbearable pain, from the welts where the cane focussed. Yet she *was* bearing it; her nipples were stiff and tingly, and her cunt slopped with juice. Vip!

'*Ah!*'

Come squirted from her gash as her bottom squirmed.

'You want me to give head, is that it?' she gasped, to Rev Ellum. 'I've sucked bigger cocks than yours.'

Rev Ellum laughed; Tracee writhed on the sofa under Mickey's tonguing, her clit stiff and a pool of come staining the fabric beneath her cunt.

Vip!

'Ooh!'

The cane whistled before each lash, and Cherri's ass clenched convulsively between strokes. Her fesse-muscles strained, the crack of her ass tightened, but still the wood found a deep welt and cut it deeper, making her gorge rise. Paula masturbated as she caned the squirming red buttocks of her naked victim. Cherri's cooze dripped come onto the sofa, and her cunt-basin wriggled on the sofa back, rubbing her stiff clitty. Rev Ellum stood with his giant cock inches from her face.

Vip!

'*Ahh!* Please, please, stop!'

Tracee groaned in orgasm as her cunt juice slopped Mickey's face; Paula whinnied as she masturbated to come, and said Cherri had taken twenty-seven cane-strokes.

'I'll bet she's longing to orgasm,' Rev Ellum said. 'Go ahead, Cherri, and diddle yourself.'

Cherri groaned in shame as she slid her fingers into the wetness of her brimming cunt and masturbated. Caned and in pain, incredulously, she pressed her stiff clitty and stroked the wet pouch, longing for the orgasm welling in her fluttering belly to explode.

Vip! Vip! Vip!

'*Ahh!*'

'The beating is complete,' said Rev Ellum, 'and the lord's service may commence.'

Cherri's fingers still diddled her cunt and clitty as Paula and Tracee knelt before Rev Ellum, each in turn taking his cock to the back of her throat and sucking for a minute, titties quivering. Droplets of come splattered the floor beneath the parted thighs of each fellatrice. Cherri masturbated faster and faster until she screamed. Hard, hot cock-meat rammed the exposed hole of her own anus, and got an inch – two inches – then, all the way inside her asshole, thudding against her root.

'*Ah!* No, no, *please, no.*'

The pain of her anal penetration by the monstrous cock was terrifying, yet she continued to diddle herself as Rev Ellum buggered her, slamming her rectum in hard thrusts, which oiled his cock with Cherri's ass-grease. Her buttocks squirmed, rising to meet the male's ramming cock; Cherri felt her whole anus and belly, filled to bursting, would explode. Come flowed in a torrent from her cunt; she longed to climax as the massive cock stretched her ass-hole and filled her with hot cream.

Rev Ellum grunted and she felt the first droplet of sperm wet the root of her anus. She thrust her ass harder, squeezing the cock with her anal elastic, and feeling the member tremble and stiffen as it slid in and out of her anal hole, now slimy with ass-grease. Her own orgasm burst on her just as Rev Ellum's cream jetted hot in her ass, and so powerfully that sperm bubbled from her anus into the come dripping onto her thighs. Rev Ellum's cock, slamming the root of Cherri's ass, delivered the last of his sperm, and Cherri groaned in orgasm, as her anus frothed over with copious creamy spunk. She slumped, gasping.

'Please keep her, master,' panted Tracee. 'There's so much to do with that tight pussy, and those sugarbuns.'

'She can stay locked in the dungeon,' said Paula, swishing the cane. 'I want to work on those titties and that cooze.'

'No!' Cherri cried. 'You're horrible.'

'Horrible things await a scapegrace,' said Rev Ellum. 'Look at your computer-projected probable futures.'

Cherri saw herself on the video screens: toiling, bare to the waist, in a prison chain gang, with a guard's whip striping her back; chained to her bed, buggered, and sucking endless cocks, in a roach-ridden whorehouse; masturbating alone, in solitary confinement, in jail; then, a radiantly nude princess, enthroned above a green pyramid, attended by naked slaves. Rev Ellum frowned and turned the computer off, but the last image would not go away.

'Get the fucking witch out of here,' he muttered.

'Want me to call the sheriff?' said Tracee Pyle.

'Yes, call Josie.'

'Fuck you, creeps!' said Cherri. 'And piss on you, Mickey!'

Cherri bolted for the door. She scooped her clothing from the Corvette and began to run towards the interstate. Rev Ellum's curses followed her, promising the highway patrol would get her wherever she fled. Cherri crashed through the forest, lungs bursting, her naked body stung and bruised but free. She knew how to run; now, there was no question of doing anything else.

A truck stopped, and Cherri awoke from her nightmare reverie.

'Why, you're an early bird,' said a woman's voice from the driver's seat, as the door swung open. 'Get in.'

Cherri got in.

'Some suntan!' said the trucker. 'Plenty of sun where we're going. Need it for the grapes. Skin like that, you must get plenty of sun. That is a nudist's tan.'

She put her palm on Cherri's bare upper thigh and stroked her. Half awake, Cherri shifted, revealing her bushy mons, straggling moist under her skirtlet.

'Mm-mm,' she murmured. 'Is this California?'

'Oregon.'

'Sure looks like California.'

'It's east Oregon.'

The sun was crimson, low in the cloudless western sky. Ahead, stretched a plain of scrubland. Cherri sat up, rubbing her eyes. They were on a blacktop highway, its ribbon empty of vehicles. The driver let her palm slide further up Cherri's thigh, touching the lower fronds of her pubic forest. Her knuckles moved under Cherri's skirtlet.

'You don't look like a trucker,' Cherri said, shifting her buttocks for air and opening her thighs wider.

'You don't look like a hitch-hiker.'

Cherri liked the caress of the older girl, and let it excite her sexually. Far from the hellish scene, the weals on her bare bottom and her orgasm under buggery, from which her anus still smarted, no longer seemed invasions of her person: rather, submissive accomplishments. *Tracee Pyle gets caned every week, and likes it. I feel good, whipped and butt-fucked, now that it's over with. That's kind of shaming, but maybe a girl can have*

28

fun with shame. Cherri opened her thighs wider, and raised her buttocks, so that the trucker's hand could stroke her bare bottom and play with the lower lips of her vulva. Her cunt-lips moistened.

The truck-driver, in her early twenties, wore a short pink linen skirt, its suit jacket hanging neatly by the bunk at the rear of her seat. Under the skirt was a flounced petticoat in white cotton, protruding three inches from the skirt's hem. Her long legs shone in white, fine-mesh nylon stockings, and her feet were encased in shiny pink stilettos. Auburn hair bounced in a perfect straight wave over her white satin blouse, with two buttons loose at the neck, where a choker of pearls sparkled on big, jutting breasts, upthrust by a crimson latex bra-corset, tightened to eighteen or nineteen inches at the waist, to her evident discomfort.

'You've been asleep all day,' she said. 'I expect you'll want to pee. Use this.'

She reached behind her and gave Cherri a rose-patterned porcelain jug. Cherri did need to pee urgently and the truck showed no signs of stopping. There was ample room for her to hunker down in front, hoist her skirtlet and piss copiously into the vessel. The driver watched, lips pursed, as the golden spray hissed from Cherri's tight gash-flaps, its arc so wide that the jug only just contained her fluid. When Cherri had finished and resumed her seat, taking care to hold her moist quim away from her skirtlet, the driver lifted her skirt right to her waist, showing her white lace garter belt and straps, but no panties at all, only a mons with a brown forest as luxuriant as Cherri's own. She took a wad of pink toilet paper from her stocking-top, and wiped Cherri's pussy dry. After placing the soiled paper in a satin-lidded box, and emptying the jug onto the roadway, she replaced her hand on Cherri's body, but this time fully on her wet cunt-thatch, and with her fingertips brushing the girl's extruded clitoris and moist quim-lips. She did not replace her skirt over her own bare pubis. Cherri gasped and relaxed her buttocks, leaving her thighs parted. Her nipples tingled as the driver began a slow massage of the exposed vulva.

'You have a good bush,' she said. 'I just knew you and I'd get on. No panties is the only way I can relax. But if the boss found out! I'd be spanked on the bare, at least. The rules say we must always dress in ladylike manner. Those titties of yours must be at least a 42.'

'44,' Cherri said.

'I'm a titty 40, but I have to beat you for ass. I'm 41.'

'44,' said Cherri. 'Sorry.'

'It's OK! At your height, you can handle it. I noticed the way you peed. You must be very tight down there.'

'Is that good or bad?' said Cherri.

'Good, I'd say. Assuming you like guys.'

'I guess so. They're all there is.'

'Not all the time. I'm Billie, short for Wilhelmina.'

Her massage of Cherri's quim became more intimate and Cherri's clitoris began to stiffen as her gash seeped come. She murmured her own name. The pleasure in her cunt-basin at Billie's expert caress removed any objection to such sudden intimacy. *I'm a scapegrace, so might as well enjoy it*. Billie's fingers traced the weals on Cherri's ass.

'You've been whipped or caned recently,' she said.

Cherri nodded.

'Proper spanking keeps a lady in order. Want to tell me about it? We've an hour to the winery.'

'You mean we're not going to California?' Cherri said.

'Wycherley's winery, Oregon, is where *I'm* going,' said Billie. 'You can come and work, if you like. Way I read you, no job, no money, and on the run. Yeah?'

'Something like that.'

'Meaning completely like that. Being a wine girl isn't too bad, if you obey the rules. Correct dress is one – Wycherley's wine is for refined folks, so all our girls

30

must dress right – trash chic is definitely out in east Oregon, however de rigueur it might be on Rodeo Drive.'

The name meant nothing to Cherri, but she didn't care as the fingers caressed her vulva, already oozing come at Billie's insistent pressure on her tingling clit. Cherri brushed her stiff nipples under her flimsy blouse. Billie did not attempt penetration of Cherri's tight quim, but squeezed her come-soaked gash-flaps while pressing hard on the swelling clitty.

'Sure, I'll try it,' gasped Cherri. 'Oh, you're making me so wet. You've such sweet fingers.'

'Why, thank you for the compliment,' said Billie. 'A girl gets lonely on these long runs.'

Gingerly, Cherri's hand slithered across Billie's nyloned thigh, and found the girl's own cunt as moist as her own. She began to thumb the hardening clitoris, and two fingertips penetrated the wet lips of Billie's gash. Her cunt-bush was soaked in perspiration and come.

'That's nice,' she moaned. 'You can tell me your story, if you like. See, mostly what I do, driving long hauls, is diddle myself, and it's good to have – *oh!* Yes, that's good.'

'I diddle myself a lot,' Cherri murmured.

Cherri's thumbnail and forefinger pinched the girl's stiff nubbin. Cherri began hesitantly, then blurted her whole story as the two females frigged their cunts. She did not omit her buggery and shame at her whipping, nor her resentment at being thus victimised, yet described her pride at being able to stand a naked flogging.

'A trailer park?' was Billie's only comment, delivered with pursed lips. 'You seem to have manners, but be aware, the rules allow corporal punishment – a mere formality – if wine girls are unladylike. Is it true, you're a seasoned masturbatress? I have to be sure. Many girls play with themselves, but less than dutifully.'

Cherri said masturbation was her only pleasure in South Chehalis.

'I knew it when I saw you. I just delivered a cargo to Seattle, and I passed you on I-5, went off at the next exit, and doubled back to pick you up. You're one of us.'

She had four fingers stroking Cherri's anus and cunt-lips, and was thumbing her erect clit, so that rivulets of come soaked Cherri's torn stockings. Billie's quim drooled juice over her cotton petticoat.

'I'd say you can take more than mild corporal punishment,' Billie panted, cupping Cherri's entire cunt, perineum and wealed lower buttocks. 'Even I get caned bare-ass, if I'm bad. As in, forgetting my manners, like, asking if you're a virgin? I saw how fine your piss was. That slit looks as if it's never opened to cock, and your clitty's so big, you must give her a real pounding, to get off.'

Her masturbation of Cherri was feverish, and Cherri responded. Billie's petticoat was wet through with come, while Cherri's puddled the truck seat.

'I don't mind,' Cherri moaned. 'Sure, I'm a virgin.'

'You liked anal?' murmured Billie.

'What?'

'Butt-fucking. When you took cock in your asshole.'

'No!' Cherri whimpered, as the woman frigged her clitty, with a severe pinching between finger and thumb. 'I mean – oh, don't ask, please.'

'You mustn't be ashamed, Cherri. Like girls masturbating each other – it's no sin, despite what the maidmaster and all those other preachers think, or profess to. I'm butt-fucked regularly. There!'

Billie flushed.

'Men round here are not exactly sophisticated, but willing enough. The boss doesn't mind.'

Cherri thanked Billie for her plain speaking, but said she had had enough of preachermen for a while.

'If a guy was kind, though, and had a really awesome cock . . .'

'You *are* one of us,' purred Billie, and both girls giggled.

Cherri told Billie about her anus and its elasticity, and said she guessed her pussy would not be so tight if she were deflowered. She said she knew men desired her, but feared her shiny bronze skin, her *difference*.

'Quite a paradox – never been fucked, because of your tight hole, and a tight hole because you've never been fucked,' said Billie, 'even though you look like every guy's dream centrefold, in the flesh. There are some things a male is good for. Butt-fucking is one of them, and preaching the lord's soothing word is another. Girls together can get a little antsy. The maid-master doesn't visit as often as he'd like. He has several states to tend. He's a celebrity.'

Billie pushed two fingers into Cherri's wet slit and stroked her anus with her pinkie finger, lubricating the hole with Cherri's gushing cunt-slime, before penetrating the anal shaft to an inch. Cherri moaned, her buttocks writhing against her masturbatress, whose wrist rubbed Cherri's throbbing clit, as she finger-stroked both cunt and anus. Ahead of them in the heat haze lay a valley, with vineyards stretching to the horizon and a gateway announcing 'Wycherley's Winery'. In the centre stood a big house, all white, with turrets. Cherri pressed on Billie's clitoris – her skirt was fully ridden up, revealing her whole tan buttocks, without bikini marks, and the writhing wet mass of her gash-lips and clit. Billie's belly quivered under the latex corselet and she hissed through her teeth, yelping, as Cherri's fingers brought her flowing cunt to orgasm. Cherri squeezed her bare ass-globes on the fingers that probed her holes, bathing them in her cunt-juice. Her own climax followed Billie's and, after Cherri whimpered eight or nine times in spasm, Billie at once scooped a palmful of her come and pressed her lips to it, sucking in the fluid and swallowing it.

'Mm,' she said. 'Not bad at all. Should make for an interesting vintage. I'm chief taster, you see.'

They slowed, and stopped at the gateway to the white castle, and a female guard saluted. Apart from a green peaked cap and boots, and a green corset, that pinched her waist to no more than eighteen inches, she was nude and golden-skinned. Hair poked in tufts from her armpits and her legs were downy and unshaven, like the rampant curls of her pubic bush. Her mane flowed, a cascade of gold, over nut-brown skin to caress the swelling of her huge bare breasts. Her body was superbly buffed, yet her woman's curves flowed and swelled smoothly, with massive breasts and buttocks – in particular the breasts, which stood like two perfect, slightly conic pyramids of taut flesh, pointing straight up from the ribcage, and almost as big as Cherri's. The hard crimson nipples were like miniature pyramids, softened at the edges. Her name-badge, pinned through her left nipple, identified her as Orchid Sommer. She was all muscle, with a centrefold's figure – Cherri felt guilty at her pang of envy. Orchid was 39-23-39, and hailed from Casper, Wyoming. She was twenty years old, and carried a cane under her armpit.

'Evening, miss,' she said. 'Fourteen minutes late. That means fourteen strokes. Sorry.'

She began to stroke her breasts, one after the other, as though she were touch-typing, ending with gentle taps to each rock-like nipple. Billie bit her lip, and sighed.

'I had to stop for a hitcher,' she said, with a winsome smile. 'A new recruit.'

'Sorry, miss. You know the rules,' said the guard, blowing a droplet of sweat from her nipple.

'Of course,' said Billie. 'You're quite right, officer.'

The guard saluted again, her breasts snapping to attention, and the truck resumed its progress towards the immaculate white castle.

'It's marvellous,' gasped Cherri. 'That fabulous girl, what was with her breasts? Like, she was diddling her nipples?'

'The guard girls have their breasts surgically enhanced,' said Billie. '100% organic, growing fibre-optic material, grafted into the lactic glands. Each breast is a terminal, connected to our central computer, and has its own code. The central computer can transmit coded information to the guard girls, which they feel as a series of intricate electrical pulses, like tickling. Each guard girl has her own codes, one for each breast. It's hacker-proof, so that no one escapes discipline.'

'That's spooky.'

'This is America,' said Billie.

'I guess so.'

'You must take your work and the rules seriously, and accept whatever correction you may earn, if the boss is displeased. Frankly, few of our butts are unmarked by the cane, and it can be pretty hard, as all canings are on the bare – always. Fourteen! I'll be sleeping on my belly, tonight.'

She shivered.

'I guess I can take it,' said Cherri. 'I took thirty on the bare, from a girl I thought was my friend. Sure, any place needs rules. But who makes them?'

'Why, I do. I'm Wilhelmina Wycherley. I'm the boss.'

Frigg Heidahl was Cherri's roommate. They shared a small apartment, with one double bed, and two identical closets, in the wine girls' turret of the replica mediaeval castle. CCTV cameras surveyed the room from each corner of the floor and ceiling, with green blinking lenses. An unsmiling guard girl, nude but for boots and pinching corset, led Cherri through the maze of corridors. Frigg opened the door at once, and introduced herself. She was Norwegian, from Duluth, Minnesota, and said she was pleased to have company. Completely nude, and seeing Cherri's surprise, she laughed.

'We don't wear clothes, daytime,' she said. 'You'll see why. It's messy work! Your formal things are all in there.'

She pointed to the second closet.

'I guess they're the same as mine. They told me not to peek, or I'd have my ass striped. I'm just dying to compare. I've never had so many beautiful things! Miss Wycherley has America's biggest collection of, you know, pre-owned intimate garments from European royalty! Like this castle, it's a replica of a real French cha-too from history.'

'I never thought about history, much,' Cherri said, sitting on the bed.

'Back in Duluth, we always lived in some trailer park, and I never had things of my very own. I had to share my sister's panties even. Is that gross, or what?'

Cherri made a face.

'Supper's in an hour,' Frigg said. 'The bell rings, and we have to report within three minutes. Yesterday, I got lost, and I was late, and –' she shivered '– well, you can see.'

She swivelled, showing Cherri her bare buttocks. They bore dark, unfaded cane-weals, about ten in number, Cherri estimated. As well as her buttock-weals, swollen to crisp ridges of skin, there were fresher, broader whipmarks crimsoning her bare back.

'Messy work?' murmured Cherri, trying to ignore the quickening of her pulse, and the fresh seep of juice in her quim, at the sight of the girl's bruised naked body.

'Yeah, and more,' sighed Frigg, shrugging. 'I guess you want to shower? Why don't we shower together? It would be fun. Am I going too fast? I mean, your driver explained, didn't she?'

She blushed, suddenly.

'She did more than that,' Cherri replied.

'Then you understand,' said Frigg, swallowing, her eyes on Cherri's pubis. 'We're supposed to be best friends.'

36

'Sure, I'll shower with you, Frigg,' said Cherri, standing, and letting her skirtlet fall, then sliding off her top. 'Friends are something I can use, right now.'

Frigg nodded agreement, then whistled.

'Wow! You've been whipped,' she exclaimed. 'With a bod like that, you'll be everyone's friend. That ass just begs for thrashing, and there are plenty of guards who'll love to watch those melons squirm. I hope you can take caning on the bare. I guess I should envy you. I'm sure I'll love it, once I'm broken in. It's what I've always fantasised about, having my bare ass spanked – I mean a proper lady's spanking. Back home, I got hit, but that's not the same as baring your ass for a real, shivery set from a cane, is it?'

'I guess not,' said Cherri, her cunt juicing more heavily as she saw the girl's own obvious excitement.

'Not many girls understand,' said Frigg.

'I'm beginning to,' Cherri said, 'I think.'

Cherri showed her own buttock-weals, and stroked the ridges left by her thrashing, to Frigg's excited pleas that Cherri tell her everything. She let Frigg touch her bottom. Frigg was smaller and wirier than Cherri, with an ash-blonde mane that brushed the unusually large, plumlike nipples of her conical breasts, twisted slightly upwards, jutting firmly without support. Her figure was 37-22-38. Her legs and bottom were hard muscle, like her arms, and her belly was flat, but the big fesses swelled dramatically from her tiny waist into long, coltish legs, almost the equal of Cherri's own. Her armpits were befurred, like her pubic bush, which was fleecy rather than curled, and drooped over her gash, well down her thighs, which parted in a gap. The quim-lips were fleshy and slack, showing her shiny pink pouch, unlike Cherri's thick but closed gash-flaps. Cherri laid her hand on Frigg's ridged bottom.

'Your butt already has friends, then,' she said.

The girl's bottom began to undulate gently at Cherri's touch and Cherri stroked the hardened cane weals.

Cherri felt Frigg's fingers exploring her own bruised bare buttocks. The pressure of the girl's fingers caused a seep of wet in her slit; Frigg's glistening pouch was as red as her face, and come gleamed on her inner thighs.

'Not so many as yours, I bet,' Frigg blurted. 'Want to trade stories while we shower?'

Cherri outlined her torture, butt-fucking, and escape, but Frigg expressed no surprise. The bathroom, too, had cameras, with tiny windshield wipers to desteam the lenses. There was no shower curtain: the girls were clearly visible as they soaped each other's nude bodies. Frigg learned that Miss Wycherley herself had picked up Cherri.

'So the boss has masturbated you already!' she cried.

'How did you know?' Cherri blurted, adding, 'dumb question, huh?'

'She didn't spank you?'

'No.'

'I would have.' Frigg giggled.

Cherri squatted on the toilet while Frigg ran the shower, explaining that it was a Turkish squatter: not a normal toilet with a bowl and seat, but a hole in the floor, with a pair of footrests for the user to position her anus over the hole, leaving her entire operation on view. A floor pedal flushed the hole. Frigg blatantly watched as an enormous dung formed and dropped with ease from Cherri's anus.

'Wow,' Frigg exclaimed. 'That monster must have hurt.'

It was Cherri's turn to blush.

'No,' she said. 'It tickles. It's nice.'

'I bet you liked your butt-fucking.'

'*Liked* my ass fucked? Get òutta town!'

Didn't I, though?

There was no toilet paper, and Cherri started to wipe herself with her hand before Frigg showed her how to squirt her anus and cunt with a separate spray nozzle. The girls climbed into the steaming hot shower.

'Miss Grayfold inducted me,' said Frigg, her fingers soaping the outside of Cherri's slit. 'She finger-fucked me all the way from Idaho, it felt like. I've been travelling ages. On the interstates, mostly – 60, 15, 84. I was hoping to get to Reno, or Vegas. Anywhere a girl can earn a living, and anywhere away from my shit-head husband. Man, all those truckers I had to fuck, or go down on, just to get a ride! I was only butt-fucked twice, but I earned every fucking mile. I was so glad when a woman trucker picked me up, and she was so sweet, just wanted to diddle, and I came and came! I never juiced so much – I never came once with a *guy* before! Dumb fucking Minnesota Lutherans! Hey, you're tight.'

Cherri told more of her life candidly, including her pride in her virginity. Frigg was no virgin, but thrilled to hear of Cherri's matter-of-fact account of sucking cocks. She refused to believe Cherri's half-hearted denial of anal pleasure, and got two impish fingers inside Cherri's anus, making Cherri squeal, closing her fesses tight and squeezing her hole on the girl's fingers to trap them.

'You don't mind sharing a bed?' whispered Frigg.

'Might not sleep much.'

'And we could, you know, spank each other, for fun. There are straps and paddles and stuff.'

'Yes, we could.'

'We have all night.'

'We have right now, too,' Cherri said.

3

American Meat

Cherri began a slow, teasing caress of Frigg's wet gash
and swollen clit, alternating with her rock-hard nipples,
which Cherri soaped, adding her own cunt's come to the
lather as the girl gasped her story. Frigg's marriage at
eighteen had meant no more than switching trailer
parks. Her bare ass no longer squirmed under her
stepmother's or sister's strap, in Duluth, but under her
new husband's belt, in South Itasoa. Cherri kept
soaping Frigg's body, running her hands over the
quivering hard fesses and cleansing the crack of her ass,
the perineum and cunt-lips, while masturbating her own
clitoris, and careful not to get stinging soap into either
of their mucous holes.

'I didn't mind the strapping so much,' Frigg said,
'because he was usually drunk, and maybe I deserved it.
He was kind of weird, even for South Itasoa. Used to
stuff my cunt with chilli peppers. He was mad, see, that
fucking wouldn't bring me off, but I could make myself
come by masturbating. He wouldn't go down on me,
said it was dirty, but that's Lutherans for you. He
taught me to break eggs in my cunt, for his breakfast
scrambled. I learned a lot about my pussy. Then he used
to tie me up. He was real careful about tying me up, first
just to the bed, but then he studied a book of knots and
had me bundled up just like a package, with only my tits

40

and butt bare for whopping, so I couldn't get free, even if I wanted to.'

'Even if,' Cherri said.

'I kind of liked it, after a time,' Frigg admitted. 'If only he'd beaten me more like a real gentleman would have. And he liked to watch while his buddies sport-fucked me. I hated that part, except for Nestor, who had a real big dick, and was pretty good, but Bobby got jealous, sometimes, because Nestor's cock was bigger than his. That was when he whopped me raw, and left me hogtied for a whole day, because he figured I liked fucking Nestor better than him – which, truth to tell, I did. Nestor was Swedish, from Amnicon Falls, and Swedes and Norwegians don't mix well. We used to go fishing when the lake froze over in winter, you know?'

Cherri said that it didn't freeze in winter where she came from, and Frigg pulled a face.

'Really? Anyway, guys cut a hole in the ice and build a hut round it, to last the winter, and have a camping stove with the heat high up, not to melt the ice. Bobby didn't even make a hole, but he tied me up and put a dinner heater on the ice, beside me, with the flames real close to the ice, and he'd sit there drinking with his buddies while the ice melted around me, and I'd fall in the hole, all hogtied. My ass had a plug in it, lashed to a rope, and when I was ten feet deep, he'd leave me down there for a minute, then haul me up. I had to hold that butt-plug tight! That water was so cold, I came up blue. He'd strap my ass and tits to warm me up, and he and his buddies took turns at fucking me. Hey, that's nice.'

Cherri was gently slapping Frigg's bare soapy buttocks while running her thumb up and down her cleft.

'Nestor would bring his girl Anita, sometimes, and they'd make us do a twosome, like, we diddled with our fingers and the girl who came last got hogtied and sunk. That was OK, because I got some beer to drink. They'd all fuck Anita, too, after whopping her. She was Armenian, from West Duluth. I can understand trading women, if you're not married, but isn't it really gross for a guy to fuck another girl in front of his wife?'

'I'm not surprised you ran out on him.'

'Oh, that was because he wouldn't buy me things. Boy, was he cheap! But I kind of miss being tied up.'

'I'll tie you up,' murmured Cherri, 'later.'

'Yeah!' cried Frigg, hugging Cherri, so that their wet breasts, cunts and bellies sloshed together. 'I'll be your friend for ever. Hey, Cherri, let's diddle now. You've made me so wet.'

'While we dress,' said Cherri, rinsing them both, with her hand already fully penetrating Frigg's dripping cunt.

'Yeah!'

The two dripping girls opened their closets, and at once Frigg positioned herself behind Cherri, pressing her breasts to her back, and cupping Cherri's breasts with both hands, the fingers trapping Cherri's stiff wet nipples in twin vices. Cherri felt the lush jungle of Frigg's massive pubic bush scrub the bare skin of her buttocks in a rhythmic, circular caress. Frigg craned to look over Cherri's shoulder.

'Wow,' she said. 'You have more than me.'

Cherri said she had never seen so many clothes before, nor such a variety of underwear.

'Yeah, well, it's weird here; when you dress for supper, if you have really tight things on, uncomfortable things that pinch your skin, you get more to eat. You dress up, but when you get to the great hall you strip off and sit down in just your lingerie, if you know what I mean. You have to cover your titties and pubies, but if you wear like a really tight corset or garter belt, you get extra servings of food. We have to leave a lot of skin bare, because they cane us at table if we've earned a punishment during the day. Miss Wycherley has a collection of some lovely canes – one belonged to the

42

Count of Flanders, for beating naked girls while he dined. Isn't that so romantic? Better than some grungy old biker's belt.'

Frigg rolled off the names of some of the exotic garments in Cherri's closet – a pelerine cloak, cut away to show the buttocks, a Medici collar of stiffened lace, skirts long or minute with accordion or knife pleats; teddies, camisoles, basques, bustiers, stockings and lingerie in silk, satin, Venetian lace, Brussels lace, sheer voile or crêpe georgette; a mass of corsetry, garter belts and straps, S-bend corsets, thrusting out the breasts and buttocks while compressing the waist with bone stays.

Cherri said she was suddenly hungry.

'What's that?' she asked.

'I think it's called a waspie corset,' said Frigg. 'I wouldn't dare wear that.'

'I will. You'll have to help me into it.'

'Can we do each other, then? I'm so wet.'

'Yes.'

Frigg heaved, panting, as she knotted Cherri into the tightest eyeholes of the peach-coloured corset, which strained even Cherri's narrow stomach. Cherri gasped as each eyehole was fastened by Frigg, giving herself leverage with her sole on Cherri's bare bottom and tickling her ass-crack with her toes, twining her big toe round a long wet strand of pubic mane, and poking it into Cherri's butthole. The corset closed at seventeen inches, pinching her waist to a finger, but as her body started to like the constraint Cherri's quim dripped more copious come, and Frigg's foot played at the cleft of her lower cheeks, teasing Cherri's swelling wet cunt-lips until her foot was glistening with Cherri's juice.

'You'll need panties,' she said. 'Stockings, garter-straps and all.'

After choosing, Cherri soon stood in complete under-things, the corset complemented by a peach bra way too

43

small and which thrust the teat-flesh up until the nipples were only just covered. She had matching panties, a string around her waist and tight in her ass-crack. Peach, too, were the tightly chafing garter belt and straps; her stockings were chocolate brown, in voile silk. Cherri chose a pair of pinching stiletto shoes, so high and narrow that walking was painful and only just possible. She looked at Frigg, in her own underclothing: no corset, but white bra and panties too small for her; matching stockings and garter straps, and a long peignoir of transparent voile.

Beneath the clothing in each closet were spanking paddles, ropes, cuffs, canes, and a variety of devices made of rubber to resemble the male organ. One device had two such dildoes set in a shallow rubber cup, shaped to fit across the vulva and buttocks, and with a waist strap, with the angle of the shafts suggesting its use lying down. Frigg explained that it was a come pot. Every night, wine girls were to masturbate, alone or with each other, and store their come for collection each morning by the guard.

'Better put something on top,' said Frigg. 'How about we both wear pelerine cloaks? They leave your ass exposed so you can wiggle, you know?'

Cherri chose a Medici collar, too, the stiffened lace-like spikes encircling her neck, and obliging her to maintain a stiff, storklike gait.

'I can't wait forever,' Frigg said.

Cherri did not demur when Frigg knelt before her, pulling down Cherri's loinstring, and plunging her tongue to its root into Cherri's soaking pouch. She swallowed Cherri's come for minutes before clamping the stiffened, extruded clitoris with her lips and starting to chew. Cherri moaned and pressed Frigg's hair to her cunt. She parted her thighs as far as her stretched string permitted and caressed Frigg's hair with her quim and buttocks, until Frigg's mane was soaking and glistened

44

with Cherri's gushing come. Frigg masturbated her own clitoris with backhand and forehand wipes, until Cherri pulled her onto the bed, keeping her back straight, so as not to twist her collar. Cherri buried her nose in Frigg's flowing gash and began to rub her whole face across the girl's anus, perineum and cunt-flaps, pausing alternately to stick her nose fully into the soaking pouch or the wet mane of cunt-hairs, to sniff deeply or to lick the girl's asshole as Frigg chewed on Cherri's throbbing wet nubbin. The two girls caressed each other's bare buttocks, cupping them in their hands like wine goblets, while they drank come from each other's cunt. Frigg moaned, her loins writhing, as she pressed her gash to Cherri's hungry face.

'Tongue-fuck my asshole,' she whimpered.

Cherri got her tongue a good two inches into Frigg's anus, and began to bob her head, like a pigeon's. Frigg's anal elastic contracted round her tongue; the hole tasted faintly acrid, like vinegar. Ass-tonguing made Frigg's come flow faster from her cooze, and her clit banged against Cherri's face while her teeth bit Cherri's swollen nubbin. The corset was so tight around Cherri's waist that she could not stop her quim erupting in a steaming burst of piss, which stained her peach panty-string, spanning her quivering thighs. Frigg opened her jaws in a cavern to catch the fine golden spray and swallowed almost all, the rest dribbling on her chin and breasts. Otherwise, Cherri would have soiled their bedlinen.

'Mmm,' Cherri moaned.

Cherri's belly heaved: the girl's submission, in drinking from bladder as well as cunt, excited her to the point of no return. Cherri cried aloud as orgasm flooded her, and the hot piston of her tongue pounded inside Frigg's writhing anus.

'Oh! Ah!' Frigg gasped and began to buck and squirm as her own climax took her, and her nails clawed Cherri's shuddering, come-soaked buttocks.

Cherri opened her mouth wide and swallowed the girl's torrent of come as Frigg's whole cunt shook in spasm, spewing the oily liquid from every crevice left momentarily unchewed by Cherri's lips, teeth and tongue. Frigg gasped that she deserved a hard spanking from Cherri, but longed also to spank Cherri's 'fantastic' brown globes. Cherri whispered that was OK, if it pleased her new friend. They lay together, come-wet bodies clinging, until the bell for supper rang. Hastily, they wrapped themselves in their cutaway, butt-revealing coats, and Frigg opened the door. Outside, stood a booted guard girl, Bev Ellerbee, hand blatantly at her cunt, naked under the severely laced corset that fixed her waist at nineteen inches. Her face was flushed but stony; beneath her dripping cunt, strung from her waist, was a brimming rubber come-pot. She began to rapidly touch, pat and stroke her breasts. Like the guard Orchid Sommer, she was tanned all over, with a mane of long chestnut hair that swept across her teats; though slender, she was heavy-titted, her breasts and buttocks ripe slabs of rounded muscle, with the nipples perking up like little flowerpots. Her figure was 39-22-39, and she was twenty-one, originally from Toledo, Ohio.

'Masturbating, wine girls?' Bev said.

'Why, sure,' said Frigg uneasily.

'Your come-pots, please.'

'Uh, they're empty just now.'

'You know the rules. Slurping is only permitted once the come-pot is full. I watched through the keyhole.'

'But, officer, Cherri's only just –'

'Hurry, or you'll be late for supper and earn a caning,' said Bev, as she tapped each nipple, 'in addition to the one I've just posted.'

Frigg led the way through winding corridors, which echoed to the girls' high heels, clacking on the stones. She said this was a special supper for a Japanese guest, an important buyer. They arrived last to join a line of

46

twenty-three girls, including Miss Wilhelmina Wycherley herself. The girls were spaced at three-feet intervals along a corridor wall, with the first girl at the dining-room door. The line was a fashion parade of plumes, stoles, fur, and even gowns of shiny rubber. Beneath their showy outerwear all, like Frigg and Cherri, wore only bras, panties, and stockings. Two guard girls, in boots and corsets, patrolled, with canes ready to flick the buttocks of any girl whose head moved. As Frigg and Cherri fell in line, there were 'vips' as canes laid thin lines on buttocks already bare, or hastily bared, in expectation of the stroke, so as to protect flimsy silk or satin panties from ripping.

Another guard stood by the door: completely nude, and with mane hanging flat over jutting, massive breasts, right to mid-thigh. Her hair was jet-black, but her skin the same bronze as Cherri's. Her pubic fleece hung in a mat to the same point as the mane: amidst them glistened a large extruded clitoris, nestling in thick, lustrous gash-lips, which replicated her wide mouth. Her eagle nose jutted like Cherri's own, the nostrils large and flared. Her darkly glowing skin was silken-smooth and rich as chocolate. She wore a whip, glittering with studs, looped at her waist. That guard had no boots: she was barefoot. Her green eyes met Cherri's and glowed.

Each wine girl had to disrobe on entering, and hand her outer garment to another guard, similar in long mane and bronze skin. In her underthings, she passed a third barefoot exotic, whip coiled at waist, and a short wooden cane dangling from her vulva, with its handle lodged inside the cunt. The bronze girl's buttocks clenched, her haunches tensed and spun, and the cane sprang – vip! – to slice the bare or pantied croup of each entrant. Billie Wycherley, clad in yellow bra and panties, with stockings and garters in crimson, clenched her buttocks and quivered like the rest. Cherri trembled as she handed over her pelerine cape, showing her pantied buttocks, and just in time pulling aside the fragile cloth to take her stroke on the bare. Vip! The cane, swinging from the glowing girl's cunt, thrashed Cherri squarely at mid-fesse, making her jump and bite her lip at the sudden, searing welt. Her painful stilettos gave accent to her buttocks, thrusting them up, while her corset ensured the posture of her belly and spine, but the long-haired girls, even uncorsed, had S-curves, with firm, bulging teats, flat bellies, long legs, and full, ripe buttocks, all that despite bare feet. They did not stand on their feet, but rather rolled on the balls of their feet. Repantied, Cherri's buttocks trembled at her cane-stroke, but her Medici collar kept her head erect. Frigg took her stroke with a grimace.

As she was about to enter, Cherri felt a silky forearm restrain her waist, while Frigg passed in front of her. A barefoot guard knelt, and with deep breaths, began to sniff Cherri's pubic and anal region. She was the tallest of the trio, with the fullest buttocks, and larger breasts even than Cherri's, with wide, dark crimson nipples. Her lookalikes joined her, and the three girls crouched, parting Cherri's thighs and smelling her cunt and anus. They bared white teeth in rictus and their green eyes sparkled, with the flared nostrils opening wide. They licked the points of their teeth with glistening pink tongues that seemed to uncurl right from the backs of their throats.

The dining table was long, only three feet across, and the place beside Frigg's was empty. As Cherri was about to sit, Frigg whispered that she had never seen the 'exquisites' sniff a girl's ass before. Billie Wycherley sat at the head of the table, with a Japanese girl at her right. The Japanese wore a pleated grey skirt, white shirt with bow necktie, and white ankle socks over black school shoes. Her petite 36-20-36 figure was tightly encased in the schoolgirl uniform, revealing, in outline, constricting bra, panties and elaborate corset, at no more than sixteen inches, painfully small even for her svelte young body. Her mane was a crown of black gloss, wreathing bright eyes and full, sensuous lips, and showing the bare nape of her neck. The three long-maned girls entered, and eyed Miss Wycherley, who blushed, and went to occupy the vacant place, while the anus-sniffers ushered Cherri to the top of the table. She stood, and found *she knew what to say*.

'Ladies of the vineyard,' she declared, 'a round of applause, please, for our honoured guest, Miss Ona Takira, of the Takira Beverage Corporation.'

Miss Takira rose, and bowed, to the clapping, and only then did Cherri blush. Of course she knew what to say! It was written on Miss Takira's place card.

'During supper, there shall be three chastisements: Miss W. Wycherley, fourteen strokes of the cane, for unpunctuality, Misses F. Heidahl and C. Black, twenty strokes each –' her voice trembled, as she heard the words from her own lips '– for improperly masturbating. Now, before supper, a toast to our guest, Miss Ona Takira, at eighteen years old heiress to Japan's largest beverage company, who intends to finish school while controlling her business.'

She had known to say that, as well. Miss Takira clapped, licking her teeth at the word 'cane'. The three bronze girls attended Miss Takira to deliver a toast. Each girl squatted, with her naked buttocks an inch from the Japanese girl's face; parted her silky bronze ass-cheeks, and broke wind, in a long, musical whistle. Miss Takira's nose wrinkled, sniffed, and flared, as her eyes closed in delight. The air was filled with a salty perfume, like crabmeat. Cherri felt the same need. Shivering, she followed suit, pulled aside the narrow thong of her panties, and spread her buttocks wide. She delivered a long trumpet of wind straight to the nose of the Japanese girl, who smiled, and clapped her hands.

'Mmm, thank you so much for that humiliation,' said Miss Takira, in a flawless Bostonian accent.

Supper began. Three grossly hairy, muscular young studs swaggered into the dining-room, all wearing T-shirts, jeans and boots, with their zippers undone, and huge cocks protruding, stiffened to erection. Each bore a silver tray of food, suspended by a chain looped around the neck of his stiff cock-helmet. The wine girls crossed hands behind their backs as they were served platters of burgers and fries doused in ketchup, and each girl lowered her head to seize the plate's rim in her teeth, then manoeuvre it onto the table. When service was complete, the males returned with bowls containing a cola beverage. At no stage did the fed girls remove their hands from behind their backs, nor look at the huge cocks inches from their faces. The corset girls on patrol waved canes if any girl's eyeball strayed, and one guard, Tara Flick, a short-cropped brunette, twenty, from Kansas City, Missouri, with a lithe 37-21-37 figure, standing 5′4″ tall, caned Mandi Graham four strokes across each nipple, ripping both bra-cups, because she had her thighs pressed too tightly, with seepage of come at her cunt. Blond Mandi, an eighteen-year-old from New London, Connecticut, with a 36-24-38 figure, burst into tears over the shreds of lingerie, and the weals on her teats that made crimson starfish of her bruised bare nipples.

'The studs are on ration, Mandi,' Tara snapped. 'Got to work for your thrill-meat, bitch. Feed your face, go back to your room, get dreaming, and fill your come-pot.'

The best-hung male of the three served Cherri and her neighbours: Miss Takira, and the girl named Roslyn Grayfold. Cherri got the biggest and juiciest burger of all, and she, too, kept her hands behind her back. She saw Billie lower her face and rip at her food with her teeth. The others did likewise, and so, clumsily, did Cherri. Only Miss Takira used her fingers, but her food was mostly raw fish. She said she so wished she could acquire the American taste for meat. The room buzzed

50

with the day's gossip: who had crushed the most grapes, whose ass had taken the most stripes, or which girls had masturbated with the best come seepage. The girls ate greedily, yet with exquisite manners: not a drool or stain marred their underwear. Cherri blushed as she felt a slice of pickle slip from her mouth and wedge itself in the cleft of her titties. She asked Roslyn Grayfold if the barefoot girls were Mexicans. She'd heard Spanish back in the trai –

'*Trailer park?*' Grayfold sneered.

'Yeah,' Cherri muttered, blushing furiously.

'Our exquisites aren't Mexicans,' sneered Grayfold, 'and don't speak Spanish. They don't speak at all.'

Grayfold was scarcely older than Cherri herself, but spoke with assumed authority. Her auburn hair was in a mannish, scooped-back 1940s style; she wore a satin bra, panties and stockings set in cream, with a chocolate backseam up each fishnet stocking. Her shoes were cream; the bra, a scalloped sliver that thrust up and exposed almost to the full her large, conic breasts, the wedges of her nipples clearly outlined under the satin. Her breasts, though full and well rounded, were inferior to Cherri's, and her buttocks were smaller. Grayfold frowned at Cherri's whole bronze body: her own tan had bikini-pale patches. She was a trim 39-22-36, from Elgin, Illinois, and her pink corset did not pinch her waist below nineteen inches.

'I believe tonight's floggings are going to be special, miss,' Grayfold said, turning to Miss Takira.

Lips dripping ketchup onto her breasts, Cherri felt herself rise.

'Ladies,' she said, 'the first miscreant shall take her caning. Miss Wilhelmina Wycherley, please take position.'

Was that right? She looked at the tallest exquisite, who did not smile but fixed Cherri with her opalescent green eyes until Cherri turned away. Billie stood, trembling, her lips pale. She unsnapped her crimson garter straps, lowered her yellow panties to her thighs, then stretched her belly across the table and placed each palm under the croup of a girl opposite. She lay, spreadeagled and trapped by the seated girls' asses, with her head resting on their shoulders, and her bare buttocks exposed.

'Volunteers?' Cherri heard herself say.

Every girl's hand shot up, including Roslyn Grayfold's. Cherri's eye caught Frigg's, and she nodded to her roommate. Frigg sprang from the table and bowed to the tallest exquisite, receiving her cane, its handle moist from the folds of cunt-flesh. She positioned herself with the cane raised over Billie's quivering bare buttocks and looked to Cherri. Cherri ordered the guard girls to hold down Billie's feet, then nodded to Frigg. Frigg's teeth gleamed.

'One,' said Cherri.

Vip! The cane whistled, then streaked Billie's bare ass, making her jump, and laying a raw pink weal on the quivering skin.

'Oh! Thank you,' she gulped.

'Two,' said Cherri.

Vip! Billie's bare buttocks clenched tight as Frigg lashed across the globes in the same welt. Billie gasped, and her ass-cheeks writhed, grinding her cunt to the tablecloth. The two girls whose fesses trapped Billie's hands were squirming, their faces pink, as they shifted croups to press the victim's fingers to their coozes.

'Mm! Thank you,' Billie gasped.

'Three,' said Cherri, her own cunt starting to moisten, as she watched the bare bottom of the girl squirming.

Vip!

'*Ah!* Thank you,' she whispered, her buttocks clenching, and her pubic bone slamming the table as the third stroke sliced her naked rump just below her spine, where her skin was tenderest.

'Four.'

Vip!

'*Ah!* That hurt! Thank you.'

Billie shuddered, with her breasts almost squeezed from her bra as the caning slammed her body against the table.

'Five.'

Vip! The cane lashed her thigh-tops, just above the stockings; Billie's bare croup, wealed pink, was darkening to the same crimson as her stockings and garter belt.

'*Ooh!* Thank you.'

Miss Takira had her hand below her skirt, the fingers moving more and more urgently between her thighs on her exposed wet panties. She hissed her pleasure at the spectacle as she masturbated.

'Faster,' murmured Miss Takira.

Cherri's cunt was flowing now with hot come that visibly stained her panties, keenly watched by Roslyn Grayfold. She felt that caning etiquette did not permit her to sit, and cover her wet cunt-basin.

'Six – seven – eight!' Cherri barked.

Vip! Vip! Vip! Three strokes took Billie on the left haunch, the delicate skin of that area striping at once.

'*Oh!* Thank you.'

'Nine – ten – eleven!'

Vip! Vip! Vip! The same, striped her right haunch.

'*Ah!* Th–thank you.'

The girls seated on Billie's hands had to press their whole weights on her as the beaten girl's body shuddered, trying to free itself from caning position: her legs jerked wildly, feet crushed by the two guards. Miss Takira had her skirt up, and her panties' thong poked aside, revealing her hairless quim, with her fingers stuck inside her heavily juicing cunt. She swayed, moaning softly as she rubbed her glistening pink clit protruding like a thumb from her gash flaps. Cherri's cunt oozed come; she dared not meet the green eyes of the

53

exquisites. Her fingers moved inside her panties, twitching at her extruded nubbin, and bathing in her oily gush of come. Pleasure flooded her, and she had to stammer the final command, while masturbating:

'T-twelve – th-thirteen – f-fourteen.'

Vip! A vertical cut took Billie in the crack of her ass, with the cane's tip hitting between the furry cunt-lips and reaching her stiff, exposed clit; the table beneath Billie's writhing cooze was soaked in her come.

'*Ah!* Oh, please have mercy, Frigg! Thank you.'

Vip! Frigg caned Billie the thirteenth stroke at top buttock, the area already wealed with crimson bruises. The bare fesses danced, slamming her cunt on the table in paroxysm.

'*Oh! No! Ah!* Thank you!'

Vip! The fourteenth stroke lashed the writhing girl in the same weal the first stroke had laid, deepening it visibly, and her cries filled the room as her fesses squirmed, crimsoned by her caning, and the bruises a meld in her buttocks' puffy mass of bare flesh.

'*Ah! Oh!* Thank you. Oh, how can a girl be so cruel?'

Billie's striped bare ass continued to clench after Frigg, panting, had laid down her cane. Her cunt and stiff clitoris churned the tablecloth, soaked in her come, and she moaned shrilly as her belly began to heave and she cried in climax. The girls sitting on her hands gasped, come dripping from their panties to the floor, as they squeezed Billie's fingers in their cunts, churning their thighs to rub clitties on the trapped knuckles and bring themselves off. Above the canee's whimpers sounded a hissing, and from Miss Wilhelmina Wycherley's jerking cunt flowed a hot, steaming flood of golden pee. Roslyn Grayfold was masturbating with eager, rapid strokes to her wet panties, and rubbing the rock-hard nipples under her thin cream satin, deeply dented with the nipples' imprints. She thrust her breasts at Miss Takira, with a lick of her teeth, but the visitor was busy with her own clit-rubbing and stroking Cherri's thigh beside her. Cherri worked her hand inside her panties, rubbing both her clitoris and the swollen lips of her gash, and with three fingers a painful inch inside her pouch; she heard her own moans and whimpers of climax join Miss Takira's as the Japanese girl masturbated herself to come at the same time. Takira's hand stroked the twitching bare orbs of Cherri's bottom, fingered the cleft and come-soaked pubic bush, and wrenched Cherri's cunt-fronds, matted in come, at her anus and cooze-flaps.

'American meat is so toothsome,' said Miss Takira.

'I'd have done a better job,' spat Roslyn Grayfold. 'Only pissing herself, the bitch! I'd have made her dung, and earn a whipping as well!'

The guard Tara Flick, and a wine girl, Elise Wuliger, nodded agreement, which Grayfold acknowledged. Cherri sank to her chair, numbed, and blushing. The tablecloth was replaced by the male servants and Billie resumed her seat with a whimper as her ass touched wood. Chocolate-chip ice-cream was served for dessert, and Cherri got herself even messier. Flustered, she had to announce Frigg's caning, but did not ask for volunteers – appointing, as a safer course, Orchid Sommer, one of the corset girls. Guard Tara held both of Frigg's feet, while Orchid administered the flogging. It was not necessary for Cherri to call the strokes. She gazed as her friend's bare buttocks jerked and squirmed under a full twenty strokes of the cane. *And it's my turn next*. Frigg's yelps of pain, the tears glazing her face, her wriggling bare skin beaten to crimson, her sobbed thank yous, were as sincere as Miss Wycherley's. Miss Takira masturbated herself smoothly and efficiently to further climax as the last stroke landed on Frigg's blotchy dark behind. Her screams seemed to come from far away. Cherri dribbled ice-cream and chocolate mess all down her breasts, where the obstinate pickle still lodged, and onto her bare thighs. At last Frigg's agony was over and, after coffee, the table was cleared completely. Cherri rose unsteadily to her feet.

'The final chastisement, twenty strokes on the bare buttocks, shall be to Miss Cherri Black,' she said, 'and delivered with a studded flail. Followed by a whipping of fifty strokes, on the bare back, for sloppy table manners. She shall be strung up naked and shackled, on the whipping tripod, with her legs and arms fully stretched, and every part of her intimate body exposed to the instrument of correction.'

Cherri's heart pounded, and her come flowed, as her voice pronounced sentence on herself. Whoever had drawn those words from her, they were *her* words, and – her nipples and clitoris tingled, as her quim juiced – she meant them. She wanted to be whipped.

'Is that meant to ease the pain?' whispered Cherri, as Frigg anointed her trussed, nude body with cold lotion.

The tripod had a wheeled base, carrying three wooden poles nailed together at the top. Cherri's body hung by the wrists, roped to a ring at the top of the tripod. Her hair was knotted in the same ring, forcing her head straight up. She wore nothing but her Medici collar, stained with food. Her back, buttocks and torso hung free, while her legs thrust sharply out, each roped to one pole, with one rubber thong buckled at the ankles and one on the thigh, just below her fesses. Her feet twitched two feet from the floor. Added to her shame, and the pain of being stretched, was the sixty-five-degree angle at which she leaned.

'No,' said Frigg. 'It's a saline water-based jelly. It's meant to make your weals sting more.'

'Why?' Cherri sobbed. 'Why *me*?'

'You ordered the flogging,' Frigg replied, grimacing, as she rubbed her own bottom.

'It was those exquisites. They made me say those things!'

'You said them, anyhow,' said Frigg. 'They can read you – like, see into your mind.'

'That doesn't make any sense.'

'It will, when you've been whipped. Why do you think Miss Wycherley gave up control of her own winery so fast? The exquisites arrived, wearing nothing, except jewelled whips as G-strings, and just stared her down, and the next thing, she was bare-assed, too, strung up, and having her back and bottom striped, the way you're going to. Grayfold is jealous because the exquisites haven't whipped her. Those girls' floggings have a special edge that's like no other. After her whipping, Billie knelt and literally kissed their bare asses, tongue right in their cracks, and from then on they were kind of in charge. Or so I hear. See the whips they're going to use? Got little pyramids studded all along the thong. Isn't that cute? It'll hurt you so, Cherri, and I'll get all wet watching you squirm, and I promise I'll come and come like all the other girls as we masturbate, watching your bare ass, and if you're ticked off at me, then you can spank my ass black and blue before we sleep.'

The tripod stood in the center of the room, with the table pushed aside; the wine girls stood in a horseshoe around them, each with quim bared and hand at cooze-flaps. Each girl wore a pint come-pot of silver, dangling from cunt-clamps, which stretched her quim lips to three or four inches. Frigg rubbed the stinging lotion hard on Cherri's cunt-lips and breasts, their nipples already stiffening. Frigg poked between Cherri's gash-flaps, wriggling her fingers in the girl's pouch, then wiped them on Cherri's lips, to let her taste her own come.

'You want this whipping,' said Frigg, 'don't you?'

'Why put stuff on my breasts?'

'That's where they'll whip hardest.'

'They?'

'You'll be flogged by all three exquisites at once.'

4

Maidmaster

'So many states to cover, and so many penitents to chastise! Do you believe people in this town will heed the lord's word, Maid Kelley?' said the young, black-robed man, tossing his shining mane of long, curly hair.

'I do, master,' said one of two young women, flanking him at the pulpit, on the stage.

'And you, Maid Joanne?' he said to the second.

'I do, master.'

Kelley Hide, twenty, of Modesto, California, and Joanne Pascal, twenty-one, of Hanover, New Hampshire, were fair and dark respectively, and their hair hung longer than their master's. They were dressed identically in blue denim halter tops, with bare bellies and cutaway denim shorts to match, revealing them pantiless. Both were firm of breast and buttock, with pencil waists and hard, flat bellies, both physiques uniformly tanned, without bikini marks. Kelley's figure was 42-21-39, at 5'9", and Joanne's 41-22-40, at 5'8", with C- and D-cups respectively, had their firm breasts needed brassieres. Both were barefoot and unhosed, their smooth tanned legs shiny as silk. Beside the pulpit stood a hardwood table, person-sized.

'You first, Maid Kelley,' said the master.

Kelley Hide leaned over the table, pressing her belly to it and grasping its sides. Joanne knelt and unbuttoned the front of Kelley's shorts so that they fell to her ankles. She kicked off the shorts, wrapped her long, bare legs round each table leg, then bent over with her chin on the table and her naked buttocks upthrust.

'Prepare her, Maid Joanne,' said the master.

Joanne curtsied beside Kelley's naked croup, lifted her arm and began to spank her bare bottom. Smack! Smack! Smack! The spanks were gentle at first, but firm, until Kelley's bottom clenched and her skin pinked. Her back arched and her legs quivered as the spanks hardened, and with each spank her breasts jiggled, threatening to burst from their slender denim fastening. By the end of the spanking, a good forty slaps, her fesses were wriggling softly and the crack of the spanks echoed through the hall.

'Your turn, Maid Joanne,' said the master.

Joanne replaced Kelley at the table, and submitted to her own disrobing. When she had taken Kelley's forty spanks on the bare and her equally pink bottom was covered, the master declared them warmed up for duty.

'You've set up a shill, Maid Rona?'

A third girl, stationed by the door, nodded. She was Rona Gumette, nineteen, of New Orleans, Louisiana, fair-haired and clad in clinging, full-length jeans, standing 40-22-38 at 5'8", with her D-cup breasts filling her red check shirt.

'Yes, master. Name of Honey Swade, 21, five-nine, blonde, 39-22-39, C-cup and a lovely spankable ass, big as watermelons almost,' said Maid Rona. 'Got her from a spanking chat room on the internet. She's experienced in chastisement and eager to help the lord.'

'Checked the licence plates in the car park?'

'Every one logged, master.'

'Then, let the people enter.'

Rona opened the doors of the hall, and a crowd filtered into the salon, dimly lit by green candles. Rona moved awkwardly in her tight black jeans, which emphasised the ripe curve of her croup. Rona had been spanked forty on the bare by the master, ten minutes before. Like the others, she was barefoot. The townspeople took their seats, gazing at the tanned, lissom bodies of the helpmaids.

'My pulpit holds no book,' intoned the preacher, 'because the lord gives us *words*, which I and my helpmaids are privileged to share with you.'

He introduced the three girls by name, age and origin.

'The lord's words are not of salvation or redemption,' he continued. 'His words are of eternal shame. There is no blessing in the lord's words, there is only *penitence* . . . for the chosen.'

The crowd stirred. Those words they understood.

'Our great nation, our virtuous republic,' said the master, 'is rotten to the core with sin. The same sinfulness led to the downfall of past republics. The Roman republic's virtue was gnawed away by the fancies of *women*, craving silks, perfume, and jewels, until women's debt destroyed Rome by luxury and ease. The same, my easeful friends, happened to all great nations which perished of depravity. I speak not of the rich, I speak of the sin which lurks in the heart of every man and woman in this room – the sin you commit every day, the sin of sloth. Sloth makes women buy labour-saving appliances, to make their idle lives still easier. It is easy to be sinful, to buy imported foreign things, in pursuit of luxury and comfort – female vices. It is easier to yield to lust than to remain pure. It is easier for women to bare their bodies for easy money and inflame the lusts of men, in the indecencies of the mass media, than to work soberly. It is easy for a slothful female to satisfy those lusts by lying back and allowing males to spew their filthiness between her legs! It is easier for a woman to say yes than to say no! Easier for a woman to lewdly tease than decently cover! To enjoy temptation than to resist! To pamper the flesh

60

than to chastise it! My friends, our republic was built on male virtues of thrift and hard work. Those virtues are gone forever. We have become a nation of women! And who is to blame for that but *women themselves*? I bring you the lord's words, but if you wish the lord to hear *your* words, in these last days of our republic's depravity, he shall hear them only above the sounds *of penitence*!'

He paused and accepted a glass of water from Kelley. He sipped half and emptied the rest on her breasts. The audience gasped. The water made the thin denim cling to Kelley's ripely jutting teats and clearly outlined the full strawberries of her nipples. The master ignored her.

'What penitence does the lord demand?' he asked, at the same time drawing a willow wand, forty inches long, from beneath his robe. 'He demands penitence he can hear! He demands the sound of chastisement on naked, sinful flesh, my friends! *Woman's idle, lustful skin!*'

He waited for the excitement to calm, then continued:

'You wonder why my three helpmaids are with me, two of them clad for their shame in a way far short of decent, and the third still making no secret of her tempting female body? Are they the chosen . . . the elect? No! They have a road to travel before their cries of shame and penitence satisfy the lord. They are here to tell you of the lustful sloth from which the lord has turned them to the painful path of penitence, and to show you how the lord demands his female servants show penitence, so that each American man may become lord of his own female, and chastise her for her own sake and for the sake of our republic. Maid Kelley, will you please begin?'

Kelley stepped forwards, tugging down the hems of her denim shorts, which still left her half-bare.

'I don't rightly know where to start, master,' she mumbled.

Thwack!

The master lashed his cane across the pulpit.

'I think you do, maid,' he roared.

'I was raised on the wrong side of the tracks, master, and I beg you all to believe my badness wasn't my fault! I'm a victim of fate! My daddy was a drunk and a gambler, and my momma was a drunk too, and of easy virtue. We lived in a dirty, lowdown trailer park and I was always skipping school. The only thing I had from there was a driver's licence because my brother Jerry used to boost cars. But when I came to be a woman, I ran away rather than give up my virginity like other girls! I didn't have the chance to enjoy my blessed purity very long! I stole one of Jerry's cars and that was my beginning in badness. It broke down and I hitch-hiked to LA, had to defend my virginity against everybody who picked me up. I wasn't used to wearing under-things; see, I never had much clothing at all, so they thought I was a whore and a tramp, and they were right! May the lord forgive me!

'In Hollywood I got a job waiting tables, and I always dressed to tease, you know? One day, this good-looking dude came in, he had a big black foreign car, and said he could get me into the movies, like I wanted. He asked to see my driver's licence, and nodded, like my age was some big deal, and took me up to his fabulous ranch near Topanga Canyon, with a swimming pool and everything, and gave me champagne to drink, and said I could take a swim. I was a victim of temptation, that I was! There were a whole lot of people from the movie business, he said, and some of them were swimming in the pool, bare-ass naked! I said I had no swimsuit, and he told me swimsuits were *pass-ay* in Topanga Canyon, and anyway, if I wanted a job in movies I'd probably have to show my bod sometime. I was light-headed from wine, so I stripped off and dived in, and pretty soon this other girl about my age swam up and started to touch my breasts and ass, and asked the name of my

62

plastic surgeon. I said they were my real breasts and my real butt, and then she started to get friendly and it felt good, her touching me. Like, I'd never known anyone be nice to me before. And soon we were kissing on the mouth, and that felt good, too.

'Then she dived under, and began to kiss me all over, but especially on my butt and my pussy. She did things with her tongue. I didn't want her to stop, so I did the same things back to her. I was all wet in my pussy and so was she, and you could see our, you know, girl juices mixing in the pool water. We got out and lay on the grass and did it some more, with her face between my thighs and my face between hers, and I kind of knew people were watching, but I was so thrilled, I didn't care. I had my tongue inside her intimate place and I was slurping and licking, like it was an ice-cream! And she did the same to me, so much that I started to cry out, because this amazing pleasure just exploded in me, like I'd never known before, and I never wanted it to stop, and she said it was called an orgasm and a girl could have as many as she liked. She asked if I never played with myself, like, stroking and rubbing my intimate places and my breasts, and I said no, it was wrong, and she laughed and said having orgasms wasn't wrong. Her name was Topaz, and the good-looking dude's name was Buck, and she said she was his wife and a movie star. She said Buck liked her to get as much pleasure as possible, and she liked him to do the same, and if I was smart I could co-star with her in my very first movie, because very few girls had a bod like mine, without a lot of silicone and stuff. All that flattery went to my head! I thought it was no crime for a girl to have fun, and not suffer all the time. Oh, how wrong I was!

'Buck came out of the pool, bare-ass, and I saw his male organ was standing up. He came over and asked Topaz if I was warmed up, and Topaz said I'd just had my first orgasm and was ready for cock. Buck said that if I was old enough to have a driver's licence I was old enough to screw! I said wait a minute and tried to get up, but Topaz started licking my pussy again, and she put three or maybe four fingers inside me, and started to poke them in and out through my juicy intimate place, which was real slippery at that point. It was so fabulous, and she said this was my chance of the big time, and I said OK, because I wanted to be in the movies and I wanted another of those orgasms. You see, I looked around and there were lots of men and women screwing beside the pool or in it, even. I just gave way and took the easy path! I let Buck enter my person and burst my virginity, while Topaz squeezed and chewed on my breasts and bit my nipples, and when I felt Buck's, uh, liquid inside me I had another orgasm. I felt my virginity was no precious thing after all, and when Buck's buddies came to look at me, all of them with stiff organs, I kept my legs open because I was still wet and willing! That was the title of the first movie I was in, by the way.

'I was screwed by five or six guys and I had an orgasm every time! It was so *easy*! But the last guy was older, and took longer, and I must have made some remark, because when he did spurt he said I needed to be taught a lesson and should be spanked! I fought, but Topaz sat on me with my face in the grass, and me kicking and screaming, while Buck spanked my bare ass with his bare hand! It hurt like . . . well, it hurt real bad and tears were running down my face, and I figured this was punishment for losing my virginity and all. Buck must have spanked me about a hundred times, and my ass was smarting, and then Topaz took over spanking me! I couldn't believe that it didn't really hurt so much after all, and my bare ass was starting to feel all warm and tingly, and I was juicing up in my intimate place, as though I was going to have another *orgasm*.

'Buck came back, and this time he had a leather strap coiled round his wrist, you know, like a biker's belt, all studded. He said spanking wasn't enough for a tramp like me, I needed chastisement. Topaz got off me and Buck told me to get up and bend over with my ass high and the cheeks spread, and touch my toes, or I wouldn't get to be in the movies. I obeyed! In truth, I wanted the spanking to go on because I just knew I was going to have another of those orgasms. Buck whipped me breathless with that belt! He flogged my bare ass until I was squirming and wriggling, trying to shut out the pain on my naked skin, yet longing for it as well. Topaz had my fingers and toes locked between her legs as she sat on the ground, fingering her open pussy. She was masturbating – yes! – as her husband whipped me, and when she reached up to my own pussy, which was dripping with oily stuff after Buck had strapped me about the fiftieth time, she touched my feminine nubbin, which had swollen all big, and I came off in the biggest orgasm I'd had yet.

'I didn't show any fight when Buck turned me over and showed everyone my whipped ass, and stuck his fingers in my pussy to wet them. I squeaked as I felt him at my little hole – my asshole! He rubbed me until the place between my cheeks and my little pucker were all sloppy, and then I felt his cock, which was hard again, poke into my most intimate, private place of all! I groaned some, but opened up my hole to him, because Topaz had her face between my thighs and was tonguing my nubbin, so I was wet again. It felt weird as Buck's cock pushed inside my teensy hole, and I thought he'd split me in half, but suddenly I just relaxed and gave way, and his cock sank into my hole as far as it would go. He began to butt-fuck me. Master, forgive my coarse language, and forgive me, because I loved it and wanted more! I came to another orgasm, just as I felt Buck's hot creamy stuff spurting inside my belly and Topaz tonguing my nubbin, until I felt I was going to burst with pleasure! Anyway, I was eager to start the movie, and Buck said I'd already started as all my stuff was on film. I was so mad, I wanted to spank somebody myself, but Topaz said there would be plenty of girls wanting just that, later in the movie. And I did it! I did everything they wanted! Fucked, sucked, got cornholed, belted and whipped bare-assed, and didn't mind! I stayed at Buck's ranch nearly two years, and made twenty-one movies. After "Wet and Willing" there was "Spanking School", "Cuties Cocooned", "Whipped Witches" and "Lovelies in Latex", amongst others. I had to get away, for I was addicted to pleasure. But at last I saw sense and escaped with Buck's fancy foreign car, and donated it and my own person to the lord's crusade!'

'The lord may forgive you, Maid Kelley,' said the master, 'but I can only chastise you on his behalf.'

Kelley's loins twitched and there were streaks of liquid flowing from her pussy, down her thighs. She confessed tearfully that her narrative had excited her. The preacher nodded to the table. Kelley stepped out of her shorts, to gasps from the audience; then, with modest palms scarcely covering her bulging, wheat-coloured pubic hairs, climbed onto the table. She lay spreadeagled, letting Joanne and Rona cuff her wrists and ankles at each corner. The room was breathless as the master lifted the cane to his arm's length and brought it down across Kelley's naked buttocks. Vip! Her cheeks jerked and a livid pink weal appeared almost at once on her tanned skin, but she did not cry out. The master lashed her on the bare to twenty-five strokes, with the naked croup twitching and clenching, and Kelley's knuckles white as she clutched the table, but she made no sound until the master announced the twenty-fifth and last stroke. After the cane had cracked again on her purple-wealed buttocks, she let out a long, choking sob, then a whimper as she was released. Having dressed, she knelt by the master's pulpit, head lowered, hands at her ankles and buttocks on soles, and accepted cords to bind her in submissive posture. Joanne Pascal stepped forwards.

'I, too, have erred,' said Joanne, 'yet my deviance is far worse that Kelley's. She is decently ashamed of the foul words she must use to describe her acts, and her shame is so great that she remembers their details. I have been unspeakable beyond my own recall, and am ashamed that the words of vileness come naturally to me. Therefore, I invite your contempt for my using them. I, too, was a victim – of wealth and privilege. I went to the best prep school in New Hampshire, and was groomed for Vassar. I masturbated from an early age, both alone and with other girls. I lost my virginity as soon as possible, regarding it as an irritating discard, and in the back seat of an automobile. Vehicular transportation – our American love-affair with the car – is, I believe, the key to our lapse from decency into sloth. How easy it is for vice to travel, while virtue remains at home!

'I neglected my studies for countless sex sessions with boys, or girls, or both together. I loved threesomes, foursomes, group sex – it was quite normal, and delicious, to be fucked in the ass, while sucking cock, and with another cock in my cunt; or to lick a girl's pussy, while a man fucked me in the cunt. I always swallowed the male's sperm and, like my other degradations, it gave me a feeling of power over men – to drain them while I became stronger. They thought that in penetrating me they were enslaving me, but in my twisted mind it was me enslaving them, for my holes could take any number of cocks. I learned that men like women to dominate and spank them, and I rejoiced in reducing some male to a blubbering jelly as I paddled or whipped his bare ass to crimson. I masturbated as I flogged, for I truly adored using men and shaming them. May the lord forgive my woman's pride! Amongst eager orgiasts, I would don a *godemiché*, or rubber strap-on dildo, to cunt-fuck or bugger girls, and also to fuck boys in the ass, which I called "giving Greek". I would "pull a train", taking a dozen cocks in all my orifices, one after the other. Always, some car – that dreadful thing! – was the means to bring all those deviant bodies to the place of debauchery, although I also befouled my home. No room was left dry of my come-juice – and how I loved to surprise some male guest, bringing him to orgasm with my stockinged toes beneath the dinner table, trapping him in the bathroom and threatening to scream unless he butt-fucked me or, if he was a succulent stud, spread his own cheeks to endure my Greek attentions.

'To hurt, to embarrass, to shame – I didn't like men because they had cocks and I hadn't! My debauchery was so expert because I really liked being fucked, as I thought it a way of dominating men, by hurting them, using them, draining them, as vehicles for my own perverse pleasure. It became clear that my studies would fail and, by that time, I had decided to make a paying career out of what I enjoyed. I moved to New York where I set myself up as a dominant whore. I thought myself well versed in deviance, but New York pleasurably astounded me. In my West 72nd St apartment, I constructed a dungeon, where rich and powerful men begged to be enslaved and put to tortures: racked, flogged, pierced, chained, caged, pissed on – if they had to ask the price of their degradation, they couldn't afford it. My secret was, I wasn't play-acting – I really wanted to make those men whimper. So many controllers themselves long to be controlled, as the slave of a woman, when enslavement is woman's natural role.

'Lesbians, too, were my clients, and I took special pleasure in flogging their bare asses black and blue. Many a powerful man dreamed of watching his wife having lesbian sex, and I loved to oblige for money,

68

seducing the bitch, knowing that most women's curiosity will respond eventually to a lesbian come-on. I was no short-order whore. Some of my expensive scenarios took weeks to fruition, with all the apparatus of flirtation and dating. I devised intricate scenarios, like I would visit some swanky suburban house, then claim something was missing from my purse. It was easy to slip the item into my hostess's own purse and demand she accept a naked whipping, then and there, as punishment, after which she couldn't complain when I buggered her husband in front of her with my strap-on and whipped him too. By then, the whipped bitch would guess the set-up, and more than likely be taking part in chastising her husband, or shaming him by gamahuching me as he looked on, trussed with ropes. All of which he paid steeply for. I knew that depravity lurked behind the most respectable fronts.

'I despised lesbians as much as I despised men – may the lord forgive me! – and my own pleasure, soon, was solely in masturbating. I did that after roping some man, or man and his wife, in bondage, flogging them and pissing on them. I masturbated while whipping a man, or just thinking about it – I masturbated when I'd whipped some millionaire and locked him in his doghouse or cage, saying I didn't know if I'd release him in time for the market to open, as I had much more important people to see. He'd be sobbing, pleading, offering me, his mistress, anything I wanted . . . they thought it was role-playing, but it wasn't. I hated them, and my heart was sore at my wickedness. I had heard there was one true master, he whom you see, who could show wicked girls the pathway of the lord. One night, I'd locked a bank president in his cage, bound and dressed in my soiled panties, and he was ritually offering me anything to spare him further humiliation, which was what he was in fact paying for. His white Ferrari was in my garage: I took the keys and his money and drove to New Jersey, away from my sins, vowing to find the master and donate those emblems of ease. Yet I am but a small way along the path of penitence. Even my telling has stirred vile thoughts, which must not go unpunished.'

Joanne's bare thighs gleamed with come. Unbidden, she removed her lower clothing, and placed herself on the flogging table, where she was tied in place for beating.

'Twenty-five strokes shall not suffice, master,' she said. 'Inflicting pain on men has dulled my wicked senses. So, to atone . . .'

Joanne took eighty strokes of the master's cane on her bare buttocks. Her bottom clenched and squirmed faster as the skin reddened, then darkened to a mass of blotchy puce bruises; though her eyes brimmed with tears, she did not squeal until the eightieth, when she gasped deeply and repeatedly before hobbling to join Kelley, roped and squatting, at the master's feet. The crowd's excitement was electric but turned to awe as the master demanded volunteers to accept the path.

'Each woman amongst you,' he thundered, 'is guilty of sloth. Who has the will to be cleansed?'

Honey Swade sprang towards the stage.

'Me! Oh, master, I'm guilty as sin!'

The audience buzzed as Honey mounted the stage and began to speak. She was the picture of small-town modesty, in a pleated skirt of grey wool, white blouse fastened to the neck, flesh-coloured hose and slingbacks.

'I truly don't know where to begin, for I've done so much badness! Playing with myself –' she gulped '– *masturbating*, why, that's the least. I've masturbated every day, two or three times, ever since I can remember. I stick things in my pussy, and into my butt-hole, too. Especially when I can't get a fuck from a boy. I can't get enough of it! Half the boys in town have had me, they fuck me, and I want more, in my mouth, my pussy, my asshole, or three guys all at once in every hole. If they won't, I masturbate for them to watch, trying to get them hard, and they call me a tramp for it and treat me like dirt. I've played with girls, too. There's such a lot of badness we do in this town, and I hope some of the ladies here will 'fess up! If a whipping on the bare ass will steer me to the path of the lord, well, that's just what this girl's bare ass needs!'

Dramatically, Honey stripped, until she wore only her stockings, bra and garter belt, all in demure white lycra. Rona placed her brusquely face down on the flogging table, and bound her ankles and wrists while Honey sobbed and trembled. Rona clawed her underthings from her body, carelessly holing the garments, until Honey was stretched, quivering and nude, with the master's cane raised above her bare buttocks.

'I now ask you good people what chastisement would set the girl on the path of the lord,' said the master, mildly.

'Whip her ten!' cried a male voice.

'Twenty!' said another. 'That New York tramp took eighty!'

'But she's so young! Thirty should be OK,' said another.

'I say fifty strokes, and hard ones!' shouted a female voice.

'Yeah, a good thrashing of fifty,' said another female.

There were murmurs: fifty seemed right.

'Do you agree to fifty strokes on your bare buttocks?' the master asked.

'I guess so. Yes,' Honey sobbed.

Vip! The master delivered the first stroke to Honey's bare nates. Vip! Her bottom began to clench hard. Vip! The room was still, electric once more. Honey was a local girl, getting caned on her bare behind. They knew Honey, or thought they had. Vip! Vip! Vip! The cane landed remorselessly on the girl's squirming bare croup,

71

its moons, bikini-pale against her tanned back and legs, glowing pink at first then darkening to crimson. The audience could not see the existing network of weals from Honey's previous flagellance, some of it self-inflicted, and some of it with spanking partners. Vip! Vip! Vip!

'Oh! No!'

'You agreed to the sentence,' said the master.

Vip! Vip! Vip!

'Oh!

Vip! Vip! Vip!

'*Ah!*'

The master caned her on the bare, without pause, to the full fifty, until the entire skin of her buttocks was a blotch of dark crimson and purple bruises. Honey screamed, wept, and shuddered in her bonds; at the forty-fifth stroke, she pissed herself, a hissing stream of smoky fluid engulfing her writhing belly and quim. Vip!

'*Ah!* Stop! I can't take any more!'

It was the fiftieth. She was released, moaning and sobbing, and, unbidden, squatted at the master's feet.

'Thank you,' she sobbed.

'Who else has erred?' the master thundered.

A woman rushed to the front. She was Mrs Arlene Dow, thirty-two, a brunette, standing 5′7″, with a figure of 37-24-37. She flung herself on the table, and shrieked:

'I've been smoking cigarettes, when my man doesn't let me! Oh, chastise me, please!'

Once again, audience participation decided: twenty strokes were appropriate for Mrs Arlene Dow. She raised her skirt, was bound in ropes, and caned on her panties. Jerking and howling, she too pissed herself, soaking both panties and skirt. She thanked the master before resuming her seat. Many women demanded the next chastisement, the one chosen being Mrs Ann Rausch, blond, 5′8″, and 38-25-39. Her crime was laziness at house-cleaning, for which a penalty of thirty strokes was agreed. She chose to take them on the full bare and stripped off below her waist. Suddenly, she added that she had fucked a travelling insurance salesman when her husband was at work, 'doing it three times in one afternoon', and her tariff at once rose to sixty. She regretted her decision to bare her bottom, for every single stroke made her howl and her naked fesses quivered frantically as they darkened to crimson. She too thanked the master for her chastisement, and thereafter women vied, with increasing clamour, to take the cane on the bare in penitence.

Among those chastised by caning on the full bare were: Mrs Jaclyn Tate, twenty-four, blonde, 5'6", 36-23-37, twenty-five strokes, for serving burnt breakfast toast; Mrs Isabel Pinto, thirty-six, blonde, 5'7", 38-25-40, thirty strokes, for watching too much TV; Mrs Dorna Woods, twenty-nine, brunette, 5'10", 40-24-38, for twice fucking her regular pool cleaner, eighty strokes. Mrs Woods took her eighty with surprising calm and walked back to her seat, stripping off her upper garments, to sit nude on her husband's lap. Miss June Dommer, twenty-five, blonde, 5'9", 39-23-40, took only fifty for cheating on her boyfriend, Ron Curle, and opted for chastisement in the nude. Her example was followed by successive candidates, and after the departure of the thrilled or chastened audience, a total of forty-three females had been chastised by bare-buttock or nude caning. Honey Swade begged to join the master's maids.

'Driver's licence?' he said.

'Of course.'

'Your ass is welcome, girl.'

The master set to contemplating his laptop computer.

'Mm,' he said. 'Some 4WDs, a 'Vette, a Cadillac even. Address, serial number, workplace, personal schedule . . .'

'I don't understand,' Honey said.

'US Postal Service Inspectors, on permanent under-cover duty in the field,' said the master, 'can access full personal information, including vehicular. You hear all about the FBI, but not about *us*. I possess keys for every car in America. When a few choice wagons go missing from driveways, in a week or two, why, they'll be in Mexico faster 'n turkey turds. Serve people right, for worshipping things.'

The master parted his robe, revealing himself nude. Kelley and Joanne stripped and tickled the master's cock until it stood quivering in massive erection. Honey Swade stripped too, knelt, and licked his balls.

'Asshole? Please?' said Kelley.

'Me too,' said Joanne.

'And me,' said Rona.

'OK,' said the master. 'I wonder when you girls are ever going to vary the menu.'

'Say, I've never taken it up the ass,' said Honey Swade. 'Is it so good?'

'Watch us and you'll see,' said Joanne. 'Lucky girl gets the cream.'

'I get butt-fucked, *I* get the cream,' pouted Rona.

The master greased his cock with come from Kelley's heavily juicing pussy, plunged it an inch – two inches – then right to his balls inside her open anus and began to fuck her. She groaned and her ass began to squirm as he penetrated, with her cooze dripping copious come. Joanne, watching, began to masturbate, and Honey Swade joined her. After the girls had diddled each other's wet cunts for some minutes, Joanne said that Rona hadn't said her piece, nor been caned bare-ass.

'Huh!' said Rona. 'I don't mind being spanked, because I really do follow the lord. I've never done anything really bad, not like you whores, so I like seeing your bare asses whipped. Plus, I'm the best car thief.'

'Butt-fucking ain't *bad*?' snorted Joanne.

'Not in service of the lord,' retorted Rona.

'Tight-assed bitch!'

Joanne invited Honey to help give Rona what *she* deserved, and the newcomer accepted. As the master continued to butt-fuck the squirming Kelley, herself now masturbating, the two girls pinioned Rona and tore away her jeans, revealing stockings and garters but no panties. Joanne lifted the cane over her naked peach. Vip! Vip! Vip!

'*Oh! Oh!* You fucking pig! Let me *go!*'

Rona's helpless bare ass clenched repeatedly.

Vip! Vip! Vip!

'*Ah!*'

Joanne caned Rona's naked, reddening fesses, and Honey clamped her head in her thighs, masturbating and dripping come over her hair as she watched the buttocks squirm. The master fucked Kelley in the anus, withdrawing his massive, ass-greased cock right to the glans before plunging to the nude blonde's anal root. He smiled, watching Rona's bare ass shudder, darkening with weals from Joanne's cane. Rona's squeals were drowned by Kelley's groans of orgasm as cunt-juice squirted from the butt-fucked maid's cooze.

'It's funny, master, the audience didn't ask *which* lord,' gasped Honey, frigging her clitty with Rona's hair, as the maidmaster withdrew his erect tool from Kelley's anus and prised Honey's buttocks apart.

'They never do,' said the master.

75

5

Crush Pool

There was a stir in the dining room as Miss Grayfold argued with one of the exquisites, the tallest. It seemed that Grayfold wanted to cane the miscreant Cherri Black, as she had been most upset by her sloppy table manners.

'I know these trailer park trash!' she shrieked. 'I know how to make them squirm!'

One moment, the unsmiling exquisite stood motionless: the next, her knee-length hair was fashioned into ropes that held the squalling Grayfold by her neck and wrists. The exquisite knelt, and Grayfold was completely bound in ropes of the girl's hair, one hank filling her mouth as a gag. Wriggling, Grayfold was hoisted to straddle the girl's neck. Miss Wycherley nodded to an unspoken command, stepped forwards, and raised her arm. She ripped off Grayfold's skirt and rolled her cream panties down, then – crack! – her palm spanked Grayfold's bare buttocks. Crack! Crack Crack! Grayfold was wriggling, scarlet with rage, as Billie Wycherley's palm spanked her ass the same pink as her corset, then to crimson. The exquisite who held her allowed Billie to deliver over two hundred spanks before the sobbing woman was still and hung limp around her shoulders. Her bare buttocks glowed with the imprint of Billie's palm, and the exquisite's nape gleamed with come from Grayfold's pinioned cunt.

As quickly as she had been knotted, Grayfold was unbound, then cast to the floor, where she lay sobbing and rubbing the bruises of Miss Wycherley's spanking, while an exquisite's toes pinioned her neck. The three males approached the shivering body of Roslyn Grayfold, crushed in submission by the exquisite. Their cocks, rising from their jean zippers, were straining tubes of hard flesh. Orchid Sommer pulled Grayfold's panties right down to her ankles and, with a forearm between her thighs, raised her to a crouch. Her neck still pinioned, her ass was upthrust and spread, with the anus pucker wrinkling above the thick wet lips of her cunt, like a crimson weal in her belly. A rope snaked from the ceiling was knotted around her waist and hoisted her buttocks up, with her knees trembling an inch from the floor. The first male squatted, balancing himself on Grayfold's hips. The tip of his glans nuzzled her anus and a scream bubbled at her lips. The cock sank an inch into her, then two inches; her buttocks clenched frantically, but, at the male's thrust she groaned, and her hole sucked in the invading cock.

'Ohh!'

She shuddered, moaning as the male plunged his cock to the balls up her anal shaft and, stony-faced, began to butt-fuck her. The guard girls assisted, by pinching and clawing Grayfold's bare ass-cheeks apart. Grayfold's thighs and buttocks, quivering, slammed to meet the male's thrusts and take full cock inside her anus. She shook her clamped head, and whinnied *no, no*, yet her fingers twitched, one hand at her clitty, the other at her erect nipples. Glistening streams of come soaked her cream stockings and the panties at her ankles. Her moans turned to whimpers, then yelps, as she masturbated under buggery, her come dripping from swollen gash-flaps.

'Do me!' she moaned. 'Oh! Fuck my ass, come in me!'

Eagerly, the two other males stood awaiting their turn. Billie rejoined the masturbating wine girls as the nude exquisites uncoiled three-thonged flails, their pyramid studs glinting, and turned towards Cherri, strung alone on her flogging tripod. Craning, she glimpsed Grayfold's buggery as the male's ass-greased piston slammed her anus; heard her grunts, as he spurted his cream at her anal root; watched the froth of hot sperm that bubbled from her pucker, and the wet slapping of Grayfold's thighs and fesses, glistening with her torrent of come, as the stud's spurt brought her to climax. Cherri's clit swelled, tingling, and come dripped from her cunt, even as the exquisites raised their pyramid-studded whips.

Vap! Vap! Vap! The three quirts lashed Cherri's bare croup at the same moment, one at top buttock, one in mid-fesse, and one on the soft place on her thighs, just below her taut globes.

'Ah!' Cherri cried.

The strokes made a dry, crackling sound as they sliced her naked skin. Vap! Vap! Vap!

'Oh! Wait!'

Why wait? You want it, slave.

The thought invaded her, vibrating in her spinal nubbin, clit, and anus. Three cuts took her on the left haunch. Vap! Vap! Vap!

'Ooh!' she gasped, her haunches quivering and striped.

At once, three to the right haunch, each stroke triple pain, with triple thongs. Her fesses were two smarting, throbbing, balls of pain, the heavy studded lashes knocking breath from her. It was twelve strokes, more than half her buttock chastisement, before her gorge rose, forcing a yelp, as her bare body writhed, slapping against the poles of the flogging tripod.

Vap! Vap! Vap!

'*Ahh!* No, stop! I didn't mean it!'

Cherri's breasts shuddered like her flogged, squirming buttocks as her wrists and ankles strained helplessly in their ropes. The thongs binding her upper thighs secured her to the poles and she was unable to shift buttock position. Any jerking of her head wrenched her tied hair; only her untethered breasts expressed her agony as they shook at each whiplash. Yet her nipples were stiff and she moaned as she felt the shameful, tell-tale flow of come at her cunt. The weals on her bare croup, seared by the whips' nuggets, hurt like saws. Her buttocks wriggled and clenched uncontrollably, the spectacle of her shame: she could not stop her body's shudder. Tears blurred her eyes and she felt the liquid dripping onto her nipples. She gaped at the girls, all with fingers at quims, jerking in eager masturbation. Each girl had a steady silver drip of come from her gash shining between the labia.

The girl slave likes her whipping.

She will reach her plateau soon.

Then she will know her truth, in part.

The flogging had lasted only four minutes, yet Cherri was beyond time. She saw the throng of masturbating girls, panties down or discarded completely, and her trio of nude whippers, their breasts quivering as their arms delivered the whipstrokes. Their huge jungles of quim-hair shone brightly with oil, and their own bare buttocks seemed to clench as Cherri's clenched. Cherri heard the triple whistle of the whips then, as though from afar, the crack on her naked flesh. Vap! Vap! Vap!

'*Uh*,' she moaned. 'Mmm.'

Hot come trickled down her inside thighs and formed a stream to her calves and ankles. Her clitoris was fully stiff and throbbing. There was a tingling in her anus, massaged by her clenched buttocks and lubricated with her ass grease, as though ready to dung, or be penetrated by cock. She saw Grayfold writhing under butt-fucking from the second male, who had plunged his cock into her anus, still creamy from the first. Cherri's sphincter tightened and dilated, longing for male meat to cleave her own anus.

She is almost there . . .
Proceed without interruption to the body-whipping.
Shall fifty be enough?
This time.
Vap!
'*Ah! Yes, yes!*'

The final four strokes to the buttock region were delivered singly, each to her open gash-cleft, the tips of each whip connecting hard to her pulsing clitoris and the whipstuds slamming her anus bud. Cherri's buttocks and now her gash and perineum were bright crimson, mingled with an overall blotch of dark bruises. Through her sobs, Cherri groaned as her cunt-basin heaved and a glittering plume of spray hissed, golden, from her racked cunt-flaps. The acrid scent of her copious piss assailed her nostrils, as it pooled beneath her writhing gash-flaps reflected in the liquid mirror. If only she could hide her face – if only her buttocks were covered by the flimsiest panties, to mask her welts, her come, her helpless pissing!

Pain is naked, slave, shivered the silent voice, vibrating within her cunt-basin.

'Ah! Yes, harder!' cried Grayfold, squirming under butt-fuck, and masturbating her clitty. Vap! Vap! Vap!
'*Oh!*'

Cherri's back-whipping commenced with three slices across her shoulderblades, each lashing the same skin. Her buttocks remained a cauldron of pain but the jolting whips to her back seemed a more intimate invasion, as if the buttock-meat formed a shield but the backbone and ribs were open and raw. The cuts jolted as they stung, slamming her body forwards as each exquisite took her turn placing her stroke to weal every inch of Cherri's back and shoulders. The whips were heavy on her bare flesh, drumming her body from side to side, with her jerking head wrenching on her hair-roots.

80

Vap!

'Ah!' Cherri shrilled, as a skilful stroke snaked the whip around her ribs, to smack her erect left nipple-bud.

Vap!

'*Ah!*'

Another took her right nipple, sending shockwaves up her spine, yet causing her cunt to flow with more copious come than ever, her oily hot fluid squirting from her cooze-flaps with the remaining drips of her piss, before drooling down her inner thighs.

Vap!

'*Oh! Oh!*' Cherri heard herself yell as the tallest exquisite moved in front of her, and whipped her directly across her naked breasts, raking the nipples with the pyramid studs.

As she raised her arm for the next stroke, her fingers pressed her own plainly erect nipples and she herself winced. Cherri endured threefold flogging: on back, on breasts, and with the third whipper attending her upper thighs, inner and outer flesh, which the buttock chastisement had left unbruised.

Not spare the slave.

Stripe its skin, to its slave meat.

Make it know itself.

Cherri's head lolled, despite the pain in her knotted hair. Her whipstrokes seemed part of her. Drool slid from the corner of her slack lips, and trickled over her nipples. Her belly twitched, as her cunt poured come down her thighs.

They flogged her on a pyramid of ice, slippery and oily fragrant, and she was climbing away from the whip-strokes, biting and licking her flesh. Snakes writhed in her pubic bush and armpits, chewing her hair; snakes fastened her erect clitoris and nipples, hauling her upwards to the top of the pyramid; each whipstroke slammed her pubis against the oily surface, jarring her clit and making her come; the whips on her bare fesses were snakes. Snakes writhed in her cunt and anus, filling her cracks, obscenely mating inside her. She could not climb with her hands, but her hardened nipples were claws, gouging the ice. She knew that the pyramid's top was her true bare croup, for her to regain, to have orgasm forever.

Vap! Vap! Vap!

'Oh, yes . . .'

The whips stroked Cherri's buttocks with honey, and orgasm took her so intensely that she grunted several times, and a new piss flood sprayed from her quivering wet cunt, while a string of dungs squirted from her anus. The whipping ceased, and Cherri felt three tongues licking her flogged body: her gash and anus, her thighs, buttocks and back, her whipped breasts and nipples, covering her in oily drool. The three nude exquisites clambered up and down the tripod, tonguing Cherri's skin, finally kneeling at her parted buttocks, where each in turn thrust her nose into Cherri's cunt and anus, breathing deeply and depositing a gobbet of saliva. Cherri saw Roslyn Grayfold, crouched and still masturbating, as she squirmed on her belly-rope, begging the males' cocks to pleasure her again; Miss Takira, her nude body all shiny in a cocoon of plastic kitchen wrap, opening her thighs for a raw T-bone steak to be thrust into her anus by Billie Wycherley, who then butt-fucked the Japanese girl with the raw meat. At each thrust of the red, dripping flesh, Miss Takira broke wind.

'Ah,' moaned Miss Takira. 'American meat, very nice.'

Frigg released Cherri from her bonds, and carried her back to their room.

'You took it fine,' she said, laying Cherri on their bed and beginning to examine her wealed flesh.

'Took what?' Cherri gasped.

She did not resist as Frigg went down on her and tongued her still-dripping quim. Cherri and Frigg masturbated and gamahuched each other until dawn, Cherri on top, most of the time, sitting on her partner's face, with Frigg's tongue poking into Cherri's tight cunt or sinking to its full depth into the clinging elastic of Cherri's anus. Both girls were careful to fill their come-pots for collection at breakfast time.

'Lord! I've never come so much,' said Frigg, stroking Cherri's wealed back and buttocks. 'Your asshole tasted like honey. And your stripes, those lovely ridges, like cute little moletracks. They're so dark, but they've healed so fast. They seem to have been there for ages.'

They showered for ten minutes before the breakfast bell rang. There was no need to select clothing: wine girls were nude in the daytime. Frigg lingered, cooing in admiration as she soaped Cherri's buttocks.

'Hey, you've seen my ass before, Frigg,' said Cherri.

'Yeah, but it seems to have grown bigger.'

The duties of the twenty-five wine girls, at that time of year, were crushing the grapes, and crushing the ex-truded must to clear juice. Miss Wilhelmina Wycherley was eager to be one girl amongst equals, and although, having derogated her authority to the exquisites, she was allowed the role of their counsellor, her naked bottom was in no way immune from the guard girls' canes. In the rocks behind the castle were three scooped basins the size of swimming pools, one above the other, and the topmost, the crush pool, draining into the second, the must pool, which drained into the lower, third basin, named the come pool. A dump truck loaded the top pool with grapes, which were trodden by nude wine girls. The must, or pulpy liquid, drained through a sieve into the must pool, where more girls trod it to pomace, which settled at the bottom of the pool, the clear liquid being siphoned off into the come pool at the bottom. From the come pool, a tanker truck sucked up the liquid after the girls there had treated it.

The tanker truck sat like an octopus, its tentacles trailing in the juice, slowly sucking it up, after Miss

Wycherley, as taster, deemed it treated. Treating the juice in the come pool meant that the girls, breast-deep in purple liquid, had to masturbate and enrich it with their come. The girls were recycled from top pool to middle, to bottom, and back to the crush pool, according to need. Discipline was maintained by guard girls, wearing corsets – fastened to a nineteen-inch maximum – and boots of rubber, so that they could wade into the pools to cane the bottoms of the lazy. For summary canings, girls had to crawl out of the liquid and cling to the jagged rock face, exposing their bare nates. The exquisites were rarely seen. From dawn to dusk, wine girls remained barefoot and worked in the nude. Miss Wycherley, declaring herself just another nude wine girl, murmured to Cherri that a good worker might win a token and claim two hours' service by any of the male studs, called James, Fenimore and Cooper – 'aliases', she whispered. She had tested all three, deciding Fenimore's cock the most suitable for anus, and Cooper's for cunt, although James was, by a quarter of an inch, the best hung.

'Hard work gets you double poke,' she said. 'Cocks are just things for girls to use, aren't they?'

This was Cherri's first day. At wake-up bell, they had scarcely time to piss – Frigg went on the toilet, but Cherri, wrinkling her nose, sprayed the shower – before rushing to line up for breakfast, with their come-pots ready. Cherri, like the others, handed in her brimming come-pot to guard Orchid Sommer and took juice, coffee, scrambled egg and toast, while her nude body shivered in the unheated refectory. Afterwards, she followed Frigg in the troop to the wine pools. She and Frigg began in the top pool, with Frigg advising her to just dive in and start her thighs pumping. Three guards supervised, wearing just their boots and corsets – Tara Flick, Bev Ellerbee, and Meryl Waldegg, a long-maned ash-blonde, from Nogales, Arizona, standing 5'8", at

38-22-39. They waved their canes with haughty menace at the bottoms of the shuffling girls and tapped hesitant bare croups, threatening proper chastisement at the slightest provocation. Cherri dived and felt terror as the grapes engulfed her. She fought her way, spluttering, to air, and saw Frigg, her face and breasts already stained purple by the fruit.

'Take a deep breath, and start crushing,' Frigg gasped. 'Faster we work, faster the level goes down.'

Cherri gulped air and dived, the grapes squashy under her tread. It was difficult to maintain a foothold and the grapes tickled her feet as she swam in the shifting fruity mass. She learned to stabilise herself and pound them with her bare feet, crushing them to pulp: slowly, the lower level of fruit turned to must, and the sludgy fluid began to gurgle out through the drain. Cherri's breasts were now above fruit level and she paused, panting. Only minutes had passed, so it seemed that labour in the top pool would be over soon. At the bottom pool, about forty yards away, was Miss Takira, helping make the wine her corporation proposed to buy.

She knelt, naked, on the edge of the pool with her thighs apart and her wrists roped behind her to her ankles. Her breasts and upper body were sheathed in plastic kitchen wrap, over which more ropes bit close and bound her to twin staves bolted to the rock. A trio of come pool girls, waist-deep in juice, tongued Takira's quim so that a clear stream of her come flowed into the pool. The other wine girls remained standing in the come pool, thighs apart, and masturbating under the watchful guards, whose canes sometimes flicked the surface near a girl whose frottage seemed to falter, and if that failed struck her in her tangled wet pube-hair or on her cooze-flaps. Wycherley wine had no alcohol: its ingredient of taste was girl-come. The tanker truck's tentacles gurgled as they sucked in juice from the come pool, with the three studs James, Fenimore and Cooper,

85

clad only in jeans, holding the tubes. As he watched the gamahuching of the writhing, bound Japanese woman, each stud's cock was stiff.

'*Ah!* Such an honour!' trilled Miss Takira. 'Yes, please!'

Cherri was startled by a sudden splash and grunted as her mane was grabbed. Bev Ellerbee stood beside her in the mush, snarling that idleness had earned her a summary caning. Those canings were delivered on the spot, unlike formally sentenced canings taken at suppertime for more serious offences, such as insolence or frivolity – mere laughter counting as the latter. After kneeing Cherri between her thighs, Bev dragged her, sobbing and clutching her bruised quim, to the rock edge, where she ordered her to grasp the top of the rock and thrust out her bottom. Cherri obeyed, scarlet with anger, and clung hanging from the rock, with her feet trailing in the grape mush. Using her body as a stepping-stone, Bev climbed above her, then caned her ten strokes on the wet bare ass, from the vertical. During work, guards used canes made of braided vine branches, long, flexible, springy and hard on the buttocks. Several strokes took Cherri not on her buttock-flans but right on the anus, in her spread crack.

Her bare fesses writhed and her feet splashed frantically, kicking grapes into the faces of her onlookers, who cheered when Cherri fell, crying, into the muck. There was little sympathy amongst wine girls. She lowered her hands automatically to rub her smarting bare behind but Bev cautioned her to resume work at once, on pain of double caning. Cherri obeyed. Miss Takira watched, the Japanese girl's belly and titties quivering, as the girls tongued her from their stance in the come pool. One of the girls twisted up her mane and wadded it right into Miss Takira's cunt, wiping the hair around her pouch until it emerged soaking in Takira's own come. The girl then exited the pool and knelt, thrusting her come-soaked hair into the Japanese girl's mouth. The pool girl continued to masturbate herself as she rammed her head against Takira's face and applied further palmfuls of her come to her wet mane while Takira sucked the hair dry. That girl was Roslyn Grayfold.

There was a crashing roar and Cherri was swept off her feet: another dump truck had emptied a new load of grapes, refilling the pool; once more Cherri had to swim as she trod, the grapes slithering over her bare skin as she struggled to crush them. She looked for Frigg but could no longer distinguish one purple body from another. Cherri needed an urgent piss but feared that failure to ask permission might earn her another caning; or that asking permission would, too. She worked frantically, her sweat pouring into the mush, until her bladder could not hold out even the time to get to the bathroom: she released her full load of piss into the wine fluid, then had to suppress a laugh. *All the other girls pissed in the wine, too. And more.* In the dark top pool, no one could see.

Cherri squatted, parted her thighs, and released a copious stream into the wine mixture. She glanced to her side and saw Frigg, crouching the same, with the surface slapping her bobbing breasts. A whistle blew; it was time for them to evacuate the upper pool and go to the middle one, where the crushing was harder, as the must was finer pulp than the whole fruit. Cherri climbed out and trooped after Frigg to the must pool, brushing past Roslyn Grayfold on her way up from the masturbatresses' pool. Grayfold shot her a dirty look, but Cherri smiled back. As she sank into the pool of slimy must, it was hard for her bare soles to grip, with only slime to crush, not the fibrous fruitskins. Several times she slipped, her head splashing into the fluid to emerge, dripping, and see a guard girl's cane and titties waggling in anger. Suddenly, Cherri tripped over a girl's slimy foot and fell to the bottom of the pool, her breasts squashing painfully on the rock floor. When she emerged, dripping and beslimed, the guard girl's cane was pointing straight at her.

'Out!' she barked.

It was the muscular, cone-titted vixen, Tara Flick. The pears of her croup trembled with her conic teats in anger. Behind her, Cherri heard a giggle in open defiance of the rules. It came from Elise Wuliger, a rangy blonde, 39-22-36, from Jacksonville, Florida, with breasts a little too big for her wiry frame, and which hung, swaying like weighted balloons topped with little pink cherries, as she laughed. Tara grinned conspiratorially; so did Grayfold, immersed to her titties in grapes, in the top pool. Elise had tripped Cherri on purpose, and Cherri's bottom faced new caning. Cherri looked from one to the other, her face red with rage.

'She tripped me!' Cherri cried.

'Out now, bitch!' sneered Tara. 'Twenty on the bare, you piece of shit!'

'No!' shrieked Cherri, looking up at Grayfold's rictus of mirth. 'It's her fucking fault, Grayfold, the bitch! Why me?'

Her face pale, she clambered back up to the crush pool, dived into the grapes, and grabbed Grayfold by her bare teats, clawing and scratching the nipples, till the girl howled. Frigg waved her arms, telling Cherri to be careful, but Cherri ignored her. She fastened the startled Grayfold in a bearhug, squeezing the small of her back, while her knee repeatedly slammed her in the cunt-flaps. Cherri avoided Grayfold's flailing blows by lowering her head and sinking her teeth into the woman's left nipple, biting the teat as if biting steak. Grayfold squealed and sank under the fruit's surface. Cherri pursued. All eyes, including Miss Takira's, were on them. The wrestling girls bobbed up and down, threshing the pulpy purple mass, which soaked both their bodies. It was difficult for either to gain firm hold on her slippery opponent, despite pulling hair and slapping, punching or pinching bare titties. Grayfold smacked Cherri with jabs to the face, breasts and belly, while Cherri, the stronger, tried to renew her bearhug under the punches. She kept up a vicious barrage of knee-blows to Grayfold's groin, jamming her thigh between the other girl's and delivering fierce knee jabs to the vulva.

Grayfold snarled and shrieked as she punched; suddenly, Cherri sank beneath the surface, taking Grayfold off guard, until her shriek became a scream as Cherri got her teeth right onto Grayfold's cunt-flaps, and bit, while plunging her finger into the crack of the girl's ass. She prodded, aided by the grape-slime, and got her finger rammed right up Grayfold's anus and, with crooked stiff finger, pulled her opponent down beside her by the butt-hole. The two fighters churned the fruit. With the finger in Grayfold's anus, Cherri forced her opponent to the bottom and sat on her belly, removing the finger in order to smack the girl's bare titties with one fist, while the other thrust deep into the gash, its lips bruised with Cherri's teethmarks. Bubbles floated from Grayfold's mouth; Cherri's lungs pounded as she thumbed the girl's clitty, and her breast-mauling became a rough, then gentler caress of the erect nipples. She had four fingers of her left hand in the wet, writhing cunt-pouch, seeking and finding Grayfold's G-spot, while her thumb masturbated the girl's erect clitoris. A stream of bubbles erupted from the girl's mouth, frothing the pulpy mass of fruit, and she shuddered, writhing; Cherri had masturbated her to come. She grasped the girl's hair and wrenched her to the surface, where both swayed, gulping air. Tara quivered in rage.

'You attacked Roslyn Grayfold, new bitch!' she yelled at Cherri. 'That means a formal naked caning, tonight!'

Miss Wilhelmina Wycherley left the lowest pool, where she had been sipping the come-enriched wine, to scramble up the rock, on bare feet, her titties wobbling in agitation.

'I do think, Miss Flick, that the new girl was provoked,' she said.

'Somebody must take twenty on the bare,' cried Miss Takira.

'I suggest Roslyn,' said Miss Wycherley. 'I do believe she's jealous of Cherri's body.'

'Yeah, that's right,' declared Elise Wuliger, 'She offered to tongue me out, and finger-fuck my ass, if I tripped up the new cunt.'

'You fucking whore!' spat Roslyn Grayfold, and punched Billie Wycherley hard in the belly, doubling her up; then kicked her between the legs until she sank to the ground.

Tara Flick was able to restrain Grayfold only after Miss Wycherley had taken savage kicking to breasts, belly and cunt. Billie sat up, sobbing and clutching her bruised quim.

'Furthermore,' added the emboldened Elise Wuliger, 'I think Roslyn orgasmed when Cherri was fighting her. She secretly wants to be punished, in my opinion.'

'In that case, she should be,' cried Miss Takira.

'Bend over, bitch!' cried Tara Flick.

'Now, wait a minute! *You* were in on this –'

Vip!

'*Ahh!*'

Tara's cane slashed her across the naked breasts, and Grayfold screamed as a vivid weal striped the teat-flesh.

'Ladies –' Takira gestured to Billie and Cherri '– please join me, while Miss Flick attends to the miscreant girl's bottom. Truly, there is little honour among slaves!'

Cherri made her way down to the lowest pool as Grayfold's nude breasts slapped rock and Tara lifted her cane over the wriggling bare buttocks.

Vip! Vip! Vip! Vip!

'*Ahh!*'

90

Cherri heard the girl scream, but was too distracted by Miss Takira's overflowing cunt-lips. The cunt was massive, the lips stretched and swollen in a huge red oval, with the clitoris extruded like a thumb, the genital apparatus seeming too big for her figurine of a body. Her pubis was entirely bare, as was her entire body, except for her thick black mane. Come poured from her gash, in a straight, clear flow that shone as it splattered the rock and dripped copiously into the come pool. Takira's pert, upthrust breasts had nipples big as plums, threatening to topple the hard pale cones to which they clung.

'One delight of America is, I am free to be a slave,' she said. 'At home, I must be mistress. Miss Cherri – I am struck by your beauty – would you do me the honour of humilating me, by pissing on my face? And if you can be kind enough to really despise me, you may masturbate as you piss.'

Cherri squatted over the girl's upturned face and opened her gash, releasing a fine spray of piss and soaking the entire visage. At the same time, she broke wind, her anus exhaling its fumes right at Takira's nose. The girl crooned with pleasure, her tongue licking droplets of Cherri's pee. As she pissed, Cherri began to stroke her tingling nubbin, with long, firm rubs from her index finger, soon changing her masturbation mode to thumb-and-finger frottage when the clit was fully stiffened. Her come dribbled, then flowed into Miss Takira's eagerly lapping mouth. A pool girl continued to tongue Takira's clit and gash, which splashed her face with its increased flow of come. Cherri eyed the bulges in the studs' jeans.

'Why does Miss Takira want to be wrapped and bound like a piece of meat in a supermarket?' she whispered to Billie, and was overheard.

'Don't *you*, Cherri?' said Takira. 'To be no more than a hunk of meat, processed, prodded, tenderised – like grapes crushed in a wine press, the antique kind Miss Wycherley showed me! If only American girls admitted their desires, to be whipped, dominated, enslaved and fulfilled. Miss Wycherley, would you ask your males if they would oblige me – oh, I'm too shy! – you know.'

'Certainly, miss. A stud's condition of employment is to be on permanent stand-by.'

Billie spoke to the three studs, who stripped off and arrived, erect, to replace Cherri at Miss Takira's mouth. Above them, Roslyn Grayfold's pubis slammed the rock and her scarlet bare croup wriggled as Tara lashed her.

Vip!

'Ooh!'

Vip!

'*Ah!*'

Vip! Vip! Vip!

'*Ahh!*'

Cherri and Billie watched, each licking her teeth, as Fenimore's massive cock slid into the Japanese girl's mouth and she began sucking the glans, licking the frenulum and corona before taking the whole shaft to the back of her throat and sucking hard. She repeated that a number of times, teasing the stud as if exerting control. Meanwhile, Cherri continued to frig herself, hand sopping in oily come, and Miss Wilhelmina Wycherley, politely clearing her throat, let her own fingers stray to her gash, where she rubbed her expanding clitoris with vigour.

Vip! Vip!

'*Ahh!*'

Fwwt! Roslyn's wail as her caned bare bottom writhed was joined by a loud ripping sound, for Tara's corset split; cursing, Tara redoubled the vigour of her caning, dropping her burst corset and flogging her victim in the nude. Takira opened her mouth wide and mumbled, with her tongue slurping Fenimore's cock:

'I can't let you ladies go unpleasured! Miss Wycherley, please take James, and Cherri, please take Cooper.'

Billie sank to her knees before James's erect cock.

'I'm not entirely sure Cherri has been here long enough to earn fuck –' she began, her words stifled, as the grunting stud drove his cock into her mouth, his stiff meat filling it.

Billie tongued the piss-hole of James's hard cock before swallowing the whole shaft, and sucking it with clinging lips and teeth, sliding her mouth up and down the whole length of the cock to fasten her lips teasingly on the corona. She continued her vigorous clitoral masturbation as she knelt in the shadow of the hulking stud and gobbled his tool. Cherri prepared to kneel before Cooper, but he grabbed her between her legs, and hurled her into the pool – splash! – jumping in after her.

'Ooh!' Cherri gasped as she rose, dripping, from the slimy fluid to feel the male's cock behind her, at her ass-crack. Cooper pushed aside the girl tonguing Miss Takira, took Cherri by the hair and slammed her face into Takira's vacated, dripping cunt, saying she just had to taste. Cherri tongued the girl's swollen gash-flaps, then fastened her mouth round the entire labia and began to suck come from the gushing pouch as Takira, her own mouth sucking Fenimore's cock, squealed and shuddered. Cherri moved up her gash-lips towards the clitoris, took the juicy nubbin inside her mouth and began to chew. Cooper held her hips as she began to lick, bite and suck the girl's throbbing clitoris and rivulets of Japanese come trickled down her bare South Chehalis breasts.

'Uh!' Cherri squealed.

Cooper parted her fesses and Cherri spread as wide as she could, winking her anal pucker. The stud drove his glans between her ass-cheeks; his hard cock tip nuzzled her anal opening and stove in.

'Mmm!' Cherri grunted.

Thank the lord, he won't know I'm a cunt-virgin.

6

Vintage Threshing

Cherri gasped, relaxing, as it was clear Cooper had neither habit nor intention of cunt-fucking. The tip of his glans probed her anal bud and she relaxed her sphincter to let two, then three inches penetrate her asshole and then moaned, her voice vibrating through Takira's cunt as the Japanese girl squealed at the simultaneous penetration by Fenimore's cock of her own anal shaft. The pool fluid splashed at Cooper's jerking hips as he butt-fucked Cherri; his cock slid in and out of her hole, right to the tip, before he drove it back into her anal elastic, slimed with her ass-grease. As Fenimore's cock slammed Takira's asshole, her cunt-flaps clung to Cherri's face, trapping her mouth on the shivering Japanese girl's clit. Cherri sucked and swallowed come as she saw, above her, Miss Wycherley kneeling to take vigorous butt-fucking from James. The force of his buggery made her titties flap back and forth like balloons in the breeze. There was a plop as Fenimore removed his ass-greased cock from Takira's anus and plunged it once more into her throat.

Vip!

'*Ahh!*'

'That's all for now, you fucking retard,' snarled Tara Flick, terminating her caning of Roslyn Grayfold.

Grayfold clung sobbing to the rock, her naked bottom crimson interlaid with purple blotches. Gasping as Cooper's cock hammered her tripes, Cherri masturbated more vigorously. She sensed Takira was going to come, so heavy was her juicing and so violent her wriggling. The Japanese girl's sucking throat trapped Fenimore's cock, and the stud began to groan, finally spurting his cream. The sperm bubbled and frothed at Takira's mouth, dribbling down her chin over her breasts and her body in plastic as he squirted in her throat. Miss Wycherley, masturbating as she was buggered, groaned as her belly and cunt fluttered; her ass-cheeks squeezed the cock that butt-fucked her, until James grunted and ejaculated his spermload inside her writhing anus. Cherri's sphincter tightened on Cooper's cock, trapping his glans at her anal root, where she roiled the hard meat until she felt the first hot droplet of sperm from his pee-hole. Then her own orgasm shook her and she squealed into Takira's cunt, which erupted in a flow of come so strong, Cherri almost choked as the Japanese girl shrieked in her own orgasm.

Slap! Slap!

'*Ohh!*'

Roslyn Grayfold fell on Miss Takira, slapping her breasts, and wrenching her hair.

'You bitch!' she howled. 'You let that whore eat you?'

'Like any female, I merit chastisement,' the girl said as Roslyn's sharp toenails clawed her cunt. 'Shouldn't you be punished for letting a whore bring you to orgasm?'

'Yes, Roslyn did come while illicitly fighting and must be punished,' snapped Billie, rising. 'Boys!'

James, Fenimore and Cooper, impassive, seized Roslyn and plunged her into the pool. Fenimore went under the surface; Roslyn came up again, spluttering curses, and was hoisted ashore, trailing two of the suction tubes from the tanker, now stuck in her cunt and anus. Her limbs flapped like a rag doll's as she lay writhing on the grass.

'Help! I can't move!' she pleaded.

The suction tubes gurgled inside her holes. Fenimore pushed the tubes to the maximum in both cunt and anus, while James held her wrists behind her back. Fenimore went to the tanker's controls and pushed a lever: a gush of wine surged through the tubes and Grayfold's belly swelled as her anus and cunt filled with fluid. She groaned until the suction was reapplied, and then shrieked as the tubes sucked her cooze and rectum. Cooper retrieved his studded belt from his jeans and folded it in half, stud side out. As James sat on the girl's face and Fenimore alternately flushed and sucked her holes, Cooper delivered a vigorous whipping to the writhing bare buttocks. Thick pink stripes soon appeared, etched with lumps where the sharp belt-studs lashed, and which soon hardened into ridges, the bruises expanding to crawl over the increasingly uniform pink of the flogged ass.

'Well,' said Miss Wilhelmina Wycherley, 'she got no more than she deserved. I'm not sure you did, Cherri.'

'Huh –?' Cherri began.

'I intend to flog you to the bone, young lady, for your behaviour this morning. Not tomorrow, but some day, and when you least expect it.'

'Yes, to the bone,' cooed Miss Ona Takira.

Three pairs of green eyes, glittering in bronze skins, watched the scene from a slit window in the topmost turret of Miss Wycherley's castle. The eyes glittered most brightly when they fell on the body of Cherri Black.

'My addiction to bondage may be blatant, for I have no reason to conceal it, but in my culture it is far from strange,' Miss Takira said. 'In the orient, packaging is an art; thus a girl bound is a living artwork. I say addiction, for bondage without addiction is not the real thing. An unbound girl must crave binding for true

96

satisfaction, when she gets it. The sign of addiction is panic when the object of addiction is absent, be it coffee, tobacco, or other substance. I panic if my flesh goes too long unbitten by ropes, or unswaddled in plastic or rubber. In America, both art and sex are broad canvases – more is better. To us, art is minimal: our drawings suggest by a few brush strokes, our poems by few words. Genital orgasm is pleasure, but holistic orgasm a gift: a girl in bondage, her nerve-ends tortured to her limit, is in a continuous orgasm of joy at her own crushed beauty. A girl bound is minimalised: she is helpless, immobile; her breasts and cunt, the organs of femininity, are crushed or clamped, and thus bondage robs her of all being. Bound with her release at a master's whim, she is in the no-world of no-time, which we call nirvana. Even naked, you westerners have your identity; even dressed, we eastern women are mere slaves of the male principle which breathes life into the world and expresses itself through power of the cock. Whipping on the bare buttocks, their round fullness a symbol of our earth mother, is part of good bondage. The whip is male, the buttocks helpless emblems of the female. Women are only happy as slaves, our natural state. We are the base of a huge pyramid, crushed by the weight of our lord and master at its peak. Yet without our support, the pyramid would crumble. We must be crushed, bound or – subtlest of oppressions! – adored. Forced to live in so-called freedom, we submit to ritual bondage, to remind forgetful masters and mistresses of their duties! How unhappy American women are, with their freedom! They use it to lust for possessions, crueller bondage than the tightest ropes. The bound slave is free of lust; her only reality is the agony of her thongs and fetters, the world of things an illusion. A girl slave relishes her bound body and submission to the lash, making her the pure object of another's power, and freeing her of all freedom.'

97

Miss Takira sighed.

'How hard it is to find a good master or stern mistress! To be roped and displayed for all to scorn, for all males to fuck or whip, while the gagged slave cannot even squeal in protest; her body swaddled in a humiliating and painful array of straps, thongs and pincers, her crimson bare bottom smarting from the cane of a merciless or, better, cruelly indifferent, dominant! The old arts are forgotten.'

The Japanese girl spoke hanging upside down by her wrists and ankles on ropes stretching from a low tree branch. Her lips and chin dripped with James's sperm, for she had just finished sucking his cock. Her legs, arms and torso were enclosed in a rubber sheath with zip fasteners at each side, but leaving holes for her bare breasts. Her cunt and bottom dangled inches from the ground, so that Fenimore was able to bugger her from one side and Cooper fuck her cunt at the same time. It was lunch break. The wine girls watched, smiling and masturbating.

Vip! Vip! Vip!

'Ah! It hurts. Oh! Harder, please.'

Tara Flick caned her bare breasts with a sheaf of vine branches and the titties were already a tracery of crimson bruises around the stiff nipples, caned with a corona of wealed purple.

'Why, thank you for sharing that, Miss Takira,' said Miss Wycherley. 'We do our best to satisfy your needs, though they may seem a little extreme to Americans.'

Vip! Vip! Vip!

'*Ahh!* I appreciate it,' gasped the Japanese girl.

Billie Wycherley was still panting from her ascent of the turret staircase as she fastened her ankles in the ropes on the end of the wire bedframe. The frame was four feet high and she had to clamber up, then kneel on the wire and reach behind her, for she was to lie face down.

When her two ankles were tightly roped, she lowered her nude body onto the frame and roped her left wrist to the corner, using her teeth to draw the knot tight. The three nude exquisites watched her, standing around the bedframe, their canes dangling from their vulvas, and one completed Billie's binding by roping her remaining extremity. Her body was stretched tight by the knotting, with her head hanging over the edge of the bedframe. The wire net was wide enough to let her bare breasts and the fat slices of her labia extrude beneath it. Having greased it with slime from Billie's anus and quim, an exquisite inserted an iron butt-plug studded with tiny sharp pyramids into Billie's anus. The butt-plug was of one piece with a sheer iron corset which another exquisite simultaneously locked above Billie's hips, to bite and restrain her pubis and lower belly, and force her buttocks to swell. The corset constricted her waist to seventeen inches. A chain from the butt-plug stretched taut and looped through a ceiling hook, with its other end knotted to Billie's mane, wrenching her head inches up from the bedframe. Billie's body was unable to arch upwards to ease her constraint, for the third, tallest, exquisite reached beneath the frame, holding an iron clamp which she bent into a U-shape and fastened over Billie's bare teats beneath the wires. The clamp squashed her teat-flesh in a vice, right at her ribcage, pumping her teats and nipples to bulge like fruits. She applied a similar clamp to the protruding folds of Billie's vulva, ballooning their swollen skin beneath the wire bed net. Billie was pulled three ways: by the single chain, linking her hair and anal plug and drawn tight through the ceiling hook; by the clamps to breast and cunt, which stretched her titties and gash-flaps and prevented her from rising to ease the pain in her hair and anus; by the ropes on her wrists and ankles, stretching her limbs in a cross and permitting no easing of bondage.

'You summoned me,' she gasped.

Obviously.

It was Billie's own voice that whispered the word. Then she screamed, and her naked buttocks jerked, clenching around the studded butt-plug, whose pyramid nodes bit into her anal elastic. No exquisite had moved.

'*Ah!* Mistress, what have I done wrong?'

You address us as slave. We have no name but slave.

'Slave, how can I serve you? *Ah! Ah! Ah!*'

Her bare buttocks clenched a further three times, jerking more convulsively, at each stripe from the unseen cane. True pink weals glowed on her bottom.

You should know by now. Your pain nourishes us, as our beauty nourishes you. You masturbated at once on seeing the perfection of our bodies. Mere orgasm can never express your longing for our silken breasts, our ripe bellies and thighs and buttocks, our nipples, fruit for the sucking. Only pain of the lash can express your longing to be us.

Billie's naked buttocks began a dance of spasm, jerking and clenching, for a minute and twenty seconds, with her body straining her teat- and cunt-clamps against the bedframe's mesh and her hair pulled to its roots as her head rocked in agony. She writhed and her buttocks squirmed as if under severe bare-bottom caning; no instrument touched her, yet fresh weals joined her existing stripes. Her cunt-lips, clamped tight by the iron pincer, oozed oily come, which dripped into a silver come-pot beneath her loins, and her swollen clitoris poked bright red between iron thongs.

This is the mildest bondage, yet you juice.

'Am I wrong?' exclaimed Billie bitterly. 'Wrong, to be one of those girls who submits joyfully? *Ah! Ah! Ah!*'

Her body shuddered, buttocks churning, and a dribble of come seeping between her clamped cooze-flaps. The bedframe shook in the rhythm of her torture, and that torture continued for two hundred seconds.

During it, each glowing bronze exquisite had her fingers dancing beneath her pubic fleece at her glistening labia as she masturbated. Billie's eyes flowed with tears and her voice was a choking sob. Her bare ass rippled with welts.

'Why me?'

Why not? You have accepted our discipline. Discipline is ongoing, as you Americans are fond of saying. It gets more, not less, painful. How, bitch, can a submissive girl be wrong? A slave cannot be wrong, because she cannot be right. She is slave.

'Beat me as you please, then! I know that's why I'm here. I once thought spanking was just kidding around, then, soon after college, I was crazy enough to accept caning on the bare, and now I need weals so badly, despite myself. You must understand, it's not my fault! I was crazy about this guy in New York, once, and he would spank me, kind of playfully, lifting my skirt up and giving me a few slaps on my panties. It turned me on – he could see my juice at the panties gusset. Then, he started to spank me bare-assed, and harder, after every date before we fucked. Then the spanking was the date, and it developed to caning on the bare. I had to bend over and hold my knees with my bare ass stuck out and I said, kind of joking, I thought girls always got tied up for that, and he said, no, it is usually one or the other, and caning and bondage together are a potent cocktail only for the truly initiate. That word should have warned me. My first bare-assed caning, he gave me twenty strokes, and I cried afterwards, because it hurt so and my ass was all blotchy and crimson, and he didn't want to fuck. I thought I hadn't taken enough, so, next time, I said I wanted thirty. Then it was forty; at fifty strokes, I begged him to tie me up, because I squirmed so violently and my knees buckled so much and my bare butt clenched and hurt so that I was afraid of collapsing. That's when I began to enjoy the potent

101

cocktail, and became addicted. Only when I'd taken fifty or more canestrokes on the bare, hogtied or swaddled in rubber and chains, or in suspension, would he fuck me. Best was suspension, where he could push me back and forth like a swing, and fuck me in the cunt and anus alternately. One swing, then I would sail back, my cunt all sloppy, and be impaled on his cock; next swing, he slid all the way up my asshole, his cock oiled with my come. So, in suspension, I learned to crave the whole cocktail: bondage, whipping and caning on the bare, titty and cunt torture, with buggery and simultaneous cunt-fucking, my nips and cunt-flaps stretched to ribbons by heavy weights, or pierced by thumbtacks, or even stapled together by an ordinary office stapler, which hurts like nothing else. He abandoned me after addicting me. I made the mistake of saying that, for truly shameful submission, I should suck another cock while he was fucking me behind. He slapped my clamped titties, left me hanging there, and just walked out, I had to scream and get the super of the building to release me. That was my boyfriend's ultimate power trip: addicting me, awaiting the excuse to deprive me of what I craved. Now I need it. I was a sadist's victim. I thought such things couldn't happen in America, but they do. I was only looking for love!'

You need it because of yourself. Such things happen everywhere, when girls know their true natures. You are here to receive command, not love. The girl Cherri Black interests slave. You promised to cane her, this morning. Do so with the utmost rigour. Test her to the limit.

'I shall obey. Why do you not test me to the limit?'

You could not endure it.

'Try me. We have all night.'

Very well. You shall be further bound, and further punished.

The three dark, nude girls masturbated in harmony, their cunts audibly dripping come onto the cell floor.

102

'Thank you, slave. *Ahh!*'

Billie's body was lathered in sweat. Her loins slammed against the metal as her buttocks twitched. Ropes, studded with tiny pyramid clusters, began to uncoil from the ceiling of the cell, wrapping themselves around Miss Wycherley's shuddering nude body to bind her immobile. A frond inserted itelf into her vulva, filling her pouch; another snaked around her extruded, pulsing clitoris. Three pairs of green eyes glittered.

A man will come, calling himself master, who is a false power. If he enthrals your maids, he may demand a sacrifice. You will offer him Miss Cherri Black.

'But why? *Ahh!*'

The bare fesses twitched violently, and the strapped girl strained against each of her bonds, her clenching buttocks roiling the inside anus with the studded butt-plug, and her jerking head pulling her hair fully. The cunt- and breast-clamps banged against the bed-frame as her body arched.

'*Ah! Ah! Please! Ohh!*'

The tallest exquisite flicked her buttocks, and her cane sprang to erection from her cunt, whistling in the air, to lash Miss Wycherley's croup. Vip!

'Ohh!'

A jagged crimson weal, from real wood, appeared on the writhing bare bottom.

Do not ask why, slave. Obey. Give Cherri to the false master.

Vip!

'*Ah!* Yes, anything. *Oh!* Lord, that hurt!'

Vip!

'*Ahh!*'

Miss Wycherley's naked buttocks danced as the air filled with the whistle and crack of three rods, held in three wet, swollen cunts beneath rippling bronze bellies, the muscles of their bellies and croups writhing as the three exquisites masturbated their stiff, juiced clits.

103

Come oiled the cane shafts as they whirled in gash's grip. Their breasts quivered, the engorged nipples of all six teats gleaming rock-hard. Canes seen and unseen lashed Billie's bare globes, until her belly, and gushing cunt, convulsed in orgasm. Her caning did not stop.

Cherri scratched Miss Wycherley's door with her fingernails and, after twenty seconds, was told to enter.

'Come in, Cherri. I think you know why I've summoned you.'

'Yes, Bill – I mean, Miss Wycherley.'

'I dare say you've been apprehensive.'

'A little.'

'And uncomfortable, in the costume I commanded?'

'More than a little, miss.'

Cherri poured wth sweat.

'Good.'

The girl wore a flounced French maid's outfit with teetering high heels, a ballerina's black chiffon skirt and a white frilly blouse, buttoned to the neck, and two sizes too small so that her breasts bulged, straining beneath. Her hose were a fine mesh of woven black rubber cord, the bottom of a one-piece sheath covering her entire body to the neck, which she had spent all that morning weaving around herself, with her current bedmate, Priscilla Pritz, unravelling the ball of rubber cord. Priscilla was a petite brunette, from Glendive, Montana, with a 38-22-37 figure. Under the rubber mesh, Cherri wore a black waspie belly-corset, also rubber, its eyelets knotted to seventeen inches. Priscilla had had to floor Cherri and stand on her back to get the corset properly knotted, and its pressure made Cherri wince. Also worn under the rubber mesh were white panties, in clinging odorous latex. Billie Wycherley wore only her undergarments, a satin bra and panties set in peach colour, with nylon stockings and garter apparatus to match, and cradled a cane, three feet in length, with a crook handle.

She wore laced-up running shoes and white fluffy ankle socks over her stockings.

'You understand the reason for today's chastisement?'

'Yes, miss. My behaviour on my first day's work, last month.'

'So we'll get this business over with quickly. You won't sit down for a while, but you'll have the satisfaction of penitence. I assume you have no problem with caning? You've been caned so often.'

'Most days, miss, by all the guards, and – you know – playing spanking games, with my bedmate. Frigg Heidahl first, then Rosee Tupa, then Lara Dasso. I've had so many bedmates. Frigg was miffed she had to leave, and said that she was victim of my beauty, and I'd soon learn to be its victim as well. I've played games with them all. Sometimes me spanking them and, you know, doing intimate games, and sometimes me being spanked.'

'Which was more often, spanking or being spanked?'

'Being spanked, miss. They all go for my bottom.'

'Were you spanked by anyone else?

'You mean the exquisites, miss?'

Miss Wycherley trembled slightly.

'I prefer to think of them as helpmaids.'

'No, miss, they haven't chastised me. But . . .'

'Go on.'

'They sniff me. They caress me.'

'Masturbate, you mean?'

'Kind of. It comes to the same thing. I climax when they touch my ass, miss. The exquisites come to my room most nights and watch as I play with my bedmate. They bring themselves off, mutually masturbating, while they watch; then, when I've come and my bedmate has come, they sniff me down there. They drink my come and lick my anus too.'

'Not your bedmate?'

105

'Only me, miss.'

'Do they touch your breasts?'

'Oh! Yes, there too. Less than my ass, though.'

'I have to ask – *are* your breasts real? Not implants?'

'No, miss!'

Billie Wycherley stroked Cherri's buttocks.

'Anybody would think your behind had implants, too.'

'Miss Takira thought so. She visits, sometimes, but only to watch and bring herself off. She doesn't touch. She likes us to tie her up but leave her fingers free to masturbate.'

'Miss Takira was one of several to remind me of my promise to cane you and to urge severe chastisement,' Billie said. 'A vintage threshing should clear the air.'

Cherri sighed.

'Vintage threshing? More than caning on bare?'

'I'm afraid so. It's a beating *to* the bare, flogging your underthings to shreds. When you are whipped to the bare, your chastisement begins. Cherri, I'll know your pain.'

Miss Takira, secreted behind the spyhole, beside the pink velvet drapes of Miss Wycherley's rococo apartment, smiled as she fingered her stiffening clitoris. She was bound head and foot in four knottings of curtain ropes, with iron vices, a foot long and with fully tightened screws at each end, clamping her nipples. Her wrists were front-roped, with fingers pressing against her gash-flaps. A spray of peacock's feathers danced above her buttocks, their bound quills fully penetrating her rectum.

'You shall lift your skirtlet and bend over my flogging-stool, where I shall bind you for a caning on the buttocks,' said Billie. 'My *tabouret de fessée* is eighteenth-century French.'

'What then, miss?'

'The whip next, on your back. Your legs and bottom remain on the stool, but your arms are raised, and tied

106

to twin posts, raising your back to an angle of sixty-five degrees. When your rubber mesh and panties are completely shredded, I shall lower you again and tawse you with those thongs. The implement comes from seventeenth-century Scotland and can be more painful than the cane over a lengthier chastisement. The sting is in the tail. The tongues inflict a smarting only felt several seconds after the stroke. After that, the birch.'

She pointed to three instruments placed on her escritoire: a leather bullwhip, with splayed tongue, six feet long, and the flat rubber thong of a tawse, narrowing to a handle and widening into three tongues, the tawse being four feet long and four inches broad. The birch was a sheaf of slender branches, bound at the handle and splaying to three feet long. Cherri blushed. Her body trembled, yet inside her latex panties a seep of come added to her copious sweat at her perineum and the cramped folds of her vulva and ass-cleft.

'I've never been birched, miss,' she said. 'Is it painful? Oh – dumb question?'

'A birching on the naked buttocks is the most painful and exquisite torture a girl can imagine. As I birch you, you'll beg for the whip or even the cane. A girl never forgets her first birching. We have all afternoon.'

Cherri lifted her rubber skirtlet high above her buttocks and bent over the tabouret, with a seat curved for belly and crotch and four splayed legs. Billie laid down her thin, springy cane after swishing the air, making Cherri shudder, and roped Cherri's wrists and ankles to the pink befrilled satin stool. She wound the coarse hemp several times round Cherri's wrists, tightening it to the maximum.

'Itchy?'

'Yes, miss.'

'Good. Now, your ankles. A waist strap is optional, if you fear you might squirm too much and fall off.'

'No, thanks: I'll be OK, miss.'

'I'll cane and whip you until your rubber has shredded right through and I reach bare meat. Once I'm hitting on bare, you'll be tawsed, then birched.'

Her cane whistled in the air, flapping Cherri's raised skirtlet. Billie applied a strip of tape, fixing the skirt up and exposing Cherri's latex buttocks for full caning.

'Let's begin, shall we?'

Miss Wilhelmina Wycherley did not await a reply. She withdrew several steps, then her rubber soles pattered the floor, and the cane whistled.

Vip!

Cherri's cheeks trembled only a little, for the cane slice, right across mid-fesse, stroked her buttocks through the armour of rubber mesh and latex panties.

Vip!

'Ooh.'

The buttocks clenched.

'Hurt you?' said Miss Wycherley. 'I'm caning you as hard as I can, with a good run-up.'

'I can feel it, miss,' Cherri gasped.

Miss Wycherley withdrew, ran up, and delivered a flurry of cane-strokes to the girl's raised buttocks. There were snapping noises as the cane broke through Cherri's rubber knotting. The routine remained the same throughout the caning phase of her chastisement: run-up, strokes, and the snapping of rubber. After the twelfth stroke Cherri's buttocks began to clench without cease, and by the seventeenth, her caned fesses squirmed violently.

'Uh' she whimpered. 'It's getting there, miss.'

'Good,' panted Billie.

'Miss – I just want to ask – when's payday?'

'Hey! Good question.'

Vip!

'*Ah!*'

A section of knotted rubber sprang loose, revealing Cherri's clinging white panties, no more than gossamer-

108

thin. Vip! Vip! The cane concentrated on Cherri's haunches and inner thighs, until the whole mesh of rubber suddenly sagged to her knees, leaving the panties a white streak on her bronze skin. Vip! Vip!

'*Ohh.*'

Cherri took the strokes right across her fullness of her ass, and her wriggling became jerky.

'It does hurt, doesn't it?'

'Yes, miss. These panties are no protection.'

Vip!

'*Ah!*'

A strip of bronze skin appeared, as the cane ripped Cherri's panties clean in half. Vip! Vip! The flogged bare bronze wealed crimson. Vip! Vip! The panties, shredded completely, dropped away, and Cherri's bottom was naked, her bronze bottom purpling with welts. The rubber mesh slithered to her ankles, completely baring her legs and buttocks. She squirmed, wrists and ankles straining in their bonds and her come-moist pubis slapping the stool. Vip! Vip! Vip!

'*Ah!* I'm bare, miss! For pity's sake!'

Vip! Vip! Miss Wycherley added stingers to Cherri's purpled bare buttocks, which shuddered, squirming, as each stroke deepened the same weal mid-fesse. Then two slices each to the naked thighs.

'*Ah! Ah!*'

Cherri's bottom writhed, and she began continuous sobbing with loud, choking gasps.

'That was over forty with the cane. We must leave some work for the tawse and the birch,' Billie said. 'Your whipping shouldn't take long. I reckon thirty lashes will get me to your bare back.'

Cherri's skirt fell back into place over her scorched nates while Billie released her wrists, rebinding them at once to movable cuffs on the whipping-posts, then adjusted and locked the cuffs, perching Cherri's body at sixty-five degrees. Billie stepped further back, the bullwhip making a run-up unnecessary. Cherri's tight latex blouse stretched across her back, etching every rib and muscle above the biting corset that ground her waist beneath her rubber mesh. Her hair hung low, masking her head as it sagged between her wrenched shoulders. The whip flew, making an eerie, buzzing moan.

Vap!

'Uh.' Cherri grunted, her body slammed forwards by the whip, whose first stroke tore her blouse.

Vap!

'*Uh.*'

Cherri's back wriggled, flinching, as the whip hummed, for her blouse was half shredded and the whip sliced the mesh beneath.

Vap!

'Hurt yet?'

'Sure, miss. *Ah!*'

The whip ripped the latex blouse, and the rubber sheath. She wriggled as the whipstrokes rapidly shredded the sheath, until the thong struck only the purpling bruises on her naked skin. Shards of blouse fluttered to Cherri's ankles. Vap! Vap! The whip descended to Cherri's waspie corset, which shredded, sprang apart, and fell from Cherri's flesh, revealing dark corset bruises. Vap! Vap! The leather thong laid deep weals across Cherri's shoulderblades, and her back shuddered, discarding her last shreds of rubber.

Vap!

'*Oh!* Oh! I'm bare, miss.'

Vap!

'*Ahh!*'

Cherri's naked back arched and shuddered, as the thong lashed the exposed skin.

'*Ahh!* I'm bare, miss, *I'm bare!*'

Cherri jerked her head up and saw that Billie's peach-coloured panties were stained dark with liquid;

that Billie had her hand inside the panties and was masturbating herself vigorously as she flogged. Come dripped down her nyloned thighs and calves into her fluffy white ankle socks. Observed, Billie halted in mid-stroke.

'Oh,' she exclaimed, 'I –'

She glanced at the stool beneath Cherri's vulva, where Cherri's seeped come stained the satin. Cherri gulped.

'Whipped to thirty-six. Tawse on the bare, Cherri.'

Groaning and nude, Cherri bent over the tabouret for Billie to rope her wrists and ankles. The tongues of the tawse slithered over her ass-cheeks and she shuddered.

'Thinking on it should frighten you,' Billie said. 'Three tawse tongues on your bare, then the birch – and you wonder when payday is!'

'I just thought . . .'

The heavy tawse flapped the air, whistled, and lashed Cherri's bruised bare globes.

Thwack! Thwack!

'*Ah! Ah! Oh!*'

Cherri reacted instantly: her body jerked in her bonds and her voice screamed hoarsely as three broad tawse weals appeared over her canewelts. The trickle of come from her swollen red cunt-lips became a torrent.

'How many, please, miss?' she sobbed.

'Till you come, you submissive bitch,' hissed Billie, her own fingers masturbating quickly beneath her come-soaked panties. 'You're wet! Your clit's throbbing, isn't it?'

Thwack!

'*Oh! Oh!*'

Thwack!

The tongues of the tawse bit the same weals as the cane, overlaying the purple welts with broader, crimson weals.

'Isn't it?'

'Yes, miss.'

'So I masturbate as your ass squirms and reddens and weals?' Billie hissed. 'What do you *want*, slave?'

'I don't know, miss.'

Thwack!

'Not good enough, bitch!'

Thwack! Thwack!

'*Ah!* I want you to beat me raw, miss. I really do.'

Thwack!

'*Ahh!*'

Billie's panties stretched across her thighs as she openly masturbated her exposed vulva, her massive pubic bush dripping with sweat and come.

'We all do, bitch!' she hissed, tawsing Cherri long and hard, across the entirety of her buttocks and thigh-tops, with the inner thighs and haunches blanketed in welts. 'This is your payday, slave! This, and every day!'

Thwack! Thwack!

'*Ah!* Yes! I'm coming!' Cherri shrieked, after 108 strokes of the triple-thonged tawse. Billie took her to one hundred and thirteen.

Thwack! Thwack!

'*Oh! Oh!*'

As Cherri orgasmed, Billie brought herself off, the tawsed girl's cries drowning her own whimpers. Her pubic jungle dripped come into her panties held at mid-thigh. Cherri's melons glowed purple on bronze, melding into a new, luminescent colour, pulsing beneath her skin. She touched them, then spread wider for the birch.

'You lucky bitch,' said Billie. 'You've reached plateau. If only I could.'

She did not pull her panties up but lifted the birch and, without preamble, swished Cherri's welted fesses. The crackling kiss of the twigs embraced Cherri's entire bare and she yelped, clenching her globes tight. Under Billie's birching, Cherri's buttocks swelled to a ridged, blotchy mosaic of bruises, with tiny vein-like weals made by the birch twigs. Seventeen strokes of the birch sheaf brought her to climax. Ten further strokes, and again orgasm; thereafter, Cherri's birching was accompanied by her wail of climax, and a permanent shiver of her birched bare buttocks, while Billie masturbated her sluicing cunt faster and faster, trying to come a second time.

Swish! Swish!

'*Uhh!*'

Swish! Swish! As Cherri's birched ass writhed and glowed, Billie brought herself off by vigorous clit-fisting, but the birch sheaf did not falter. The ass-cleft beneath dripped with Cherri's sweat and come. In her nook, Miss Takira, breathless in bondage, took her hand from her throbbing clitty, which she had masturbated to repeated orgasm since the cane first sliced Cherri's croup. She held her hand an inch from her juicing cunt and closed her eyes a moment, then gazed at Cherri's squirming bare bottom and yelped in excitement as orgasm flooded her, clitoris untouched.

'Oh! Yes!' Cherri groaned, her teeth bared in a rictus of ecstasy. '*Yes!*'

Her buttocks were a painting of bright purple, crimson and black welts, many already hardened to crusty ridges. Her last birch stroke was the forty-fourth. Billie's arm stopped, frozen in mid-air.

'You have to go now,' she gulped. 'I've had a communication. It's suppertime. Shower, but don't dress. Go nude into the dining-room. *They* want the girls to see your slave's marks.'

7

Miss Fornication

Back in her room, Cherri conferred with Priscilla Pritz, who was selecting her own underthings for the evening's meal. Priscilla saw Cherri's wealed, glowing bottom and at once fell to her knees to press her nose into the cleft of Cherri's fesses. Cherri assented, sobbing and shaking.

'Oh!' Priscilla cried, 'you're the girl! I just have to do myself! That ass! I've never seen anything so beautiful!'

'It isn't a thing,' gasped Cherri. 'It's me, thrashed raw.'

Priscilla was smaller than Cherri, but her figure had the same ripe proportions: full ass-melons, the breasts heavy yet jutting without support, the nipples pink plums. The distended swelling of her vulval apparatus confirmed her as a skilled masturbatress. Her glossy brown pubic fleece matched her all-over worktan. Stroking Cherri's weals, she masturbated herself to climax and did not take her fingers from her cunt but continued to masturbate until she came a second time. Priscilla had been a wine girl for three months – or, as she said, a slave.

'I'm so wet,' she gasped. 'Of course we're slaves. What else should girls be? Our pay is spiritual, getting our asses whipped, the most spiritual thing there is. The exquisites helped Miss Wycherley understand.'

'Where do they come from?'

'They arrived just after I did, and I didn't know girls should be enslaved, then. I thought I was just an American working girl! They've made us real girls, and the winery a success. People like to drink slave wine.'

'That doesn't answer my question.'

Priscilla leaned closer, stroking her engorged vulva and Cherri's bottom, and licking Cherri's jutting bare nipples.

'A girl can be really, really, beaten for questions.'

'I just have been really, really, beaten,' said Cherri.

'Cherri, what's America? A society of robots. Produce, consume, conform, obey! We are all slaves, if only to the almighty fucking computer. Even the winery wouldn't function without the central computer. The guard girls, slaves themselves, bio-wired to report, command, obey.'

'Yeah, that's so weird, I mean, I've heard of bionics and stuff, but I thought that belonged in the distant future.'

'I think it belongs in the distant past. The exquisites *are* the central computer. They communicate by thought, and by cunt, and by their asses. Women aren't allowed language, wherever or whenever they are from. They are pure slave, pure woman. That's the source of their power. Slavery unrefined. Girls. Like us.'

'How do you know that?'

'The exquisites felt me.'

Priscilla touched Cherri's bare bottom, and Cherri's hers, and both girls orgasmed, together.

In the weeks following her thrashing, Cherri worked hard, took her daily canings with humility, and tried not to clash with Roslyn Grayfold. She won tokens for 'stud visits' to the shacks where the three males lived. She was frightened to use them, fearing the redneck trio might have a mean side in private. They might be the kind of guys who liked to slap a girl around. Yet the events of her first day proved a one-off and, with public butt-fucking unlikely, she could no longer deny her need for anal penetration by cock, be it in private. Cherri confessed what she did, and Pris made a wry face.

'Our games not good enough?' she said.

'It's not that.'

'I know. Time to get your ass to boy's town.'

Billie Wycherley arranged for Cherri to see Fenimore, at 11 p.m., after supper, on an evening when several girls were planning to sneak out to some revivalist meeting with a guy called the maidmaster. Cherri refused, saying she'd have nothing more to do with preachermen. She wondered if Billie knew of this excursion but wondered, more importantly, what to wear for her fuck session – underthings, full dress, or nothing at all? She decided on a teasing bra in see-through voile, which hardly covered her nipples – just its cling made them stiffen to bricks – and matching panties, a triangle that covered a third of her pubic fleece. She chose a lacy garter belt, fishnet stockings and high stilettos, painfully tight and awkward to walk in over the scrubland. She saw lights of the studs' tarpaper shacks twinkling nearer, beneath the shadowy hulk of a barn, and wondered if Fenimore's cock would be as big and brutal as Cooper's – if he would fuck her ass harder, out of macho pride.

I hope so. I need butt-fucking so bad. Slave or no slave, I'm a trailer park girl.

She scratched the door of the middle shack, Fenimore's. The door slid open. She had expected a room full of guitars and beer cans and male stuff, but she entered a single room, softly lit by green candles. All three studs stood, naked, and legs apart: before them knelt the three exquisites, each cupping her own buttocks in her palms, and her mouth vigorously sucking cock. The exquisites' heads hung low, their long manes piled on the floor at their feet and their pubic manes

116

wound up around their breasts. The studs gasped as tongues slid over frenulum, shaft or corona of rigid cock. Each girl fellated in the same rhythm, drawing her lips over the swollen purple glans, licking the piss-hole, then letting her lips slide down the helmet again, her drool shining on the bursting cock until she clamped the neck of the glans to tongue its ridge; then a swift plunge down the drool-shiny cockshaft to engorge the entire flesh with her lips pressing the male's ball-sac, and the cock's head filling her throat.

'Fenimore?' Cherri said, her gash starting to seep come as she observed the nudity of the three girls in the candlelight, which illumined starkly their muscular, writhing spines, the clefts of their massive buttocks and the harmonised bobbing motions of their heads.

'Yeah?' said the male, sucked by the tallest exquisite. 'Lord, girl, I hope I got juice left for you.'

Like the others, he appeared nonchalant, pushing the girl's head down on his cock in mastery. Yet her tongue held him in thrall. Cherri's fingers crept between her thighs and she began to masturbate her swelling nubbin through her panties. Juice dripped from her rapidly swelling gash-flaps as she thumbed her clitty and poked her fingers an inch, as far as they would comfortably go, into her virgin slit, stretching the panty fabric.

What if Fenimore wants cunt-fuck? Not too late to run.

Each male gasped harder, and his cock quivered and bucked, as the exquisite's lips squeezed the glans neck: the three fellatrices sucked and licked, making all three males sperm into their mouths. The girl's throats jerked as they swallowed the studs' sperm, although the males spurted so powerfully that sperm frothed at each girl's lips. Fenimore groaned; the girl released his cock, which flopped to dangle massively under his balls. The two other studs emitted rebel whoops. Cherri paused in her masturbation and withdrew her stud token from her panties, now soaked in her come.

117

'I have an appointment, Mr Fenimore,' she said.

The three exquisites turned to face her, eyes glittering, and each spread the flaps of her cooze, revealing glistening red meat, while pinching her nipples to fullness. Cherri's fingers were once more at her throbbing clitoris, which she began to rub, gasping. In panties, bra, stockings and high-heeled shoes, she stood masturbating in front of the six nude individuals. The exquisites stood and masturbated their own crimson wet pouches.

Squat, slave, like a bitch.

The voice resonated inside her clitoris. Cherri crouched on the floor, her buttocks raised and spread to the males. The exquisites moved. Cherri felt two naked cunts pressed to her lips, a pair of thighs trapping her head, and a mouth, that of the tallest girl, at her own pantied cunt. She did not resist as she was knotted in the long braided tresses of the exquisites. Her wrists and ankles were secured, then a rope of hair coiled across her breasts, squashing them, with another around her face. The three cocks swayed above the naked girls, all gleaming with sperm and girl-drool. Three exquisite cunts squashed Cherri's face; her tongue darted from one swollen clitoris to the next. She felt a stab in her own cunt as the tall girl's tongue penetrated the panty-fabric, and entered her virgin gash. She couldn't cry out as her face was bathed and pinioned by the gushing coozes of two girls, but she mewled as the tallest girl's tongue unrolled inside her naked cunt and penetrated her to the neck of her womb where nobody, not even Cherri's masturbating fingers, had ever penetrated.

'*Mm!*' she squealed at the tickling at her wombneck, and her belly fluttering as the tongue slid rapidly up and down her slit, cunt-fucking her for the first time, and then she gasped, chewing and sucking and licking the two cunts smothering her face as her own cunt exploded in orgasm.

My pussy's not virgin, now.

'Well, I'll be . . . look at *this* for wood!'

She heard Fenimore's voice, and then shrieked, as his cock pierced her panties. He was ramrod stiff and quickly found her anus; she relaxed her sphincter, allowing the cock two inches inside her anal hole, and on his second thrust Fenimore penetrated her to the root. He began a vigorous butt-fucking, while the tall exquisite, sucking and swallowing Cherri's flowing love juice, continued to tongue-fuck her cunt. Cherri squeezed and embraced the cock, teasing it with her anal elastic and frotting the glans with her rectum. Fenimore buggered her fiercely for fifteen minutes before he grunted and Cherri felt the hot spurt of his sperm. No sooner had the stud withdrawn his softened cock, than another – Cooper's, she was sure – stabbed through her panties and renewed her buggery. He butt-fucked her for sixteen minutes, before spurting a huge quantity of hot cream into her anal elastic, and then the third male's cock replaced his. Cherri was buggered for forty-eight minutes, while tongue-fucked, and herself gamahuching the two exquisites; the tall girl masturbated her own cunt, positioned under Cherri's hair-bound breasts, and squashing them with her labia. She and Cherri came together.

You are crushed, burst, filled by the cocks of male power, ready for vilest shame, whenever master desires. You are slave of cock. Slave submits. In submission is power.

'That never happened before,' said Fenimore. 'Course, normally I'd get it up in about ten minutes, but . . .'

'Yeah, said Cooper, hastily. 'Ten minutes is about right.'

'Maybe less,' said James.

'Those girls work magic,' Fenimore said. 'Yet they're no more 'n slaves, like the rest of us here.'

119

Slavery is power, said the voice in her clitty. *Use your power to resist the domination of a false master, who will try to take you soon.*

Cherri strode back to the castle barefoot and got an hour's sleep, before sunrise.

'OK?' said Billie Wycherley brightly at breakfast. 'Want to show me your spank marks?'

'Why, I wasn't spanked,' said Cherri.

'Next time, you should insist.'

There may not be a next time, said the voice vibrating in her vulva.

'Hey, are you my friend, or my enemy?' blurted Cherri.

'What a curious question,' said Billie. 'I'm your friend, of course.'

We are slave together.

'Slave? Together?' said Cherri.

'Who, me?' exclaimed Billie, nervously.

The thing that was Cherri. Slave.

'No, not you, miss,' Cherri said.

I should have run the moment I lined up for supper, Cherri reflected, *somewhat later. The exquisites were gone and I knew something was wrong, the way everybody looked at me. They were all chattering about that maidmaster, and how they wanted to do his bidding, and all.*

Tara Flick, Bev Ellerbee and Meryl Waldeck all lashed Cherri's buttocks with canestrokes before she entered the dining-room. She winced as the rods struck her butt, bare but for a thong in her ass-cleft, of one piece with her high, Victorian 'S' corset in titanium-ribbed black satin, that metal's lightness and strength allowing a greater cluster of painfully thin stays than most and constraining her waist to eighteen inches. It left the teats bare and squashed upwards, and over it she wore a cashmire wrap. She sat at the end of the table; at the head sat Miss Takira next to a nervous Billie

Wycherley, and Roslyn Grayfold, smirking. The three studs, in blue jeans, served tomato soup and corned beef hash. After the meal, Miss Wycherley stood.

'I wish to announce,' she said, blushing, 'that I have agreed to some changes around here. The girls we called exquisites are no longer with us. The majority of you wine girls have persuaded me to adopt the program of the maidmaster, whose expertise, in running the winery on sound business principles, without fee, we shall warmly welcome. We are all Americans, with Miss Takira kind of honorary, so must accept democratic decisions. This arrangement is to commence as soon as the maidmaster has received a gesture of our goodwill. I am informed by my good friend Roslyn Grayfold, and endorsed by Miss Takira, that the gesture should be spectacular.'

She looked straight at Cherri, who was at once overpowered by the studs and dragged from the table, with Fenimore and Cooper each hauling her by one clawed breast, while James wrenched her hair. Cherri didn't even try to stumble, but let herself be dragged, as it was painful to walk, with the corset thong chafing the crack of her ass, and her cunt-lips. They dragged her across the scrubland to the barn behind their shacks and the wine girls followed in an excited, squealing troupe. Priscilla Pritz and Cherri's former roommates, including Rosee, Lara, and Frigg, whooped at her constraint. The barn housed the antique and now disused wine-press. Outside were parked a white Rolls-Royce, a Porsche, and a pink Corvette. The males dragged her inside where the maidmaster awaited, attended by his maids Kelley Hide, Joanne Pascal, Rona Gumette, and Honey Swade, all bare-breasted, in cut-off denim shorts, with arms folded under silver rings dangling from pierced nipples.

The iron wine press was dusted, oiled, and ready for use. It was a circular basin the size of a person, with a rim two feet high, and runnels to let crushed juice escape; above it, the grinder was a slab with geared teeth. A screw lowered the grinder to press the fruit in the container, a second made it rotate to grind the fruit when pressed. Across the surface of the grinder were slots containing a hundred and twenty pinwheels, half an inch in diameter. Roslyn Grayfold and Billie Wycherley grasped the gears and began to lower and rotate the grinder, while the three studs roped Cherri's arms to her sides, binding her ankles and wrists together and placing a brown supermarket bag over her head. Like that, she was lowered into the crushing basin and her wrists and ankles further roped to rungs at the basin's rim. The grinder hummed, coming nearer to Cherri's roped and helpless body.

'Crush the bitch!' shrieked Elise Wuliger, and the wine girls screamed approval.

'But slowly,' purred the maidmaster. 'Let her enjoy, while you maids pleasure yourselves.'

'*This isn't right!*' Cherri screamed.

'Why not?' purred the maidmaster.

Suddenly, there was a sharp swishing sound, and the girls shrieked. Cherri's ropes, severed, sprang away from her flesh. She ripped the paper bag from her head; the grinder, its pinwheels spinning, was inches above her and, rolling aside, she escaped from the crushing slab. Before her, the three exquisites, nude, and with scythes held in their cunts, faced the gasping crowd, and copious fluid squirted from their coozes, flaps apart, to bathe the dirt floor in a shimmering, oily lake, glowing green, and illuminating the gloomy barn. Roslyn Grayfold rushed forwards, to slip and fall headlong in the lake of cooze fluid; Ona Takira, masturbating like the other girls, slipped too, and so did Tara Flick and Bev Ellerbee, joined by the snarling James, Fenimore and Cooper. Cherri's only escape was through the ever-widening lake of girl-gush. Gingerly, she took a step and found the liquid sticky, like glue. She looked at the howling faces, the stony maidmaster and his four bare-breasted maids, too busy masturbating each other's cunts under unzipped jean shorts to notice. The exquisites were nowhere to be seen: only the lake of shining cunt-ooze evidenced their presence. She took another sure step forwards, and another, through the acrid pond.

'Get the bitch!' screamed Roslyn Grayfold.

'Shackle her!' added Billie Wycherley.

'Crush her!' shrilled Ona Takira.

Cherri put the puzzling exquisites from her mind, reckoning they must be illegal aliens or something. Barefoot, bare-breasted, and wearing only the painfully tight corset with its thong chafing agony in her exposed ass-cleft and cunt-flaps, Cherri did what she knew how to do best. She ran.

Cherri ran, until the lights of the winery were far behind her. At first she stayed on the scrubland but, after a few miles of running, found a blacktop and entrusted herself to the roadway. There was only starlight to guide her and the road led towards a range of rolling hills where a few lights twinkled, reflected in the ripples of a distant lake. Still sobbing, she slowed to a walk, and blinked as a car's headlights stopped behind her. She turned to look, trapped in the beam.

'Getting in?' said a girl's voice. 'Must be cold.'

Cherri approached the station wagon, nervously, and peered inside. The driver was a slim girl, her own age, with bobbed black hair and a hard, moulded figure, 36-23-38, with conical jutting breasts half bared under the straps of the cream satin nightdress, which was her only clothing. Her bare leg on the accelerator pedal was long, sleekly tanned, and powerfully muscled. The wagon was piled with boxes. Cherri climbed in and sank into the velour passenger seat. The car moved, the girl's buttocks rippling as she drove.

'You're out pretty late. I had to go to the city, see,' she said, without looking at Cherri, 'to get some supplies for Mom. She takes a lot of looking after, and I'm the only one who can. You can stay the night at the inn, if you want. I can offer you a job as live-in housemaid. We're always short-staffed; in fact, we've only the twins at the moment and they are, well, as you'll see. Then there's Cal, but he's from Arkansas. Is that sexually provocative garment your normal clothing? You'd better cover up, because Mom doesn't approve of sex, and neither do I. There are some pajamas and stuff in the back. If you want to stay bare-breasted for the ride, that's your privilege. Funny weather, for the time of year.'

'Bare-breasted?' Cherri said, looking down. 'Oh, yeah.'

'That corset looks painful. Is it?'

'Yes, it is,' Cherri replied.

'I'd say you've been whipped.'

'Some,' Cherri blurted.

'You must be wicked. Most girls are. You'd better take the job, for it'll make you less wicked. We're vegetarian – also, we're clothing-optional, and for women only. Nudity is healing, and cleanses the female of sex impulses. We call our hotel "Inn Health". Mom's idea.'

Cherri said she could use some healing.

'We have hot pools and tubs, sun-bathing lawns, river, lake, gardens, mud baths, lacto-vegetarian dietary facilities, and total seclusion at the hilltop, which is the crater of a dormant volcano, its lake having plentiful grey sand beaches. The marines have an isolation training centre a few miles away; they practise running up hills or something, not that I care. There is little to distract from the healing process. You seem to have no ID or possessions, so I assume you are wanted by some law enforcement agency. My name is Miss F. E. Lee. I hope you'll take the job; the pay is adequate, and the work will heal you. Our guests are women who want to get in touch with their real, naked selves. F. E. Lee is my maiden name, as my husband left me with our marriage unconsummated, so my vagina has never spliced with a male sex organ. I dare say you have spliced often, being low in moral quality. I have often wondered what it's like. Tell me how you got those whipmarks.'

Law enforcement? Yeah, that Corvette Mickey boosted. And the fake video of me stealing from the NeedaBurger cash desk. I'm wanted.

Cherri said she wished to reach California, but was soon blurting out her angry tale of victimisation at the winery. Miss F. E. Lee interrupted.

'So, at this winery they were all full-bodied girls.'

'I guess so,' said Cherri. 'Pretty well built.'

Miss F. E. Lee shifted her skirt, to reveal the smooth, amputated stump of her right thigh, sliced at her groin. Her pubic fleece was untrimmed, and coarse black thatch straggled over the thigh stump.

'Are you apotemnophobic? I mean, do I shock you?'

'Why, no.'

'Many of our guests are apotemnophiles, or real apotemnasts – we prefer that to amputees, or amps. "Apos" is the acceptable short form.'

Miss F. E. Lee kept her stump and her naked vulva displayed, and stroked the stump. Cherri's fingers joined hers. The skin was soft and downy, like a breast.

'It's kind of beautiful,' Cherri said.

'Don't flatter.'

'I wouldn't. Honest.'

'Mmm. In fact, I like what you're doing. Mom named me after old puritan custom, by sticking a pin at random in the bible, and taking the words the pin fell on. So my given name is Fornication. This is California, by the way; that's Goose Lake over there.'

'It doesn't look like California,'

'What does? My second name is Evil. On my driver's licence it says Fornication Evil Lee, but you can call me miss.'

Cherri continued to stroke Miss F. E. Lee's stump, as the car began the winding ascent of the mountain range, and the girl's breathing became heavier.

'I have an organic prosthesis, but I prefer the natural look. As do most of our guests. We reject American society's prurient hypocrisy about the unlimbed, and wish to be ourselves, free apotemnasts. Apos with attitude.'

'Yeah, I suppose it's kind of clumsy, like, having to strap it on and all.'

Miss F. E. Lee laughed.

'We've no strapping, in that sense,' she said. 'An organic prosthesis clings by itself. They grow so well, on a titanium boneframe, they function better than the original. Illegal in the United States, but not in Mexico.'

'Grow? Cling?'

'You've seen geckos on the ceiling, upside down?'

'Sure. They have suckers or something.'

'No. A layer of space one molecule deep separates the gecko's feet from the wall. Within that molecule, gravity is polarised to the gecko's position. A gecko controls its own gravity – it is never upside down. An organic prosthesis fits using the same principle.'

'Controlling gravity? Then people could go to Mars and stuff.'

'Maybe people did. They have pyramids on Mars.'

The air was much colder, as they spiralled, fast, up the hillside. They passed a floodlit metal gate that read 'US Marine Corps – NO TRESPASSING', then a few straggling shacks, and then, neon splitting the velvet darkness: NEEDABURGER!

'Hey, geckos or no geckos, I'll take the job,' Cherri blurted. 'I need money to go to LA, and get an acting job, you know? I'm pretty broke.'

126

'*Pretty* broke? I'd hate to see ugly broke.'

'About the law, well, I'm not sure.'

'The law usually is. Maids have to observe strict rules of service, and there are penalties for infractions. Now, your frankly recounted story suggests you are far gone in wickedness, in fact, that you are addicted to buggery, masturbation and spanking. Think before answering.'

'Addicted? Never!'

'That proves it. A submissive addict always denies her addiction. You will have to accept therapy.'

'What kind?'

'A cure usually resembles the affliction.'

There was a faint smile on Miss F. E. Lee's lips, which grew wider as Cherri's fingers continued to tease the soft skin of her thigh stump. A pool of shiny liquid dribbled from her vulva, wetting Cherri's wrist. It was come. F. E. Lee's belly began to quiver, then the swollen lips of her cunt parted to expose a hugely distended red clitoris and the drip from her gash became a flood; at Cherri's touch, Miss F. E. Lee's breath became a harsh flurry of yelps, and Cherri exclaimed in surprise.

'*Ooh,*' the one-legged girl gasped. 'Surprise is part of the therapy.'

She parked the wagon and whistled for the boy Cal to unload it. She nimbly hopped out on her single leg, and said that she must get Cherri fixed up, before showing her round her new workplace. She hopped into the building, casually holding her prosthesis, a perfect bare female leg, under her arm, and scarcely bothering with her crutch.

'You have a lovely croup,' said Miss F. E. Lee, a while later, as Cherri followed her into the vestibule. 'It's so pear-like, round and firm, and so big, yet the two fesses moulding in perfect, succulent harmony. The skin, so bronze, yet creamy in texture. I can well understand the temptation to which others have yielded, to spank or whip you, to leave their marks on beauty itself.

Titties and legs in perfect harmony, and your sheer, uniform skin colour adds lustre, deliciously offset by that jungle of hairs at the pubis, hanging quite superbly, to embrace the folds of your labia, and brush those silky thighs. I sense great healing power.'

Dawn was breaking, a vivid lemon sun in big sky, and Cherri had exchanged her corset for a pair of skimpy voile pajamas, which clung to her body as tightly as her corse. The shorts were scarcely more than clinging panties, the fabric tickling the bare skin of her bottom and rubbing her vulval lips, so that there was a damp patch at her gash. The top was a mere halter that left most of her cleavage and her belly bare. A festive note were the hems of fluffy white cotton on pants and sleeves. Apart from the aluminium elevator, the vestibule was all of wood, without decoration, save for a wooden carving on the reception desk of a nude girl squatting on her buttocks, beneath which both legs were amputated to the hip. She had her arms outstretched, palms facing upwards. Her long tresses teasingly covered her breasts, but parted, to show erect nipples; her open vulva and luxuriant bush were exquisitely depicted, the gash almost seamless with her fesses and stumps, and a few droplets of liquid oozing from her vulval crevice. Her wooden clitoris was massively extruded. Miss F. E. Lee wondered if Cherri had a twin, as the statuette looked just like her. Cherri said, not to her knowledge.

'It's great,' Cherri cried, as they exited the vestibule, and viewed the volcanic crater, its lake and grey sand beaches, ringed by wooden cabanas, about fifty in number, pyramidal in shape, and garlanded with flowers and fronds.

Her breasts expanded against the thin pajama cloth as her lungs filled with crisp mountain air.

'Inn Health owns the entire mountaintop,' said Miss F. E. Lee. 'Its bowl is a suntrap, permitting sunbathing

128

even in winter, and both lake water and hot mud pools are heated by the magma beneath, although there has been no eruption since the end of the Miocene era. Our baths are heated by earth steam, which we also use for cooking. The tepees are living, sculpted trees, those nearest us being housemaid accommodations. You may rest a few hours before starting duty, when you must exchange pajamas for formal maidwear. Now, your therapy shall not be the agony of sudden withdrawal from your addictions. You are free to masturbate, for example.'

'Well, uh, thanks, miss.'

Cherri stooped, to enter her tepee. From other tepees came female moans.

'Neither shall your other addictions sudddenly be withdrawn,' said Miss F. E. Lee.

Cherri did indeed masturbate to calm herself after her ordeal, requiring few strokes to her clitoris to bring herself off before falling soundly asleep on her futon. The earth floor was hot and she slept without covering. When she awoke, Miss F. E. Lee stood before her and ordered her to remove her pajamas. She was nude, but for the very same painful corset Cherri had previously discarded, and that pushed her pert, hard-nippled breasts up like pears. It also accentuated the taut melons of her bare ass, which swayed lop-sidedly, compacted by her single black rubber boot with high spiked heel. Her pubic bush was combed and teased up with hairspray on either side of the corset's thong, so that her thick cunt-folds, with the inside pink meat clamped by the thong, were fully exposed. She walked with a wooden crutch and carried a second crutch and a roll of duct tape under her arm, as well as a bag of clothing and a short cane of stiffened rubber. Cherri stepped out of her pajamas, with Miss Lee's eye on the stain of come at the gusset of her shorts. She stood nude before her new mistress.

'You masturbated,' said Miss F. E. Lee.

'You said it was OK, miss.'

'Describe your fantasies.'

'I was caned on the bare, miss, by girls, three of them, nude and tanned like me, and there was a man with long curly hair in a robe, and I was on my knees, sucking him off as the girls stood over me and caned my buttocks. He came in my mouth, all hot and creamy, so his come dribbled over my titties, and I rubbed the welts on my ass, it was smarting so! Then I came.'

'You *are* an addict. I'd better give you light discipline, so you can do your duties without the cravings of withdrawal. Bend over, touch your toes, and spread your cheeks.'

Cherri obeyed, her legs and buttocks trembling, as Miss F. E. Lee swished the cane in the air. There was a whistling swish; Cherri clenched her fesses and her gorge rose as the cane wealed her spread bare.

Vip!

'Uh,' she gasped.

Vip! Vip! The second and third strokes followed, almost at once, and Cherri's bare buttocks began to squirm, her ass-crack clenching continuously.

'Uh,' she gasped, again, 'those really *stung*, miss!'

'Good.'

Vip! Vip!

'*Ahh*!'

Cherri's bare flesh writhed, seared by slices of the short, whippy cane, until she had taken the remainder of a set of twelve strokes on the bare. She rose with a groan, rubbing her fesses and wiping the tears that stained her face.

'Hurt a lot?' said Miss F. E. Lee.

'Yes, miss,' Cherri whimpered.

'Touch yourself between your legs, then show me your fingers.'

Cherri's fingers delved beneath her cunt-bush, and found her vulva oily wet. She held up two shiny fingers.

'Yes, a bare caning turns you on. You have a lot of therapy ahead. Feel better, now?'

'A little, miss.'

'That dozen will serve for the moment. You pink nicely, and should show good ridges when the skin hardens.'

Miss F. E. Lee gave her the crutch and duct tape, explaining that maids thus deferred to apotemnast or apotemnophile guests. Cherri had to wedge her left foot in the cleft of her buttocks, and tape calf to thigh, so that she seemed amputated from the knee. The clothes bag spilled its contents; Cherri wrapped her breasts in a strip of black rubber, three inches wide, which just covered her nipples, and fastened with velcro at the back, squeezing her teats so tightly that they pouched into two separate plums. She had to wriggle into a tight black latex skirt which clung to her buttocks and taped leg, and clamped her thighs together so tightly that her monopedalism became irrelevant: she could scarcely have walked, even with both limbs. Her last accoutrement was a single surgical boot in black rubber, with high wedge heels and soles, which she had to buckle as tightly as possible. She tucked her crutch in her left armpit, whose bushy hairs shrouded the rubber grip. Cherri looked behind her, and said she looked deformed, as if her ass had three cheeks.

'Some would call that beauty.'

The mistress allowed her a few minutes of practice hobbling before leading her out of the tepee into the noonday sunshine. A few women swam nude in the lake, or sat in mud pools; others, nude also, played volleyball, with artificial or organic prostheses, although a few monopedal girls had discarded their replica limbs and played at the hop. They proceeded to the restaurant adjoining the vestibule where, the mistress explained, Cherri would take charge of the lunch cart, to serve certain apotemnophiles in their tepees. Two girls were

131

busy at the buffet counter. They were identical twins, both in the nude. One had hair cropped short, and the other long blonde tresses that extended over her massively jutting breasts to her extruded navel. Both were tall, long-legged and with ripe buttock peaches, and the crop-haired twin had a huge pubic bush and armpit hair, completely untrimmed, while the long-maned sister had her body completely shaven, the swelling of her pubic mound as bare and shiny as porcelain. Both had all-over golden nudist tans, and identical figures of 39-20-39. They stepped forwards in unison, to shake Cherri's hand.

'Meet Greta and Garbo Cuman, of El Paso, Texas,' she said. 'Greta is the twin with the shaven pubis. Both enjoy clothing optionality, for, as you can see . . .'

Cherri shook their hands. The girls were physically joined at the buttocks.

8

Fullbody

'Greta and Garbo are Siamese twins,' said Miss F. E. Lee, 'joined by a gusset of gluteal muscle, easy to remove surgically, except they wouldn't be any other way. Would you, maids?'

'No, miss,' chorussed the Texan Siamese twins.

'We do everything together,' said Greta.

'Everything,' drawled Garbo, staring at Cherri.

'Except, I like to dress up,' said Greta, pouting, 'but *she* doesn't, and we can't easily wear panties, so I have to stay bare-ass like her and catch cold and all.'

'It's much healthier to be nude,' said Garbo.

'Says who?'

'Says Miss F. E. Lee, *that's* all.'

'Then why's she wearing that corset, with her titties all squashed up?'

'You questioning *Miss F. E. Lee?*'

'Girls,' said Miss F. E. Lee, 'I'm leaving you in charge of Cherri Black. She takes the lunch cart, so I can help Mom with her bath upstairs.'

'Thank goodness! Those tie-ups give me sore nerves.'

'Garbo, are you being uppity?' said the mistress. 'What do uppity girls get, Greta?'

'Why, bare-assed caning, miss.'

'Same as when they aren't uppity,' said Garbo.

As soon as their mistress' back was turned and she hobbled towards the elevator, the twins smirked.

133

'You're not a real apo,' said Greta. 'Must hurt, having your foot stuck up your ass. But the guests, see, they have to feel superior, like, you're worse off than them. And attitude! A thigh-amp sneers at a knee-amp, a double-amp at both of them. As for Feely, she's not tracking right, half the time. I guess she gave you that crock about no splicing and no guys, like, the US marines aren't guys, or what? Even that fucking Cal's a guy, if you give him the chance to show off his humongous fucking dick. Like, he's fun up your corn-hole, with his head in a bag, and the lights out, you know? Feely just gets off on different shit, like caning girls bare-butt. We don't mind, do we, Garb?'

'Surely not,' said Garbo. 'We're submissives, see. Hardcore. That means, our bodies are pleasure things for others, and if they get off on making us squeal, that's what we get off on, too. Cane us bare-assed, if you want. You're a fullbody! We'd *love* to play games with you. You got to study the rules, so's you know how to break them. We're bound together and it's the best bondage. We pleasure ourself and, the more we're whipped, the more we like it. Caning or binding aren't just pain, but shame, melting you down, so your true self fucking *screams* for mercy, and you're no more than a pair of spanked bare butt-plums and a soaking cunt – pure girlmeat. That's all men are for, see, to fuck our holes with stiff cocks, and be our masters. A girl can orgasm till she drops, but a guy shoots one lousy load, then he has to take a rest. A posse of guys, that's different. That reminds a girl she's just pure cunt and asshole.'

'Or pure slave, I guess,' Cherri said.

'You have a problem with that?' said Garbo.

'No, I don't.'

Both twins reached out to claw the balloons of Cherri's pinched bare breasts. She shivered, but did not protest.

'Hey, maybe you understand already. A hardcore apo considers limbs unnecessary things, even inconvenien-

134

ces, like, a girl's only real stuff is her ass, and her cunt, the things of her master. The tied-ups you're going to serve lunch to, the apotemnophiles, are just wannabe apos.'

'Say,' said Greta, touching Cherri's clinging latex skirt, at the swollen pubis, 'do you shave your mound, or are you a fullbush? Garbo plucks my cunt hairs with pincers, then shaves me, with my come for shave cream. She'll do you, if you want.'

'Fullbush,' Cherri replied. 'I'm not ready for anything else just now. Miss Lee already accused me of addiction to spanking, and buggery, and masturbation.'

'And you aren't?'

'Look, I just don't know. I'm kind of confused about myself. I hear voices, in my clitty or my asshole, telling me I'm a slave, and should enjoy it. Sure, I masturbate a lot. Don't all girls? People just seem to bully me. I've been whipped, tied up and buttfucked, but I've never been fucked in my pussy.'

'Oh, *that*?' snorted Greta. 'I mean, bitch, *get a clue*.'

Cherri hobbled awkwardly, swinging her crutch like a baton, and pushing the lunch cart with her pubis or belly. She had four deliveries to make, with precise instructions. She stopped at the first tepee, and announced herself. There was no answer, so she opened the swing doors, and saw that Melanie Messer, a twenty-three-year-old brunette, from Janesville, Wisconsin, had her mouth closed with several layers of duct tape. A similar bandage covered her eyes. Her meal was a bowl of broth, with a straw for the hole bored in the duct tape at the girl's lips. Melanie's 38-22-37 nude figure was seated, cross-legged, in a lotus position, her ankles roped together in rubber thongs, while her arms were raised above her head, the wrists knotted together by a rope from the ceiling so taut that her buttocks hovered a tenth of an inch from the rocky floor. Her puffed nipples peeped from her breast vice, a horseshoe of flexible metal which squashed her titties to swollen red pouches, as Cherri's rubber teat-pincer squashed hers. A coarse hempen rope looped her waist, biting the open lips of her gash, and its itch making Melanie constantly wriggle. Cherri looped her broth bowl around her neck and put the straw through the mouth hole and, at once, Melanie began to suck. When the bowl was empty, after only a minute, she broke wind; then, a heavy stream of pee spurted from her roped cunt. Melanie's 'mm' of satisfaction was the only communication.

Cherri's next customer was Torrie Chute, a petite twenty-four-year-old blonde from Wilmington, Delaware, whose 37-23-37 figure was encased entirely in a one-piece rubber costume that included a hood, open at eyes, mouth, pubis and nipples. Torrie knelt on the floor, with her arms suspended behind her in a sheath and her wrists cuffed to the end of a chain from the top of her tepee. Her ankles were fastened in bolts hewn into the rock and a shaft of cast iron, also embedded in the floor, was plunged fully into her cunt, with another similar shaft filling her anus. Come or ass-grease shone on both tubes. Before her lay a laptop computer, whose softouch keys Torrie pressed with her stiff nipples, by twisting her upper body, which thrust the metal tubes in and out of her cunt and anus. Every word typed brought her a metal ramming of her holes. Her meal was a platter of tofu and bread sticks, and she curtly ordered Cherri to put it down, then go, as she was busy trading.

Cherri obeyed. In the next tepee, twenty-two-year-old ash-blonde Emilia Lovisec, of Lawrence, Kansas, with a 39-22-39 figure, was able to lunch more conventionally. She leaned on her elbows, reading a book, her breasts in a pink brassiere dipped in the dirt. Her back was raised, and her hips wedged on a rail two feet high, with her bare buttocks upthrust and her legs spread ramrod straight in ballerina's splits. Her feet seemed nailed to the floor: in fact, wide-headed tent-pins, hammered into the floor between each toe, pinioned her bare feet. The puffy and ripely swelling bare buttocks bore stripes of recent caning; above her, suspended from the roof, a bar of six industrial candles placed horizontally dripped hot wax directly into her ass-cleft, spattering her open cunt and anus. The congealed wax formed a pyramid beneath her gash, about a foot high, and the hot wax dripped, mingled with come from Emilia's gash. She grimaced at Cherri and accepted the cutlery and napkin which accompanied her salad platter.

'Am I due another spanking?' she said, fearfully. 'I got thirty bad weals with the hickory switch, not an hour ago.'

'It doesn't say so here,' said Cherri.

'Glory be,' Emilia sighed. 'Hickory switch is the worst.'

'You've never been birched,' Cherri said.

'Why, no!' Emilia's eyes lit up. 'Does it really hurt?'

'And leaves marks,' said Cherri, licking her lips. 'Really beautiful marks, like your bare ass has been kissed by a bunch of flowers. But I guess that wax is painful, too.'

She felt moisture seep at her cunt and was glad of the rubber sheath dress, which would not show any stain.

'I'm doing research for my master's degree,' Emilia said. 'It's titled "Orgasmic Dysfunction in the Assertive Female." Pain helps me concentrate.'

She looked up, and licked her lips.

'Are you sure you wouldn't like to spank me?' she said.

Cherri looked at the firm, wax-spattered melons of the girl's bare ass, and felt her come gush.

'I have no orders,' she said.

'Then do me one favour, princess,' said Emilia. 'Clear the solid wax out of my asshole. It's blocked up, and not painful. I can only feel the drips on my cunt.'

Cherri clambered over the girl's stretched legs and jammed her fingers in the open anus. It required laborious clawing at the anal elastic to free the shaft of every crumb of wax, and during that time Cherri winced as scalding wax spattered her own face and her breasts, bulging beneath their thong prison. She felt a powerful urge to masturbate as the girl's bare bottom writhed and her cunt dripped blatant, copious come at the pressure of Cherri's fingers in her anus.

'Another favour,' Emilia murmured.

'I'm running late,' Cherri protested.

'It won't take long. You see my clitty?'

'I think so,' Cherri said and, indeed, Emilia's plainly erect clitoris was a whorl of congealed wax.

'Scrape me off,' said Emilia.

Cherri put her fingernails to work on the distended nubbin and Emilia started to groan, then pant, whimpering as Cherri's fingers touched the naked clitoris and tiny shards of wax fell away from the red, glistening flesh. Emilia's come flowed copiously; as the bare clitty was fully exposed, Cherri scraped away the last chip of wax and Emilia groaned in a long, belly-fluttering orgasm. She was still whimpering her thanks as Cherri hobbled out of the tepee to her last call.

Rochelle Amygdale was twenty years old, auburn-haired, and 5'8" tall, from Palos Verdes, California. Her figure was full but unharmonious, due to breasts measuring 56", while her waist was a whipcord 24", and her bottom a hard 40" peach. Her frame was a rippling slab of muscle, betokening a body-builder's, and her breast melons were thrust forwards by massive pectoral muscles. She knelt with her spine bent backwards. Her head rested on a breeze block on the floor behind her ankles, fastened on a wooden hobble bar. Also knotted to the hobble bar were her long auburn tresses, while her arms were stuck to her spine with hospital adhesive tape, and her wrists cuffed, sticking through her spread thighs, with her palms cupping her vulva. Her breasts were clamped in nipple vices, each fastened to a ceiling cord, and pulled tight into strained white envelopes of meat that contrasted with her all-over nudist suntan, while the puffed, clamped nipples protruded red and swollen from their vices. Her lunch was in a styrofoam cooler: a tub of cherry-flavoured ice-cream and a thick white popsicle on a stick, both items covered by a mound of ice cubes. Rochelle said cheerfully that Cherri was supposed to untie her hair. Cherri found that those were her instructions, so obeyed. Rochelle's muscles tightened as she forced herself half upright, using fingers on pubic bone for leverage, so that her face was squashed against the massive, stretched flans of her clamped breasts, now taking most of her weight. She instructed Cherri to scoop the ice-cream onto the breasts beneath her mouth. Cherri did so, wincing as the cold burned her hands, and dolloped the frozen ice-cream onto the girl's nipples, from which it slid into the bowl of her breasts.

'Now my popsicle,' she said. 'My treat. I've saved up for it, at the tree!'

Cherri unwrapped the creamy-coloured popsicle, and proffered it to Rochelle's mouth, but the girl laughed.

'Not there,' she said. 'In my cooze, silly. It's what I call a spermsicle. Ram it up me as hard as you can, till you can only see the stick.'

She spread her palms so that Cherri could manoeuvre the frozen tube of sperm into her dripping wet cunt, and found it slid in easily, though it as twice as thick as any male's cock. Cherri was ordered to place the empty ice-cream box beneath Rochelle's cunt. Rochelle gasped, and cried 'yeah!' as the frozen sperm penetrated her, and then grasped the stick with her fingers and began to thrust the sperm popsicle in and out of her cunt. She licked the slab of ice-cream, which was beginning to melt and drip from her massive teats, until it drooled across her stretched belly, onto her pubic forest, and into her vulval cleft. The popsicle, too, melted rapidly as it poked her cunt, and melted sperm, mingled with her own copious come, dripped into the box. Rochelle's face grew flushed, and her masturbation faster, until, with the popsicle and ice-cream almost entirely melted, and her teats and belly slathered in oily cherry-coloured fluid, she cried several times, in climax. The box contained her come and sperm from the popsicle in equal portions; Cherri raised it to Rochelle's lips, and the bound girl drank the entire contents, gurgling as the sperm dripped over her chin and titties to mingle with the cherry ice-cream and form a streaked pool of liquid.

'What tree?' asked Cherri, as she reknotted Rochelle's hair to the hobble bar.

'You're new, aren't you? The suckhole tree! It's only the hottest place to meet the US Marine Corps.'

The rest of Cherri's first day was constant, repetitive, work: cleaning, washing, or polishing. She hated scrubbing the toilets, even though, nude, she was free of prosthesis pretence, for she had to clean and polish them, using her own head hair and pubic fleece as cleansing implements, possibly being permitted to shower afterwards, at Miss F. E. Lee's discretion. Her brief glance at the thick rulebook gave her its gist, which the twins confirmed – a maid at Inn Health had neither rights nor privileges, only duties, and corrective punishments for dereliction thereof, and was thus a slave.

'At least the pay's OK,' Cherri said, sitting, at sundown, in a hot mud bath, with Greta and Garbo, allowing strength to seep back into her unbound limbs.

All three girls were nude, and giggled, slapping each other's face, hair and breasts, with the hot, aromatic mud. Greta's, or Garbo's hand, occasionally dipped out of sight, and the girl's writhing limbs would churn the mud, as she blatantly played with her own, or her sister's cunt.

140

'But you don't see it until you leave,' said Greta.

'And you don't leave,' said Garbo. 'Or, not righteous-ly.'

Cherri smiled as fingers touched her already tingling clitty, which she had on purpose exposed, spreading her thighs so that hot mud seeped all the way inside her cunt.

'I hope I get to visit the suckhole tree,' she said. 'It sounds kind of Californian.'

The twins looked at each other warily.

'Sure, sucking dicks through a knothole, only in California,' sneered Greta. 'Those marines are heavy comers, but if Feely catches you . . . a *real* whipping.'

'I thought you liked that.'

'It's still scary. I don't know if you understand how a girls wants to *be* caned, but fears the caning. You're too new to trust, anyway.'

'I'm trusting you down there,' said Cherri, blushing as her cooze seeped come into the mud under both twins' fingering. 'You're going to make me come, for sure, if you rub my clit like that.'

Her own fingers found Greta's cunt, and she felt a finger – either one of the twins' – getting its full length into her anus. The girls mutually masturbated, until an apotemnast joined them, unfastening her bikini top and bottom, and imperiously pushing Cherri aside with her crutches, before lowering herself into the hot mud. She was twenty-one-year-old Eve Carnuntum, blonde, of Boston, Massachusetts, and her 40-22-39 figure ended abruptly at her hips, for she was a double amputee. Yet her truncated body emphasised her ripe, jutting breasts, the full-muscled pears of her croup, and the garish red slit of the glistening gash that was the girl's centerpiece. Her cooze poked from a massive, glossy blonde fleece that encompassed her befurred stumps and crawled up her belly, almost to her navel, and likewise her tufted armpits were the equal of Cherri's. The twins leaped from the bath, and stacked the newcomer's crutches and swimsuit neatly, asking her permission to bathe, before sliding back into the mud with a plop. Eve looked suspiciously at Cherri.

'A maid?' she snapped.

'Why, yes, miss,' Cherri said.

'You should have vacated this pool and begged my permission to reenter. From where are you?'

'Chehalis, Washington, miss.'

Eve Carnuntum grimaced.

'Some *trailer park*, I assume.'

'Yes, miss.'

'Maids should have manners, even those from trailer parks. This benighted *West*! Back east, we wouldn't tolerate such sloppiness. When I was monitor at Livingshurst prep in Boston, I whipped girls, nude and hogtied, and more, for lesser insolence, and they thanked me! One of my girls, Ona Takira, in only a year, rose to become preceptress of the school, and said she owed her fortune to my strict discipline.'

'This girl's new today, miss,' said Greta.

'Then she can be spanked today,' Eve said. 'Bare me your bottom, maid.'

'It's in the rules,' said Garbo. 'Show butt, Cherri.'

Trembling, Cherri raised herself from the pool, and presented her mud-splattered bare to Eve Carnuntum, who began to spank the wet flesh with sharp slaps. She continued to spank Cherri for some minutes, while the twins diddled each other, laughing at Cherri's discomfort: Eve was a deft spanker, and Cherri's bottom glowed pink as the mud dripped from her. Suddenly, Eve pushed Cherri's head towards the mud.

'Eat me, bitch,' she snarled. 'You can come up when you bring me off.'

She pushed Cherri's head beneath the surface, while continuing to spank the bared buttocks, the only part of Cherri's body still visible. Cherri's face was pushed between the apotemnast's stumps and her tongue found an engorged clitoris, which she took between her teeth, and began to chew. The flurry of spanks on her wet backside doubled in speed as she tongued the swollen cunt, almost sheer with the thigh-stumps, and chewed the throbbing stiff nubbin. Even with the mud slopping her mouth, she tasted the heavy flow of girl-come from Eve Carnuntum's cooze. She opened her mouth wide, her bottom squirming under the spanks, and took the whole cunt in her mouth, sucking powerfully while flicking the clit between her tongue and teeth. The twins' fingers had already excited Cherri's clit, and she continued to masturbate with her own, rubbing her engorged nubbin in a circular motion. Come oozed from her cunt as her bared bottom wriggled under Eve's spanking. Eve's whole trunk jerked and her belly heaved as her spanking grew erratic, and her stumps threshed the mud in the intensity of her climax. Cherri's hair was wrenched until her head, gasping, emerged into the air; she gave her clitoris a powerful thumbing, and her own belly jerked as her buttocks and dripping cunt, beneath the mud, writhed in orgasmic spasm.

'You're better than that bitch Takira,' Eve Carnuntum panted. 'You may hoist me back to my tepee. I'll take you to the suckhole tree, sometime.'

Cherri did her best to learn the 'Rules of Servitude', like:

'A maid shall obey her lord or mistress in all matters whatsoever, on pain of chastisement with a cane or other implement of correction, applied to the bared sensitive portions of her body, viz, the buttocks, breasts, and pudenda, with or without bondage extreme of ropes, brank, boots, hobble and shackles. Errant maids may be publicly whipped and strung, or publicly strung, to receive corrections.'

'A maid derelict in her duty of obedience, self-abasement and servitude, and the good care of those of nobler rank, shall receive punishment at the discretion of the master or mistress superior.'

'Maids subject to complaint by penitents superior, scribes or masters of art, shall suffer chastisement of naked flogging and bondage, equivalent to that for dereliction, insolence or disobedience.'

'A maid may not raise her voice in complaint at any corrective treatment whatsoever, on pain of further correction, and stilling of her voice. A maid must keep righteous silence in respect of the lord, and may not express herself unless called upon by one of the elect.'

'A maid found with soiled underclothing shall wear the offending items around her neck, or over her face, or wadded in her mouth, while she undergoes appropriate chastisement, and for a time thereafter, to be determined by master or mistress.'

'No maid shall take pleasure in touching her intimate body, or that of another maid or penitent, and any maid conspiring to gain or cause impure pleasure shall be subject to rigorous and prolonged discipline, especially whipping of the parts wherein impure pleasure resides, and not excluding bondage in suspension, as tidy, firm and rigorous as that of packed goods, than which a maid is nothing more.'

'The rules governing maids also govern penitents superior, who, though provisionally elect, are no more than maids in the eyes of master or mistress, and must submit to a maid's chastisement if causing offence to good discipline. Penitents and maids must cleanse themselves of impurity and vileness by submission to just chastisement.'

The list of rules was long. Eve quickly befriended Cherri, appointing her 'special mud bitch'. Her duties were masturbatory: clitoral or anal, involving stimulation of Eve's befurred cleft with tongue and fingers, and also breast-spanking. Eve liked it when Cherri was invisible under the mud, diddling her anus, cooze and stumps. Who, Cherri asked Eve, as she was assisting her one day, slapping the amputee's nipples clean of mud, were the scribes and masters of art? And the lord?

Eve laughed.

'You mustn't take the rules seriously,' she said.

'They seem to mean I can't talk without being punished, and can be punished for anything at all.'

'They do,' Eve said, sighing, as Cherri squeezed her gash, 'but – *ooh* – the rules apply to us all. They are a copy of rules from some order of flagellants, at the time of the Spanish *conquistadores* in California – maybe from an older source. Seems the Spaniards met a glamorous tribe of females, not Aztecs, but who lived in tunnels or something, and implored the Spaniards, their new lords, to spank and whip them, naked, for penitence. The Spanish didn't mind, I guess. So, technically, we guests are penitents. *Oh! Mmm!* Spank me, bring me off, Cherri.'

Cherri slapped the mud-splattered buttocks of the double apotemnast, with her fist inside Eve's cunt and her thumb pressing the throbbing clit, until Eve shrieked in her climax, swearing that no fullbody had ever made her orgasm so deeply. Eve befriended Cherri as far as she could, since Miss F. E. Lee actually scolded Eve – a guest and double apo, one of Inn Health's mutant aristocracy – for being too friendly with the staff, so Eve had to be cautious, even while sneering at 'western rednecks'. Over weeks, Cherri worked to the bone as maid – cleaning, cooking, serving, joining the apos in baths and games. In fact, most of her time was abetting the punishment and bondage of guests, or else submitting to her own. There was, she said to the twins, little time for fun. The girls in bondage didn't seem grateful for her meal service, not even Torrie Chute, who complained one day that she couldn't eat her tofu, wasting valuable trading time, without help. Cherri was clad as on her first day, in her tight rubber skirt, and

145

simulated amputation, and submitted to Torrie's request. She knelt on one leg, supporting herself by holding Torrie's shoulder, and shifted her strapped foot the fraction necessary, from its position in her ass-cleft, to bare her anal bud. She rolled up the rubber skirt to bare her buttocks, then filled her anus with the bean curd, wadding the substance right to her root, until her rectum was packed.

'OK, bitch?' grunted Torrie.

'I guess so, miss. It hurts. I'm not comfortable like this.'

'Well, good! You think *I'm* comfortable? Get going, bitch.'

Cherri evinced no reaction when called 'bitch'. With buttocks upraised, she forced the food from her butthole, as if dunging, a mouthful at a time, for Torrie to swallow, and when Torrie had emptied Cherri's hole, she licked the rim and bud clean, with Cherri's anus dilating and contracting as the tongue tickled her pucker; a trickle of come began to seep from her pussy.

'Like it up the ass, bitch?' snarled Torrie, rubbing her nose in Cherri's perineum.

'What if I do, miss?' Cherri blurted.

'Your cunt says you like it a lot. It's wet, like a sponge. I like to drink a bitch's come. You think you're better than other girls? We all like it up the ass, bitch.'

'OK, miss. It's just that I've a really big asshole, you know? And I've never found a man big enough – *oh*!'

Cherri squealed as Torrie fastened her teeth to the swelling flaps of her gash and held on, chewing, until the girl's face was lathered in Cherri's copious come, which she drank, before requesting more refreshment. Cherri opened her thighs and directed a full jet of piss to the bound girl's face. Torrie swallowed most of the acrid pee, the rest dribbling on her rubber sheath. That became Torrie's ritual, no matter what Cherri's costume on any particular day. Other wannabe apos devised their own methods of troubling Cherri, usually involving the disposal of food from her anus, and quenching their thirsts with pee, so that Cherri was obliged to ration her liquid, and proceeded from tepee to tepee, bladder bursting with the agony of holding in sufficient piss for all her clients. Her submission did not stop them calling her 'bitch'.

'You got to make it fun,' Greta said. 'That's the whole point. Girls are supposed to be submissive.'

There was still the tantalising trip to the suckhole tree, promised by Eve – even more tantalising, as Cherri was often too tired to masturbate at night after a hard day's labour in partial apotemnastic bondage, at Miss F. E. Lee's whim. She might be roped, titty-bound in rubber, swathed in hospital bandages, or even be obliged to hobble with her leg encased in plaster. The arcane rules always provided an excuse for Miss F. E. Lee to cane Cherri's bare, loudly regretting that Cherri was doing nothing to cure her addiction. The mistress said a cure might be effected by satiety, so Cherri's tariff of bare-bottom cane-strokes rose from ten, to twenty, and then forty, or even sixty.

The beatings were in the dining room, outdoors, sometimes in the vestibule, and always with an audience of masturbating apos, thrilled by Cherri's shame. Eve, the most eager masturbatress, said that rules for maids' pain counted, but not those restricting guests' pleasure. Cherri usually took her canings in restraint, fully nude, and bent over a simple four-legged diner stool, with her wrists and ankles roped to its legs. The implements varied: sometimes a cane of willow or elm or hickory, but always applied with full force by Miss F. E. Lee, who stripped to bra and panties, usually dark green or wine-coloured, for more comfortable delivery as she clung to her crutch. As Cherri's fesses squirmed helplessly under the cane and the stool rattled at every lash to her naked bottom, her choked, tearful pleas that she

147

wasn't addicted to pain or bondage or spanking in any form only made her beatings worse. Once, Miss F. E. Lee abandoned her crutch and stripped off her panties. Wearing only her bra, she caned Cherri while balancing on her single leg, inviting the sobbing, squirming maid to consider whose was the greater discomfort: her own, belied by the juicing of her bared cunt, as her rod wealed the maid's buttocks.

Greta and Garbo admired Cherri for taking such brutal bare-bottom caning, with her legs firmly gripping the stool, and not buckling as she was striped to purple, with most of the watching apotemnasts and the apotemnophiles in partial bondage masturbating openly. The caning of Cherri Black's bronzed ass-pears and their metamorphosis to two glowing crimson suns encouraged many apo fingers to stray beyond their owner's juicing cooze into the folds of her neighbour's. Garbo said Cherri was becoming a tourist attraction; grumbled that Cherri had begun to earn generous cash tips by taking chastisements in place of apos who had erred with some insolence or other to Miss F. E. Lee. Guests or penitents were technically subject to maids' rules, and often, Cherri would take a flogging of twenty or more strokes, only to bare her bottom again to take a further ten with the cane, as a proxy for an errant apo, or 'limb-free'. The proxy beatings had Miss F. E. Lee's approval, as she averred Cherri's vice-addicted bottom would soon tire of the cane; Cherri squirmed and sobbed at every beating, but took it, never collapsing as her bare fesses reddened and squirmed under the flogging-rod, and never confessing either that afterwards she masturbated.

She was often strung, and so were the twins: nude body stretched, with the ankles and wrists bound to branches of separate trees, and flogged on the bare back, or on back and buttocks, with a rawhide whip. That was especially painful for the conjoined twins,

148

whose central limbs were roped together with their outer limbs tree-roped. The twins' routine bare-bottom canings were generally during mealtimes, when some fault in service obliged them to bend over their customised caning pushcart, for twenty each on their bare fesses, which turned to four glowing red gourds. Sometimes, there was nobody in the tepees, and all the apotemnophiles would eat communally, although Torrie Chute was never without her laptop; however, the girls Cherri normally served in bondage always appeared with some slight restraint, whether a loosely tied ankle string, paperclips or hairpins fastened to bare nipples, a waist cincher, pinned cunt-flaps or an inner-spiked corset.

When she could, she joined the twins in the mud pool, and generally achieved satisfactory orgasm, or paid turnabout visits to their separate tepees, where they spanked each other, bare hand on bare ass. Cherri's work was double, for she had to spank four buttocks at once while the twins masturbated beneath her; sometimes, they would make a 'bod sandwich' of Cherri, since the twins could fold themselves on their gluteal flap at any angle. They liked to trap her upside down, with both twins tonguing Cherri's open cunt, while her own tongue licked one girl and the other rubbed her clitoris on Cherri's hair.

The twins possessed a quadruple dildo they had hewn from wood, with which they masturbated both anally and vaginally; they enjoyed doing it as Cherri watched, rubbing her own clit to come. The prongs of the *godemiché* were sculpted as a male organ, and Cherri wondered if such a massive thing existed naturally.

'Cal? Natural?' sneered Garbo. 'It's a moulding of his cock, see. The fucking midgethead will come sniffing round your pussy one day, when Feely's mom lets him out of her butt. Fuck knows how many times he dicks her ass every day, up in that penthouse.'

'But Mrs Lee senior is an invalid,' Cherri protested.

'You'll be a fucking invalid when that midget gets his horn up your hole, bitch. We don't need the little fuck anyway, we have each other.'

The twins were able to twist completely, so as to face each other, which they did, with a flexible twin-pronged dildo of ribbed black rubber inserted in their cunts. Like this, they spanked each other's bare bottoms with a short cane or wooden paddle while they gamahuched, slapping and rubbing their coozes together. They remained evasive about a possible visit to the suckhole tree, despite Cherri's open acknowledgement that she wanted cock, without specifying buggery. Cherri did not tell them of Eve's promise to take her there, but gradually revealed more of her history, and did eventually describe her extreme elasticity of anus, and her shameful craving for anal sex, despite her denials to Miss F. E. Lee. Each twin expressed envy of Cherri's croup, its endurance, and its apparent ripening after each flogging.

'I feel I'm kind of atoning for bad things I've done,' Cherri said, 'like, helping the guests? They're so brave.'

'Fucking apos!' sneered Greta. 'Listen to the bitches, how they put each other down! "I lost mine in a Mercedes accident!" – "*Oh, I* lost mine in a *Ferrari!*" Fuck 'em.'

'Right,' Garbo agreed. 'I don't think they lose them at all. I mean these people aren't fucking *normal*. I think the bitches have cosmetic fucking *surgery*.'

9

Dirt Eater

On the thirty-seventh day of her maidservitude, Cherri served at lunch, with both her legs strapped by surgical bandages to her buttocks, and swaying on double crutches. Her false amputation was concealed by a tight nurse's skirt in white latex that clung to her bottom and thighs, with her bandaged feet clearly outlined against her buttocks, so that her rear portion looked a natural deformity or huge bubo. The skirt left her knees bare. She wore white rubber nurse's boots and a nurse's cap, like an old swimming cap, moulded tightly on her scalp, and with flaps like fangs that clung to her cheeks, almost to her lips. Her breasts and shoulders were naked, the teats thrust upwards by a full corset in white rubber with titanium bones that pinched her belly to eighteen inches and bunched her titties into a bowl. In her teat-crater was a pile of grated carrots with mayonnaise, and her task was to hobble around the tables while the apos scooped food from her bare breasts. It was called salad bar duty.

When her breast crater was bare, save for the slime of mayonnaise, she returned to the serving bar. Miss F. E. Lee was caning the twins, and their quadruple bare nates bounced to an extra-long cane of 4'9". Several lunchers stroked each other's groins as the twins' titties bounced in the rhythm of their caning. Cherri saw a single, enormous carrot, too knobbled for easy carving, left in the sink. She snatched it and hid it under her skirt, where it went unnoticed in her gluteal deformity. After lunch, and before her afternoon duties, she sneaked back to her tepee and hid the carrot under her straw palliasse. The afternoon passed routinely. Having earned no punishment herself, she nevertheless had to endure two separate canings, one of ten strokes on the bare, for Miss Jen Hauptli, a long-maned, timid blonde from Framingham, Massachussetts, a twenty-three-year-old fullbody, 37-22-38 in figure, for whom no bondage seemed tight, shameful, or punishing enough, and who would accept severe and painful whipping through layers of rope or latex, but dreaded the touch of cane on bare skin; the other, of twenty strokes for the impetuous Miss Valarie Turnwood, twenty-two, from Paducah, Kentucky, a pony-tailed brunette with a sumptuous 39-21-39 figure, and her left leg scythed at the hip, who enjoyed being caned naked, even on her breasts, gash or stump, but enjoyed paying to watch a fullbody take her stripes on occasions, when she would incur punishment for just that purpose. Cherri's tariff was now a generally agreed $5 per canestroke, so for these two beatings she would receive $150 to add to her stash of bills buried in the dirt under her palliasse. Her caning stool was out in the open, by the lake, under a cloudless sunny sky, and Cherri walked regally nude towards it through the crowd of girls. She received applause, and blushed.

'Pleasant afternoon for a caning, Cherri,' said Miss F. E. Lee, flexing her long willow wand. 'Mind if I touch the skin I'm going to thrash?'

'No, miss.'

The mistress brushed Cherri's bronze bare buttocks with her fingertips, and cooed.

'Mmm,' she said. 'Bigger and better. 44-22-44, you said, but I'd guess a 21″ waist and a good 47″ at teat. Time to bend over, maid.'

Cherri grimaced as the ropes bound her ankles, then her wrists, Miss F. E. Lee having announced her policy of henceforth binding her tighter than a calf for branding.

'It really does hurt, miss,' Cherri gasped. 'Just the roping, never mind the cane.'

'A maid in bondage, or unlimbed, is a maid superior,' said Miss F. E. Lee. 'Whipped, she is an icon to be worshiped.'

Above them clattered the rotors of a USMC helicopter. Miss F. E. Lee swished the cane in the air, as if threatening to attack the vehicle. She wore the corset she had sneaked from Cherri, which squashed her bare titties, and she was bare-legged, wearing her prosthesis. The heavy growth of her pubic forest crawled over her upper thighs, making any join invisible, and her grown leg flexed as sturdily as her attached one as she spread thighs in caner's stance. Her mood was friendly as Cherri was taking proxy, not earned canings.

'Let them watch!' she snorted. 'We'll put on a show, won't we, Cherri? Damn US Postal Service snoopers.'

'What, miss?' Cherri blurted, as the cane hovered over her buttocks.

'That's Chopper Bukowski's bird up there. Lesbian voyeur bitch, she's a postal agent for sure. Directional microphone in there, hears every word we say. Don't you, bitch dyke? Well, Wanda, suck on this!'

She held up a finger. Cherri said it looked like a marine helicopter.

'Marine Corps, my ass,' said Miss F. E. Lee. 'Just a front for the US Postal Service. Didn't you know postal service inspectors have more powers than the FBI, CIA and NSA all in one? They control this country. By federal law, every urban area has a mailbox every eight blocks – you ever tried to look in one of those mailboxes?'

'No, miss,' said Cherri. 'They open so as you can't see inside.'

'Exactly!'

The cane whistled, and Cherri's bare buttocks jerked, as the rod sliced upwards – vip! – in her exposed ass-cleft.

'Ohh!' she groaned, her gorge rising in shock at the searing force of the cut on her tenderest bare.

'*Oh*! Please, not so hard, miss.'

'That cissy bitch from Framingham needs hard! Lord, you all do, wicked bitches every one!'

Vip!

'*Ah*!'

Cherri's caned ass writhed, the emblems of past canings marbling her translucent weals on top of her bronze ass-globes. Come dripped from her cooze and her nipples were erect, cooled by the breeze. Cherri's belly knotted as her naked buttocks smarted and clenched, awaiting the next canestroke. Apos gazed as come seeped down Cherri's thighs from her wriggling cooze. Greta and Garbo, their own bare asses scarlet from their lunchtime caning, pissed on the grass, soaking their wrists as they diddled each other's clit. From the vestibule, a bare-torsoed male rubbed his hands in glee. Vip!

'*Ah*!'

The helicopter swooped lower, as if focussed on Cherri's bare bottom wriggling. The hard caning of the Framingham sissy, Jen Hauptli, rolled over into the harsher caning for the 'sassy bitch' from Paducah. Cherri fought back her tears of shame at the flood of cunt mucus dripping from her cooze as her cane-seared naked buttocks squirmed. Everyone smirked, as the humiliation of caning excited her. *Girls may be bitches, but I'm a slave.*

Moonlight sparkled at the string door of her tepee as Cherri reached for her carrot while rubbing the congealed welts of her buttocks, smarting from the after-

154

noon's caning. She had been permitted to remain in the nude and unbound, save for a ringer rope on her titties which made each bronze breast bulge out scarlet, like a giant tomato. The ringer rope was gone, and her breasts were their normal bronze, but its bruises on Cherri's breasts were livid as cane weals. She lifted her palliasse and took out the giant carrot concealed there. It gleamed like red flesh in the moonlight as she sank to her knees, fingers already at her vulva and, spreading her thighs, began to urgently masturbate her clitoris. Her come oozed and Cherri transferred it to the carrot's lumpy surface and to her anal pucker, wiping the oily come all up and down her perineum and spread ass-cleft. Her clitty throbbed under frottage and when the carrot shone with come she reached behind her, sinking her face into her palliasse and inserting its tip into her anus bud. Shuddering, she continued to pinch her clitty and pushed harder. The carrot penetrated her asshole about two inches, then met resistance; Cherri relaxed her sphincter and sucked the carrot inside her. The makeshift dildo sank into her writhing butt-shaft, right to her root, with an inch of carrot extruded from her clenched buttocks.

Moaning, she began to bugger herself with the carrot, drawing it fully to the tip before ramming it back into her pulsing butthole, which greased the carrot with anal lubricant at every poke. As she butt-fucked herself, she continued pinching her stiff clit and rubbed her nipples on the coarse canvas palliasse, bringing them to firm erection. Her cunt gushed come, wetting her palliasse; the dildo slid rhythmically in and out of her writhing butthole. Cherri's gasps were harsher and harsher, and her belly heaved.

'Need any help?' drawled a male voice.

'What? Who?'

Cherri twisted, to see a figure silhouetted amid her doorstrings.

'Name's Cal,' said the male, advancing towards Cherri's body, frozen in fear. 'I saw you steal that carrot, today. Yeah, steal. I'm no snitch, girly, but why use a damn toy, when you can have the real thing?'

Cal was bare-torsoed, barefoot and wore only jeans, which clung like rubber and, as he patted his massive cock-pole – *no, it can't be, it's obscene*! – that extended from ball-sac to knee, he began to unbutton them. Cal was exactly five feet tall, but his body was whipcord muscle.

'Get out of here!' Cherri spat.

'You don't mean that,' said Cal, dropping his jeans, and stepping above her naked butt, with his monstrous tube of a cock already stiffening. 'I'm no snitch, but as a matter of local policy, more than general rule, you understand. I mean, there has to be a trade-off, satisfactory to both parties. I've been watching you diddle yourself, and I know what you want.'

'No,' Cherri moaned, as Cal removed the carrot from her anus and sniffed it, but she did not alter position, and the cavern of her anus and her dripping cunt remained spread as he straddled her, lowering his now stiff cock to her ass-cleft.

His prepuce was drawn fully back, exposing the huge shiny glans, which nuzzled the nubbin of her spine. He took a bite from the carrot and began to crunch.

'Bet your asshole feels as good as it tastes,' he said. 'I do two things: I suck good and I fuck good.'

His cock moved, and Cherri gasped. Cal laughed.

'I'll be back,' he said.

He knelt and his face sank between her thighs, with his mouth on her swollen labia. He opened his mouth wide and clamped her entire genital apparatus between his teeth, so that Cherri's whole cunt was trapped by the boy's mouth. Then he began to suck her vulva while his tongue penetrated her cunt. He slobbered and grunted, still crunching on the carrot, bits of which intruded into Cherri's pouch, tickling her cunt walls.

156

'Pussy's way tight,' he laughed. 'You one of them near-virgins?'

'Don't laugh!' Cherri cried. 'Please! Do me if you have to. Do me in the ass, where it hurts most. I stole the thing, and I deserve to be punished.'

Cal swallowed the last of the carrot.

'Told you I'm no snitch,' he said. 'No evidence left. Pretty weak case.'

He went down on her cunt again, taking the whole swollen mass of wet girlmeat into his mouth and chewing on the extruded clitoris until Cherri's come gushed in torrents and her moan became a whimper. As he gave her vigorous cunnilungus, Cal brushed his huge stiff cock up and down her thighs and calves.

'Please,' she begged.

'Please what, bitch?'

'Please do me.'

'Can't hear you, bitch.'

'Please fuck me in the ass!'

There was a sucking noise as Cal removed his mouth from Cherry's gash-flaps and rose to straddle her. He wrenched her mane and pulled her face off the palliasse, pressing it onto the ground. The boy mounted her quivering croup and Cherri's scream was muffled by the earth as he penetrated her with his entire glans. With his free hand, he grasped Cherri's wrists, and twisted them behind her back in a half-nelson, forcing her face into the dirt.

'Ahh! Ugh!'

Cal panted as he rammed his cockshaft further and further up her butthole, and grunted at the automatic invitation of her anal elastic, which dilated and squeezed, drawing the tool towards her root. Cherri groaned, with the boy's hand pressing her face down and her bare ass wriggling, slapped by his balls as his cock steadily drove home. She squealed as the tip of his glans slammed her anal root, and then Cal slid his cock in and out of her squirming asshole in rhythmic, powerful buggery. Her squeals were drowned by the mud floor.

How could I want this? It's too awesome. It's worse than anything in the world. Yet I do want it. Slave merits pain.

'Eat dirt, bitch!' snarled Cal, as he butt-fucked the girl.

'Hm?'

Vap! Vap! Vap! Cal spanked her bare moons three times.

'*Oh!*'

'I said, *eat dirt, bitch*. Chew real good, and swallow.'

Cherri began to bite and chew the caked dirt of the floor, filling her mouth as Cal slammed her head to the ground. Vap! Vap! Vap! A flurry of spanks seared her bruised bare ass, and she shrieked, involuntarily swallowing her mouthful of dirt to avoid choking. Her teeth began grinding into the dirt, and after she had wet it with drool it became pliable enough to suck and chew, until finally he could force the muck down her throat.

'Good Arkansas dirt's a meal fit for a queen, or a marine!' he crowed, his body dripping sweat onto her writhing bare ass, and dripping to mingle with the come that flowed from her gash, lathering each inner thigh in a frothing oily drool. 'This is only cheap hippy-dippy fuckin' California dirt, but you're no queen, and I'm no marine! Fuckers wouldn't have me, called me shorty. *You* gonna call me shorty? Are you, babe? *Are you?*'

'Mmm! Mmm!'

Cal's belly and ball-sac hammered Cherri's buttocks, so fiercely did he fuck her, with her buttocks now rising to meet his cock-thrusts; her anal elastic tightened as he penetrated her hole, trying to clutch his cock-tip at her anal root and milk him of sperm.

'Ever had dick like this up that lily-white asshole, bitch?' Huh? *No*, you have *not*, miss!'

He's splitting my asshole in two. Lord, how I want it. Want his sperm up my ass, hot and creamy and never stopping. I want to be butt-fucked for ever, and whipped raw for taking it, for ever.

Cherri mechanically chewed and swallowed the dirt, her stomach expanding with its leaden, curiously satisfying bulk. The excruciating pain and pleasure of her submission to this male animal seemed happily joined by her utter shame at eating dirt, like some . . . some . . .

Some trailer park trash, bitch. Fit to be stripped and hogtied and butt-fucked raw. Trash bitch, slave bitch. Slave.

'Mmm!' Cherri cried.

Cal butt-fucked her, the strength of his penetration unvarying, for twenty-five minutes, before Cherri's belly began to shake and heave and she felt the first sperm droplet spurt from Cal's cock into her rectum. The piss-hole of his cock slammed hard into her midchamber rectum, which made her buttocks writhe and heave and clamp on Cal's cock, while her pussy gushed come and a massive orgasm filled her shuddering body, pouring with sweat and love-juice; the male's sperm jetted hard, hot and strong inside her rectum, sliming her whole anal canal, and Cherri swallowed her last mouthful of dirt before sinking to her palliasse as the male released her wrists and withdrew his cock from her hole with a squelching plop. He used her hair to wipe himself clean.

'I hate those fuckin' amps, girly,' he said, 'but I hate you more.'

'Why?' Cherri sobbed.

'Your ass, it's too fuckin' spankable. I'd love to see those plums properly whipped, not just to the bone, but to the fuckin' marrow. I won't snitch on you for thieving, but Miss F. E. Lee won't be pleased to hear one of her maids is a fuckin' *dirt eater.*'

159

'Our customs entitle you to trial before a jury of your peers,' said Miss F. E. Lee, stroking a cane of exceptional length, five feet long, and springy enough to count as a whip, its wood freshly oiled. 'Eating dirt is behaviour of the lowest slave, and subject to a slave's punishment. You do not deny the accusation that you ate dirt, yesterday.'

'Mmm! Mmm!' Cherri gurgled, shaking her head.

She was gagged with a tennis ball, jamming her teeth apart, and fixed around her head and nape by duct tape. Her jaws gaped helplessly. She stood naked beside the lake, beneath a gibbet, to face the makeshift court. A hobble bar, three feet long, held her ankles apart, while a rope hung from the gibbet's crossbar, fastened to her cuffed wrists and holding her arms up behind her back at a forty-five-degree angle. The simple restraints prevented her from moving. Miss F. E. Lee herself, bipedal for the occasion, wore a black rubber waist-cincher with inturned spikes that pinched her belly to a wrinkled eighteen inches, and on her head a black rubber mask, with holes for eye and mouth; on her legs, black rubber thigh boots, whose skins ended just below her glistening cunt-flaps. Otherwise nude, she explained that her painful waist-cincher was to spur her on, in execution of presumed punishment, for her pain could be no less than the prisoner's.

'I invite the members of the jury to deliver their verdict. Guilty, or not guilty?'

Rochelle, Emilia, Torrie, Melanie, Eve, Jen, and Valarie sat on a row of white metal lawn chairs before Cherri, with their arms and wrists strapped behind them in rubber double-tube sheaths, closed by zip fasteners in the central gussets. Their nude bodies were identically crisscrossed in white binding ropes that wound several times around their thighs and arms, also looping through spiked dog-collars round their necks. Ring-cords puffed their naked breasts to swollen redness, and their nipples were clamped in mousetraps. The white

160

chairs had no seats, so that buttocks and cunts were bared beneath. Mousetraps were pinned to each of their cunt-flaps, holding the vulval meat open, and from chains looped through the mousetraps hung porcelain piss-pots, pulling the gash-lips to four or five inches. Each girl wore a gag of ropes that fastened around her mouth and nose, with the ropes tied well inside her palate, flattening her tongue. Eyes blurred with tears, the girls moaned in their hempen gags.

'I take that as a guilty verdict,' said Miss F. E. Lee. 'The prisoner shall be prepared for punishment.'

Greta and Garbo swivelled Cherri's ankle hobble, so that she faced the gibbet and lake, and presented her bare back to her watchers.

'The sentence is fifty strokes of the cane, on the bare back,' said Miss F. E. Lee.

Cherri moaned behind her gag.

'Followed by one hundred strokes of the cane, on the bare buttocks,' the mistress continued, her breasts bobbing in excitement and the nipples hard as brick, with a seep of come shiny at her cooze-lips. 'The sentence to be followed by bondage in ropes, wet with fluid of disgrace, and suspension until darkness.'

The empty seats of the lawn chairs presented the girls' buttocks, pressed beneath the frames, as twin plump melons. Cal, in jeans, western boots, and bare-chested, patrolled the line of girls, brandishing a short scourge: from its handle radiated fourteen thongs of stiffened rubber, a foot long. He paused at each girl's chairback and stooped so that the scourge lay beneath her nates and cooze; then, with a deft flick, lashed upwards, flogging one stroke to cover buttocks, thighs and gash-flaps. Each girl moaned at her stroke. The piss-pots beneath the jury-girls tinkled as fluid dribbled from their cunts. The twins knotted Cherri's wrists to a hook descending from the gibbet, winching her arms higher to present her full bare back.

'Mmm! Mmm!' Cherri sobbed, shaking.

The cane whistled through the still air. Girl-piss and girl-come tinkled in the pots, in heavy flow. Vip! The rod lashed Cherri's bare back, just below her armpits.

'Oh!' she moaned, and a spray of golden piss erupted from her cunt.

Vip! Vip! Vip! The strokes followed, hard and precise, until Cherri's shuddering bare back was a morass of cane-marks; then her buttocks took chastisement. Her complete flogging took forty-five minutes, and by the last stroke of her bottom-caning a whimper escaped her drooling lips as her wriggling purple buttocks danced, reflected in a lake of piss and dung beneath her holes. Tears coursed down her face from eyes wrinkled tight. When Cherri's whipping ceased, so did Cal's methodical scourging of the jury-girls' bare buttocks and thighs, now scarlet or crimson beneath their white chair-rims. The girls sobbed and whimpered; their piss-pots overflowed.

The twins assisted Cal in lowering Cherri and began her bondage in coarse hempen rope, snugly wound into her weals. Her arms were bound, crossed behind her back, and her thighs stretched backwards, ankles over wrists, for her roped hands and feet to be attached to the same hook which held her hair. Ropes ringing her breasts and puffing them out to hard scarlet balls were looped through the hook. Several waist-ropes bound her to the gibbet, one veering to loop through the spiked iron collar, holding her head up. A second rounded hook was lowered from the gibbet and inserted into Cherri's anus, while her cunt was held open by clothes pegs, stretching the vulval flaps several inches, with a piss-pot beneath. Cal fetched the jury-girls' piss-pots, and emptied each one over Cherri's ropes, ensuring the stinking fluid drenched her. Her gag remained, and the twins winched her up.

'The inverted crab,' said Miss F. E. Lee. 'One of Mom's favorite positions.'

As Cherri's body was hoisted to limbs-back suspension by anal prong, waist, hair and ankles, Miss F. E. Lee rubbed herself, adding new come to her glistening thigh boots, and gazing defiantly at Chopper Bukowski's helicopter, above.

'Hey,' said Greta, loud enough for Cal to hear. 'While you're up, think of the suckhole tree! We'll take you *tonight*, along with the Eve Carnuntum bitch! She has a car, so we can stop off for some good American red meat first, at NeedaBurger.'

Cherri hung in bondage for four hours and thirty-two minutes.

'Three,' said Greta, in the driver's seat.

'Three,' said Garbo, licking her teeth, beside her.

'Two,' said Eve, from the back of her silver '11 Cadillac.

She wore her party dress, of a single white rope coiled around her nude body, just covering her titties and cunt, but leaving her thigh-stumps bare. She said it was her custom to use both prostheses when visiting alone, but company made a visit special.

'One's good,' Cherri said, forcing a smile.

The big-titted blonde NeedaBabe flicked an errant bra-strap, and swivelled to serve the pyramid cartons, her mostly bared teats garish under the neon NeedaBurger pyramid. Her filmy skirtlet allowed generous view of her thighs and underfesses firm as plums, and with recent spankmarks the colour of that fruit. The staring eye of 'We Got 'Em!' gleamed under the northern California night sky, as throughout the whole United States. Behind their car was a solitary personnel vehicle with military plates. Apart from Eve, the girls all wore identical strapless halter tops, plunging to show breast, and brief cut-off shorts, hugging the vulva and buttocks, the garments in blue denim; with bare legs and histiletto boots in black rubber. None wore panties. Greta had offered Cherri her costume, vague as to its provenance, but glad she agreed it was kind of cute.

The girls demanded separate checks, and waited, while Cherri extracted Eve's money from her pussy; the blonde NeedaBabe accepted the oily bills without blinking. Greta gunned the car and they sped towards the suckhole tree. It was halfway between the marine camp and Inn Health, she explained, turning off onto a narrow dirt track that soon became no track at all, just moss and bushes, and then trees, spaced just wide enough to allow passage. She stopped the car and they proceeded on foot, with Eve carried on Cherri's shoulders, her stumps draped on her neck and the gusset of her shorts moist on Cherri's nape. In a two-acre field stood the bole of a redwood, truncated by ancient lightning, so that only the massive stump was left, the size of a room and twelve feet high. The twins threw a rope ladder over its rim and the four girls clambered up and into the secret bole, pulling the ladder behind them until only one rung peeped, sporting a pair of pink panties, heavily soiled at the gusset, looped there by Greta, the last girl to climb in. That, Garbo explained, meant someone was home.

The pink panties were, in fact, Eve's donation, and were prettily trimmed in white lace, contrasting with vivid crotch-stains. Custom forbade visitors from climbing into the bole; sexual contact was anonymous, for the extra excitement of both parties. The floor of the bole was planks laid on a deep carpet of moss, which was dry and springy. A patch of wall was shaved thin as board, with a carved knothole big enough for the largest cockshaft. The twins showed how a girl could kneel on the cushion of moss, with her lips right at the knothole; or fashion a platform of planks to present her cunt or anus to the visitant member. There were also broken chairs and stools for that purpose.

'That's kind of laborious,' she said, 'and those marines are usually a posse in a hurry; they just want a straight blow job, each one of those suckers blowing his wad right after his buddy, though technically speaking it's us who are the suckers. Fact is, NeedaBurgers taste like shit, less you have some sperm sauce.'

'Yes,' said Eve. 'I wouldn't eat a NeedaBurger in Boston, unless, of course, there was cock in the box. My, don't I sound *western*?'

The girls laughed, but Cherri shivered.

'Scared, hon?' said Greta. 'Hey, you took that stringing like a pro today. Not right, that shit-kicker Cal making you eat dirt, then snitching on you! Hell, every girl likes to eat dirt once in a while. We'll fix Cal's ass good.'

The twins winked at Cherri, suggesting that El Paso girls possessed some terrible secret for use against shit-kickers.

'It's not that,' murmured Cherri. 'I wanted *more* of it. His cock up my ass, eating dirt, everything. Even my punishment was worth it. But I guess he was just fooling with me, and won't come see me again.'

'Men!' said Eve. 'They're all the same. Butt-fuck and spank a girl till she screams for mercy, then never call her.'

They heard a vehicle stopping outside, doors slamming, and raucous male laughter. The twins hoisted Eve onto a chair, propped against the shaven bole, so that her face was inches from the knothole. After some more male lewdness, the glans of a bare cock poked through; then the whole length of the cock appeared, in a semi-rigid state. The organ was huge, even when flaccid; as Eve grasped the shaft, drew back the prepuce to expose the helmet fully and began to flick the piss-hole with her tongue, the cock swelled to full stiffness, almost filling the knothole. Eve rubbed the shaft with vigorous strokes, but her tongue lightly danced on the exposed glans, licking alternately the frenulum, the neck and the corona of the shining crimson helmet. A groan was heard from the other side as the cock trembled.

Cherri's pussy was seeping come as she watched Eve's careful tonguing, and her fingers slipped beneath her clinging blue denim shorts, stroking her sweaty pube-hairs on their way to her unpantied cunt. Greta and Garbo did the same, save that each twin was masturbating the other's cunt, her knuckles digging like moles under the rapidly-moistening denim. Eve had her fingers delving between the ropes that strapped her cunt tight, and was rubbing her clit, with the white of her bondage soon staining wet with come. Her licking of the cock, eleven inches in length, gave way to harder sucking, but with dramatic pauses to tease the rigid male. Suddenly, she took the whole glans into her mouth, sucking it like a popsicle; swooped to engorge the entire cockshaft, right to the back of her throat, and hummed as her tongue moved under her cheeks, massaging the glans. Finally, she withdrew and squeezed the cockshaft hard, wrenching it towards her so that she pulled the male's entire ball-sac through the aperture, completely filling it. He squealed, his balls and cock now trapped, until the softening of the cock would let him exit. He squealed again as four unexpected spanks from the twins on the unroped portion of Eve's bottom-flesh caused her to jerk and bite his cock. Slap! Slap! Slap! Slap!

'Mmm! Do me!' Eve cried, her bare ass quivering.

Her fingers continued to masturbate her cunt more rapidly as the twins picked up dead tree branches and began to whip her naked buttocks, while her free hand cupped the man's balls, stroking and squeezing them with her mouth still sucking on the neck and frenulum of his straining glans. There were moans from the trapped male. Swish! Swish! Swish! Eve's stumped buttocks writhed as a tapestry of thin pink wealed her skin under her bondage party dress, its rope coming undone as she wriggled. She drew back, then dived to enclose the huge swollen balls in her mouth, sucking them while continuing to rub the cock and slicing the piss-hole with sharpened fingernails. Swish! Swish! Swish! The twins masturbated vigorously as they whipped Eve's bare. A droplet of sperm appeared at the cock's piss-hole and Eve's mouth returned to the glans, now slamming her face forwards to engorge the whole cock with the spurting piss-hole in her throat. She drained the male of sperm with bobbing motions of her head, the lips gripping the cockshaft, while her throat constricted around the glans, and trembled, as she swallowed cream. Swish! Swish! Swish! Her bare scarlet buttocks squirmed under the rods of the twins, who continued flogging her ass and stumps, after she had swallowed all the male's ejaculate; her own masturbation grew more intense as she cooed dovelike under her beating.

'*Whoo-ee*, marine!' gasped a male voice.

'Man, you shot your load like some fuckin' sailor-boy!' responded another. 'I'll show you the marine way.'

Eve licked her teeth, as the limp cock and balls withdrew from the knothole, to be at once replaced by a second cock, almost as large. This one was erect upon entrance and the twins knelt before it, with Greta beginning the tonguing, while Garbo rubbed the cockshaft with her lips. The girls mutually masturbated, each with two buttons loose on her shorts and the curly wet jungle of pubic hair peeping out. Eve had a NeedaBurger opened and was feasting; Cherri, gasping, ripped open her own shorts to plunge her hand through her wet pube-jungle to her swollen cunt-flaps, pouring juice. She masturbated hard as the twins deftly sucked cock, changing tongues and lips in military precision. They waggled their denim asses at Cherri, who picked up their discarded rods and pulled down their shorts to reveal the bare joined croups. Despite squeals of protest, the twins were preoccupied, milking the giant drool-slimed cock that poked their faces.

'You bitches were cruel to Miss Carnuntum,' Cherri murmured.

Vap! Vap! Vap! Her strokes were harder than those Eve had taken, and the twins' squirming bare bottoms quickly reddened with weals. Eve eyed the punishment as she chewed her burger. She continued her cunt-frottage, watching the conjoined brown asses of the twins wriggling under Cherri's forehand and backhand cane-strokes, until Cherri abruptly terminated chastisement after thirty-five strokes to each girl's bare bottom. She approached Eve, kneeling, to get her tongue between her loosened wet bondage ropes and find the swollen stiff clitty. Eve stroked the bare moons of Cherri's bottom, while Cherri caressed the stumps of the apotemnast and sucked the come from her cunt. Eve's belly began to heave; her fingers brushed the nubbin of Cherri's spine and ran up and down her ass-cleft, getting a forefinger inside Cherri's anus and, as Cherri spread her buttocks, joining it with two more. Anally impaled, Cherri writhed, frotting her soaked cunt with her knuckles as she worked on Eve's stumps and clitoris with her lips and tongue.

'Oh, yeah, baby, do me, yeah,' panted the male. 'I can keep it up for ever, bitch.'

The twins began teasing and licking and brutal squeezing, finally tugging the second male's balls through the knothole and trapping him.

'Aw, sheeoot,' came his apprehensive voice: an apprehension fully justified as the twins' treatment of his balls was more subtle and more savage than Eve's.

Garbo chewed, sucked and nibbled the taut orbs, making him beg her to bring him off, while Greta amused herself by tonguing the glans neck and corona, followed by vigorous rubs of the shaft. Garbo slapped finger-spanks on the tip of the glans as soon as Greta had released it from her mouth. As they chewed the cock and balls, they writhed, frotting their wet coozes, and with angry slaps to already wealed bottoms disputed who should swallow the ejaculate. Garbo surprised her twin by pausing in the spanks to plunge three, then four fingers, into Greta's dripping cunt, finally getting her whole fist in and balling it. She punched Greta inside her cunt and Greta squealed as her sister's knuckles slapped her wombneck. She yielded and it was Garbo who slammed her head up and down on the jerking cock, which spurted cream into her mouth with such force that frothy dribbles of sperm moistened her chin and plopped onto her heaving titties. Cherri's masturbating fingers swam in a flood of come from her pulsing cooze. She groaned as orgasm racked her; the twins, and Eve, followed her example, and the four gamahuching females squealed, mewling, in climax.

'You havin' a good time, you fuckin' amp bitches?' snarled the first male. 'Hey, *we're* doing youse a *favour*. What cock you ever get, 'sides marine cock?'

'Let's get out of here,' said the other. 'That fucking Bukowski's overhead. She catch us, man, we're in the brig.'

'Don't that fuckin' dyke never sleep?'

'May be a dyke, least she got two fuckin' legs.'

'Four, more like. And a fuckin' tail.'

A car door slammed, and the vehicle drove away, leaving the girls in silence, and Cherri's pussy still dripping come. The twins assured Cherri that there would be more, for sure. Her companions wolfed food as Cherri approached the knothole, carrying a chair, and a third cock appeared, this one more massive than any before, fifteen inches long, and four inches thick, filling the knothole in its erect state.

10

The Suckhole Tree

Cherri took the massive cock in her right hand, and began to rub, allowing her fingers to press firmly on the glans and shaft and pulling the prepuce back and forth to its full length, at each stroke. There was a gasp from the other side. She took the massive cock-shaft with both her hands, and wrenched the balls through the knothole, so that the monstrous erection was now fully in her power. With twiglets, she fashioned a miniature scourge and began to tickle the balls while applying her lips and tongue to the swollen glans, slurping and drooling as she chewed, licked and sucked the massive helmet. Sometimes she raised her lips from the glans, leaving just her tongue penetrating the piss-hole, and whipped the glans with her tiny crackling scourge before returning it to the balls.

'Wow,' he moaned, as the twiglets scourged his tightly swollen orbs. 'Ooh, that's weird.' His cock throbbed under Cherri's tonguing.

Cherri did not kneel to fellate him but wound a length of rusty copper wire under the ball-sac, fashioning a ring thick enough to prevent escape from the knothole. She ringed the shaft of the cock above the balls with a similar wire coil, to stay ejaculation while keeping full erection. His balls were sandwiched, helpless, between the two wire restraints. Cherri climbed a chair and, lowering her denim shorts to her ankles, presented her naked fesses, with her anus crammed against the pulsing stiff cock.

'Cherri,' Eve whispered, 'that's not a marine. It's Cal's cock! That ungrateful Arkansas shit-kicker, why, I pay him $100 a fuck!'

'I know it's Cal,' said Cherri. 'He overheard we were going to party tonight, and anyway, I, uh, recognise the cock. He snitched on me! That's why I was strung. He's a marine wannabe, and marines have leather balls, so I'm going to give him blue balls. He's going to butt-fuck me till his cock's raw, and not come till I let him.'

She slopped her fingers in her wet cooze to oil her anus bud and Cal's cock, before squatting on the glans and sucking the cock into her anus. She spread her buttocks to full width and, with two more heaves of her ass, had Cal's cock trapped inside her, right to his twin wire cock rings. Her gash-flaps, spread thick and wide, swallowed the balls whole. The twins and Eve stared, masturbating vigorously, as Cherri bucked and squirmed, squeezing and teasing Cal's cock-meat until it was raw, bruised, and flaming scarlet. The weals of Cherri's flogging by Miss F. E. Lee glistened in the runnel of sweat down her writhing spine into her buttock cleft, and joining the flow of come from her cunt as her anus bud shone with the ass-grease that now coated Cal's cock. Her buttocks pumped as the whimpering shit-kicker begged for orgasm and release of his cock and balls from their prison of girlflesh. The louder he pleaded, the more vigorously Cherri's anus roiled his glans and shaft, the harder she thumbed her swollen clit, and the more copiously come flowed from her cunt into the sodden denim at her ankles. The moss carpet of the tree bole was soaked in girl-come. There was the throb of a helicopter overhead, growing louder as the aircraft approached and landed. Its rotors slithered to a halt, the cockpit door slammed, and footsteps marched slowly towards them.

'Yo, Marine! Buck-ass naked, you fuckin' some damn fuckin' *tree*, you scumbag piece of shit? You fuckin' disgrace to the corps, you corn-holin' fuckin' disgrace to whatever shit-patch your mom drug you from under, you too much a fuckin' disgrace for me to take cognisance of, you fuckin' little *tree-fucker*. Don't *move*, marine!'

'Lieutenant Bukowski, ma'am,' sobbed Cal, as Cherri continued to grind his raw cock with her elastic anus meat, 'I ain't, I ain't really a, I mean, I'm the *victim* here!'

'I don't care what you are,' thundered the woman's voice. 'What you gonna be is whupped and chastised, in that order, and then some, scumbag fuckass no-good redneck shit-kicker piece of stinkin' fuckin' scumbag *shit*!'

Vap! Vap! Vap! A baton whopped bare meat.

'*Ah*!' Cal yelled.

Cherri continued to enforce her buggery by the trapped male, masturbating her clitty furiously and her cunt dripping hot come as she heard the slap of hard baton on bare buttocks. The other girls, drooling over their trembling teats, jerked in threefold mutual masturbation at the spectacle of Cherri's pumping buttocks and anus and at the squeals of helpless male anguish.

Vap!

'*Ah*! That hurts! Oh, please, Miss Bukowski, I'll do anything, just don't whip me.'

'I like whipping bare ass,' said Lieutenant Bukowski, 'and watch it get all red and blotchy, and squirm like bats in a bag, specially a scuzzy, cheatin' *male* bare ass.'

Vap!

'*Ah! No! Please*!'

The flogging of Cal, and his enforced butt-fuck of Cherri, continued for thirty-five minutes, by which time Cherri had masturbated herself to four comes and the other girls to three, their eyes bright, cunts gushing and

172

nipples erect, and each licking her teeth at the vap! of the baton on naked male buttocks. Cherri reached behind her bottom, and unwound the wires that held Cal's balls and cockshaft tight. With a final thrust of her buttocks, she pinned herself to the tree wall and churned her fesses on the trapped cock, while squeezing the naked balls between her thighs. Cal's cries grew shriller as he spurted his cream into Cherri's sucking anus, so that bubbles of brown creamy froth dribbled over her pumping thighs. Despermed, and freed from the prison of Cherri's anus, Cal's cock and balls shrivelled and disappeared, as did Cal himself, fleeing after a final flurry of spanks to the bare from Lieut Bukowski's baton.

Moments later, a female appeared over the bole rim, and sprang down to the come-soaked mossy floor. Her hair was long, blonde and flat-combed, reaching her breasts, swelling braless under her shirt, with unusually wide strawberry nipples plainly visible in erection. She was 5'10" tall, twenty-four years old, and 39-23-40. She wore a dark blue uniform with shiny nylon blue stockings, gleaming high heels, and a white shirt with a flounced neck. Green jade pyramidal earrings sparkled on her lobes.

'Is that a NeedaBurger?' she cried. 'I'm just starved!'

'It's mine,' said Cherri. 'You're welcome to it, ma'am.'

Twirling her springy rubber baton, three feet long, Lieut Chopper Bukowski wolfed the NeedaBurger and drank the NeedaCola in one gulp.

'Thanks, but I must ask you ladies to leave now. US Postal Service business never ends, I'm afraid, although I do enjoy whipping men on the bare. I have to discipline those marines – darn grunts, think they own the country. You're not trespassers – as taxpayers, you are entitled to visit unposted federal facilities, but not to observe operations therein. This happens to be one of

173

several US Postal Service emergency facilities, which is all I may tell you. Otherwise, civilians are free to use it for recreational, non-postal purposes.'

She eyed the dripping cunts of the orgasmic women, Cherri's, in particular, and the soaked moss floor.

'I watched you thrashed the other day, miss. Hard affair, but Miss F. E. Lee's First Amendment right, and, I might add, your own. I must say I enjoy female chastisement too.'

She shrugged.

'I'm glad to see you've enjoyed your recreation, ladies. You have adequate transportation? '11 Caddy, excellent vehicle, I keep one at my country place near Montauk, Long Island. If you'd be so kind as to exit, I have US Postal Service business.'

From the shelter of the Cadillac, the four girls watched as Lieut Bukowski opened a door built invisibly into the tree bole and emerged carrying a carpet roll: the entire moss floor, soaked in girl-come, which she stowed in her helicopter before replacing it with a fresh moss carpet, relocking the suckhole tree, and taking off.

'I've a NeedaBurger left, if anyone wants it,' said Greta.

Cherri grabbed it, stuck it between her buttocks awash with sperm and come, and rubbed it there until it was drenched in fluids. She scarfed the NeedaBurger, the first she had ever finished, in four seconds.

'Don't bother to strap your leg up, Cherri,' said Fornication E. Lee, peering through her tepee drapes, as Cherri rubbed her few hours' sleep from her eyes. 'You have an audience with Mom. You can do breakfast in the nude, today, just in surgical boots, as a courtesy to our guests. I hope you don't hurt too much from yesterday's chastisement.'

'A little, miss,' Cherri said. 'What the –?'

She shook her legs, to find her ankles clamped in a four-foot hobble bar.

'And after your suspension bondage, you slept well?'

'Yes, miss,' Cherri. 'My ankles –'

'I wonder where? You weren't here, when I called to cane you ten strokes, at 2 a.m. I'm of the new school of thinking, you see, I don't believe in pure bondage as an end in itself. The thrill of restraint is far greater, if a maid knows chastisement awaits its termination. Mom and I differ on the question. *You* were at the suckhole tree last night. No! –' she held a hand up, her single leg trembling '– don't tell me any lies. That's why Mom wants to see you, so that she can pleasantly get the truth from you.'

Cherri hobbled to kitchen, goosebumps all over her nude, shivering body; her hobble bar and the hideously thick and lumpy surgical boots in which Fornication had encased her bare feet making disobedience unthinkable. The twins were already there, cooking vegetable fritters, with hot oil splattering their naked bodies, but too nervous at Cherri's presence to mind. Cherri performed the breakfast service robotically, with no appetite, as the NeedaBurger of a few hours previously still clung in her stomach. When she smiled at Eve, the double apotemnast looked away. Fornication was on crutch, wearing black rubber panties and bra, and one black rubber thigh boot, with her stump bare. Cherri asked for permission to visit the bathroom, but permission was refused.

'I'm bursting to dung, miss.'

'You can talk to Mom about things like that,' said the mistress, leering. 'My husband has opinions of maids who can't control themselves, or so he said, when he left me.'

'I'm sorry, miss.'

'Silence, bitch!' spat Fornication. 'A maid is not permitted sorrow, unless her bottom smarts! As yours assuredly –'

175

Panting, she caught her breath, and leered again.

'But let's leave that to your pleasant chat with Mom.'

'I guess it was Cal who snitched again,' said Cherri bitterly as they approached the elevator, after breakfast.

'Not exactly snitched,' said Fornication. 'Mom saw the state of his ass, last night, and Mom can be very persuasive with males. He knew you were in the suckhole tree, because he recognised your anus. He couldn't identify your co-conspirators, though.'

The elevator doors opened, and Cherri hobbled, trembling, after her mistress. The elevator hummed upwards.

'I have no doubt Mom will persuade you to identify them,' hissed Miss F. E. Lee, as the doors whirred open.

'No!' Cherri wailed; suddenly, her bowels gave way.

Automatically, she squatted as steaming brown dungs plopped from her anus onto her hobble bar and the elevator floor.

'I'm sorry, miss,' she sobbed. 'I'll clean it up. I know I deserve chastisement.'

Miss F. E. Lee shrugged.

'Fouling an elevator is the least of your worries right now,' she said. 'In a few minutes, you'll be riding a rail.'

Cherri's unhobbled nude body lay quivering, straight, and roped to a two-by-four wooden plank, six feet long, supported by two pairs of splayed legs, also two-by-fours, and holding the rail four feet high. Her back and belly were swaddled to the rail by white ropes, with each wrist and ankle roped to a splayed strut. An extruded knot in the wood bit into her gash, although her squirming, to ease discomfort, only increased it. Her chin hung over the rail's edge, facing Mom's bed.

Her breasts hung below the rail, with her nipples clamped by clothespins, fixed to separate chains from two floor-bolts, four feet apart. The titties strained to narrow envelopes of pale flesh, maintaining Cherri's balance on the rail. Her cunt-flaps were likewise clamped and pulled by two separate chains on either side of the rail, each chain bolted to the floor, and stretching Cherri's gash-flaps to four inches. Below her wrist and ankle bindings, her fingers and toes were screwed in individual vices, bolted to the floor. Her mane was wrenched into two hanks, knotted together through a ring suspended from the ceiling, and holding her head up. After dunging in the elevator, she had not been permitted to wash before Cal and Miss F. E. Lee bound her; her nostrils puckered at each breath. The edge of the two-by-four was gnarled, and the portion biting Cherri's naked gash was a knothole, which pushed up her cunt-basin and buttocks; however, raising her gash-meat from the jagged wood placed unbearable strain on her stretched cunt-flaps. Combinations of three simple knots – sheet bend, sheepshank, and catspaw – sufficed to hold her body rigid and helpless.

Cal scowled at Mom's bedside, wearing only his jeans and rubbing his ass. Mom, a fullbody, was nude, suspended in bondage. over her colonial four-poster bed. At thirty-eight years of age, Mrs Lee had lush auburn hair, and a firm 39-24-40 figure above long, coltish legs, topped by a jungle of pubic curls that stood a good three inches out from her hillock. She hung with legs and arms twisted behind her, in the same suspension used on Cherri the day before – the inverted crab. As well as the ropes cross-fastening her wrists and ankles, and the hook pronging her anus, she wore a rubber thong and ring harness, with a ceiling chain clipped at her spinal nubbin. Clamps pinched each gash-flap, with dangling lead weights that stretched the flaps to four inches. Below her spiked iron collar, to which her mane was knotted, an iron breast fork squashed her titties to puffed red balls of flesh, the nipples pinned, weighted and stretched, like the cunt-lips. Mom hung, sobbing and moaning, from a hook on the four-poster's top crossbeam; a second bed had a crutch stand, laden with whips and canes.

'Cal, you still here?' barked Miss F. E. Lee. 'Your ass want another beating?'

'No, miss,' Cal muttered.

'Then go fetch the marines, and make sure they stash their uniforms neatly.'

'There's twelve of them, miss.'

'A round dozen, then. Less you want to make it a baker's dozen. Got enough juice left in those balls?'

'You fuckin' bet.'

'Go first, then.'

'Please, no, Fornie,' cried Mrs Lee.

'Swallow his load, bitch,' snapped Fornication, and her mom wailed.

Cal unzipped his jeans, and lay beneath Mrs Lee, with his stiffening cock inches from her mouth. He propped himself on his elbows, raising his hips, and thrust his cock between Mom's lips. Groaning, she engorged his entire cockshaft in one swift, bobbing movement that made her ropes squeak. Cal's erect cock bulged against her cheeks as she sucked him off, her tongue probing the upper glans and piss-hole while her throat squeezed the cockshaft. She strained and got his entire ball-sac into her mouth, with the helmet now deep in her throat, and began to move her head up and down, her eyes moist with tears. Fornication stared with one hand rubbing her pussy beneath her black rubber panties, from which seeped a gleaming trickle of come. Cherri blushed furiously, not least because her own cunt, helplessly bound, also began to ooze. Cal grunted and Mrs Lee's throat quivered as she swallowed his ejaculate. She opened her mouth wide, drooling sperm and saliva, and freed Cal with a grimace. Her cunt wriggled, exuding droplets of come.

'Oh, Fornie, please don't torture me any more.'

'You, tortured! My own mom, a fullbody – the shame – and a tramp, who had me in her teens, and didn't care who daddy was. I have to live with that embarrassment.'

'I know I'm guilty, and deserve chastisement, but leave that poor girl alone. I hate to see suffering, it just makes mine worse.'

'Exactly,' said Fornication, continuing to flick her clitty. 'Mom knows the art of gentle persuasion. Any man's a pussycat, when a bound bitch desperms him. Bondage of a female, and shaming herself the dirtiest way – swallowing a man's come, after sucking his dick, why, that's perfect submission, Cherri. That's what the maidmaster preached, right, Mom?'

'It wasn't like that. Oh, please let me down.'

'What was it like? Did you know who was buttfucking you?'

'Yes,' groaned Mrs Lee.

'So, you connived in my husband's anal adultery.'

'No!'

'Then you're a tramp who'd fuck anybody.'

'I was a victim. The maidmaster beguiled me; he said he'd spank my wickedness away, and caned my bare ass a hundred strokes with a hickory switch. It hurt so much, and all I ever wanted was to please!'

'Miss Fornication gave me to understand you were disabled, ma'am,' said Cherri.

'Lord, girl, don't I *look* disabled?'

'Personally, I am happy without the maidmaster,' snorted Fornication, 'free to do my own thing.'

'He sure didn't stay around long enough to let you do *his*,' said Mrs Lee, and her daughter flushed.

The door opened and a male entered, naked but for the USMC cap he held covering his cock. Fornication took his cap and placed it on Cherri's bottom, then motioned the male to lie down in Cal's place.

'Or you may sit while Mom services you,' she said. 'Whichever position makes you feel more in control.'

The marine sat up against the bed's headrest and the bound female's mouth took cock. Mrs Lee swung, jangling her restraints as she sucked, engorging the entire shaft. Her daughter discarded her crutch and leaned at Cherri's head, balancing on her single leg and rubbing her cunt, with come dripping down her tangle of pubic fronds. Her mother's quim glistened with her own come, belying her snuffles of distress. The male began to whimper. Mrs Lee's fellation was expert, and in four minutes he ejaculated his spermload in her throat. Fornication masturbated, her rubber panties strung across her thighs, and Cherri felt her own cunt ooze as she watched the cock emerge drool-slimed from Mrs Lee's lips. The marine stood at attention by the wall near the daughter's bed, while a second marine entered. His cap, too, was placed on Cherri's bottom, and he took his fellation lying down. Mrs Lee sucked him off in three minutes, her face twisted in anguish. He got up, and joined his comrade standing at attention.

'Please, no more,' sobbed Mrs Lee.

'Do it, bitch!'

'Make my knots a little tighter, then,' she whimpered. 'I can't manage, otherwise.'

Her daughter obliged, tightening Mrs Lee's bondage until she squealed.

'My hair's coming loose; you'll need to reknot it.'

Fornication tied the tresses to the spiked collar, fully wrenching the roots. The third marine presented his stiff cock and Mrs Lee sucked him off in four minutes; the fourth, in six minutes; the fifth, in two minutes, to the smirks of his fellows. By the end of an hour, twelve fellated marines stood to attention beside Fornication's bed, and Mrs Lee's mouth and chin shone with sperm. Fornication was pantiless, masturbating herself to a third orgasm, with come streaming down her single leg and spraying her stump at the frantic jerking of hand on swollen clitty.

'How you shame me, Mom,' she said, as her fingers dripped cooze-oil. 'Watch what I learned from you.'

Cherri was wet with come, dripping from her rail, to pool beneath her wrenched cunt-flaps. Fornication hopped to the marines with their caps, knelt and licked their balls until their cocks rose, then placed a cap on each erection. She lay face down on the bed and raised her ass and stump, spreading her buttocks so that her wet vulva and asshole gleamed slimy and red. A marine placed his cap on his neighbour's hatstand and straddled her, his cock brutally penetrating her anus, with the muscles of his ass clenching as he pumped. He butt-fucked Fornication for five minutes, before sperming, and his place was taken by another marine. Fornication had her elbow propped and diddled her clitty during each of a dozen butt-fucks.

'Oh!' wailed Mrs Lee, squirming in bondage, but with her cunt juicing. 'My own daughter!'

Cherri writhed, her clitty throbbing.

'Who was with you in the suckhole tree, Cherri?' gasped Fornication, as the seventh marine buggered her. 'These boys have cream for you, if you'll 'fess up.'

'I was alone, miss,' she groaned.

'You shan't escape whipping,' said Fornication as the eighth marine rammed his cock up her asshole, 'but you could sweeten it with grunt sperm.'

'Grunt?' cried her mother. 'Boys, that's an insult!'

The butt-fucking marine frowned and spanked Fornication's stump, then her fesses. He spanked her bare to crimson until he spermed in her anus, then spat on her cunt as he withdrew his tool. The rest did the same, spanking as they buggered, to over one hundred slaps on her squirming bare. Spanked, she masturbated harder, whimpering, with her blotched bare bottom darkening to a crimson tapestry of fingermarks. Cherri jerked her streaming cunt on her rail and, as the last marine spanked Fornication to tears, exploded in orgasm, her come splattering the floor.

'I never heard the word grunt before!' cried Fornication, and pointed at Cherri. 'That bitch said it! She said grunts at the suckhole tree didn't know how to buttfuck.'

The marines looked at Cherri's splayed, helpless body and spat on her. Mrs Lee begged them just to tickle the girl's ass with a hand-spanking. They spanked Cherri, and at first, it was tingly: her clitty throbbed, and she juiced. After one hundred and fifty spanks, she gave shrill cries of surprise, and spread her cheeks to show the marines her anus bud.

'Now cane her,' said Mrs Lee, eyes gleaming. 'Aim for the welts of yesterday; open them up nice and fresh, and then, if she's still conscious, the cattle whip.'

'No! Wait!' Cherri pleaded. 'This isn't right.'

The marines reached for the canes, beside Fornication's crutch. At the first canestrokes to her bare, Cherri's bare ass jerked, slamming her erect clitty on the come-soaked rail, and she shrieked.

Vip!

'Oh! Please! Don't! I was whipped only yesterday!'

Vip!

'*Oh!* Please! *Please, no!*'

Cherri's naked buttocks writhed in her ropes, binding her so tightly she could scarcely even clench them to ease her agony as the marines caned her.

Vip! Vip! Vip!

'*Oh!*'

Cherri was whimpering by the fiftieth stroke on her bare, quivering globes, a hundred seconds into her caning.

'*Ah!* Enough!'

'I don't think so,' said Mrs Lee, pausing in her fellation of a marine, kneeling at her lapping tongue while another lay beneath her cooze, his cock ramming her furry wet gash with come pouring over the whole cockshaft and balls between the weights stretching her gash-flaps. 'Look how I suffer! That fucking bitch can suffer some.'

Each canestroke slammed Cherri's bruised cunt harder against the wooden rail, so that the agony of her bare bottom mirrored the pain in her slit. Fornication stood on one leg, handing the caners choice rods, so that Cherri's bare nates writhed under maple, elm, willow, hickory, oak; always, Fornication murmured her invitation to betray her conspirators at the suckhole tree.

'A dirt-eater, and a meat-eater!' she accused.

'NeedaBurger isn't exactly meat,' Cherri sobbed.

'Insolent bitch!'

In the middle of Cherri's caning, her body wracked with spasms, and her ropes drenched in sweat, come and piss – she lost control of her bladder at her thirty-fourth and fifty-seventh strokes – Cal entered the room and whispered to Mrs Lee, still filled by two cocks. Mouth bulging, she nodded assent and Cal exited. Mrs Lee tongued the fellated marine to powerful spurt, swallowing rapidly, with his cream bursting from her lips to splash her chin. Her cunt-basin writhed on the cock below, bucking hard into her dripping wet cunt, until that marine spermed and she moaned, drooling as her belly quivered in climax, with her copious come mingled with marine cream sliming the giant cock.

'If only my daughter had satisfied the maidmaster,' she said, licking her lips, 'he might be here to guide us.'

'You fucking hag!' cried Fornication, suddenly, grabbing a cattle whip. 'I stayed unspliced, while he fucked *you*, and I had to watch!'

The whip snaked across the room and Fornication lashed her mother on the bare cunt.

'*Ah!*' Mrs Lee wailed, jerking in her suspension.

Crack! The cattle whip lashed her naked vulva again, before a marine snatched the instrument, and said whopping bitches was man's work. The vip! of Cherri's ass-caning echoed the crack of the cattle whip as marines flogged the mother's vulva. Mrs Lee groaned, bucking in her bonds, and at the twenty-second whip-lash to her quim a copious stream of piss splashed the marines. The double beating abruptly ceased when a newcomer entered the scene. Torrie Chute was radiant. She swept aside her fur cloak, to show herself nude, save for lacy white bra and panties. Fornication fell to her one knee, to press her mouth and nose to Torrie's panties.

Fornication tongued Torrie's vulva through her panties, while masturbating her own clitoris so that her cunt juiced into Cherri's pool of piss and come. The marines looked at each other until one leaped onto Cherri, balancing himself on her shoulders and calves, and rammed his erect cock between her wealed buttocks.

'Uh,' Cherri moaned, her cunt juicing hard as she relaxed her sphincter.

The grunt penetrated her to the root, and began deep butt-fucking. She thrust her caned ass up to meet his thrusts, while squeezing his cock with her sphincter, and milked him of his sperm after a severe buggery of five minutes. Come splashed from her cooze.

'Bitch can pull a train!' the marine growled.

The marines buggered Cherri in turn and, in ninety minutes, Cherri's anus was penetrated by all twelve marine cocks, while her clitty and come-spewing cunt writhed on the rail, bringing her off three times. Fornication and Torrie were nude, gamahuching each other, their faces buried in each other's cunts and mouths sucking wet red pouches, oozing come. The eleventh marine prised open the lips of Cherri's anus and finger-fucked her. First, he had two fingers in her anus, then four, and finally he slammed his whole balled fist inside her.

'*Ah!*' Cherri groaned, as knuckles filled her rectum.

During the anal fisting, Cherri rubbed her clit against her rail, bringing herself off, despite the pain of the wood on her soaking vulva. The grunt fisted her for five minutes, jabbing her rectum, and opening his fingers inside her to ream her anal cavern, slimy with ass-grease, before withdrawing his fist and replacing it at once with his stiff cock, which butt-fucked her for eight minutes before ejaculating sperm so copious, it dribbled down her thighs.

'Oh, my asshole,' Cherri sobbed. 'My asshole . . .'

'Look at the bitch!' crowed Fornication. 'It's too late for her to confess, now. If Torrie can make the submissive sacrifice, that dirty little tramp must. Join the unlimbed, bitch, from the hip! Get rid of the thing.'

'*No!*' Cherri wailed, as the twelfth marine filled her anus with sperm, a slimy overflow of bubbly brown froth staining her ropes.

'Yeah,' said Mrs Lee, 'as an apo, the cunt will stay with us forever.'

'What about you, Mom?' snarled Fornication.

'I suffer enough as a fullbody; I'm scared to be an apo.'

'I promise I won't torture you if you get it done.'

'No deal,' Mrs Lee said.

'Let me go!' cried Cherri.

'Not on two limbs,' said Fornication.

Up high, a helicopter's buzz approached.

'Shit,' said the twelfth marine, his cock slimed with Cherri's ass-grease, as he withdrew from her sucking anal hole with a loud plop. 'Not that fuckin' Bukowski again!'

The roar of the rotors was right above the roof, drowning all sound. A rope ladder snaked down at the window and the glass shattered, smashed by a gleaming scythe. Three nude bronze girls leaped through the opening, and, while the others menaced the marines' exposed balls and cocks with their scythes, the tallest hacked away Cherri's bonds and unscrewed her clamped fingers and toes. Her scythe cut through Cherri's ropes, the blade dancing a quarter inch from her cunt, from her nipples, from her anal cleft, and Cherri felt the wind of the metal on her skin. The tall exquisite's green eyes met hers and the eyes smiled, mocking her, as she delicately untied Cherri's hair after a pretend movement with her scythe. The girls lifted Cherri and wrapped her in the rope ladder, then, clinging to her, were winched up to the helicopter.

'Hi, Cherri,' said Lieut Bukowski. 'I heard everything with my surveillance devices, and had to intervene, to prevent possible violation of your constitutional rights. Darned if I shan't force-march those grunts, ball-shackled behind a two-ton truck. Did they fist you?'

'One did.'

'Did you mind?'

'Not really.'

'I hoped you wouldn't.'

Cherri crouched, shivering, until she felt three hot girls' tongues licking her naked bottom, and her ass-cleft, and the dripping flaps of her vulva, and her anal pucker distended by her multiple buggery.

The exquisites! Are they looking after me?

Her body glowed, with the warmth spreading from her caressed bare buttocks and cunt. She shut her eyes.

The tongues of the bronze slaves heal me, make me whole again, a true slave, like them.

Cherri moaned as the tongue of the tallest exquisite penetrated her cunt, its tip caressing her wombneck for an electrifying moment before the tongue slithered out of her slit and resumed licking her thighs and bottom. The helicopter flew low, over a lake. Lieut Bukowski wore a denim halter top and cut-off denim shorts over her naked flesh, without underthings or other clothing. Her body was uniform gold, almost bronze.

'Kind of a disguise,' she said, 'but cute, huh? US Postal Service inspectors must be careful. There are impostors. I think those Lee bitches listened to some impostor.'

Cherri's pussy began to juice, her come flowing heavily, until the licking ceased. She looked round: the exquisites were gone. Their bodies spun in the air, then splashed into the lake below. Ripples danced from three bronze figures, their pubic fleeces and long manes spreading around them in the water, like black lilypads.

'They sure like to swim,' said Lieut Bukowski. 'I can't tell you who they are. Plausible denial! In fact, I don't know exactly who they are. They just kind of appear when you need them. I can't take you much further, but I'll drop you, where you can hitch-hike to the interstate, give you some money, and you can take my clothes. I have several uniforms.'

'Are you really a marine lieutenant?'

'Or undercover postal inspector, tracking impostors? "Who, then, shall inspect the inspectors?" I could have been a princess, once, but a girl has to do her duty. I don't know where you think you're headed, but a righteous girl gets where she wants, in the end.'

She stripped, controlling the aircraft, and handed her denims to Cherri along with her black rubber boots. Her nude golden body gleamed in the lights of the instrument panel and the sun overhead. The breasts jutted over the instrument panel, shadowing the flat belly and lush tangle of blond pubic hairs; thighs, rippling with muscle, squeezed the crimson slash of her quim, shiny with come. The nipples were quivering and erect, with goosebumps across the red blossoms of their areolae. Her green eyes gleamed. Cherri hugged her; then her head fell to lick the silky, jutting breasts and chew the stiff nipples. It was a short scented slide down Bukowski's belly to the jungle of her pubis and the wet cunt-lips.

'I was hoping you'd do that, ever since I saw you,' said Lieut Bukowski. 'And if I may kiss your slave's ass?'

187

'Oh, wow! There's nothing I'd like – I mean, I've wanted to – you're so beautiful, lieutenant.'

'Even out of uniform?'

'Especially.'

Cherri moved her buttocks to the girl's face.

'Yeah, that's it. Mmm, whipped slave-ass tastes so good.'

In true whipping, slave will know joy.

That voice vibrated in Cherri's clit. Cherri sucked the naked pilot's own clitoris, swallowing the copious come her cunt gushed; Bukowski tongued Cherri's anus, then fingered her there and finally got her fist inside the yielding anal elastic. She fisted Cherri while sucking her clitty, with her face buried in the wet cunt-curls that draped Cherri's cleft and perineum. The girl's tongue made Cherri writhe until she flowed and shivered in orgasm. Bukowski pressed her naked cunt against the cleft of Cherri's ass, and rubbed her juicing slit over Cherri's globes until she, too, climaxed. She returned to lick Cherri's cooze, swallowing her come before finally raising her glistening face.

'There's no end to that love-juice of yours,' she said. 'And your pube hair is just so gorgeous, it's so long!'

'I loved it when you fisted me,' Cherri said. 'It's a slave's submission. And you called me "slave".'

'Are you ticked off?'

'No. It gives me a kind of thrill – like, it's my real name.'

'It comes to me, when my helpers are around, because they're called "slave". Their beauty *is* their enslavement. They always swim away, before I can ask why.'

Cherri looked down at the vast expanse of lake, receding behind the helicopter. The bodies of the bronze slaves were unseen. They could not have reached the shore in the time elapsed.

'They didn't swim away,' said Cherri, pulling tight denim over her buttocks and teats, as the helicopter descended. 'They went down to the bottom of the lake.'

11

Cloister of Clyster

Cherri squatted by the highway, under a broiling noonday sun. The road was empty. She felt the bills in Bukowski's denim pocket, totalling $988. The interstate lay over the horizon, at least, *an* interstate. Beside her was a creek, the first sliver of freshwater that broadened into the lake, where the bronze girls had vanished, many miles back.

Hey, I'm in California!

Cherri stripped off, and dived nude into the creek, which proved surprisingly deep. She swam down as far as her lungs would permit, and glimpsed a glowing green light way beneath her. She stayed under for over a minute, until she came up for air. She dived again, two minutes now, trying to get nearer the light, but it seemed as distant as ever. The water was cool on her fesse-weals and soothed her buggered anus. She dived again, relaxing her muscles, to let the water bathe her rectum and cunt as she sought the green light, but she couldn't hold out more than three minutes, with her lungs bursting.

She sloshed up from the water and her blurred eyes saw a horned animal chewing the tatters of her clothing. She shouted, and the beast raced away. She stared, aghast. Her clothing and money were torn to shreds. She tried to fashion the rags into the semblance of a bikini, but not enough fabric remained, even for that. There were no leafy plants in this scrubland, only a few bushes and spiny cacti.

Alone, in the nude, in the middle of California, with no money! The last part's bad.

A vehicle appeared, to the northeast. It was big, shimmering in the heat haze, but too big for a truck. As it approached, its enormity became clearer. The thing was an RV, a long, rounded cylinder of shiny metal, with wheels and windshield like an aircraft's: a submarine on wheels. The windshield was black. Cherri stood akimbo on the roadway, her legs firmly apart and, smiling, stuck out her thumb. The vehicle did not slow as it approached, growing bigger every second, and Cherri stepped back until the giant RV silently braked from full speed to stopping on a dime beside her. It had North Carolina plates. A door, invisible from three feet away, slid open to a twelve-foot aperture, above Cherri's head.

'Hi!' called an unseen girl's voice. 'Jump in!'

The base of the door ejected a grey metal ladder, which anchored itself to the ground. Cherri climbed to the sixth rung, to see into the cab, and the ladder coiled itself up to her heels.

'Don't be shy! We're all nudists, like you! It's just so *cool* that you dare to be bare! I'm Poppy. What a fabulous tan you have! I'm *so* jealous! But wait till we get to Mexico.'

Cherri ascended a few more rungs and saw the driver. There was a whir as the ladder rolled up after her, and she put a foot inside the cab. The driver was nude, an elfin blonde girl, Cherri's age, 5′5″ tall, with a svelte young body from which sprang a pair of massive dugs with sprawling raspberry nipples – or would have sprung, had they not been encased in a safety belt of several crisscrossed rubber strands, like a parachute harness. In fact, Poppy Bush's figure was 38-22-38, but her ripe ass-pears were hidden under the massive

190

webbing that enfolded her body, pinning her to the seat. The safety harness was fastened very tightly, so that faint bruises were visible on her teats and thighs where the straps bit. Her pencil of a waist broadened into a generous pelvis and bulging pubic hillock, topped with a massive pubic bush, like a blonde yule tree. Around her neck was a foam cushion eight inches high, holding her neck straight, with her mane pinioned in a pony-tail by a green jade clasp. She operated the foot controls with long, green-polished toes. Her body had an even, California-credible nudist's tan. Cherri stepped aboard, and at once the door whooshed shut behind her. The cab was as big as a room, its seat a plush davenport. Cherri sat down and introduced herself.

'Wow, Cherri, you have just a perfect figure! Sometimes I wish I was a guy, then I could – well, if you know what mean. Could I – would you mind showing me that ass of yours? I drive better when I'm madly jealous.'

Sighing, Cherri showed her bottom.

'Hey, that's something else! You're all glowing, as if you've been spanked! I mean, it can't be sunburn, with that tan. And your skin. Beneath the glow, there's this kind of cool marble, like peach and strawberry ice-cream.'

'Yeah?' Cherri said.

'Look in the mirror.'

'I haven't been spanked, exactly,' Cherri said.

She knelt on the seat, and thrust her buttocks up to the panoramic driving mirror, and gasped. Poppy was right. There were no whip or cane welts on her skin's surface; rather, they had been subsumed into her flesh, under the skin, like the filaments in tiger's eye, and the skin's surface glowed a uniform pearl crimson, as if just spanked.

'I guess it *is* just sunburn,' she said, sitting down. 'Even, um, a long-term, committed nudist like me gets sunburn, if she has to wait too long for a ride.'

191

'I can't believe you haven't been spanked, Cherri. Well, it's your butt, and a glorious sacred part of your personal you, so if you're sure nobody's spanked it recently . . .'

Poppy's mischievous laughter made it clear she didn't believe Cherri, but didn't mind, either.

Mexico! Cherri figured to humor the girl and whatever weirdo nudist crew she was part of. *Mexico, away from the law.* Poppy told her to fasten her safety belt, and Cherry manipulated the web of straps until the apparatus clicked, self-locking. She had to sheath her neck in the foam rubber neck brace, part of the safety harness, in case, Poppy assured her, of whiplash effect. The vehicle accelerated fast and smoothly, in silence.

'So, how long have you been a nudist, Cherri?' Poppy bubbled. 'I mean, how liberating, hitching round America in the nude, it's so great. Did you get hassled? I bet the cops didn't dare bust that fabulous butt of yours! I'm sure Bud'll want to write your adventures into the script. We're going down to Baja to make a proper movie, with a story and everything, about nudism in the wilderness. It's kind of a thriller, I think, I mean a real blockbuster; the idea is, girls function better in the nude, because it's so empowering for girls to get naked, free of all the, you know, *materialism* and stuff. Hey – I'm sure Bud won't mind – I mean, maybe you could be in the movie? I bet you can run some, with those long legs, for action scenes. We're getting paid American union rates, like, for a real job? I'd love to get really naked with you. I mean, I know we *are* naked, but, you know, *doing things* together, in the nude?'

Poppy blushed.

'Sure, I'd like that,' Cherri replied, 'but I've no ID. I mean, that's part of nude hitch-hiking round America, to, um, give the whole materialist thing the finger, you know?'

'All the girls will love you, Cherri! You're such fun, and so clean. That's one of Bud's things, nude living is

192

clean living. I'm nuts about your body, I mean, how did you get such an even tan, with no strapmarks? It's to die for!'

Cherri shrugged.

'You'll love travelling with us. There's everything a girl could want, it's like a hotel – and if girls ever spat, Bud sorts things out cleanly. He calls us the cloister of clyster. Isn't that so spiritual? You don't need ID to go to Mexico, they're *spiritual people* in Mexico! Now, Cherri, do tell me how you became a nudist.'

Cherri told Poppy that she was from Washington State, and liked to run in the woods, and swim nude.

'With boys?'

'Uh, yeah, I guess, sometimes.'

'Did you used to *do it*?'

'No,' Cherri said. 'Just being naked was fun enough. I don't need boys for that.'

'How thrilling! I'm there myself.'

'You never –?'

Poppy shuddered.

'I did, way too much! That's why nudism's so good for me, it's cleansed me. I used to fuck and masturbate so much! I couldn't say no to cock. Now – well, I can't say I don't think of it, but if I do, Bud always cleanses me with a spanking. You're not shocked, I hope?'

'It's the cleanest way, I guess,' Cherri said.

'I can talk, then! Bud Packer is our master. Girls close together always need a master to spank them if they get out of line. Spanking's so holistic, especially when it really hurts, and your ass feels tingly and warm and fresh. All of us agree. You've been spanked, Cherri, don't tell me no.'

Cherri admitted she had occasionally been spanked, and did regularly masturbate.

'You'll come much harder when you are properly spanked, with irrigation. Masturbation, girls diddling, is more wholesome than sex, that's what Bud teaches. Were you spanked a whole lot?'

'Some.'

'On the bare?'

Cherri pouted.

'Yeah, Miss Curiosity. You know another way?'

Both girls, giggling, agreed that only a spanking on the bare hit the spot. Poppy said there were four other girls in the cloister, as the RV was called: Cayenne Strahl, Marsha Quimby, Suze Thoroughgood, and Ginny Catepan, all of them, like herself, from North Carolina, and loving to be spanked. She said that there were freaks who liked whips and chains and rubber and stuff, which was really dirty, and in the cloister of clyster everything was clean. America was so full of weird cults and phoney preachermen, and only the cult of clean was true. Poppy was brought up to be clean, though she had a kind of rebellion thing, when she went with bikers, who used to make her do all kinds of stuff, like go down on them one after the other, or else bend over his *scooter* to pull a train, being gang-fucked from behind. She didn't mind that part, only they never washed. Cherri asked if Bud contented himself with spanking, and Poppy assured her he was the best master and totally righteous, disapproving of sex.

'He only spanks us for our own good and if we agree,' she said. 'It's so lovely to watch your ass squirm on video, afterwards, and your face all crunched up in pain, same as when the cheeks of your tush clench! Bare spanking is part of being a girl, because her bottom is her essence. Also, a girl is like fruit, and must be properly irrigated. There are so many airheaded girls who just won't understand. Spanking is a reward, not a punishment. I mean, what girl ever thought bare-ass spanking was punishment? Some people!'

'Don't you get weals from spanking?' Cherri said. 'Big red ridges, sticking up like blisters?'

'Yuk! That's only for weirdo caners! Spanking gives you a healthy pink glow, is all.'

194

'Are the girls allowed to spank each other?'

'Sometimes, when Bud wants to watch.'

'Wow, spanked all the way to Mexico!'

'Honestly, it's way cool, Cherri.'

'I mean, only being spanked. Spanking gave me an appetite, see –' Cherri gulped '– for harder than spanking. I've been victimised so much by control freaks that I'm kind of used to, uh, caning, you know? I can't help it.'

Slave wants it.

'I've been whipped with a cane, on the bare. It's not so bad. Imagine, Poppy, one hundred cane-strokes on your bare ass.'

Poppy shuddered.

'That's awful. Did it hurt?'

'Yes, that was the whole point. Doesn't a spanking hurt?'

Poppy frowned.

'I guess it must. But caning –' she shuddered '– that must hurt a whole lot more.'

'So you'd be cleaner.'

'Yeah, I never thought of it that way.'

The rear door of the compartment opened and Bud Packer entered. He was massive and heavily-bearded, twenty-eight years old, in jeans, red check shirt and dirty western boots, with lank greasy locks draped at his shoulders.

'Never thought of what, what way?' he growled.

'Oh!' said Poppy, starting. 'I was just telling Cherri that I've never imagined people not wanting to be cleansed.'

She explained Cherri's presence and their conversation, and that Cherri was already into spanking and nudism and would love to be a movie star. Bud leered.

'Lot of sows get their clothes eaten by critters,' he said. 'You clean, sow?'

'Clean enough, I hope,' said Cherri, brightly.

Bud produced a key and unlocked Cherri's safety harness.

'Aren't you overdressed for a nudist?' Cherri said, and Bud promptly slapped her face.

'Please don't be angry, Bud,' said Poppy. 'I've been good, I said what you told me to.'

Bud slapped Poppy's cheek and told her to watch the road. He ordered Cherri to lift her ass. Trembling, Cherri raised her buttocks to a squat and Bud sniffed her seat, warm from her behind. He wrinkled his nose, then pushed it right into the tangle of moist pube-hair at her anus and took a deep breath. He smiled.

'Fuckin' disgusting,' he said. 'Get aft, and I'll cleanse you.'

'You mean, spank me on the bare?' said Cherri, trembling, and rubbing her slapped cheek.

Bud grimaced.

'Spank a sow with stinkhole? You out of your mind? I'll spank you after irrigation,' Bud said.

He looped a rope to her neck and wound it round her breasts, pinning them in several coils, before pulling her down to the floor.

'Down on your fuckin' trotters, sow, and follow master to your girl-sty. You can snuffle and squeal and grunt, but no fuckin' sowtalk, 'cause it gives me a headache.'

Cherri stumbled, naked and roped, on all fours, after her new master, into the cloister of clyster.

It's not right. It's just not right.

Cayenne Strahl, nineteen years old, 38-24-39, and 5'10" tall, was a full-breasted, full-maned blonde, with a big butt, long horse-riding legs and toes, with a golden tan, and faint bikini strapmarks. Her cunt-fleece was thick, tightly trimmed in a crew-cut that hinted at its luxuriance if left untrimmed. The gash-flaps were straight and long, like a precisely-cut red jelly sandwich. Her armpits were trimmed to lawns of wheaty stubble. Marsha Quimby was eighteen years old, 38-22-37, and 5'5" tall. Her compact figure, like Poppy's, carried outsize breasts, and a ripe ass that tapered neatly into long colt's legs, with small feet. She had bikini strapmarks at titties and ass, indicating a microscopic bikini, the pale zone now overlaid with tan. Her nose was aquiline and her wide lips turned down in a sulk. Lank brown hair flopped to just above the big conic nipples of her breasts, like a male bodybuilder's pecs. Her cunt was like her mouth, an unruly slash of red amid an untamed pubic jungle, the inner and outer labia large and flabby, as though imperfectly glued together, and leaving an inch of her pink tunnel on view. Her armpit tufts were as dense as her cunt fleece.

Suze Thoroughgood, twenty years old, 36-23-37, and 5'4" tall, was an hourglass figure, with ash-blonde hair short and boyish, as if in mockery of her rosebud lips, pert, jutting breasts and big red plums for nipples, and her ripe bottom-pears. Her skin was tanned, without strapmarks. She had high cheekbones, long neck, and wide lips, that added to her tomboyish demeanour; like Marsha's, her cunt and armpits were untrimmed, and there was a fine coating of blonde down all up her legs, arms and spine. Her pubis was an untrimmed chaparral of wiry fuzz, and her tufts spiky blonde fleece under their pits. She had a gap of three inches between her powerful thighs, just below her cunt-flaps, where the blonde hairs hung in a weedlike tangle, and a one inch gap between her big and second toes. Ginny Catepan, eighteen years old, 36-23-37, and 5'8" tall, sported a lush auburn mane that caressed her wide crimson nipples, with the buds jutting from the areolae like grapes, on her hard breast-pears. Her body was completely shaven, the lips of her cunt folded like orchids. Her body rippled with athlete's muscle and especially the taut globes of her buttocks, where the creamy skin of her all-over suntan overlay gluteal fibre taut as wires. None of the girls had ever left North Carolina before.

All were naked, and squatted in a long aluminium pigsty filled with slimy wet clay, two feet deep. There was a gurgle as the slime drained from one end of the sty to be constantly replenished from shower heads that drizzled a spray of muck onto the bodies of the girls. The nozzles varied in fineness, so that some sprayed watery mud and some dripped slow, viscous gobbets, like dung. Each girl's hair colour and other distinguishing marks were only scarcely visible to Cherri at that time, as each body was covered in the muck. The four sowgirls were tethered like marionettes by ropes to each wrist and ankle, the ropes suspended from a galley of movable ceiling hooks, and their ankles strung to three-foot hobble bars of flexible rubber which, with their slack binding, allowed them limited freedom of movement, but placed far enough apart that they had to strain to touch each other. They were in constant motion, vainly wiping their faces, hair and breasts clean of the muck that showered them, and which at once dirtied them again.

They were roped so as to part the legs wide and tilt the pelvis, and it was hard for any girl to keep her cunt empty of dirt. At one end of the girl-sty was a toilet trough, with running water; fresh dungs swam towards its gutter in their yellow pond. Opposite, were two empty feeding-troughs. There were water nozzles and hoses at each end of the sty and, beyond the sty, bolted to the floor, a tubular aluminium table with splayed legs, festooned with rubber tubes. Beyond that was an aluminium stool, also bolted. Three video cameras rotated from drop-hooks on the ceiling. A spiral staircase led up to a second floor.

Even filthy, the girls' bare butts were discernibly red from spanking, although no girl's buttocks carried the same pattern of bruises, but bore mosaics of fingermarks. Each girl bore welts mostly on one side of her haunches and fesses, although Cayenne's buttocks were marked equally, indicating a double-side spanking, and were, in fact, the most blotched, her crimson bruises nearing purple. The marks of chastisement, though livid, attested to basic spanking, the narrow weals and sharp crusted ridges of cane or whip being absent.

'Got a new piglet for the sty, sows,' Bud drawled. 'Aren't you happy?'

Cayenne squealed; Marsha grunted, sullenly; Suze snuffled, and Ginny held her nose, crying, 'Oink! Oink!'

'That's good,' said Bud. 'You can watch the new sow's butt broken in, then all chow down together.'

He dragged Cherri forwards, helping her with a kick of his pointed bootcap between her cunt-lips. She shrieked, and Bud said she had the makings of a good pig.

'Pigs don't talk, but they're clean and behave, long as they're spanked regular. Have to spank a sow's butt, teach her to squeal good and suffer good, but that sow-butt still got to look good for when she goes to market.'

He lifted Cherri and slammed her belly-down on the tubular table, hooking her tit-rope underneath, so that escape, despite her wriggling, was impossible. He tied her legs apart, each ankle knotted to a table leg, and her arms straight in front, wrists roped together to a ratchet, which Bud tightened to rack her spine and legs, while spreading her cheeks to show full cooze and anus.

'Please,' Cherri blurted. 'This isn't right! Poppy said –'

Bud slapped her several times on both cheeks, hard enough to make her head rock.

'That's the last time you speak anything but pig talk, you fucking sow,' he snarled. 'I got gags upstairs. I got all kinds of things upstairs. Never mind what Poppy said about no movie or stuff. Her job is to put you pigs at ease, because she's so innocent, see, not like you stinking sows. I'll have you gussied up for G-Mart, though. Won't I, sows?'

The four other sows, eyes wide, agreed with squeals and grunts. Cherri shuddered, feeling the thick, greased rubber tube fill her anus, penetrating to her ass-root, and gasped; hot fluid sluiced into her anal cavern, filling it until she felt her belly would burst. Bud held the tube rammed in place for two minutes, then withdrew it and ordered Cherri to evacuate. She obeyed and the liquid jetted from her writhing anal pucker into a funnel that dropped her effluent into the girl-sty. That was repeated several times, with each enema different in heat, viscosity and discomfort. Bud favoured a chilli-pepper mix, which left Cherri scarlet and gasping for breath: her buttocks wriggled as though under canestrokes. Her irrigation lasted nearly an hour, until she jerked as a jet of icy water soaked her and was left, sobbing, to drip dry before Bud pronounced her clean enough for spanking. He untied her limp body, only to rerope her at once to the stool in a simple wrist-and-ankle tie that bent her over the seat, with her bare buttocks high. The stool placed her ass at Bud's waist, and her toes dangled inches from the floor. Bud lifted his arm.

'There's something I don't hear,' he snarled. 'A good sow says thank you after cleaning, and before she gets her butt reddened, and her hot NeedaBurger for chow. I don't hear thank you, no sow gets chow!'

Sobbing, Cherri parted her lips to speak, but only managed to gasp.

'I don't hear you, sow!' crowed Bud.

'Oink!'

'Eeeh!'

'Ghhh!'

'Nhhk!'

Cayenne, Marsha, Suze and Ginny began a frantic grunting and snuffling, urging Cherri to comply.

'Listen, sow, sooner your ass is fuckin' *red*, sooner you all get fuckin' *fed!*' Bud crooned.

Cherri pursed her lips and nose, tightening the back of her throat.

'Oink! Oink!' she sobbed.

Crack! Crack! Crack!

Bud's palm and fingers were hard as wood, and Cherri clenched her bare as he spanked.

Her smarting buttocks writhed.

'What I hear, sow-girl?'

Crack! Crack! Crack!

Tears blurred Cherri's eyes as her seared nates squirmed, helpless in her tie.

'Eee!' she cried.

'That's better,' Bud grunted.

Crack! Crack! Crack!

His heavy spanks thrashed her right across both quivering naked globes and Cherri squealed high.

'Eee! Eee!'

'Better settle your ass in for a long session, sow,' said Bud. 'It's the finest I've seen in a long while, and she pinks up nice and deep under that nudist tan you got. Why, I'd swear you have spankmarks under that skin, like they grew there already, or whipmarks! You a *pervert*, girlswine? Have to spank that perversion out of those wriggly little buns. In the cloister, you get decent American spanking, bare on bare, way it should be.'

The metal stool rattled as each spank enflamed Cherri's bare buttocks, clenching and squirming, with the bronze skin of her peach marbled deeper and deeper crimson.

Crack! Crack! Crack!

'*Nnnk!*'

Cherri's spanked bare bottom began to writhe more slowly as Bud's palm-prints blotched her ass-skin, and her squeals deepened to a low, snuffling ululation. Cayenne, Marsha, Suze and Ginny grunted in approval at the newcomer's distress; each of the roped girlswine had her hand between her muddy legs and was rubbing her dirt-filled cunt and slimed clitty-button, masturbating, eyes wide, as Cherri's bottom wriggled and reddened.

'*Eek! Nnk!*'

Drool dripped from Cherri's frothing mouth as Bud continued to spank her past two hundred slaps. The drip of saliva onto the metal floor merged with a spreading pool of oily fluid from her cooze. The four frigging sows grunted gleefully at Cherri's spanking. Bud switched sides for each fiftieth slap, so that an equal, blotchy, chastisement was applied to the entire expanse of Cherri's fesses. The spanking included slaps to inner thighs and thigh-backs, as well as stingers with straight fingers to the tender haunch-skin, and particularly strong spanks right at the top buttock under her spinal nubbin. Cherri's bronze bottom became a kaleidoscope of shifting crimson and purple blotches. She gasped hoarsely, not even moaning any more, as the spanking passed five hundred. Forty-two minutes had elapsed. Bud slowed the spanking to work on Cherri's perineum, gash-flaps and anus bud, which had so far escaped slaps. With Cherri's buttock-flesh widely marked, Bud searched for crevices incompletely darkened. He spanked, stabbing in the tender area of perineal skin, at her cleft stretched between the spread ass-flans. Crack! Crack! Crack! Three stingers caught Cherri squarely on her swollen gash-flaps, and she howled.

'*Eek!*'

Bud laughed.

'Thought you were dreaming, sow?' he said. 'Plenty do. I know what a cunt thinks, as she's spanked. She thinks, *this is my secret blossom, all for me, it shows my man cared enough to punish me, and I want to see my ass all red in the mirror, and diddle my clitty, watching my*

202

blush quiver. Spanking is mind-pleasure, see. Good ropes and a firm hand on her bare ass, that's all a sow needs to make her happy, apart from swill and slop. Spanking sow's ass is no different from painting a barn red; got to make sure every crack's filled. I never spanked such a ripe pair of lower titties before; just look at how my sows are diddling their cunts, watching your ass wriggle! I swear you're winking – what a mare's quim does, when she's on heat, steaming and glowing and kind of pulsating. Hey, swine-girls, this sow's ass is on heat for spanking!'

That discovery enthused Bud to increase the force of his spanks; he did not neglect slaps to Cherri's vulva and anal crevice, sometimes two or three in ten seconds, which had her jerking and shuddering, with a froth of drool bubbling at her lips. Her tongue was shut behind a rictus of teeth or, at an intimate spank which touched her crevice or cunt lips or even her clitoris, it poked between her teeth in a silent scream. Crack! Crack! Crack! Bud spanked her past the seven-hundredth. As her bare buttocks squirmed to deepening crimson, and her strained ropes rattled the stool, only gurgling piggish noises emerged from her throat, and nose: '*nnnh – eee – gggh!*'

She was joined in squealing, first by Marsha, then by Ginny, Suze, and at last Cayenne. All squealed and grunted as their squirted come mixed with the mud-spray, unwiped from their naked bodies; the pool of come widened under Cherri's legs, and the spanked sow's squeals grew long and whimpering until, at the thousandth slap, her red bottom was clenching frantically and she slapped her dripping cunt against the hot metal of her stool.

'That's your thousand,' said Bud, and untied her. 'One hour and twenty-three minutes exactly.'

Cherri, her bonds loosened, still clung to the chair-stool, rubbing her engorged clitoris against the hot metal and whimpering, drool frothing her mouth. Bud raised both his hands and, with a lightning-fast crack, delivered two dozen further spanks to Cherri's flaming red buttocks, in the space of six seconds.

'*Ahh!*' she squealed, as her clenched bare nates slammed her throbbing clitty against the stool.

Come drenched her pubic jungle, dangling beneath the quivering cooze-flaps, and flowed down her thighs as she moaned, then yelped aloud in a rush of orgasm.

'Eek! Oink!' squealed the masturbating sows as their come sprayed from pulsing wet cunts, and each swine-girl brought herself off. Bud leaned back with a satisfied grin and untied Cherri's ropes.

'That's what we call the "tarheel surprise", back home,' he drawled. 'We're called tarheels, and a real North Carolina spanking is on a girl's tarred bare ass.'

He flung Cherri over his shoulder, then into the girl-sty, where she landed with a splash of muck that coated the naked captives. The mud was warm.

'Fix her up good, sow-sluts, and you'll get your slop.'

Straining at their slack ropes, Cayenne, Marsha, Suze and Ginny tussled for the honour of tying Cherri up the tightest, and the sobbing new sow was fastened at wrist and ankles like the others, with her vulva open to the incessant spray of muddy water and gobbets of clay that splattered them.

Bud whistled, clapping his hands. An awkward click of heels came from the spiral metal staircase, and a girl appeared, her face bright red and twisted in pain. She was swaddled from neck to knee in a sheath of tight latex, which did not hide her big breasts and ass, but beneath which bulged several protuberances, like humps or similar derformities. Cherri gasped.

'Why, Karen! Karen Souter! Don't you remember me? It's Cherri!'

'Shut that sow's snout!' bawled Bud.

'Eee! Oink! Eee! Oink!'

Straining on their ropes, the four North Carolina sowgirls fell on Cherri in a furious splash of mud. Cherri overbalanced and fell backwards into the slimy muck, only to be turned over with her bare butt sticking in the air. One girl sat on her head, immersing her in the liquid, while two more held her down by the ankles and waist and a fourth slapped her muddy bare buttocks. Wriggling, Cherri opened her mouth to squeak, as new spanks added to the smarting of Bud's thousand-slapper, but choked on the slime that flowed into her mouth. Her bottom squirmed helplessly as all four girls helped to spank her, clawing at the stiff ridges Bud's palm had raised on her bare ass, until Cherri went limp. At that, they let her up, and she gulped air, but when they realised she had tricked them, they grabbed her again, and while Cayenne Strahl spanked her bare titties and pinched her nipples, the others wadded her cunt, anus, and mouth with gobbets of the thicker, dunglike clay. Cherri's cheeks and both her holes were packed with the slimy muck.

'Don't you move, sow!' barked Bud.

He began to unroll the latex sheath from Karen Souter's body, which was nude, and patched with steaming lumps of food which Cherri recognised as NeedaBurgers. They were hot from the microwave, and Karen had held the hot burgers against her nude body, lodged at her nipples and her cunt, until Cherri's spanking was over. Karen shook herself, and disgorged her load of slop into the feeding trough, while Bud opened a tap and NeedaCola streamed into the parallel trough. The girls fell to, oinking and slurping. While they were occupied at trough, Karen quickly wound herself in her rubber robe and tottered back up the stairs, but not before Cherri had glimpsed her full nudity. Cherri stared through her tears at the sneering Bud, and began to chew and swallow the clay that wadded her mouth. She worked her teeth around the muck, and avoided gagging, until the last of it was in her stomach.

'Eek,' she said softly, to Bud, while licking her lips.

'Shee-oot! A fucking dirt-eater! Maybe you're a North Carolina tarheel after all!' he whooped. 'Don't try any more talking, nor sign lingo, because I'll be watching on the video monitor, see? And you don't want to go *upstairs*.'

Bud followed Karen Souter up the spiral staircase. The NeedaBurgers were gone, but Cherri was able to refresh herself with a suck of NeedaCola. She began imitating the other sows, wiping the sprayed mud from her titties and face, but gave up, and dozed, her hair in the warm slime.

What is Karen doing here? And why is her whole body covered in cane welts? I do want to go upstairs ...

The cloister of clyster took the long way to Mexico, meandering through California, Nevada, Utah, and as far as Arizona, always keeping off major highways. Poppy explained, as she administered one of the sows' three daily spankings, that Bud's purpose was to break them in, to be perfectly docile for market. They made daily stops for exercise in the nude, in desert or by a lake, with spankings averaging five hundred slaps, and two enemas daily for each sow, the clyster usually applied before her spanking. During outdoor excursions, the sows could pick wild fruits or berries to supplement their NeedaBurgers. Generally, a source of fresh water was available to replenish the RV's tanks, the vehicle being fuelled by solar panels on its roof. Before leaving the RV, sows were hosed down and unroped, the places chosen always off-road and desolate, but the sows remained hobbled. At dusk, the spanked bottoms of the girlswine glowed like red lanterns. They slept, roped, in their warm mudbath, but with the mudspray closed. Reveille was the brown fluid again squirting their bodies.

The spankings took a long time, and there was no time at which the sows were not busy or exhausted. Speech was impossible as, even at night, surveillance monitors covered them. Sows communicated by grunts and squeals, and Cherri found herself initiated into sow language, in which there was very little to say: spanking hurt/spanking mild, mud warm/mud cool, enema burn/enema icy. Bud said little while spanking or administering colonic irrigation, but Poppy was a chatterbox, talking to herself as much as to her victim:

'My, your ass looks good enough to eat! Redder than yesterday, I'm sure. You're coming on, sow-girl.'

Poppy's own buttocks bore livid spank-blossoms, but her spankings of sows were not vengeful. Her hand was lighter than Bud's and sometimes she used a rubber glove, weighted with metal, so that her spankings were in fact more feared, and left much more ragged blotches than Bud's palm, although sometimes she liked to raise a uniform glow by spanking light slaps in longer duration. She also used a leather slipper, rubber-soled sneaker, or wooden butter-pat, permitted by Bud as 'organic'. The sows' bare bottoms squirmed, and reddened equally.

'It's always so,' said Poppy. 'When you're spanked with rubber, you wish it was hand, and when you're hand-spanked, you think slipper would be kinder. But a spanking's a spanking, and it's what a girl needs most, especially a sow-girl.'

12

Spanked Sows

If she pleased, Poppy openly masturbated when she spanked a sow's bare, and always when spanking Cherri, who received the longest spankings, often over a thousand. Playing with her extruded clitty, as she spanked Cherri's bare, Poppy mused about her days as Miss Nudist North Carolina, and how she won the special 'pink bottom crown' for spanked girls, added at her own suggestion.

'There's an art to blushing a bottom,' she said, 'so that it's the same pink all over. Spanking's healthy for a girl, like nudism. If she has fifty pairs of shoes, or fifty dresses, she frets because she doesn't have fifty, when what she needs is to get naked, and have her cares spanked away! Possessions don't make a girl happy – only a bottom spanked hard, bare, and often, can do that.'

Cherri also received the longest and most painful enema, as Bud discovered her rectum could accommodate over a quart of liquid, and that Cherri obediently held it in as long as was ordered; while other girls, notably Suze, squealed and squirted before command, earning further spanking. The spanking methods varied, from stool-strapped to plain over the knee with the spanker in an easy chair, or to double spankings, with two sows strapped bottom-up over the enema table, and both Bud and Poppy in spanking action, exchanging bottoms at intervals. The RV still moved, so Karen Souter must be driving, Poppy thought; until, on her third day, she was taking a double spanking along with Cayenne Strahl when Karen appeared, sheathed in her rubber garment, with their slop. There was another person aboard.

The Carolina sows soon accepted Cherri as one of the sty, and spankings were taken in a playful though never totally trusting atmosphere, with sty-sows urging on the spanker, and cheering the spankee's squirming bare fesses with gleeful squeals. Cherri relaxed into the unchanging routine. The breaks for fresh air seemed bliss, and a few berries, clawed while jumping in her hobble, a feast. Yet, after their breaks, the sows sighed with relief as they were roped back in their familiar trough. That was part of a girl slave's breaking in, Poppy explained, like training birds not to stray from their open cage. Cherri's endurance of anal cleansing and bottom-spanking, after provoking sneers of envy, soon made her popular, because it was her buttocks and anus which exhausted their hosts' punishment energy. If a sow was 'uppity', even after a long spanking, further restraint could be applied: she might be fully hogtied, her trotters roped together either behind her back or in front of her, and during such restraint she was unable to wipe herself clean of the sprayed muck.

Bud sometimes belted a sow, which meant fastening her waist in a belt, tight as a waspie corset, and leaving her belted for a day or more. He explained that females could as a rule be reduced to 74% waist size; Cherri thus found herself gasping, as her twenty-two-inch waist was pinched by a belt tightened to seventeen inches. At no time did Bud behave improperly towards sows; he did not consider masturbating sex, but healthy animal behaviour, and organic, and insisted the sows masturbated regularly. Diddling was a sow's privilege, enjoyed, too, by Poppy, who claimed she was 'just a sow like you, don't forget', and showed off the plentiful pink weals on her own fesses as she played with her clitoris and squeezed drips of come from her gash.

'Be glad you don't have to sit bare-ass on that itchy driver's seat!' she reminded them, dramatically.

Bud and Poppy had quarters in the rear of the RV. The girls were all so tired from their routine that sleep came easily, especially as the lights were not dimmed until every sow had masturbated herself to Poppy's or Bud's satisfaction, allowing her come to drip into the food runnel, whence it dripped into a green Tupperware dish. On her twenty-fifth night, Cherri was awoken by her bladder; she felt too drowsy to lift herself from the mud, so peed into it, as she suspected the other sows did. Above the humming of the RV, the hissing of her own pee, and the slopping motions of sows in mud, broken by occasional anus wind, rose a different sound: a dry, rhythmic tap-tap-tap, which seemed to come from upstairs. It was so regular, it might have been engine noise; suddenly, the taps were drowned by a choked, piercing sob of agony. It was Karen Souter's voice.

Cherri sat up. The other sows snored and did not awaken as Cherri gnawed through the ropes at her wrists and ankles, her face half-immersed in the mud to reach the ankles. She chewed carefully so that the severed ropes could be reknotted and her hobble replaced and pass unnoticed in the slime. She squatted on top of the toilet sluice and rinsed herself clean of mud, which took over five minutes. She dried her feet on her pubic bush, then padded on tiptoes to the spiral staircase. The tapping sound grew louder, as she approached, and placed her toes on the first step. She started as a light blinked: the night video! There was no going back. Punishment would surely follow her misdeed, but what could Poppy and Bud do? Spank her? Sear her insides with chilli enema? Tap-tap-tap, came the sounds, and then another strangled sob from Karen Souter. Cherri shuddered, and climbed.

They could whip me.

She peered into the top deck, and gasped. The tapping was now a loud vap! vap! vap! A tawse of three leather tongues lashed the bare back, thighs and buttocks of Karen Souter. There was a pillory with holes for arms and neck, and a splay-legged flogging-rail attached behind its headboard; on the wall hung an assortment of crook-handled wooden canes, leather and rubber whips, pincers, hobbles, and cuffs. The naked girl was tied to a pyramid of four metal struts, waist-high, with one arm or leg fastened to a single strut. Each wrist and ankle was locked to its strut in a rubber cuff and the apex of the pyramid pierced her cooze, with the orbs of her bare buttocks thrust high, crowning the punishment frame. The struts of the pyramid shone with her come. Her head and back hung low, with her mane brushing the floor, and her dangling teats were pulled away from her ribs by a taut violin string to a point directly under her anus. The violin string, fastened between struts, pierced each nipple, so that every shudder hurt the pierced titty-buds. Her naked buttocks and back were dark crimson, streaked with purple ridges rising three-tenths of an inch from the surface of her skin, and growing with each lash. A lit green candle, four inches wide, was inserted in her anus, its scalding wax dripping onto her stretched nipples and underteats, with drops from its base seeping onto her perineum and lower gash-flaps. Behind her stood a large freezer. Vap! Vap!

'Unggh!' Karen sobbed.

From the bulkhead, Cherri saw only the flogging implement and the partial body of the naked flogger. His cock was monstrously erect and Cherri moaned, for at the sight of the huge cock come seeped between her gash-flaps and a tingle went up her spine. She looked at the empty pillory and stepped into the chamber.

211

'Eek!' she said.

'What the fuck?' said the male.

Cherri squeaked again, then grunted, her cunt dripping with juice as she eyed the nude male tawsing Karen's naked body. He laughed.

'Fucking pig-girls, forget how to talk,' he sneered. 'Like what you see, sow? Want some?'

'*Mickey!*' she cried. 'Oh, *Mickey!*'

'You know this pig?' Karen gasped.

Vap! The tawse flogged her striped thighbacks.

'*Ah!*'

'Shut up, cunt. Yeah, I remember. *You* know sweet little Cherri Black, the cock-teaser virgin. Bitch the cops are after! Sure I remember, Cherri; I remember you said to piss on me, and that wasn't ladylike at all. That was scapegrace, trailer park trash talking. You've grown – at least, your tits and butt have. Just ripe for that whopping I've saved up for your dirty fucking whore's ass, when I've made *this* piece of shit faint.'

The tawse lashed Karen's squirming bare buttocks, right on the high purple ridges at mid-fesse.

'*Ah!*' Karen sobbed, shuddering as the candle flame seared the down on her anus pucker and puddles of hot wax blobbed her pierced titties.

'Want my dick, bitch?' Mickey said. 'I can do you in the cunt, when I've done her in the ass for maybe an hour. Or you can suck me off, once I'm good and slimed off her stinking asshole. You always were a cocksucker.'

'Oh,' Cherri sobbed. 'Mickey, how could you leave me in that mess, with that Ellum Tod? It wasn't right!'

'*Nnnh!*' squealed Karen, in a choked sob, as the tawse snaked under the pyramid, to thrash her naked breasts, and come poured from her impaled cunt down the pyramid struts.

Cherri gazed mesmerised at the stiff tool throbbing almost within reach. She slowly sank to her knees and, as she sank, her lips parted.

212

'I'd have done anything for you, Mickey,' she murmured, 'you know that.'

'Well, suck on this,' he ordered, grabbing her mane and forcing her head down on his cock, so that Cherri jerked convulsively, almost choking on the glans as it filled the back of her throat.

Her head began bobbing up and down and her lips clasped the erect tool, sucking vigorously on the shaft, before raising her lips to the glans and tonguing its corona and neck. When her tongue flickered over the thin membrane of the frenulum, Mickey shivered.

'Yeah, you always did give good head,' he said.

Cherri licked his piss-hole before plunging her mouth on the cock until her lips pressed his balls; she recommenced her powerful sucking.

Four savage strokes of the tawse added further purple to Karen's jerking bare rump.

'*Ah! Oh!*'

'Quiet, cunt!'

'They'll hear everything now,' Karen sobbed, then squealed as the candle flame reached her anus, spluttered and went out, leaving a greasy hot mush of wax in her asshole to drip, slowly congealing, into her perineum and coat her swollen, come-soaked gash-lips.

'They're asleep,' Mickey gasped. 'Anyway, they can't mess with me, I'm a –'

Cherri moved her head faster, then felt Mickey's hands pressing her hard against him, trapping her.

'Oh, *yeah*, bitch,' he moaned.

She constricted her throat so that her uvula embraced and squeezed his throbbing glans, and felt the first droplet of his sperm. His cock started to buck and quiver as he pushed her face against his balls, her head acceding willingly. Her lips caressed the balls with firm pressure as her throat filled with his first jet of sperm, and Cherri began to gurgle as she swallowed the whole spurting volume of creamy ejaculate. When Mickey's spasm was over, he smacked his lips and lashed Karen's bare bottom three more strokes with the tawse.

'*Ahh!*'

'That's your two hundred, bitch.'

Mickey unbuckled Karen's bonds, whipping the teat-wire smartly from her pierced nipples, then pushed the remnant of hot candle all the way up her anus.

'*Ah!*' she wailed.

'Now I've got real business,' he said, licking his teeth.

He wrenched Cherri's hair, twisting it.

'Oh! Mickey, you're hurting me!' she said, her lips drooling his sperm down her chin.

He pulled her by the hair towards the pillory, and opened the jaws of its headpiece.

'Mickey, no!'

'It's what you came for, bitch, right?'

'No!'

Mickey slapped her mouth, then punched each of her bare breasts, smack on the stiff nipples.

'Not like *this! Oh!*'

He pushed Cherri's head and wrists into the pillory, then slammed the headboard shut. Cherri's head and arms were trapped. Mickey grabbed her by the pubic bone with his fingers in her cunt, and hoisted her belly onto the padded flogging rail, holding down her buttocks while he swiftly buckled each of her ankles in rubber cuffs to the base of the wooden legs. Cherri's buttocks wriggled frantically, exposed to the full and raised by the padded rail, which sliced her cunt-flaps. Her naked breasts hung on either side of the flogging rail, the nipples eight inches beneath the bottom of the headboard, and her spine arched for her head and wrists to fit through its holes. A trickle of come from her cooze wet the rail. From the implement rack, in front of Cherri's imprisoned face, Mickey selected a thin crook cane, four feet long, then swished the air, so that Cherri's hair danced.

'Bare-ass caning. That's what you came up here for, right, you fucking sow?' he said.

'Yes, Mickey,' she whispered. 'Yes, *fuck you*, it is.'

The cane rose and whistled. Vip! The rod sliced Cherri's bare bottom on the fleshy mid-fesse, raising a crimson weal over the glowing spanked pink of the croup.

'*Oh!*' she moaned, her buttocks clenching furiously. 'Just tell me, why won't Bud and Poppy mess with you? What are you today – a cop, a federal marshal, a fucking CIA agent or something?'

'Better than that,' hissed Mickey, his flaccid cock now stirring to semi-erection as he raised the cane over Cherri's helpless bare croup.

Vip!

'*Ah!*'

Her buttocks squirmed, wealing instantly, with a long crimson gash from haunch to haunch.

'I'm a US postal inspector,' Mickey said.

'I don't believe you.'

'Shut your fucking mouth, cunt.'

Vip!

'*Oh!* How are you going to make me – cane my bare ass, or what?'

'Good idea, cunt.'

Vip!

'*Ohh!*'

Cherri's belly slapped the flogging rail as her caned bare buttocks jerked under Mickey's slices; her balled fists, imprisoned in the pillory, punched the air and her head jerked in its opening, just an inch wider than her neck. Karen Souter, groaning, removed herself from her come-slimed perch on the pyramid, whose pointed summit left her cunt with a squelching plop. She hobbled to Cherri's pilloried face, dragging the pyramid with her, and sat down with its tip stuck once more into her gash. She squatted, wriggling on the point with her

215

gash oiling the struts, and stayed at a crouch, holding her knees to her titties and her face in front of Cherri's. She pushed back a lock of her lank hair and wiped tears from her face as she smiled at the pilloried girl. Then she produced the stiff breast wire and plunged it through each pierced nipple, grimacing.

'Mmm, that's better. It's true, Mickey *is* a US postal inspector,' she said, reaching behind her to the punishment rack and walking her fingers over the implements, until she stopped at a short quirt of fourteen stiff rubber thongs. 'He carries top-secret mail that you can't entrust to mailboxes, unless they're deactivated. They're all spying devices, see? That's why you can never see inside.'

'See?' said Mickey, flicking the freezer door open; inside were stacked green tupperware dishes with lids. 'I'm the Pony Express and Wells fucking Fargo!'

Mickey's cane again lashed Cherri's bare.

'*Uhh.*'

'Starting to hurt?' Karen asked.

'Yes,' Cherri gasped, through clenched teeth.

Karen took the fanned rubber quirt from the rack, and showed it to Cherri.

'This'll hurt you some more,' she said. 'The thongs are stiffened with titanium wire.'

She slipped the stiff rubber thongs beneath the pillory's head and tickled Cherri's breasts and nipples. Her free hand caressed her own pubic fur and crept to her cunt-lips, which she opened between finger and thumb, wriggling her cunt-basin, so that her juices sparkled to Cherri's gaze and her erect clitty was extruded. Cherri's mouth was a rictus as Mickey's canestrokes lashed her bare ass, methodically covering all of it. Her cries had slurred to an unbroken, sobbing moan. Karen held her clit between finger and thumb, and began to roll it, masturbating. A flick of her wrist placed the rubber quirt four inches below Cherri's teats. Cherri gaped.

216

'No!' she sobbed. 'Please, Karen, no!'

Karen's wrist flicked up. The fan of thongs lashed Cherri's bare breasts. Cherri yelped. Karen whipped her titties and Cherri cried out again. The crack of Mickey's cane on Cherri's bare ass, accompanied the tap of Karen's quirt-tips on Cherri's nipples. Karen's own breasts were etched with a lattice of whipmarks, the largest concentration being around her big plum nipples, their areolae widened by crimson whip-scars. Helplessly trussed, Cherri squirmed under double flogging.

'*Ohh!*' she cried. 'Why, Karen? What happened to you?'

'I'll *tell* you, bitch,' Karen hissed. 'I found what I am, and what every girl really is. Spanking, caning, bondage, submission, punishment . . . *I'm a girl slave*. Those fucking hypocrites in South Chehalis, they used me and my mom, but they didn't like us enjoying it. Do you know how big the spanking and caning scene is in the US? Huge! Everybody's into it, but doesn't dare tell. Every girl's bad, like me, and needs her ass whipped. Girls pretend if they possess enough things they're not bad. But they are.'

Vap! Vap!

'*Oh, no!*'

Cherri's titties quivered like red grapes at each thrash of Karen's quirt.

'Piss on me, huh?' Mickey snarled.

Vip! Vip!

'*Ahh!*' Cherri sobbed, as her buttocks throbbed to her chastisement's rhythm, with the scarred ass-globes rising, clenched, to Mickey's cane. 'I'm sorry, Mickey, I didn't mean it! It was those girls, Tracee and Paula – I thought they were my friends – and that mean Ellum Tod.'

'Rev Ellum taught me about fucking bitches,' said Mickey, 'that they're all whores and have to be whipped and treated like slaves, for them to be any use to a guy. Course I knew that already. I whipped their asses raw, after they made me swallow the sump oil from their dirty fucking pigs' cunts. Yuk! Cooze-ooze is *merchandise* – for lamebrains, not righteous Americans. They saw reason after Rev Ellum let me hang them up in ropes, and give them real mean titty torture before I butt-fucked them. They were my slaves after that. Rev Ellum knows a mite about bitches.'

'I would have been your slave, Mickey, if you'd treated me right.'

'Too late now, bitch.'

'I know.'

'You what? Since when did a fucking cock-teasing whore bitch from South Chehalis fucking know anything?'

Vip! Vip! Vip!

'Ah! That's too hard!'

Her naked, flogged ass-globes churned and shuddered in an incessant quivering, under the canestrokes.

'*Anyway*, Bud took me back to North Carolina,' Karen continued. 'He's a fine master, and kept me as a sow, but he only spanks and clysters, which is kind of OK, you know? Then he bought Poppy at G-Mart, and she's a nudist, and he made us mud-wrestle and diddle each other, charging the rednecks money to watch. That was fun, too. I wanted more and harder spanking, and he said I was an insolent bitch, and I dared him to spank me to fainting, but he never could, and said he was going to auction me at another G-Mart. I didn't like that – smart, huh? So I stole a car and took off. It was an old '03 Ford. I dumped that in Arkansas, and stole an '05 Chevy. Fucking state trooper bitch stopped me for speeding, and said she'd let me go if I took a whipping, naked, instead of jail time. I figured she was a dyke, but so what? We went to her lakeside cabin. She whipped me, like, a hundred on the back with her police belt, and me strung naked between two trees by the lake. Then she caned me on the ass, and that was another hundred, and my cunt was squirting come, and my welts were really hurting, and she said did I like it, and I said it was OK.'

Vap! Vap! The whip struck Cherri's nipples.

'*Ah!* Oh, Karen, please stop!'

'Hurt too much, Cherri?'

'You know it does.'

'That's nice.'

Vap! Vap!

'*Ohh!*'

'Well, this cop bitch wasn't a total dyke. We went inside to see her old man. She had a real torture chamber, a dungeon, with racks and pillories like yours, titty-screws and cunt-pincers and everything. I was scared! But I stayed because I was curious. The police cunt said if they couldn't find a girl slave, then she had to be the slave, and she showed me her weals and pierced cunt and nipples for suspension games. All her femme-flaps were pierced, and that's where I got mine done. It doesn't hurt as much as you'd think, or like. I had to sleep with her and her old man, and lick her pussy, while he butt-fucked me, and they did all these tortures on me, and watched me masturbate, while I took bare-ass caning. I was caned bare-titty, bare-cunt, bare everything. Her shit-kicker laughed at me because I was juicing so much, being caned bare-ass and bare-titty, tied up like a hog, and begging him to touch me off. That's when I knew I really liked being a plaything, whipped and helpless and all, so I didn't regret running off from Bud. They made videos, and I wasn't acting at all, squirming and screaming, I just loved thinking of horny cowboys drooling over my bare ass covered in purple stroke-weals, you know?'

Vap! Vap! The quirt flogged Cherri's bare breasts.

'*Ahh!* Karen, please stop.'

'That's not a good idea, Cherri. I wanted to stay, and be their slave, but they changed girls every weekend, so the fucking shit-heads left me on the fucking highway, with enough dollars for one fucking NeedaBurger and a smarting butt. I started thinking, I kind of missed Bud's clysters and spanking. I was squatting outside the NeedaBurger place, eating a fucking burger, and my T-shirt all sloppy from it, so you could see my tits, then this dude drives up in a US Postal Service van, says do I want a job? Called himself the maidmaster, so I figured he was no postal dude, and all I had on was really tight cut-offs and a wet T-shirt, so he could see my thighs and most of my ass, pretty bruised up from my whippings, and I didn't mind telling him my true story. Turned out he ran a revivalist meeting scam with these slave maids who confessed their sins and got whipped as penitence and then, due to being a postal inspector, he could get a make on licence plates while the fucking small-town hypocrites were drooling over nude maids being caned, *and* their own bitches offering their sinful asses to be whopped, and come back later and boost cars from their driveways, see? They'd end up in Mexico or Canada, or in a chop shop, I guess. I said I knew about whipping and boosting cars, so I got to be one of his star turns, and went just about every state west of the Mississippi, which was fun, except Nebraska was kind of flat.'

Vap! Vap! Vap!

'Oh . . . oh . . .'

'Your tits are really purple, Cherri. Thing was, the other maids got jealous, because I always wanted more whipping, and the maidmaster said I'd have to keep door only, as my body was too scarred and would scare the righteous folks. That was in Utah, I think, so I took one of his boosted cars, a white Mercedes convertible, and got to Nevada. I drove past this neon sign, "TORTURE SHACK – Drive-Thru Spanking, Whipping,

Bondage, Muddy Girls" and things like that. Prostitution is legal in Nevada, see? This naked babe in a studded harness asked my pleasure, and I said I wanted a job. I got one! I was "Miss Analla" and had my own torture shack, where guys could cane me and give me enemas and just everything. I didn't mind switching; I'd beat them, piss on them and stuff, and I always took their cocks in any hole, and they paid per service. That lasted quite a while, until one client happened to be the owner of my white Mercedes! Hypocritical fucker, just after he'd caned me a hundred on the bare, and I'd sucked him off, he said he'd call the cops. I ran out of there and hid in a truck out of Phoenix, whose driver had caned and butt-fucked me a few times, and he wanted a freebie for getting me away from the law, so I sucked his dick while he was doing eighty on the freeway, and then he suggested I try a slave market, which is a western name for a G-Mart. He was kind of nice.'

Vap! Cherri's naked titties shook.

'*Ahh!* Please stop.'

'You don't mean that. I knew all about the girl marts, from Bud – you'd be surprised how many girls are traded as voluntary bondage slaves, and they have G-Marts all over the country. So we got to this rancho dump, out in the desert near Vegas, with a lot of girls in the raw, strutting their stuff, getting whipped, or muddy, or cattle-prodded, or whatever their thing was – some were French maids, with frilly dresses that showed their buns for caning – and I chose bare-ass caning, unlimited strokes, and said I did everything. A guy asked if I did spanking, and I said yes sir, I can take any number of spanks your hand is good for. It was Bud! I could have hugged him. He bought me and a few other slaves, and we made the run down to the big slave mart down in Baja, where anything goes. Hog girls are a North Carolina speciality, see, and Bud had gone into the slave business full-time, and Poppy, being a nudist, liked the Mexican sunshine. I told him I needed more than just spanking, and he made me swineherd, in charge of the girls at mart, plus which, I'm the draw, I take really savage beatings before I herd the sows on, to get the bidders horny. You get all kinds – movie people, ranchers, and all. Plus, I can pick up studs for myself, like Mickey, to do me while Bud and Poppy watch and make videos. I *enjoy* being a girl slave. It's *me*.'

Karen punctuated her story with flicks of her quirt to Cherri's naked breasts, with Mickey caning the buttocks. Her breast tally was eighty-three strokes, and the croup, a hundred and six.

'You bitches done squawking?' snarled Mickey, 'Now I'm going to butt-fuck this sow till she squeals. I got interrupted the last time, so this is unfinished business.'

'Oh, no!' Cherri sobbed, as Mickey rammed his erect tool into her anus, penetrating the root of her rectum with his second, come-greased thrust.

Cherri thrust her raw fesses up in time to his fucking rhythm. Her face creased in a rictus. Mickey butt-fucked her for over twenty minutes, slamming his hips against her bruised buttocks, while she squealed as each savage penetration of her greased anus rattled her head and wrists against the pillory and Karen deftly whipped her naked breasts. When Mickey grunted, filling Cherri's bruised rectum with his sperm, she squealed 'Eek! Eek!' several times, reaching her own, simultaneous climax, her face a mask of pain.

'You're no slave, Karen,' she panted. 'A girl slave doesn't enjoy.'

Cherri was punished for speaking, and leaving the sty. Bud thought her blotched bottom would be unmarketable, but relented when her weals sank into the rich marbling beneath her skin.

'Sun doesn't seem to blister your butt, nor your titties,' she said, herself in the nude. 'You lucky thing!

I'm covered in sun-blocker, and that's a fact. Your ass seems bigger and riper every time I spank you. I can see traces of my last spanking growing inside you, like flowers in a terrarium. And your pubic! Most girls' quim fur peaks, but yours seems to grow longer and thicker, your armtufts too. I'm jealouser than ever!'

Cherri groaned, her butt still wriggling from the spanks, and Poppy hosed her down with cold NeedaCola, then applied the pipe to her lips so that Cherri could drink. When the cola dried on her skin, it left streaky smears. Sometimes, after a spanking, Poppy masturbated the bound girl to orgasm, masturbating herself at the same time by rubbing her wet gash and clitty against Cherri's nipple. At night, Cherri was unbound for two hours' exercise, running barefoot after the RV on the roadway. She was attached to the rear vehicle by a rope, fastened to two metal nipple clamps, and by a second rope, attached to pins, holding her gash open by the inner labia. Her pube-hair was thicker and longer than ever before, and the cunt-pins had to penetrate its huge golden jungle, to reach the pink slit-meat. During exercise time, the vehicle moved at eight miles an hour, and Cherri ran with wrists roped behind her back. Apart from the hum of the cloister of clyster, the only sound to disturb the desert air was the seldom interrupted whipping of Karen Souter in the torture shack beneath the sun roof. When her days of punishment were over, Cherri was readmitted to the sty and the familiar embrace of slime.

'Learned your lesson, sow?' Bud said, as he applied his palm to her squirming bare rump.

'*Eek! Oink!*' Cherri squealed.

It was the last of their spankings, as Bud announced they would be crossing the border in a week, and he wanted their asses pristine for the G-Mart. To compensate, the sows' enemas became more severe, with chilli clysters applied routinely. To slake the sows' thirst for bare-ass spanking, Poppy's croup now publicly squirmed under Bud's spankings of a thousand or more, which the sows watched with nimble fingers at frottage, and their coozes emitting copious cunt-slime into their mudbath. At last, Poppy announced they had crossed the Mexican border at Mexicali, and were now in Baja California, on the road to Tijuana. The news was greeted with excited squeaks, including Cherri's. Karen served them their food, as always, but now, when she opened her rubber punishment sheath, did not bother to don it again and allowed the sows to inspect her spectacularly welted nude body. Poppy said that once at mart, Karen would be their mistress, and they must trot after her like good pigs: if they were lucky in their new owner, their bodies might become like Karen's, which was an example to the sows and prospective buyers of what a girl slave could endure. For auction purposes, Bud presented his North Carolina sow-girls as spank virgins, unbruised asses on which a new owner could etch at will. Cherri's flogging by Mickey had left her bottom wealed but in a rosy blossom, rather than Karen's fretwork of ridges and welts, and after days unspanked the glowing marble of her buttocks was finally deemed nudist blush, rather than fruit of spanking.

One morning, the mudspray awakened them as usual, but the RV had stopped, and the rear door was open. A 4WD pickup stood at the base of the ramp, loaded with supplies, and a wheeled bathtub of slimy mud for each sow. They were beside the Mexicali-Tijuana road, a moonscape of jagged rocks and fissures in the desert, with arroyos, caves and phallic pinnacles of volcanic effluent. One of the caves, halfway to the crest of the mountain, emitted a pale green glow. Karen appeared, wearing a rubber blouson and thighboots, with her ass and cunt-basin naked, and carrying a cane. After they had eaten, and – on Karen's instruction – masturbated, to keep them quiet, she ordered them to climb into their mudbaths, where each sow was strapped in a wooden yoke that forced her arms over the side of the tub, while a rubber vice attachment clamped her breasts, to prevent escape. The truck's flatbed carried a styrofoam chill box, into which Karen placed the Tupperware dish full of come from their recent masturbation: the box was filled with identical vessels from Mickey's fridge, upstairs in the RV.

Bud drove, with Poppy in the nude and strapped in a safety harness beside him, wearing a spray of spiky cactus in her hair; smirking, jeaned and booted, Mickey sat on the box, dangling his own cane over the muddy sows. The truck started up a dry riverbed into the moonscape. It groaned and wrenched, bumping on the rocky surface, passing the cave of glowing green hue, jolting the trussed sows in their tubs, with slime slopping their hair and faces. It crested the hill, and lurched into descent, towards the crater, where a mass of shiny, swanky limos, sports cars and RVs clustered around a white mansion, its Grecian style incongruous in the moonscape of rocks and dust. Past it, a railroad line from the west coast snaked into the mountain. Three figures emerged from the cavern's green glow, into the truck's cloud of dust. They were bronze girls, one taller than the others, with long dark hair caressing their ass-clefts. They were nude, with canes lodged in their gashes, and whips coiled at waist, with thick pubic fleeces trailing down their thighs. The girls padded barefoot on the jagged rocks, following the truck, their rippling legs and dangling pubic forests glistening with come.

13

G-Mart

A silver-haired, tanned gentleman in a white suit spoke into a microphone. He reminded the assembly that he was Col Schuyler G. Wycherley, of the South Carolina Wycherleys, and that this faraway replica of the Wycherley mansion in Florence, SC, destroyed in the *misunderstanding* of 1865, was due to his ancestor's luck in finding a silver lode in the sierra, which he hid from both the US and Mexican governments, until the lode ran out in 1912. Normally resident in East Bay St, Charleston, Col Wycherley maintained the replica mansion for the purpose now underway, the auction of willingly bonded girl slaves. The auction chamber was decked with ferns, palms, and scented flowers. His listeners were males and females in sombre suiting – buyers, sellers or both. Some were buyers of raw product, unspanked females; they would take the product home for processing, then back to mart as a trained cane or bondage slave. Some were sellers of finished product, who, like Bud, auctioned girls already trained in submission. A stack of zoo-crates was attended by Mr Ed Larue, local rep for the airfreight experts Girlex, Inc, of Seattle, who guaranteed next-day delivery of girl slaves in bondage anywhere in the continental US. Bud and Mickey put on suits and neckties before entering the auction room, though Poppy remained nude, with

Bud holding her by a slave-leash, prettily garlanded with prickly cacti that looped round her waist and through her cunt and ass-cleft. The sows stayed outside in their baths of slop, behind the truck, and attended by Karen, wearing a rubber sheath just covering her titties and pubis.

'Although most of us are Americans, we hold our proceedings in this discreet venue,' the colonel said, 'as a safeguard against misunderstandings by busybodies, interfering with the constitutional freedom of the female American, to dispose of herself in tutelary bondage, if she so wills. The unlettered might say that girls should not be auctioned as though they were things. In South Carolina, we say, things should not be auctioned as though they were girls! Spanking of young ladies on their wilful bare bottoms, and all subsequent measures for their discipline, humiliation, pain and penitence, limited only by American imagination, which has no limit, make spankers and spankees rational beings in an irrational world.'

There was devout applause.

'Vendors may each demonstrate their girlware,' he said, 'after which bidding per item shall commence. Due to the variety of items on show, some displays shall be outside, where I might recommend that ladies and gentlemen wear sunhats or parasols. Let us start the demonstrations with a vendress beloved of us all. Those few of you unfamiliar with Miss Bowdoin, of the Newport, Rhode Island, Bowdoins, may know that her merchandise is as impeccable as her own pedigree, which goes back to Baudoin of the Iron Arm, Margrave of Flanders, who whipped all thirty of his girl slaves naked, every day.'

On the stage set representing a colonial drawing-toom, the nineteen-year old girl, 39-24-39, in frilly French maid's costume, curtsied to her mistress. The maid's russet tresses cascaded over her upthrust and half-bared breasts, whose saucer-shaped nipples peeped over her scalloped voile brassiere.

'Was tea to your satisfaction, madam?'

'No, Mimsy, it was not. My toast was incompletely decrusted. What are you, Mimsy?'

'Oh! A naughty, thoughtless girl, ma'am.'

'And what happens to naughty, thoughtless girls?'

'They are caned on their bare bottoms, ma'am.'

'Then you may fetch the maple stick.'

Mimsy handed her mistress a glossy brown cane, nearly four feet in length, and with a crook handle.

'Begging your pardon, ma'am, I took the liberty of bringing the cane. It seems that every day, I am naughty and thoughtless, no matter how hard I try to be a good girl. I know my bottom deserves thrashing on the bare, until it is all crimson with welts, and I am weeping.'

'At least you know something, Mimsy, so there is hope for your intelligence, if not for your hindquarters. Such a ripe, rounded, temptation-making, *daring* backside shall, I fear, never know freedom from caning amongst the decent folk of Newport. A certain fowl goes by the name of Rhode Island Red, but the term applies also to the blossom raised by maple or hickory wood on the naked buttocks of an errant maid. You may assume position.'

Mimsy bent over, lifting her black pleated skirtlet to reveal black satin garter straps and belt over white cotton panties. She removed her skirt, then knotted her blouse up at the small of her back, revealing a black satin waspie corset that pinched her waist to nineteen inches. She unfastened each of her four garter straps, then rolled the panties down to her ankles, and, touching her toes, parted her thighs to raise her bare buttocks spread for caning.

'Mimsy! Your corset!' cried Miss Bowdoin.

'It's laced as tight as I can stand, ma'am.'

'You are two eyelets away from that, miss. Your waist measures twenty-four inches, does it not? Therefore, you can be corsed to eighteen inches. Remedy the matter at once.'

Panting and blushing, Mimsy unfastened her corset and strained, until it was laced two eyelets tighter, pinching her waist to jagged wrinkles of flesh.

'Oh! I can hardly breathe, miss.'

'Excellent. As I cane you, Mimsy, you shall avoid shudders, twitches, squirms or unseemly wails and gasps. Otherwise, you shall incur further punishment.'

'It'll be very hard, ma'am. You cane so well.'

Her mistress stood, and flexed the cane over Mimsy's trembling bare rump, between whose cheeks peeped a generous tuft of russet pubic hair, enclosing the ripe swollen folds of a cooze, slightly moist with lubricant.

'Indelicately exposed as, perforce, you are, Mimsy, it might seem further indelicacy to suggest that the prospect of bare-bottom caning excites you in an unseemly manner. Yet what other explanation can there be for your daily offences and the effort you put me to in flogging away your miscroyance?'

'I cannot think of one, ma'am.'

Her mistress was a full-breasted blonde, of twenty-three years, and 40-23-39, wearing a grey muslin business suit, with a short skirt that showed her seamed black nylon stockings to half-thigh.

'In that case,' said the mistress, 'I am going to make your punishment a long one, Mimsy and, for greater efficacy and painfulness of strokes, shall put myself at my ease. You may not peek, on pain of further punishment.'

'No, ma'am.'

Swiftly, the blonde stripped off her business suit and stood in peach-coloured bra and panties, with black garter ensemble to match her seamed hose. After a moment's hesitation, she unhooked her bra and let her full breasts jut naked, with the big pink cherries of her nipples quiveringly erect. The perineal thong of her string panties, between her starkly outlined cunt-lips, was stained wet with her exudation, and the panty silk clung wetly to cover a small portion of her bottom, her figure excelling her slave's. Her peach-coloured corset was laced to seventeen inches. She lifted the cane above Mimsy's bare cheeks.

'Sixty, Mimsy,' she murmured, stroking her nipples as she spoke, 'including an extra ten for your improper corsing.'

'Oh, ma'am!'

Mimsy's bare ass clenched violently, wealed by a pink stripe all across her middle fesses.

'I said, no noise! Your beating shall start *now*.'

The bidders and their slaves at auction watched the maidservant take, in silence, a bare-bottom thrashing of sixty strokes that coloured every portion of her ass, plus an extra punishment of fifteen, for the wriggling and squirming Mimsy's buttocks had been unable to avoid during their naked caning. By the end of the flogging, the girl slave Mimsy's fesses were quite unrecognisable as the firm pale globes they had been, ten minutes before. Her blonde mistress had flogged her while caressing her own bare breasts, and allowing her hand to brush the growing wet stain at her panties, as if to emphasise that the joy of caning such a slave as Mimsy afforded more than merely disciplinary pleasure. Her owner, not bothering to resume her business attire and, by her smile, aware her delicately quivering bare titties, tight corse, swollen cunt-mound and delicate underthings might not deter bidders, led Mimsy around the auction room, allowing prospective purchasers to touch the purpling ridges raised by the cane on her naked skin. In high heels, Mimsy was obliged to proceed at a hobble, with her panties still at her ankles. Her costume was quite in disarray, and the massive nipple of her left bubby peeped entirely free of its restraining brassiere. Tears glistened on her face, lowered in shame.

'Only time prevented me from giving Mimsy a really adequate thrashing of at least a hundred and fifty strokes, strung up with apparatus from my collection, such as nipple or quim-clamps,' whispered Miss Arabella Bowdoin, amid the throng. 'This girl is a most obedient item, capable of standing any punishment, of which caning its bottom to purple is certainly the mildest. I shall leave it on show until the bidding.'

Arabella ordered Mimsy to prostrate herself and place her wrists and ankles in the apertures of a wooden stocks, a single hinged bar that snapped and locked, imprisoning the girl with her bare bottom up for spanking and her arms stretched between her thighs, with her chin on the floor. Mimsy's face was blank as buyers fingered her cane-weals and private parts, or twisted and pulled tufts of her pubic hair, sniffing their fingers, moist with the girl's continuing exudation of come. Col Wycherley invited interested parties to step outside for a demonstration from Idaho. An area of pavement had been laid on the desert floor and furnished with simple properties, such as poles, crossbars, whipping stools and frames, for the convenience of vendors.

The portly and moustachioed Mr Theodore Buchanan, from Pocatello, Idaho, displayed three nude nineteen-year-olds. 'Frisky as rabbits, so I call them rabbit girls,' he said. The lithe girls, cousins, and all with large, muscled bottoms, large pubic tufts, and pert conic breasts, were closed in a hutch of bamboo bars and munched sullenly on carrots, with their hands roped behind their backs, each to the next. Each carrot was inserted into a girl's anus, so that the chewer had to contort herself to feast. When each girl had swallowed the last shreds of carrot from another's anus, Mr Buchanan opened the top of their hutch; they leaped out, and it was seen they their cunts were stuffed with broccoli, "an

231

Idaho delicacy",' as Mr Buchanan boasted. He had a bucket of baked potatoes steaming in tinfoil, another delicacy of his state, and extracted with tongs three of the potatoes, which he placed in a row on the pavement, after removing their wrapping. He cracked a long cane, marking the three girls' fesses, at which command they bent backwards, pointing their coozes at the onlookers, and shot broccoli spears, gleaming with their fluids, a good ten feet. They squatted to pick up the three potatoes with their cunts and stood still. Mr Buchanan cracked them across the nipples with his cane, and again across the cooze-lips, then turned them for a vigorous caning of their bare bottoms. They stood and took the strokes, trembling and with faces twisted in anguish, but not one dropped her potato.

Mr Buchanan pursued them with his cane, obliging them to hop on one leg or two around the arena, bend back and forwards, do somersaults, always clutching their potatoes, and under repeated canestrokes, until they bent over and their owner extracted the potatoes from their cunts. The tubers were shown, drenched in come, before each girl had one thrust fully into her mouth, and bent over for a triple caning, of forty individual strokes to each naked croup. Bottoms livid with crimson welts, the sobbing girls, drooling come from half-chewed potatoes, hopped back into their hutch. Mr Buchanan announced that his rabbit girls were available singly or as a lot and that, like Miss Bowdoin's property, could stand far more punishment than time presently allowed.

The next exhibitor was Mr Claude Murphy, an eager young man from Dubuque, Iowa. His femmeware was two teenage housemaids, their breasts and asses measuring in the high thirties, in serving wenches' uniforms of latex and denim scraps, all scuffed and shredded so as to reveal large portions of 'bare, spankable meat', as Mr Murphy put it, as well as vividly stained bras and panties, often holed.

'These are what Iowa folks call fieldmice,' he explained. 'Dirt vermin, but trainable as live household appliances and furnishings. Don't need to dress them fancy, as plain folks can't well afford the expenditure, so you don't worry about shredding their frillies during discipline. As long as they are well bound, caned bare-ass every few hours for their circulation and, most important, have a mirror to look in, my cuties are happy with cast-offs. A fellow can arrange his basement to look real homely, with a few fieldmice in ropes.'

The girls were displayed thus: a rusty bathtub was filled with water, and the girl's shabby shirt, skirt, bra and panties ripped off. Her wrists were roped behind her, and she lay on her back in the bathtub. Mr Murphy folded her legs over her belly, roping them around her lower back, and tying her feet, thence winding the rope around her breasts in several layers, until the puffed breasts and nipples, squeezed to balloons, went bright red in color. Two chains dangled from a crossbar; he screwed a vice on each distended nipple, with each vice hooked to a chain. Then he tied a breeze-block to the other end of each chain and released both breeze-blocks together. The chains went taut as the breeze-blocks fell from the crossbar to swing below the bathtub's edge, jerking up the girl's breasts, and changing them from glowing red puffballs to stretched white envelopes of skin. The girl gasped for breath as the operation lifted her head and breasts above water level.

'Peggy needs spanking, of course,' Mr Murphy added, 'and we can't get at her ass this way, so here's a variant.'

He pinned open her cunt-flaps, bunched between her strapped thighs, and held them open with cooze-clamps, strung to her bound toes. Her inside pink slit was amply revealed, and Mr Murphy took a long, five-footer cane. Vip! The cane sliced the water, and thrashed the girl across her thigh-backs several times, then across the pinned-open cooze-lips, on the shiny wet meat of her cunt.

'*Unnhhh*,' the girl whined, shaking her head, and her ass banging the bathtub as each canestroke sliced her bare cunt; her shaking breasts made the breeze-blocks careen, and she was rewarded with lashes of the wet cane to the stretched titty-flesh.

'*Ah!*' she shrieked.

'Almost forgot, folks!' said Mr Murphy, and rapidly gagged the girl with her own ripped and stained panties, securing them in her mouth with duct tape.

He caned the girl for several minutes, until clouds of her come floated in the rusty water.

'Mmm, mmm,' she moaned, behind her gag.

The second fieldmouse, smoking an unfiltered cigarette and quite blatantly masturbating under her dirty rubber panties as she contemplated her sister vermin, squealed as Mr Murphy grabbed her long mane and twisted. He ground her cigarette butt on the crotch of her rubber panties, which sizzled, and stank.

'Debbie's a little sassier,' he confided. '*She'll* get her ass spanked, and a lot more.'

'Oh! Now, just a minute! *Ah!*'

Debbie protested, squealing, as Mr Murphy ripped all her clothing to shreds and wadded the remnants of her slimy latex panties in her mouth, tying it with wire around her nape, with her hair looped around the wire and wrenched to its roots. He slapped her hard on the face, then the big bare teats.

'Shut the *fuck up, bitch!*' he snarled.

Debbie had to content herself with sobbing gasps.

'City folks favour all kinds of fancy bondage,' said Mr Murphy, 'but there's plenty ordinary Americans can do in their own basement or workshop. Now, I guess most of you have some spare plastic drainage tubing for that rainy day. Case it in a simple readymix concrete plinth, and it keeps the mouse's ass good and high for caning.'

234

He maneuvered a length of grey plastic tubing, three inches wide, under Debbie's cunt, by now dripping steadily with her come, and stuck the tubing into her slit, ramming it, until it bent, and would go no further. Debbie's come rapidly oiled the intruding cunt-tube.

'Mmm,' she moaned, her eyes rolling.

'Course,' said Mr Murphy, 'you can likely spare just six or eight inches of the same tubing.'

'*Mmm!*' Debbie screamed, as he oiled a short length of pipe with her come, and plunged it into her anus, to the hilt. He filled her anal shaft to the brim with green slimy Play-Doh.

'Now she looks pretty enough to cane,' said Mr Murphy, licking his teeth, as he picked up his five-footer.

Vip!

'*Mmm!*'

It was the first of thirty strokes to Debbie's bare. At each stroke, her bare ass squirmed wildly, she screamed, or gurgled, as drips of the viscous green slime spat from her writhing anus, and a spray of come cascaded from her cunt-flaps, oiling the grey drainpipe that transfixed her. Her spine arched, wrenching her nailed breasts against their thumbtacks. She pissed herself twice. The thirtieth stroke, an upender, took her on the gash-flaps and perineum, and she orgasmed, explosively.

'People say we're flaky in California,' said Mr Frank Lamarck, an intense young man in wire eyeglasses, and a powder blue linen suit, 'but we prefer, like, in tune? Melanie here is a zoo girl, and one hundred per cent eco-friendly.'

The blonde girl, with the suntan heightened by pure white bikini areas, pouted sullenly, as he roped her ankles to a four-feet-wide hobble bar, so that her spread thighs showed pink cunt-meat in her white bikini zone, under an immense, and untrimmed golden fleece. Her torso was then sheathed in a thick knotting of white ropes, which crisscrossed her forty-one-inch breasts, compressing them to huge crimson bulbs. Melanie's face assumed a grimace of distress. Her arms were spread behind her shoulders, through the holes of a yoke, so that her throat rested on the central indentation, hinged with a brace which Mr Lamarck locked over her neck. He took a short, springy little cane and tickled Melanie's engorged crimson dugs.

'Melanie likes breast enhancement,' he said. 'Don't you, Melanie?'

'Yes, master,' Melanie murmured.

Vip!

The cane sliced across both her swollen bare nipples.

'Uhh,' Melanie groaned.

Vip! Vip! Two cuts, one to each upper breast, made the bulging, roped teats wobble.

'Uhh.'

'Not hard enough?' said Mr Lamarck.

'N-no, master,' she whimpered.

Vip! Vip! Vip! The naked teats shuddered, livid with red weals.

'*Ah!* Yes! Oh, please!'

With Melanie's cunt tightly closed, he caned the tip of her swollen, extruded clitty, then the cunt-flaps and hairy inner thighs, the cane tip making a circuit of her perineal zone before returning to lash the nubbin. Come squirted from Melanie's cunt as she cried out, at last, writhing in orgasm; her cunt flapped open, releasing a flood of come.

'The modern office, too, can use Melanie's training as a phone girl,' he said. He thrust a cell phone into the pink maw of Melanie's cunt, and told her to dial a number. Her belly and pubis writhed, and clicking sounds were heard, then a buzzing tone, and a voice answering, 'That you, Frank?' The voice was heard clearly, amplified through Melanie's swollen bubbies. Mr Lamarck asked his interlocutor to call him straight back. A buzzing emerged from Melanie's cunt, and Mr Lamarck told her not to answer right away. The phone continued to buzz, while Melanie's belly danced, drool frothed at her lips, and her cooze slopped with love-juice.

'Oh! Oh! I'm going to . . . *Oh! Ooh!*' she shrieked.

Mr Lamarck told her to answer the phone. Her cunt jerked, and after a click, the voice said, 'Hear me, Frank?'

'Sure,' said Mr Lamarck. 'Congratulations, you just phoned Melanie to come.'

Displays followed from Maine, with a nude red-haired girl in scuba helmet and fishing-net bondage, her huge breasts growing more freckled under a drip of scalding red candle wax. An Arizona stage magician, the Invincible Marvell, in a frock coat, introduced a surly nude blonde, twenty years old, 38-22-38, with much-wealed back and bottom, whom he whipped on a gallows, with a hangman's noose slack around her neck. Her hands were roped behind her back, up to the elbows, and she received fifty strokes of a cattle whip on her naked shoulders, before a further fifty on the buttocks, followed by a caning on the buttocks, also of fifty. Her back became a streetplan in weals, and her wriggling ass-globes a relief map in troughs and ridges of crimson and purple welts. Her unbound bare feet danced as the whip lashed her naked skin to a tapestry of purple, with the girl screaming and sobbing, and onlookers crowding to inspect her genuine facial expressions of agony.

'Oh!' she cried, at last. 'I'd rather be hanged, than endure this dreadful pain!'

Suddenly, Marvell jerked the lever; the trapdoor opened, and the nude girl was hanged. Her body plunged into the darkness, and the rope tightened, swaying and jerking back and forth, for two minutes, to awed silence from the onlookers. After that, the rope ceased moving. Suddenly, the nude blonde appeared, unbound, from inside the Wycherley mansion.

'The female Houdini of Flagstaff!' proclaimed Mr Marvell, and invited bidders to check that her whipscars were real.

A Texas girl was caned seventy on the bare, while riding a rail biting deeply into her cunt, with her ankles roped beneath her and her arms stretched above to a gibbet. Two twin maids from Tennessee were suspended in breast torment, one's weight taken by a wrist suspension, with the ropes criss-crossing her teats, and inflating them to red bursting tomatoes. Mr Duplessis, from Chicoutimi, Quebec, displayed nude girls Yvette and Rose, who wrestled in a tub of maple syrup, nipple-gouging, gash-clawing, wrenching hair, and mashing each other's cunts and titties before they gamahuched to orgasm, while slurping maple syrup and come from their dripping coozes. Still sticky with syrup, they were put in the stocks, bottoms up, and caned on the bare, their mouths gagged with whole apples, the quickfire caning to last until each had crunched and swallowed her apple. Rose took sixty-two strokes to Yvette's seventy-one. Then, it was Karen's turn to display her North Carolina sows.

She and Mickey trundled each bathtub into the arena, as Bud explained to the bidders that their slimy cargo was trained to obey, but were, as yet, virgins to spanking. Therefore, there was a high reserve price. The sows left their mudbaths to be sluiced clean, and their immaculate tanned bottoms presented for inspection, while Poppy proclaimed the taming and healthful values of a nudist regime. Bud hogtied the sows, binding them thigh-to-ankle and ankle-to-wrist for full quim exposure, and with breasts roped in especially tight knots, so that the dugs and nips swelled and reddened. They were displayed in rope suspension four feet up, from gibbets: Cayenne and Suze face up, weight on hair, wrist and ankle knots, and Cherri, Marsha and Ginny face down, weight taken by hair, wrists and waist. Karen slithered out of her rubber sheath and stood nude before the bidders, who gasped at her whole-body tracery of welts.

'Virgin sows is what we offer!' she cried, 'and I'm the finished product, for I was a spank virgin once! Any lady or gentleman may put me to any test, and I mean any! These sows, though virgins, are totally docile.'

'North Carolina,' said Bud, 'has Virginia up above, and South Carolina beneath. We are called a trough of humility between two pyramids of conceit, and my sows are guaranteed humble.'

'Then,' said Col Wycherley, coloring slightly, 'let us test your display sow in Carolina fashion. She may ride a rail, and be ridden.'

Karen was bundled towards the railroad track and roped, crouching, between the rails, with her neck tied to one rail, her ankles to another and her wrists roped beneath her shins. Her buttocks thus thrust upwards, at a suitable angle for spanking, with her perineum spread, helpless to resist penetration of either exposed hole. Her neck rope also filled her mouth, gagging her. Cherri watched, helplessly swaying in shame from her gibbet as bidder after bidder brushed Karen's ass-skin, or prised open her cunt and anus, the latter particularly interesting to a male and female with California tans.

'That butt's made for camera, Buck,' said the female.

'Your call, Topaz,' he replied. 'You'll be the one doing her.'

Cherri's shame was greater as she felt her own quim ooze at the sight of Karen's degradation. Suddenly, she jerked: amongst the bidders was Miss Grayfold of Wycherley's winery, accompanied by a young man in a dark robe and with flowing curly locks. The curly man led a ropeline of teenage girls, barefoot and wearing only denim halters and shorts that revealed most of their bodies and, in particular, large portions of breast and buttock with obvious recent cane stripes. The visitors seemed in animated conversation with Mickey. Mistaking the cause of her emotion, a quim-prodder asked her if North Carolina cunts were especially modest.

'*Eek!*' Cherri answered.

'You see, sir?' crowed Bud. 'My sows are so submissive, they've forgotten how to speak English.'

Whap!

'*Ah!*'

All eyes turned to Karen Souter's bottom, lashed by a long cattle-whip. Cherri watched the girl shake against her ropes under the whip's battering, her bondage the more horrifying as, like a stocks, it consisted of so little, yet rendered her completely helpless. Mr Murphy wielded the whip for twenty or so lashes; he yielded to Mr Lamarck, for the same; then, Mr Buchanan, Mr Duplessis, and Miss Arabella Bowdoin, her whipping the subtlest and causing Karen to howl the loudest, as drool slimed her rope gag and cunt-juice soaked her ropes. In the space of ten minutes, Karen Souter took sixty-five whipstrokes, on bare back, buttocks and haunches. Her existing patchwork of welts glowed with new, sullen fire as her nude body writhed. Her howls rent the desert air and her face glistened scarlet with tears. Cherri's cunt flowed come as she watched the whipping proceed to a hundred, then a hundred and thirty. Glee possessed males and females alike, when Mr Buchanan lowered his pants, and penetrated Karen's open anus pucker with his erect cock to bugger her vigorously for three minutes until he spurted inside her anus. Karen groaned and writhed under her butt-fucking, but spread her cheeks for the next stiff cock that slid easily into her greased anal shaft, and for the next. Come dripped from Cherri's swollen cunt-flaps, onto the desert dirt.

Poor Karen . . . it isn't right. She's no slave. It should be me.

Col Wycherley left a conference with Miss Grayfold and the curly-haired man, and approached Bud; he pointed at Cherri.

'It seems, my humble friend, your merchandise is not as virgin as you claim.'

'What?'

'That female is recognised by Miss Roslyn Grayfold and her associate from the state of Washington, County Sheriff Josiah Tod, who has the added distinction of serving the US Postal Service.'

The curly-haired Josiah Tod nodded pleasantly to Cherri, as to a long-awaited new friend.

'Both attest to her considerable experience of all forms of discipline; moreover, Sheriff Tod avers she is not from North Carolina at all. Miss Grayfold is unwilling to auction her own cargo of one dozen true spank virgins, presently expected from Oregon, if this deception continues. You must withdraw her from auction, unless –'

'I can't!' Bud gasped. 'She's my prize sow!'

Ginny, Suze, Marsha and Cayenne scowled.

'Then she must show herself equal in value to the wench currently enjoying railroad correction. Judging by the sow's quim, sir, interestingly wet, she may prove even better.'

Cherri was railroad-roped, her nude body scorched by the rails, and by the whip on her buttocks. Vap! Vap!

'*Ah!*'

Cherri heard a voice scream, realising that it must be her own. Sound seemed a poor thing indeed, to express the white-hot pain that seared her bare nates. The pain had begun as single strokes of a cane or a whip – or both at once, maybe, so fast did lash pile on lash. Soon, the pain was a constant fire, each stroke a spurt of flame. Vap! Vap! Vap! Cherri's bare bottom jerked, squirmed, and clenched, her welted fesse-skin undulating like glowing lava.

241

'Ahh! No! *Please!*'

No, not this way, it's not right. I didn't mean . . .

Again, there was a voice inside her, not in her head, but in her cunt, and her flogged bare bottom itself, vibrating her swelling clitoris. *It is right, slave.*

Distant sounds, distant voices, omnipresent pain.

'Whip the bitch raw.'

'She's used to it, the whore.'

'Some virgin! That ass is a seasoned slave's.'

'I can vouch for that!' A Boston accent, female, but with an oriental lilt. 'So pleasant to see those fesses wriggling again. My, she is far from Wycherley's Winery, and certainly merits punishment for escape. She would have been our prize girl slave at auction.'

'Yet you have brought us an admirable crop of slaves, Miss Takira,' the colonel purred.

'Ah, yes! Dear Frigg, naughty Elise, brutal Tara, thrifty Bev, innocent Meryl, sweet Priscilla, wicked Rosee, clever Lara! Thanks to your niece, sir, they are all ripe for auction – bound nude, and with hands free for pleasure since our leaving Oregon. They shall be glad to stretch themselves for whipping, after confinement in their hutches.'

Miss Takira carried a bright blue parasol shading her school uniform, of white shirt, pleated blue skirt, and fluffy white ankle socks, but her shoes had high black stilettos. Her uniform was too tight for her, as were her bra and panties, while, beneath her shirt, showed a waspie corset, pinching her waist to a seventeen-inch reed.

'I cannot excuse you from reward, Miss Takira, after my niece's recommendations.'

'Too kind, Colonel. Excuse me, to speak with the gentleman from Girlex. His slave-crates interest me.'

Cherri was helpless to move, trussed in the same knots as had trussed Karen Souter, with the whipscarred martinet abetting Cherri's binding, instructing the lustful chastisers how to make her ropes more secure and more painful. Her bondage crouch was lower than Karen's, so that her naked teats were flattened against the scorching heat of one metal rail, while her gash-flaps were squashed against the second. Her thighs and buttocks overhung the rail and strokes to her bare fesses came aslant or sideways; or, with her ass-pucker stretched and spread, the canes and whips descended vertically to lash the anus, perineum and lower cuntlips. No rope gagged Cherri, for Karen said her cries would be music.

'I adore whip music,' said Miss Arabella Bowdoin.

14

Ultrabottom

Vap! Vap! Vap! the strokes rained on her naked back and squirming bare ass, as Cherri's eyes blurred with tears, and choked screams gurgled in her throat.

'Ah! No! *Stop!*'

Vap!

'The bitch has pissed herself!'

'Whip her asshole till it puffs *right* up!'

Vap!

'*Ah! Ah!*'

Cherri's staccato screams at her cane-strokes gave way to a long groan as flesh entered her anal cavern. Her pucker opened to squeeze the stiff glans which invaded her; one thrust and the cock penetrated all the way to her root, filling her rectum with a giant shaft as its owner began vigorous butt-fucking.

'Uhh!' Cherri grunted, the breath knocked from her by the force of the male's buggery.

Swiftly, he spurted his cream at her ass-root, the copious fluid overflowing and trickling down her wealed thighs and perineum.

'Speedy enough, sir,' said Col Schuyler G. Wycherley.

Another cock, ramrod-stiff, penetrated Cherri's anus.

'Fuck her ass to ribbons! It's what the bitch wants!'

Come flowed down her twitching thighs, as her erect nubbin pressed and frotted the searing hot metal rail.

Her aroused nipples, squashed on the opposite rail, squirmed against the metal. *It is what I want*, Cherri thought, but her secret voice vibrated in her clit, anus, and flogged croup.

You want nothing, slave. You submit.

Cock after cock rammed her squeezing butt-hole as her cunt cascaded come, hissing on the rails. Her thighs were bathed in sperm and come, mingled with her sprays of piss, and her hole, filled by pounding cocks, slopped with the cream of cocks before. Her belly fluttered and her clitoris throbbed with the savaging of her cock-distended anus.

'Good slave! It's going to come,' drawled Miss Bowdoin.

'Fine merchandise, Miss Bowdoin,' said the colonel, bowing.

'Butt-fuck the bitch till she fucking faints!'

It was Karen's voice.

'No tarheel girl would pull a train!' spat Cayenne Strahl, swaying from her gibbet.

'Fucking whore!' added Suze Thoroughgood.

'*Uh . . .*' Cherri groaned as orgasm welled inside her, the butt-fucks accompanied by spanks to her purpled haunches, and spankers' fingers raking her ass-welts.

'The postal service *is* the government. Has been so, since the Roman *cursus publicus*, and the private postal monopoly which controlled the Habsburg empire. Most military inventions owe their existence to the quest for postal speed and efficiency.'

The maidmaster, Sheriff Josiah Tod's mellow voice.

'Fuck that,' snarled Mickey. 'When do I get my money?'

'Where's my merchandise, boy?'

'Box is in the truck, and the bitch on the rail, I brought her like our bargain. She's not going anyplace.'

'Except South Chehalis,' said Sheriff Tod. 'I've heard of her butt-hole's charms.'

245

'They're real, man,' said Mickey.

'I may yield to temptation.'

Cherri screamed as a cock larger and stiffer than any before penetrated her throbbing rectum. It plunged almost disdainfully right to her root and began to stab her with massive, powerful thrusts, withdrawing completely from her quivering asshole, before ramming her anew. After four thrusts, Cherri wailed, her belly tightened, and a gush of come poured from her cunt; moments later, she exploded in orgasm. Sheriff Tod laughed.

'Brother Ellum will be glad to see you again,' he said.

'No! Let me go!' she cried.

As Sheriff Josie, the maidmaster, continued to bugger her, Takira's voice floated through the clamour and heat haze and the agony that filled Cherri's ass.

'You can surely rope me much tighter than that, sir,' the Japanese girl gasped, her skirt up, panties stretched across bare thighs, arms and legs bound, and blouse ripped open, with her nipples and cunt-flaps pinned fourfold.

'It's our first overseas flight, ma'am,' said the Girlex rep. 'There's enough food and water, but are you sure about such heavy bondage?'

'Bind me tighter!' gasped Miss Takira. 'I want to come! Tighten my corset to fifteen inches, sir, and tie my wrists at my cunt. I intend to frig myself throughout my girlfreight to Japan, but wish to be otherwise helpless. Col Wycherley, you may have your niece's perverted sluts for free!'

'Too kind, ma'am,' said the colonel, bowing.

'No!' wailed Grayfold. 'I can't go back without payment! I'll be whipped!'

'So you'll be happy, you fucking douchebag, won't you?' said Miss Takira, in pure Bostonian tones.

'My box, with the sow juice!' yelled Mickey, running from the pickup. 'It's gone!'

'Deal's off, then,' snapped Sheriff Tod, butt-fucking Cherri. 'I'll take this fucking whore for free. She's going to enjoy her penitence with me and brother Ellum. She'll be squirting come for ever and a day.'

'No! No!' screamed Cherri. 'It's not right!'

From the shimmering mineshaft, into which the railroad tracks vanished, emerged the nude bodies of three bronze girls, carrying scythes in their quims. Their fists brandished whips. Behind them, in the minehole, lay the box of green Tupperware pots, with the cunt-juice of Bud's tarheel sows. They ran forwards, unsmiling, and as the tallest knelt to cut Cherri from her bonds the others drove back the crowd, with their whips whistling. They vanished into the phalanx of glittering automobiles of the slavemongers. Josiah Tod's cock trembled and bucked but, before he could ejaculate, he was wrestled to the ground and his cock, slimed with Cherri's ass-grease, poked air. The crowd advanced on Cherri and the tall exquisite, who held the maidmaster, Sheriff Josiah, squirming with her foot on his balls. *Hsss! Crunch!* Air spurted from the tyres of vehicle after vehicle, and they sank, immobilised. Only Bud's RV was spared.

'Those bitches!'

'Fucking illegal aliens!'

'But this is Mexico!'

'Then they're illegal for sure! Whip their hides raw!'

Tell your friends to hurry back to North Carolina, said the voice, vibrating in Cherri's cunt-basin and asshole. *Tell them to go home, and be happy as hogs in shit*. The tall nude nodded, without a hint of a smile, and Cherri shouted her instructions to Bud and his trussed sows. As the crowd advanced, Bud complied, and took Poppy and his sows to the safety of the cloister of clyster's RV. The vehicle revved and skidded away, kicking dust.

Slave, follow slave.

As Cherri ran alongside the exquisites, Miss Arabella Bowdoin's foot crunched the maidmaster's back, and her cane whistled above his ass. Vip! Vip! Vip!

'*Ahh!*' he screamed.

'The maidmaster mastered by the bitchmistress! That's kind of neat,' said Kelley Hide, roped to Joanne, Rona and Abigail; the maids giggled. 'Might as well watch the show, now there's no cars to boost.'

'Maybe we don't need a maidmaster,' said Rona. 'Kind of run our own show? *I* can preach, some. There's a market for girl-come, easier than boosting fucking cars.'

As Miss Arabella Bowdoin thrashed the squirming maidmaster, she lifted her skirt to show bare ass to Cherri. Her skin glowed, luminescent with a tracery of subcutaneous welts, like Cherri's own.

'This ordinary needs manners,' she cried. 'Go, girl slave!'

The green mist rolled forwards from the mine's belly, enveloping the girls. The exquisites placed themselves at the entrance, their bodies in stance for chastisement, and blocking ingress. Cherri waited, frowning, as the sound of whips began to crack on their presented flesh, and her slave protectresses shuddered, shielding her, as whips fell upon their defenceless buttocks and shoulders.

Hurry, said the voice inside her. *Take the box of girl-juices. It is slave's offering to the lord.*

'Where? How far? I'll get lost!'

Slave is already lost.

The words made her clitoris and anus vibrate. She grasped the container, and ran into the thickening green murk, away from the three bronze bodies shuddering under angry whips. She ran through the green gaseous luminosity until she faced a wall where the minehole split into four separate tunnels. Which path? She stopped and crouched, gazing at herself in the green

248

mist, so viscous it formed a mirror. Suddenly, in the opalescent light, the three nude girls faced her. All three shuddered, as if bitten.

'How –? You were being whipped, back there!'

Our second selves are still whipped.

The girls about-turned, and Cherri saw the girls' backs and buttocks quivering from unseen whips, and with real welts appearing of their own accord.

'A second self?'

Slave has no self, therefore has many.

'How many? Sorry if that sounds dumb.'

Infinite.

'Where are we going?'

Slave is going to the lord.

Cherri trembled, gasping, and sobbing.

'Oh, *yeah*,' she blurted, 'the *lord*. Excuse *me*! I mean all my life I hear so much about the fucking *lord*, and it's always from people who want to whale the fucking tar out of me, you know, so which way is this lord? Seem to be any number of ratholes here, I mean, do we have a fucking road map or what? I mean, yeah, come on, guys, show me the fucking interstate to the fucking lord, huh?'

Turn around. Look at slave reflection.

'Huh?'

Turn around.

Cherri pouted, sighed, and turned. In the sheen of green gas, she saw a perfect reflection of her naked bottom. The tracery of weals, embroidered under her skin's surface, glowed like a spider's web. The tall girl touched her spinal nubbin, and the weals changed, retracting, growing smaller, yet more numerous. The girl rubbed her spine again, and now her weals grew larger, and fewer, until the tracery enlarged to a single weal, diverging into four paths, of which the second to the left glowed most brightly. At once, the three exquisites ceased their twitching, and no further whip-weal marked their bodies. They marched into the second tunnel on the left. Cherri ran after them.

'Guys, I was only kidding! I mean, thanks!'

Slave does not thank slave. The lord decides.

'Decides what? I mean, my ass is some kind of road map? Hey, OK, I buy it! And you diddle me the other way, I kind of zoom out, and show the whole US or what? *That's* why the lord wants me! Get a clue, Cherri, you should have known!'

True slave has full globes.

'Now wait a minute. My ass is a road map, so this lord wants to fuck me in the ass? Well, my cooze has never been fucked, but I've discovered, hoping I don't shock anyone, that I like being butt-fucked. I just hope the lord doesn't mind that every shit-kicker west of Salt Lake has been there before.'

True slave bears the pathways of the people before.

'So it's kind of like the Sierra Club? I wave my bare ass, and we go hiking, to buttfuck in the mountains?'

True slave carries all pathways, hidden by the old ones, and revealed by the whip on girl's bare globes. True girl slave's croup contains the wisdom of the speedy pathways. To be certain a female is true requires time, and observation of much whipping. The female Wycherley was not true slave. At last, slave brings the lord true slave.

'What pathways?'

All through this world.

'You mean, like, planet Earth?'

Yes.

'Yeah, I mean, it's so obvious. My ass is a road map of the whole fucking planet.'

And others. Speedy pathways extend beyond the Earth. Your bottom alone contains the secret of the wormholes.

Cherri rubbed the ridges and valleys of her bottom, and looked through the luminous green mist, at her flogged, glowing skin, the marbling that pulsed within her whip-ripened bare buttocks. She frowned.

'And we're in one of the, uh, speedy pathways?'

Yes.

Suddenly, the green mist gave way to a bright white light, bathing the four girls. They stood in an atrium, square at base and rising to a pyramidal point, at which a white sun glowed suspended in air. The walls of the atrium were veined green marble; at its centre stood a pyramid, surmounted by a single green eye, and wreathed in green vapour. The pyramid was of the same marble, sculpted in clustered bare fesses, all alike: those of Cherri herself. She reached out to touch the pyramid, then recoiled, gasping at the icy shock. The marbled weals inside the naked croups began to glow in a multitude of veins.

'Oh,' Cherri said, no longer smiling. 'Of course.'

She swooned onto the warm bare breasts of the tallest exquisite, and awoke strapped face down on a hospital bed. A rubber cincher held her by the waist, while rubber cuffs held her legs spread wide, and a cushion raised her spread bare buttocks. Her wrists were cuffed and spread like her legs. Her whole body tingled, not with the pain of her whipping and buggery on the railroad, but with tongues licking her bare buttocks. Three girls in white nursing uniform knelt, attending her with tongues as long as lizards', and whose slurping soothed her whipwelts. One nurse inserted her tongue into Cherri's rectum, and Cherri gasped as it healed her bruises of the maidmaster's butt-fucking.

The white-stockinged nurses were broad of shoulder and croup, with massive breasts, straining against their skimpy nylon uniforms. Their faces were bronze, like Cherri's, but their manes were jet-black, and their foreheads bulging over splayed nostrils and full sensuous lips. Other girls, like the nurses, were nude and barefoot, swabbing or cleaning. Their nipples were hard saucers of black, and they had no pubic or underarm tufts. Their bronze bodies shone hairless and gleaming,

251

without the stubble of pubic shaving: they were natural barequims.

'Where am I?' Cherri stuttered.

'Ah, it can still speak?' said a voice; Cherri twisted her head, to see a similar woman, in doctor's uniform. 'That will pass. I'm Dr Bodace, girlslave.'

'Am I to be beaten?' Cherri gasped, wrenching vainly at the rubber straps, bruising her anew.

'Of course, slave,' said Dr Bodace, 'but not in my hospital. You're not a recruit, it seems.'

'You recruit slaves?' Cherri gasped.

'You'd be surprised how many backpackers are enticed, and never wish to leave, although we sell them after slave-breaking, as G-Mart ordinaries. So many rich people want an agrestic bondsmaiden, and so many girls want nothing less. It's easy to disappear, in America!'

Cherri said nothing would surprise her, after her ordeals, and began to describe them.

'I'd love to establish conversational rapport,' Dr Bodace interrupted, 'but it would only hurt you. Slaves must be mute and soon cannot be otherwise. Forget your ordeals, slave, for your experience here will be a thousand times worse. You are cunt virgin, for one thing, penetrated only by slave's tongue; that will mutate when the lord deems.'

'I can't imagine anything worse than what I've gone through,' Cherri muttered.

'Slave doesn't imagine, she submits,' said the doctor.

'Mmm,' Cherri groaned; the tip of the nurse's tongue flickered on her rectal root, and her quim moistened.

'Who are you people?' she moaned. 'You're not like the exquisites, like *slave*.'

'You and they,' said Dr Bodace, 'are *slave*. We healers are hybrids, that humans term neanderthals.'

'Doctor,' quavered a lick-nurse, 'may ... I ... diddle?'

'Of course, Sugarbuns,' said Dr Bodace, adding: 'My nurses have nicknames. The orderlies have numbers, and don't need permission to masturbate, as long as they remember to yield full come-pots.'

In fact, each nude orderly already diddled, collecting her seepage in a bowl pinned between her quim-lips.

Dr Bodace plunged her fingers inside Cherri's pouch and, with silken fingers, caressed her clitty. Cherri moaned again, her cunt-basin writhing, until her cunt juiced heavily under the doctor's expert frottage. Her come dripped into a green bucket beneath her loins. Dr Bodace frowned and lifted her own white latex skirt, revealing her pantiless pubis and brown hairless cunt, brown lips and pink meat inside the gleaming wet pouch. Continuing to masturbate Cherri, she began to masturbate herself, using the silver tip of her stethoscope.

'You are one the lord awaits,' she said. 'That knowledge helps me exude. I have urgent scythings to perform – to you, amputations. What you think are replacements are in fact beautiful and more efficient enhancements of the female body. I'm unsure what language remains to you, so it is timelier to transfer your slave-knowledge directly. In fact, that pleasure is lawful, for your bottom is almost an ultrabottom. Chastisement has so ripened it, and the underflesh wealing is so delicate! As slave, it will achieve completion in the pyramid. All bottoms I enhance have borne chastisement, and it is fascinating how they react. Some take sharp cane-slices, yet their croup suffuses an even crimson; some, a palm-spanking, yet grow tendrils of crimson, like a vine, or blossom, with ridges and weals that suggest the harshest cane. No two girls have the same spankprints.'

Pinning her skirt and baring her vulva, she removed the cushion from Cherri's hips and slithered under the girl until her cunt pressed Cherri's and the metal

253

bootcap touched Cherri's mouth. Their comes mingled; Cherri gasped as her erect clitoris touched the doctor's throbbing nubbin, and her belly began to tremble.

'*Oh!* I think I'm going to *come*,' she squealed.

'Orgasmic potential, in slaves of the pyramid, increases beyond the dreams of human ordinaries,' said Dr Bodace.

She gamahuched Cherri and cunt-juice bathed the writhing bellies of the two females. When their cunt-basins were slippery with ooze, Dr Bodace's gash-lips clamped Cherri's clitoris in a fleshy vice, and the doctor's pouch squirted come inside Cherri's cunt. The nurse's tongue poked and prodded her inner rectum.

'Oh, yes,' Cherri gasped.

'Open your cunt,' Dr Bodace ordered, as their comes mingled at Cherri's wombneck, 'for slave knowledge. You may chew my bootcap. What happens when you orgasm? Do you see the moon, and the stars? Does time stop?'

'Yes,' Cherri gasped. 'Something like that.'

'Well, then,' said Dr Bodace.

A jet of come spurted red-hot into Cherri's womb.

'*Ahh!*' Cherri screamed, clamping her teeth on the bootcap, as knowledge bathed her.

From above, the great pyramid looked non-fractal: its smooth green surface concealed under a rubble of boulders, like any mountain in the desert of central Baja California, three hundred miles south of Col Wycherley's slave mart. A prism at its cone-tip refracted sunlight and heat into every chamber of the great pyramid. Its green walls were porosite, allowing both light and air to pass freely, so that its servants above the earth's surface seemed to live outdoors. Slaves below lived and worked the titanium mine, in as much darkness and discomfort as the lord, or his princess, thought fit. The lord's domain was staffed entirely by females, their rank indicated by their attire, with slaves, the most numerous, passing every second of their lives in the nude, when not in bondage or their tender parts stretched by punishment weights. Those injured in the mine, or at agrestic duties, went to hospital to be licked to wholeness, along with girl slaves bruised by their whippings.

Slaves, with bottoms fully ripened by the thrice-daily beatings, were sent through the tunnels, as the lord's messengers. Beatings might be with cane, whip, paddle or tawse, at the judgement of nursing orderlies, all of hybrid stock. No hybrid was a slave, only true human girls. Slaves might discipline each other by bare-bottom palmspanks, at their own judgement, on any slave agreed to be insolent or sparing of cunt-juice. Slave spankings showed orderlies that infractions were dealt with, in hope they might mollify the thrice-daily beatings. An orderly might place a girl slave in bondage, suspension or weights, of limitless severity, and at whim, if she considered the slave insufficiently spanked by her own kind or was masturbating insufficiently for the stock of girl-come to nourish the sacred pyramid that lay in the heart of the great pyramid. Mute, the girl slaves communicated by mutually masturbating, or drinking each other's come.

The sacred pyramid stood in a chamber chilled to minus fourteen degrees centigrade, equal to Fahrenheit zero, the freezing point of salted water, and of girl-come. Girl slaves entered the freezing chamber nude, to deposit their cargoes of sacred fluid, replenishing the sacred pyramid of come ice, constantly shaved by rubber-suited orderlies, for exports to the northern land. A girl slave who did not replenish her pint come-pot by masturbating throughout the day was flogged on back and buttocks to a hundred strokes with a fourteen-thonged rubber whip, then bound under ice blocks, where she remained, and returned, between the regular thrice-daily beatings of over one hundred strokes, with a variety of thongs, rods or quirts. Other punishments included bound suspension, bondage mobile, or bondage helpless, with wire or rope, and the attachment of rocks on clamped or pin-pierced nipples and gash-flaps. Language was a hindrance to female obedience, slavery, and orgasm. Girl slaves descended of old stock had tongues mutated to eat, but incapable of speech. Newly found genebearers, like Cherri Black, soon lost their power of speech.

The pyramid existed since humankind, its empire founded on chastisement of the female buttocks and anus. Whipstrokes were to the female ass-peach as rainstorms were to the planet. The anus was the female's sacred chamber, and her dungs fed the earth. The ocean of space in which the planet floated was the life-force, cunt-juice the concentrated energy of female orgasm; ionised girl-come fuelled the speedy tunnels. Masturbation was the sacred duty of every adult female. Female whip-pain was similar energy, and harmony of orgasm and pain was stronger than gravity. Great knowledge was destroyed by the flood, twelve thousand years past, including, some fancied, the secret of wormholes, through which a girl slave whipped and masturbated to a singularity of ecstatic pain might pass into other dimensions, for her infinite selves to orgasm under infinite flagellance. Lords through the millennia sought to regain those secrets, known to survive in genebearers, females born as human ordinaries, but who retained the princess or flagellant gene. High though their flagellant orgasmic consciousness rose, most girl slaves, unlike Cherri Black, did not prove genebearers.

Human reproduction was engineered by female doctors, who engineered males to be masters, fit to enslave and chastise females. Sperm and speech were the burdens of males alone. Female sexual ecstasy was anal and flagellant, with orgasmic engineering of the buttocks and rectum an ancient art. Organic prostheses, on a titanium base, grew in tanks of girl-come. Unlike the majority population of girl slaves, medical staff – hybrids saved from destructive human ordinaries – might speak and read. Their goal being the legendary perfect ultrabottom, doctors enhanced the female croup to clitorality, with every spank or caress on the buttocks bringing girl slave to orgasm and wisdom. Female orgasmic energy fuelled planet Earth and its people.

Girl slaves, as the lord's messengers, maintained world harmony, carrying maps of the speedy tunnels implanted in their buttocks. It was speculated that speedy tunnels extended throughout space. After the great ice-melting, those girls stranded on high ground submitted to breeding with *homo sapiens*. In cases where the princess gene survived, its bearers, if properly chastised on the buttocks, could mutate and achieve the pure cunt telepathy of the people before. If their bottoms were whipped to perfection, girl slaves with the princess gene could mutate to ultrabottoms, believed capable of attaining orgasmic singularity, to pass through the wormholes of ordinary four-dimensional space-time. The lord of each cycle of one hundred and nineteen years sent girl slaves through the tunnels still known, to entice girls likely to carry the princess gene, and whose bottoms were capable through corporal chastisement of attaining transcendence.

Messenger slaves had to seek genebearers, to be reawakened by corporal chastisement, or themselves submit to splicing with post-diluvian humanity and spread flagellance. The lord's messengers were expert fellatrices, for they possessed a second stomach to store swallowed sperm, for transport to the pyramid and breeding of new female hybrids and slaves. If only one girl slave, living as an ordinary, bred a female each year, over eons, millions of human female ordinaries would secretly carry the princess or flagellant gene. Not every girl could awaken, like Cherri; yet, the lord's messengers monitored growing awareness of cleansing flagellance, popularly called spanking. Greedy false prophets abounded; yet even they preached sacred flagellance, with their excesses kept in check by the lord's messengers.

The lord was unnamed and unnameable, for each lord, since the integration of the hybrids, was a hybridic clone of the lord before. Each reawakening of a girl slave, like Cherri Black, promised rediscovery of speedy tunnels, in the veinous weals of her spanked bottom. It was fitting for the lord in the twenty-first century to target the populous power north of the pyramid and assume American identity. A tunnel ran due north from the pyramid, nine hundred feet under Interstate 5, so D. Bob Niederburger, of Seattle, a respected if reclusive businessman, and his airfreight company, Girlex, Inc, ensured supplies of girl-come for the sauce that made NeedaBurgers so flavoursome to the increasingly spank-conscious American public.

However, when slave, formerly Cherri Black, awoke from Dr Bodace's cunt-grip, she knew nothing of the above, for the knowledge was secreted in her come. Her brain knew only that she was slave, mute and female, and would be whipped for being so, for ever. Deeper knowledge was gained as cuntlore, in masturbation with other unspeaking slaves. All laboured in the hope of perfect ultrabottom, and becoming princess, able to appear and disappear at will, flitting through wormholes to coexist in other dimensions, spanked to infinity, her fesses her clit, affording her unending orgasmic joy. Mere slave might go forth, to entice, recruit or breed.

Cherri had never known true degradation before. For eleven months, she toiled in the titanium mines, joining her sister slaves for thrice-daily flogging, for slop, or the slumber dungeon, where girls masturbated restlessly to sleep, on come-stinking straw. She incurred frequent spankings from other slaves, and was flogged at pillory or in stocks, with the orderly's wand whipping every exposed part: thighs, nipples, quim, bottom. She suffered whipping in bondage or suspension, with cunt-flaps pinned, and teats stretched by nipple-clamps or pins through her piercings; flogged while yoked and hunched, her body swaddled in ropes, and her teeth holding candles, to drip scalding wax onto her nipples and into her open cunt. She visited the hospital for Dr Bodace's bottom and teat enhancement. She said slave was not far from a true ultrabottom.

'You will have to combat the lord's princess,' she explained, 'who cannot tolerate fairer fesses than hers.'

Little English remained to Cherri by this time. She befriended the nurse Sugarbuns, and they masturbated together; Sugarbuns urged her to accept scything.

'True ultrabottom,' she purred, rubbing Cherri's alpine cane ridges, as she masturbated her in Dr Bodace's office.

'Doctor dreams of finding perfect princess gene.'

She showed Cherri the photo-record of scythees. Cherri gasped, recognising Fornication E. Lee, Torrie Chute, and Eve Carnuntum; amongst the quadruple apotem-nasts, 'USMC pilot, US Postal Inspector, and lord's messenger' Wanda Bukowski, nude, and quadri-stumped. Then, Bukowski, wearing all four of her prostheses, beside Cherri's tallest exquisite, wearing none of her four prostheses, both girls nude, and oiled for combat.

'No more,' said Sugarbuns, closing the book.

'She my friend,' Cherri moaned, her first words in months.

'Silence, slave! Do you want flogging?' cried Sugar-buns, yet not ceasing to diddle Cherri's clit.

'Flog me!' Cherri hissed, seizing the book to look at *the ultrabottom* of the tallest exquisite. Bukowski was plainly submitting, though the exquisite's only fighting limbs were her massive breasts and bottom: she was quadri-apotemnast. A robed male in back of the photo watched the contest, his cock erect beneath his garment. The tallest exquisite's name was Carolanne Olsen, of Bismarck, North Dakota, measuring, at apotemnasis, 49-21-48.

'*You* are 52-20-50, slave. She is the lord's princess! But your princess gene is the stronger.'

The nurse slapped her bare bottom once, and Cherri climaxed.

Lieut Bukowski fought to become princess, and lost, to the tall exquisite!

'Insolence!' hissed Dr Bodace, entering. 'You may expect unusual flogging, Sugarbuns.'

'Yes, Doctor,' quavered the hybrid.

The two nude slaves touched cunts.

I knew I should have to fight you for my lord's favor. I always knew.

It was the tallest exquisite, the lord's princess and the lord's messenger, who thought.

Then why did you entice me?

Slave has no choice.

Both nudes shivered, in the chamber of the sacred pyramid. Above the apex of the frozen come pyramid, the robed lord sat, enthroned, on a balcony. The balcony encircled the chamber, and all around the lord naked girl slaves crouched, masturbating in obeisance and showering the sacred pyramid and the two wrestlers in a drizzle of their come. The tallest exquisite, formerly Carolanne Olsen, squatted and removed her left leg, allowing it to float an inch from the ground.

Slave prepares herself for fair contest.

She removed her right prosthesis, then her left arm.

That's no fair fight!

The slave princess shrugged.

I must give you advantage. Then my victory is fair, or my loss, shameful.

Not so fast!

Cherri squatted. The two nudes swayed with their heavy manes and cunt-bushes glistening, and their slits gleaming swollen and wet. Slave's cunt spoke.

We excite each other.

Yes. We are each other.

Of course. Yet you have ultrabottom. That is why I had to shield and entice you. I shall not lose without pain.

The two girls fought savagely, biting and headbutting breasts and quims, and rolling together in a lake of their spurted come, frozen to a rink. They slid helplessly on their come-ice, and fought as battering rams, each girl delivering bone-cracking blows, cunt to cunt. The lord decreed a caning ordeal, the first yielder to orgasm losing. Nurses held the girls squashed against the frozen come pyramid, while Dr Bodace and Sugarbuns stripped, and flogged the nude contestants with quirts, fourteen-rubber thongs, ice-hard. They flogged the girls equally, a striping to the buttocks of one hundred, followed by one hundred to the shoulders and back; returning to the buttocks. After one thousand whiplashes to back and buttocks, the two nudes were quivering, the torrents of come from their quims frozen in mid-stream and adhering to the come pyramid. The whipping went on, until the two-thousandth stroke was lashed, and each body was raw, shivering gel.

Slave shall never yield lord to slave by whipstrokes.

The words vibrated in Cherri's cunt, almost tipping her into orgasm. She swivelled on the ice, still grasped by the nurses, but with her head at Carolanne's ass-cleft. Cherri snaked her tongue between the wealed mountains of the bare ass-globes, and found the sopping cunt. She darted her tongue between the labia, and licked the clitoris.

No, not fair! Ah! You win, my princess. Slave's juice worships you. You are the lord's slave, and slave is yours, forever.

Slave sobbed, exploding into orgasm, and clawed at the come pyramid with her teeth, and stiff nipples,

261

gouging holes above her, and swinging her body up to the apex. She perched, the icy pinnacle penetrating her cunt, and, nostrils flaring, howled her triumph.

'*Eek! Nngh!*'

The lord took her in his arms and laid her on his throne, loins facing out. His massive cock penetrated her anus in a single stroke. He butt-fucked the girl for ten minutes, bringing her to orgasm three times, as he masturbated her clit, then withdrew, and plunged his ass-greased cock into her cunt. He penetrated right to her wombneck, and Cherri climaxed at once. A further fifteen minutes' cunt-fucking raised her to a plateau of rising and ebbing continuous orgasm, until the sperm spurted in her cunt; no longer a narrow channel, but fitting the cock, glovelike. The sperm poured from his balls, brimming over her gash-flaps, and congealing on the come ice beneath. Orgasm engulfed her; every whiplash her buttocks had ever received smarted anew. Cherri knew that agony of spanking, and constant orgasm, in the very nerve-shreds of her flogged bottom, were hers for life; that no whip need touch her for the smarts to sear her bottom, in her wakefulness or in her dreams. Her breasts and cunt would tingle for ever, with all the thrashings of their former selves. She was slave, princess, chattel, a female thing. She was joy throughout dimension and time and space. She was a bare bottom, spanked. Are there spanked Cherri Blacks in every world, or is every girl in this one, in her heart, Cherri Black? The lord spoke:

'You are princess of the pyramid, and man's slave. You are true female.'

Cherri could not speak for the intensity of the orgasm in her bottom, clitoris, and cunt, as the pyramid's tip began to pulse, glowing in translucence, where she saw pyramids beyond, and pyramids beyond those. Cherri did not speak again for the rest of her life. Which was for ever.

Nexus

NEXUS BACKLIST

This information is correct at time of printing. For up-to-date information, please visit our website at www.nexus-books.co.uk

All books are priced at £5.99 unless another price is given.

Nexus books with a contemporary setting

ACCIDENTS WILL HAPPEN	Lucy Golden ISBN 0 352 33596 3	☐
ANGEL	Lindsay Gordon ISBN 0 352 33590 4	☐
BEAST	Wendy Swanscombe ISBN 0 352 33649 8	☐
THE BLACK FLAME	Lisette Ashton ISBN 0 352 33668 4	☐
BROUGHT TO HEEL	Arabella Knight ISBN 0 352 33508 4	☐
CAGED!	Yolanda Celbridge ISBN 0 352 33650 1	☐
CANDY IN CAPTIVITY	Arabella Knight ISBN 0 352 33495 9	☐
CAPTIVES OF THE PRIVATE HOUSE	Esme Ombreux ISBN 0 352 33619 6	☐
DANCE OF SUBMISSION	Lisette Ashton ISBN 0 352 33450 9	☐
DIRTY LAUNDRY £6.99	Penny Birch ISBN 0 352 33680 3	☐
DISCIPLINED SKIN	Wendy Swanscombe ISBN 0 352 33541 6	☐
DISPLAYS OF EXPERIENCE	Lucy Golden ISBN 0 352 33505 X	☐
DISPLAYS OF PENITENTS £6.99	Lucy Golden ISBN 0 352 33646 3	☐

SISTERS OF SEVERCY	Jean Aveline ISBN 0 352 33620 X	☐
SKIN SLAVE	Yolanda Celbridge ISBN 0 352 33507 6	☐
SLAVE ACTS £6.99	Jennifer Jane Pope ISBN 0 352 33665 X	☐
THE SLAVE AUCTION	Lisette Ashton ISBN 0 352 33481 9	☐
SLAVE GENESIS	Jennifer Jane Pope ISBN 0 352 33503 3	☐
SLAVE MINES OF TORMUNIL £6.99	Aran Ashe ISBN 0 352 33695 1	☐
SLAVE REVELATIONS	Jennifer Jane Pope ISBN 0 352 33627 7	☐
SLAVE SENTENCE	Lisette Ashton ISBN 0 352 33494 0	☐
SOLDIER GIRLS	Yolanda Celbridge ISBN 0 352 33586 6	☐
THE SUBMISSION GALLERY	Lindsay Gordon ISBN 0 352 33370 7	☐
SURRENDER	Laura Bowen ISBN 0 352 33524 6	☐
TEASING CHARLOTTE £6.99	Lisettte Ashton ISBN 0 352 33681 1	☐
TEMPER TANTRUMS	Penny Birch ISBN 0 352 33647 1	☐
THE TAMING OF TRUDI £6.99	Yolanda Celbridge ISBN 0 352 33673 0	☐
THE TORTURE CHAMBER	Lisette Ashton ISBN 0 352 33530 0	☐
TIE AND TEASE	Penny Birch ISBN 0 352 33591 2	☐
UNIFORM DOLL £6.99	Penny Birch ISBN 0 352 33698 6	☐

- - - - - - ✂ -

Please send me the books I have ticked above.

Name   ....

Address   ....

              ....

              ....

              .... Post code....................

Send to: Cash Sales, Nexus Books, Thames Wharf Studios, Rainville Road, London W6 9HA

US customers: for prices and details of how to order books for delivery by mail, call 1-800-343-4499.

Please enclose a cheque or postal order, made payable to **Nexus Books Ltd**, to the value of the books you have ordered plus postage and packing costs as follows:

UK and BFPO – £1.00 for the first book, 50p for each subsequent book.

Overseas (including Republic of Ireland) – £2.00 for the first book, £1.00 for each subsequent book.

If you would prefer to pay by VISA, ACCESS/MASTERCARD, AMEX, DINERS CLUB or SWITCH, please write your card number and expiry date here:

....

Please allow up to 28 days for delivery.

Signature ....

Our privacy policy.

We will not disclose information you supply us to any other parties. We will not disclose any information which identifies you personally to any person without your express consent.

From time to time we may send out information about Nexus books and special offers. Please tick here if you do *not* wish to receive Nexus information.   ☐

- - - - - - ✂ -